I0690031

A MICHALE LUKE KINKADE
SERIES

BOOK I OF III

I AM APEAY

MICHALE L. KINKADE

COVER ILLUSTRATION BY, DANNA M. STEELE

ISBN: 979-8-218-82018-3

I had to tell his story... I had no choice... Well, I suppose I'm being pretentious in a way, because I could've said "no." Maybe, it was because of how I met him, what he revealed to me, telling me of all about his journeys, his countless extraordinary exploits. That, along with his sincere disposition, is why I felt obligated to share his legacy, throughout the existing world.

On one cool afternoon, he appeared in front of me as I was waking from a nap under my favorite towering tree. Initially he startled me. Then, he spoke to me in a calm voice as he extended his hand to greet me: "I apologize for disturbing you, but you're the only person I've come across all day, and I'm running out of time." He looked at me with a warm smile as if he were a close relative I had known all my life.

"Running out of time for what?," I asked.

"Never mind that," he replied. "Please, listen well, and at the end of our day here, you will understand."

His eyes were begging me with sincerity. His voice sang in truth. I sat up, now fully awake, as out of a light silver bag he handed me a large booklet full of blank pages, as well as a writing utensil as long as ones arm.

"If anyone should ask you "why", tell them, "because of this." Here they'll find me at the end."

It took from noon till dusk and then until the sun rose the next morning for him to finish. It was hard to keep up as I scribed page after page of his life in the oversized binder he gave to me. Finally, after he was done, as I recorded the last detail of his life thus far, he stood up and began to walk away.

"Hold on... wait a minute!" I shouted after him.

He turned back towards me. Then, he stopped and cocked his head, with what seemed to be mild impatience. At first, I was going to let him leave, until I took note of one thing. I had become so caught up in and overwhelmed by all he had passed on to me that I forgot to ask him one important question.

"What's your name?"

He was hesitant to answer my question. He closed his eyes and responded with a sigh. "It doesn't matter. It's just a name."

"Well, maybe to you. But, how will I tell your story without a name? When people ask, what will I say to them? You've told me the names of everyone in your life except yours. Who are you?"

He must've found something amusing in my request. He shook his head with a childish grin.

"You're already slowing me down. I thought you under-stood. Whatever...If you have to have a name *here it is*:   *APEAY* My name is *Apeay*. Fill in the blanks where you feel the need."

He gave a refined bow, dismissing himself from my presence. My eyes followed his shrinking profile through the forest until I was alone again among the trees.

I didn't understand why he left so abruptly after his last, what seemed to be, a cynical remark. But after a few more hours of following through with my commission, it began to make sense. It wasn't long thereafter that I decided to chronicle his life into a decipherable account; the story that would explain why he bothered to share his life with me in the first place.

"So,... that's who you are... I'll be sure to let them know."

CHAPTER 1

Legends are born from those who live from the heart.

It all began with that cool wind. For, the cool wind was the beginning of everything. The winds of querro blew a parting kiss 'goodbye' to the leaves of the fields as a parade of frost danced the blades of grass to an icy chill.

Around that time, there was some talk about a great monster's return, ghosts among abandoned places and mystic lands. Anyway, I'm getting a bit off track.

ΛPEAY. Yes. His birth, like much of his life, was shrouded in mystery. He appeared out of nowhere that evening. The Regalis's, Jhar'ensky and Bexhiera, were prestigious members of the community. Yet, they managed to live a humble life of nobility. They lived on the outer rim of Estellar; restored to its former glory it was the wealthiest and most grandiose region on planet Tzierhan. Their home was customized to their liking; a picturesque dwelling among the verdant forest. In their youth they desired to raise a family. But, with each passing year their hopes of having children dwindled until it was nothing more than a dream. Accepting this as their fortune, they became content with their quiet life.

Jhar'ensky was a proud man, strong-willed and reserved in his ways. At the time he was growing in favor among the Estellar Council. His early election to Council Board won him honors and the commensurate responsibility that went with it. There were days when he half-heartedly wished otherwise.

Bexhiera, the beautiful wife of Jhar'ensky, was a brilliant woman, a lead diamond-hand aeroxia, well-versed in the ways of therapeutic recovery. And, even though she was a prodigy in her field, she took care to keep herself and her career out of the public spotlight as much as possible. Her ways were simple and unobtrusively wise. Bexhiera spent her days at the Centre, discovering new remedies to heal the sick and disabled. This she and her team did, not only for their own region, but on behalf of the nearby regions that fell short in staffing and resources.

After their busy days apart they enjoyed a run through the Khalterzhan trail, weather permitting, or join the performers at their camp for a toned down training session. It was Bexhiera's passion for complete wellbeing that kept them on a well-laid path to optimal health. However, on cool evenings towards the end of a phase, they would spend a short time in the yard preparing for the coldest peak of querro to come, before finishing by tending to the fruit flowers in their nursery. Embraced by layers of warm fanzuay, they gardened tirelessly before retiring inside for the evening. Then, as routine would have it, they shared their daily trials and triumphs accompanied by groans and laughter or reveling in a game of cunning and cuddling by the fire.

On this cool, insignificant night they were enjoying a nourishing meal of veldhin leaves and zaiti froth seasoned with sweet red tarapes. Lit by the emerald fire, the dishes were alive with robust savor.

"I think I might wear out if we keep going like this; another Heliox that's sure to prove to be nothing more than a waste of an assembly. Why, I should be out on the bavajo range tomorrow enjoying a beverage, instead of attending another deliberation. You would think grown men of distinction would learn to work together instead of bickering like unlearned children. I mean, I just can't believe how much the two orders have grown apart," said Jhar'ensky "Now we have a situation where none of the elder members, with all their supposed knowledge, have yet to come to any sort of agreement on where, or even when to construct the next sioleh; the primary proposed site is causing an internal dispute. Discord is starting to set in, and we have only five days left to sign the contract before a "postpone" is issued." He let out a sulking sigh, slumping down in his seat.

"Jhar'ensky," Bexhiera said in a lightly chiding tone.

"Yes, what is it?"

"It's still today and we have a wonderful evening left to enjoy. So, how about we let that be for now? I'm sure you'll have plenty of time to muddle over the details during breakfast. Okay?"

She gave him an eyebrow raised smirk. He obliged with a slight bow and smirk of his own.

"Fair enough. Well then my lady, are you up for a game of friendly game of Jerrez?"

Jerrez was made popular by the founders of the Estellar region. Their ancestors brought it with them from their distant homeland. In the game, the player's ability to balance their "key piece's" orientation across diverse playing fields, while limiting their opponents movement is the fundamental strategy for victory.

"Sure. And we'll settle who is the best strategist once and for all," Bexhiera replied.

Mr. Regalis straightened up a bit in his seat. He was rather pleased with himself, knowing Mrs. Regalis would not back down from the challenge. She shifted over to the ensemble of glass shelves where they kept most of their games and guest entertainment. But, before she could retrieve the renowned game of Jerrez, there was a ring at the door. No it wasn't a ring. Rather, the door chimed. It was such an unusual noise that fell on Mr. Regalis's ears.

"Did we order a new artaghan for the door?"

"No, I don't believe so."

"Are you sure?"

"My love, I'd be the first to know…" She too took note of the unusual chime at the door. "Who would come on such a cool night, at such an odd time?"

Bexhiera proceeded towards the door, but Mr. Regalis interrupted her stride.

"I'll contest our strange visitor this evening. This could be someone out for trouble. And, if that's the case, they've found it with me. Bexhiera shook her head at his bravado. Though his protective disposition pleased her, they lived in one of the quietest and most spacious districts of Estellar, where there wasn't much to fear. And yet Jhar'ensky, in his duty as the protector, marched on towards the elegant cedar wood, gold-trimmed door. The weighty door had been engraved with pictures from the Book of Ascension and stained to give it a rouge accent, a fitting tint to match the temperament of a busy councilman who'd had his blissful evening interrupted by a would-be miscreant.

Looking through the viewer, Jhar'ensky saw not a person nor creature in sight. Perhaps the person was standing to the side of the door where the lacquered paneling was wide enough to hide them? "Who is it?" said Jhar'ensky in a commanding voice. The silence responded loudly. "Who is it?!", he bellowed, now with more annoyance in his voice than before. Still, the only reply was the soft breeze that beckoned him forth for further investigation. "Please take a step back," he said to

Mrs. Regalis, who was stood by his side. Then, preparing for a potential assault, Mr. Regalis made a quick tactical maneuver. He swung the door wide open as he dashed to one side. The anxiety within him was dispelled as he looked upon what lay in front of him. "Well, what do we have here?"

As he attempted to grasp what was taking place, Bexhiera peeked out from behind him. She caught only a quick view of the star lit sky above before her eyes met with another's that were looking up to her from below.

"Oh, how precious," she exclaimed in a whisper. "How did you get here, little one?"

In a shimmering lapis-lazuli cradle on their doorstep a baby man-child lay, wrapped in a dark blue shrouding garment laden with violet-pink flower petals.

"Who leaves a baby on someone's doorstep on a cold night and then vanishes like that?" Jhar'ensky was disturbed by the irresponsible behavior as he peered off into the night, searching for whoever did this.

The mysterious visitor made no sound. He lay there, looking at them as if he was expecting something. Maybe he was. Mrs. Regalis moved around Jhar'ensky and scooped him up.

"His eyes shine like starlight," said Mrs. Regalis. What's this you're wearing little one?"

In her hand she held a single braided cord clearer than crystal. Attached to it, was a small mystifying sphere. Within it a cerulean light whirled at a blurring pace, jumping about as if it were alive.

"There's something engraved on the middle portion," Mr. Regalis took note.

"Let's see."

THIZ IZ APEAY

"Hmm... why would they put it like that?" he pondered.

"Apeay..." Bexhiera's voice trailed off. It was perfect. Their wish had been granted. "This is it, dear."

"This is what?" Mr. Regalis was still trying to figure things out.

"We were just talking about it; raising a family, having a child of our own. Tonight our dream came true. Isn't that right my adorable Apeay?" She rubbed her nose against his. Apeay giggled with delight. He was happy to be so eagerly accepted.

"Hold on. We don't even know where he came from. What if he was kidnapped?"

"If that's the case then someone will come looking for him. In the meantime, he can stay with us. Who, knows. Maybe, whoever left him here couldn't keep him for one reason or another, and wanted him to have a better life."

"Honey, that's a wonderful theory. But, we're settled now you know. And with our responsibilities to the region, were not exactly ideal parents."

"Jhar'ensky, you can't be serious. We're very ideal. We're both in good health and have plenty of room here for one if not two or more in our family. No one would kidnap a baby only to randomly leave them at our doorstep."

Mr. Regalis knew what she said was true. But, it was all so sudden and he didn't like abrupt changes. He lived life by a simple rule: Make a plan. Go over the details. Review everything twice. Then, execute. There was a time during the first phase of his tenure on Council when he ignored this rule, causing him to overlook a minor detail in the Legionnaires' affairs which almost cost them their order within their region. Never again did he wish to relive that mistake.

"What I'm saying is that this is...unexpected. However, I don't see the harm in keeping him until we find out where he belongs."

Mr. Regalis leaned back, standing tall looking upon the child in Bexhiera's arms. "Apeay. Well, well. I think you may have found yourself a place to stay. C'mon, dear, let's go in. He's been in the cold long enough."

Mrs. Regalis twirled about as she carried their miracle through the door. Jhar'ensky followed behind, cradle under his arm. Feeling as if they were being watched, he turned around, taking one more glance and scanning for movement in the twilight before closing the door.

The enchanted night carried on until the dawn declared them a pristine, newly established family. It wouldn't be long before Mr. Regalis fell under the same "spell" that captivated Bexhiera right from the start.

Apeay was home.

CHAPTER 2

"Space 55 at gold level three."

"Are you sure about that?"

"Yep."

"Well then, I'll go back to 21 at diamond level five. So you my friend are boxed in the lower corner again. You'll have to stop limiting your conceptions, and work more on your abstract thinking if you want to beat me."

Three games of Jerrez in a row: Mr. Regalis: 3, Apeay: 0.

"Yes, but you have to admit dear, he's very good for his age. He even had you on the run for a jhenta, in the upper period," Mrs. Regalis pointed out. "I think you got lucky this time."

"However you'd like to put it, dear, he still has a long way to go." Jhar'ensky knew his wife was right, but wasn't going to speak on it.

Nine cycles had passed since they discovered the starlit child at their doorstep. A child whom they soon realized was a fast learner. There were times when it seemed to go beyond learning, as if Apeay knew far more than a child his age had been taught. In fact, he displayed high intelligence in all his session curriculums. Still, his parents had their concerns. Despite his brilliance, Apeay struggled to maintain focus in his studies, and showed little interest in any subject. Even in visual expression, which he liked most, was something he dabbled in rather than committed to. All of his images were vague and unfinished. His hue coordinates looked like misplaced accumulations of color. When asked what he was working on at any given time, he would always say, "You see it. That's all it is." Questioning him didn't help because the answer remained the same. Those who knew him accepted that this was his way of being; a boy with a bright, yet melancholy temperament. He was indeed a peculiar type of a "happy child."

This was the typical Setmun afternoon for the Regalis family, and a welcome day off from hectic overfilled Council meetings for Jhar'ensky. He wasn't fond of some of the new additions to Council Board. He felt they were attempting to grandfather in unnecessary stipulations wherever they saw fit. The region of Estellar was split on the definition of advancement. Many of the laymen, along with devout mystics among them argued for a naturalist movement that would require reverting to some of the "old ways." However, those of prestige who funded most Council initiatives threw out any notions of retrograding, to push on with new construction for the persistent increase in energy demands. Therefore, with an era past, the postponed proposal was back at the discussion table of an increasingly unstable Council. Jhar'ensky now held the title and chair of Council Principal, beating out his longtime comrade and close friend Valus by a small margin. And, with the last of the antiquated order from the Golden Era of Council stepping down, he felt more pressed to restore harmony and balance throughout Estellar.

Bexhiera also enjoyed her time away from the busy Centre. Today, she needed rest even more than Jhar'ensky. Growing numbers of children suffering unexplained fatigue were being sent to Estellar Centre. Whatever it was affecting the children, didn't affect most of the older adolescents, nor any of the adults.

Then, there was Apeay running here, there and back again. He couldn't wait to go out and visit with his friends. The golden light of Heyliun beamed through the hexagonal windows, illuminating Apeay's face. It was the call to an outside world of fun. He hoped he'd have a chance to meet up with the Mangiazj twins. Their usual play involved riding their mirahs up and down the Khalterzhan Trails, a vast, surreal place where the dirt paths wound in and around tall verdant driveree bushels while the silver blue kepli swam up the nearby streams. It was a favorite site of the local children, many of whom would zip around the four paths that met at Lake Hyzjozhio, where new clusters of wildly growing zaitson fruit lay. It was the result of a bold new push by the aeroxia ambassadors to Council, who had taken steps to ameliorate the natural beauty and bounty of the region. People would come to gather some of the fruit in due course and while many of those would trek to the center to collect their fruit, the mischievous trio would see who could collect the most honey nuts without stopping; the not-so-innocent game often inciting an unaware passerby to yell into the tree line, "Who's out there throwing those nuts?!" The honey nuts weren't all that big or heavy enough to hurt anybody, but still had the potential to sting. Each of them had a secret path to escape before any could catch them. The game never got old.

"Father," Apeay was prepared himself to make an important request as Mr. Regalis was deep into his afternoon reading.

"What is it, son?"

"Can I go out for a ride with Deslao and Seldao?" Apeay grinned with expectation as he anxiously bobbed from side to side.

"You sure can. After a...short but meaningful read through the Book of Ascension."

"...short but meaningful read through the Book of Ascension," Apeay groaned in unison with Jhar'-ensky. Throughout the region and beyond it was widely accepted that the authors of this book were not from their world. Or, at least, that's what the folklore said. This in itself delighted Apeay. Often he read through the various text for the sheer enjoyment of taking his mind to a place outside of the realm of Estellar. The accounts of symbolic remarks, ideas and elemental accounts intrigued him. Therefore, it wasn't that he disliked the reading it, but on a star filled, warm day as it was, Apeay became overwhelmed by a boundless energy that couldn't be contained. Bexhiera, called it "the spark of super-novas."

With a shake of his head, he did as Jhar'ensky requested. He picked up the black and platinum bound book, taking a seat on the edge of the linen chair. He opened the large book going directly to "The Account of Ancient Elemental Virtues." In a few zahmens Apeay turned a, "meaningful read" into a glancing skim-through. With that, he placed the book back on its stand and dashed out the door.

"Please, don't come back with any more cuts and bruises," Bexhiera yelled out to him.

"Okay, love you," Apeay said. Then, making a turn he yelled back, "can you make zaiti soup for dinner please?" Then making another one-eighty he ran to his mirah. He hopped on quickly, working the levers back and forth with the shifting of his hands and push of his feet cruising, down the avenue to meet up with his riding buddies. Mrs. Regalis stood for a moment at the door to watch him float off into the breeze.

"An adventurous child," she thought to herself. *"Where are you going to now?"*

The path that took him to their usual meeting place was one of Apeay's favorites. It was complete with twists and steep curves for speeding over on his mirah. The various shades of blue and purple valdiashez that filled the air with the most pleasant aroma were accented by orange tufts of grass on each side of the road. Yet, in spite of so much to look at, he had caught up to the Mangiazj twins within the blink of an eye. He saw them on the edge of the curvy path. They didn't appear to be doing much besides stooping over something on the ground.

"What's going on guys?" Apeay asked upon joining them. "I thought you'd be at the trails or at least Ausylan River by now."

The Mangiazj twins were an unlikely duo. Yes, they were identical twins, but they were everything and nothing one would expect of such a pair.

Quick to speak on any situation Seldao informed him, "Deslao's mirah is broke. So, were stuck. And I don't feel like going back home to fix it."

"You don't want to go back home because you skipped out on chores," Deslao scoffed.

Apeay wasn't fond of fix-up projects. Instead, he thought of another solution, "How about we leave our mirahs hidden in the bushes and race to the river?"

"Nah, I don't feel like racing. And I stubbed my toe on a root last time," said Seldao.

"Whatever slow boy," Deslao teased. "Not so fast without your souped-up mirah."

The game of "I'm better than your best" was underway. The twins played it so often that Seldao didn't flinch before clapping back with an insult.

"I got the Estellar City Diamond Star for symphysmatics. You still can't add simple shapes. Who's slow again?"

It puzzled Apeay how two identical twins could be so alike in looks and at the same time, on opposite spectrums of ability. Seldao was quick with tablets and numbers; his diverse aptitudes were ranged from everything and anything in between. He was invited to speak at Ajina Delta, the most prestigious of the post-succession enhancement zones, in the sister region of Sohexiah, for a delivery he wrote in his fifth cycle at Estellar Prime. Deslao, on the other hand either didn't care to delve into tablet work or anything concerning calculations or he lacked the ability to grasp it. However, he was incredibly quick and agile and strong for his age. Deslao once threw a stone about a third of the way across Lake Hyzjozhio mid-flip, landing in the exact spot from which he leapt.

Apeay truly admired them for what they could do, though he felt he didn't measure up in the area of natural talent, unless napping or daydreaming counted.

As Apeay thought of it he began to drift off until he heard Seldao say, "Apeay, what's the deal with that neckless?" He pointed towards the brilliant jewel dangling from Apeay's neck.

"What do you mean? I've had it all my life," said Apeay.

"That's what I'm saying. You don't tell us anything about it. We just see you flipping it through your fingers here and there."

"Hey...let's play catch with it," said Deslao.

"Yeah, we should," Seldao seconded.

"No way," said Apeay. "Mom said this is my special ornament." He remembered what Bexhiera said the first day he left home for his first session at Estellar Prime: "Keep this with you at all times. Let no one take it from you. Now, pay attention, do well, and come right back home when you're done. I love you."

"What? It's just a shiny blue ball," Deslao said in disbelief. Then reaching for it, "You see, all you have to do is..."

As Deslao attempted to lift the ornament from Apeay's neck, the dancing blue light within, burst out and engulfed Deslao's hand in a blue blaze. Deslao let out a yelp, recoiling from the painful shock.

"What did you do to him?" Seldao shrieked.

Apeay was horrified. "I didn't do anything. I don't know...it was the ornament?"

"His hand is smoking!"

"I'm sorry. I didn't mean to..."

"You did something! What's wrong with you?" Seldao said cutting him off.

"Nothing's wrong with me," Apeay said. *Why is Seldao angry with me?* He was dazed by his reaction.

"Well, I don't like it and I know my brother don't like it either after what you did to him. If you're going to burn up his hand over a little ball, I don't think we should hang out with you anymore."

"Yep. No more," Deslao said confirming his brother's words.

Apeay's chest was heavy. He felt like he had been hit with a mallet. All he wanted to do was help. But, the twins' displeasure kept him away. How could it be that he went from being their favorite acquaintance to a pariah in such a short time? Apeay hopped on his mirah and fled in shame. The valdiashez had lost their luster as he passed by. Nothing about the scenery was beautiful anymore. *What's wrong with you? No more...* The words echoed over and over in Apeay's mind. Tears poured like rain down his face. He rode his mirah down to the trail. But, this time he was going there to be alone.

The dinner Bexhiera prepared was starting to get cold.

"Honey, where's Apeay? Heyliun's almost set." Mr. Regalis, though outwardly stern, had a warm heart for his child. It worried him for Apeay to be out alone after dark.

"I don't know. He took off to meet the Mangiazj twins over four ahkmeres ago. They never ride that long." Now Mrs. Regalis became worried as well. "Wait a minute. Look over there, out the terrace window..."

" I know that already," he said, taking a peek out the window. "Oh, that's his mirah by the shrubbery. Why would he come back that way?"

"Look, the nursery door is open."

"I believe we've located our mystery child," said Mr. Regalis as they exited the room. They went down the stairs and out the back door. As they got closer to the nursery entrance, they could hear Apeay sobbing.

"Apeay?" Mrs. Regalis called out, while searching the rows of plants. Then, turning another corner, "There you are my baby. Come to your mother..."

"Stay away!" Apeay bellowed, and continued sobbing.

"There's a fresh bowl of zaiti soup waiting for you inside."

"I don't care!"

"Apeay, don't talk to your mother like that," Mr. Regalis said, taking control of the situation. "No one is going to hurt you. Just tell us what happened."

"You'll both get burned," Apeay cried, burying his head in his lap.

"Burned? What are you talking about?" Jhar'ensky asked. Please, my son, we can't help if you don't tell us what's the matter."

Apeay lifted his head and explained in detail what had taken place with the twins on the side of the road.

"That can't be. There was probably something nearby that made it happen. A flux in an energy transfer in the subterrain might have shot up from a deep fissure under the path," said Mr. Regalis.

"It does seem strange, but it doesn't mean it couldn't happen," said Bexhiera. "When you were still a baby, every night I removed your ornament , fearing it might strangle you. The light inside sometimes spun round or even got brighter, but I can't say I ever saw it outside the ornament."

"And, my son, I used to take it off to bathe you. I'm sure it was something else," Jhar'ensky added.

"But, it happened and his hand got burned!" Apeay was irate at his parents' disbelief over what he experienced firsthand. The frightening experience, and the state of shock from being ostracized weighed heavily on him.

"Maybe something changed Jhar'ensky" Mrs. Regalis. If that's the case, we'll soon find out."

Mr. Regalis knelt down in front of Apeay, who shied away from his approach.

"Please sit still, son. It's alright." His reassurance calmed Apeay. Jhar'ensky cautiously leaned forward and removed the ornament from Apeay.

Nothing happened.

"You see son, there's nothing to worry about. It's just a glowing ball. See?"

"Maybe," Apeay sniffled. "But, why's it do this?"

Apeay snatched the ornament from Jhar'ensky and sprinted towards the tree line behind their house. They followed closely behind him. Apeay threw it towards the woods as hard as he could. To their astonishment, the ornament froze in mid-air, spinning, shining like a star before zipping back like lightning to Apeay, settling around his neck.

Mr. Regalis was speechless.

Mrs. Regalis whispered aloud, "My goodness, Apeay, you must be so scared right now." She hugged him, comforting him. "You're going to be okay."

In her mind she was marveled, *who are you my Apeay?*

$$\pi$$

Out the window a bojo flies past. Then, beyond the distant horizon, it soars far out of view. Where it journeys after that is pure imagination. I'll leave that up to you.

"Apeay... Apeay, are you paying attention?"

"Yeah, sebah I hear you," he responded.

"Then, what's the answer?"

"Umm... Heptagon 62?"

The entire session burst out laughing.

"Quiet protozens," said Ms. Clesias, calming the room. "Awkwardly late, and no. We're at the literature portion of session, Apeay." She was displeased with his lack of focus. However, she was astounded that he gave the correct answer to the shape formation that no one knew from three stages before. In fact, she had every protozen in session record the problem in their tablet to try and solve before the next phase's session. How was it that Apeay could solve a problem that should take the average protozen ahkmeres to figure out in mere zahmens? Still, she had to reprimand him for not paying attention. "Have you even activated your tablet?"

Apeay looked down at his blank tablet. He hadn't taken a single note, and it was obvious he hadn't heard a word she said up to this point. He'd been caught daydreaming. His thoughts were focused on being everywhere but there, partly because of what happened that previous evening. Mr. Regalis got a hold of the Mangiazj twins' parents to apologize. It turned out that Deslao's hand wasn't burned at all. Whatever happed had only lasted a moment. However, they kept their distance from Apeay for quite some time as did many of his peers. And Apeay's quiet, melancholic disposition didn't help. Those that questioned him about what had happened that night were given the answer, "Not much," or "Ask someone else," as he passed them by.

The echo of the ocuroo whistled. He was saved. Session was over. Apeay grabbed up his tablet and lintighins, racing towards the door. His hot feet were quickly cooled by the sebah's call.

"Apeay, could you please approach the podium?"

Ugh. This again? What does Ms. Clesias want with me this time?

A few of the other protozens snickered insults as they brushed past "Mr. Sixty-two."

"How much is a verb plus a noun?"

"What's the sum of indentation?"

Apeay sauntered up to the podium, awaiting his doom.

"Please, look up when I speak to you. I'll accept no heads held down in this room. Internal confidence is the way to making the symbol." Her lively spiel cruelly interrupted his departure.

"You know Apeay," Ms. Clesias continued. "When you put in the effort during session, you do very well. You may not realize it, but your calculation skills are extraordinary. Earlier, you solved a gold level three alignment problem in the same amount of time it'd take a shototu. During silent symbol I've walked past your worktop enough to see that you understand linguistics on the level of an administrative council ledger. You have so much untapped talent, but you don't put effort into anything. Your symbol markings are slipping down. It's as if you're always lost in some other place. What is it that distracts you so much?"

That was just it even now, he was distracted by thoughts of leaving the session room to go for a meaningless walk.

"Oh... I guess my dreams, I'd say."

"Well, I hope that whatever they may be that they're worth the extra studies I'm assigning for personal enrichment. You'll have to catch up with the rest of the protozens before next session. I'm assigning pages 8 through 13. You will then provide me a summary resolute of the lesson. That's all. You're free to go."

Before the last syllable struck his ears, Apeay had spun around and exited the room. Ms. Clesias watched him jet out in his familiar way, as a familiar feeling came over her. "Oh..." She stood up and ran to the door. She saw the young one had almost made it to the end of the hall in rapid time. To this fleeing apparition she shouted, "Hey, I'd love to see what those dreams of yours read like someday. Chin up Apeay!"

Apeay didn't wish to be drawn into another exchange of words, so he nodded his head affirmatively and continued straight on his way. He went down the grey and pearl marble hallway that echoed with each step, then headed down the spiral staircase and out the double cedar doors. Apeay breathed a sigh of relief as he gazed upon the late afternoon horizon.

As his ritual dictated, Apeay caught the express beam mynvad to the northmost district; he made it a tradition to walk the route of the canals at the end of the phase; the canals his father warned him about and insisted he never travel alone. They were dangerously close to the site of the "Forbidden Ruins." Any citizen of Estellar with good sense knew to stay away from there. It was an old, vast place. It was so vast, in fact, that one might consider it a region unto itself. A peculiar obscurity rested over the entirety of the Forbidden Ruins, making it a thing of nightmares. There was a constant fog that shrouded its landscape at all times. Even on the brightest days, this fog created a subtly overcast environment that couldn't be ignored. Everyone native to the region of Estellar had heard of its mysterious horrors and tragedies. Combined with the terrifying tales, its desolate appearance ratified its ominous reputation. However, Apeay paid no mind to the rumors. Neither, did he have a reason to wander beyond these canals of which he was familiar with. It was nearly three cycles ago when he took his first venture through the massive tunnels. He was on his way home from the trail, when for some mystifying reason he felt compelled to take an express ride by the way of the river to its end, leading him to this remote place. For that reason alone, he decided to keep this journey secret. From that day on he continued his private walk at the end of each phase. And today, he was determined to make the trip last as long as possible. The thought of "extra enrichment" made him feel weighed down. So, up and down, zig zagging and exploring the canals Apeay went. Each canal was like the one before. They were tall brick walled fortresses. The overflow from the Ausylan River poured into them in between.

Apeay was humming away, carrying on an endless one man carnival: *"Dum dida da dah, fire fields, dida da dah on cabera wheels..."* He carried on his tireless procession until he looked up at the sky once more. Heyliun was beginning to fade in the southern sky.

"What time is it?" Apeay wondered aloud. "I'd better head home."

He scampered down the canal corridors, making his way back. Left, another left, right then left again. He remembered the route well. Another two rights, and the mynvad station would be in sight.

But, wait...what is this?

As he neared the pathway that should've taken him to where the commuters gathered, he discovered yet another canal.

Where...when did this get here?

Unlike the other canals that were made of bright red stone, this one was faded, almost devoid of color, overcast and dusty. It seemed as if Council didn't care to see that this one be kept in good condition like the rest.

"I know what happened. I took one too many right turns," Apeay said, assuring himself as he began retracing his last movements. He went back by one turn and straight forward again.

Yes, I'll still get home in no time.

Apeay was in full sprint. He approached the familiar way as it became unfamiliar once more. And now, ridiculing him ,was the same dungy canal he left a few moments ago. Apeay had never lost his way before. Not here. And if so, it was only for a matter of not caring where he was.

This can't be right. There's no way I could be lost.

An unsettling chill crept up his spine. His knees shook upon hearing the leaves menacingly scrape the ground in the dark shadows of the canal in front of him. This image he had to escape. But, the image was not done provoking him.

The wind whispered to him from behind,

"Who are you, child?"

Startled, Apeay jumped to his rear to face an empty canal.

"Who's there?" he said, his words were catching up in his throat.

"Who Are You Boy?" This time the unknown had an odd sound, like the voice of many speaking through one, raging in the wind from the other side. He spun around to meet another faceless pursuer.

"What is this? WHO ARE YOU?!"

The booming voice shook the very walls of the canal. Apeay felt gale winds whipping, cutting at him from behind. The voice in the wind seemed to be chasing him, roaring at him from all around. He dropped about all he was carrying and fled down the faded canal, while the terrifying voice in the wind urged him on.

"CHILD WHO IS NOT, RETURN AND FACE ME! WHO ARE YOU?!"

"No! Stay away from me! Help, help...someone's trying to get me!" But, there was no one to hear his cries for help as he ran deeper into the cryptic canal. Realizing this he put all he had into his getaway. He ran with unrestrained swiftness until he could feel his legs no more. His heart was surging. All was fire within him, making a blazing escape, and then...

A pause.

The clamor of haunting voices had come to a stop. There was nowhere left to run to. He had come to the end of the canal, arriving at a shining innovative place.

Whoosh... whoosh...whoosh...

Colossal mechanical delignos's flashed back and forth on what looked like glowing violet rods of steel, vanishing as they came and went. Some went up high above, until they could no longer be seen. Others sank below the horizons abyss. Each one was routed in every direction possible, some going up, down, forwards, and back and some even going in and out.

Could these be the old capsyint lines father told me about? The ones that connected Estellar to the rest of the world?

Whooooooossshhhhh

One of the speeding caberas came to rest at the platform in front of him.

"Hey there." A man with a rounded, shiny, copper topped hat popped his head out the window. His face was stern but polite all the same. His demeanor was that of one quite sure of themselves at all times.

"Me?" Apeay was leery of this funny-looking man with the squished hat. *Was this the man chasing me down the canal?*

"Well, seeing as how there ain't no other people standing out here on this platform, who else would I be referring to?"

Apeay squinted at him in disbelief, insulted by the strange man's sarcasm.

"Look kid, I'd hate to leave you stranded out here by yourself. It's not good for someone your age to be out here after dark. And, there's no more coming down this line after me."

"So, take me home!" Apeay yelled with impatience.

The man threw up his hands, "Can't take you home. You haven't told me where you live."

"Estellar, Khalterzhan district. That's where."

"You mean way back there?" The man pointed towards a populous metropolis in the mountains clouds. It was the region of Estellar, and it was nearly out of sight. How had he gotten so far away? Estellar's landmass made it the second-largest region of Tzierhan; expanding like a diamond it was 5,000 reels from end to end. It would be impossible for anyone to journey that distance in such a short amount of time. And something else about the way it appeared didn't seem right. The horizon was misty, without a rain cloud in sight.

"I understand you want to go home young traveler, but it's going to take me a while to get you back on this circuit. And, you have my word. I will get you back there. In the meantime I have a few stops to make."

"What stops?"

"Ones I'm sure you'll enjoy, my friend. There's this place called Laixfu. The palace there is packed with excitement. Then there's that sweet charming Lady of Silver Lake. Oh, and plenty of tinker shops along the way. They've got a lot more styles and colors of model glineers like the one you're holding."

Apeay looked in his right hand, and realized his miniature glineer was the only thing he hadn't dropped on the way. However, one of the sides was damaged.

"Can they fix it?"

"Oh, I know a fella who can."

Apeay mulled it over for a moment. He was inclined to find out what all this talk of palaces and silver lakes was about. Besides that, he was already lost and didn't know of any other way to get back home.

"Where do I get on?"

"The doors right in front of ya, kid." The man pushed on a string and an entrance slid open. "Welcome aboard. Name's Haru. I'm the best out here on these tracks. Sit back and hold tight. We're taking off."

"Okay, so where are we going again?"

"To where dreams are life, young Apeay."

"Hey, how do you know...?" Before he could complete his question, the capsyint bolted away into the star filled night.

Φ

"Is that right? Thank you. We appreciate your efforts. We'll be up all night. Please let us know if anything changes. Yes? Sure. Goodbye."

Jhar'ensky was exhausted. He and Bexhiera had contacted every Centre in the city. The Legionnaires had found no trace of him. Of the five Rings of Legionnaires, Ring Three was sequenced first in the duty of locating missing persons. "My... this is unbelievable. He was seen right after session. Then, he just vanishes. I'm putting all my Council logs on "hold" status and then I'm heading out. Bexhiera seemed to be unmoved by his proclamation, which irked Jhar'ensky to his core. "Why are you sitting there looking out the window? Are you listening to me?"

"Of course I am. I'm waiting my turn to make a suggestion," said Bexhiera. They locked eyes for a moment. "Why don't we ask the twins if they know where he might be? They spend most of their time together. Maybe there's some place they go to hide out?"

"Excellent idea! Grab what we need for the night and get the mynersha ready. I'll get a hold of an old friend of mine."

Bexhiera fetched a kit that contained everything a family needed to last a phase without returning home, along with guides and visual enhancements, and put them in the back of the mynersha.

Jhar'ensky came out front and hopped in. Looking at the kit in the back he said, "That's a bit much for one night, don't you think? After we stop by the Mangiazj place, we should know his whereabouts."

"Maybe so..." Bexhiera took a deep breath as they rushed into the night. However, Apeay was farther away than either of them could have comprehended.

CHAPTER 3

If there is one thing I never understood, it's how I got this far in life. I was merely resting.

A sea of iridescent gems gliding through the ocean. That was the marvel Apeay saw while peering out his capsyint window; a sensational view that made him feel at home in the amazing capsyint. His seat was absorbing his body as the capsyint pushed on faster and faster. This mighty cabera seemed to have no limits of power.

After a moment or so the capsyint reached a steady pace. The gentle sway in the belly of the beast rocked Apeay to sleep.

"Only 200 more reels to go my friend. We're almost there," said Haru.

"Two-hundred...huh?." Apeay said, with a yawn rub-bing his eyes after being woken up. Propping himself up, he turned and looked outside to see what he could see, and gazed upon a boundless lush meadow receding into snowcapped mountains. The scenery was the sound of a well-orchestrated melody. "Haru?"

"What is it, kid?"

"Where are we?"

"We, my friend, are deep within the Xenominh Meadowlands. You could say it's the gateway to the Imperial Palace."

"That's one of the places you told me about last night, right?"

"Sure is," said Haru.

He was recalling everything the man said to him before. Anticipating what was to come before returning home. Then it hit him.

"Hey, how did you know my name?"

"Oh...you fit the type."

"I fit the type?"

"Sit back and get ready! We're coming to a stop," Haru said as he pushed down on a handle from the floor.

Ssshhhh...Whooossshhh

The capsyint came to rest on the edge of deep blue waters. The emperor of Laixfu was not fond of the noise of capsyints. Therefore, he decreed that all lines would stop on the perfect alignment at the center divide of the Xonique River and proceed around the mountainside outside Laixfu.

"I don't see a walkway," said Apeay.

"Who said we were walking?" Haru waved Apeay towards the sliding door where he was standing. Within moments, a youthful, smooth-skinned lady guided her vehicle to an explosive stop on the waters of the capsyint dock. It seemed as if time slowed as she turned her head, greeting them with an enthusiastic smile. Her crystal-green eyes were aglow against the backdrop of her dark brown and ruddy hair that reached down to her copper shoulders. Her physique and posture were that of a professional acrobat.

The young lady navigated a gold imperial sea tabanger, built solely for transporting passengers to the mainland. It was eating the water and spitting it back out.

"Welcome back Haru, even though it's been forever," said the lady.

"Yeah well, it's nice to see you too, Jenshii."

Stepping out, Apeay looked up curiously at Jenshii.

"A new traveling partner, I see. Got lonely out there without us, did you?"

"Not at all, miss. My work keeps me occupied just fine."

"If you want to believe that, I guess I will too. So, who's this handsome little guy you brought with you?"

Apeay started to feel blush, and pretended to study the waters, yet he felt compelled to look up again. The moment his eyes met hers, he fell into a trance. He wanted to say his name, just to tell her who he was, but for some reason couldn't bring himself to speak.

"He's my pal, Apeay," Haru said, rescuing Apeay from the spell. "I came across him last night. He was on the outer passageway beyond Laixfu."

"Way out there? That's impressive *and* brave." Looking into his eyes, Jenshii studied Apeay for a brief moment.

As for Apeay, he wasn't sure if he saw sadness in her, but if there was, her polished speech covered it up. Jenshii was energetic and showed a great deal of enthusiasm as she continued the interview. "What's the business today, 'Haru the Everywhere Man?'

"Let's see. I have an overnight stop here…"

"Overnight?" Apeay interjected. "You said we were stopping here, and another place, and then you'd take me home."

"You're right, but it's going to take a while kid. I wasn't lying. It will be sooner than you think."

Apeay sighed. "Sure, sure. Not like I have a choice"

"Like I said, Jenshii; we'll be here long enough to get some new H-rods built for my capsyint. That will give us enough time to go sight-seeing, which includes taking this youngster for his first look at the palace."

"Sounds like fun. Hop aboard. I'll take you to shore."

Apeay tiptoed onto the sleek tabanger. After they took their seats Jenshii shouted, "They call me the speed demon of Xonique River! Whoo yeah!"

"What's that supposed to mean?" Apeay said under his breath to Haru.

"It means you better strap in, or get tossed out the tabanger."

Apeay, taking Haru's advice, quickly harnessed himself to the tabanger's body restraint.

The tabangers large appetite for the pure crystal waters steadily increased. They could feel the tremoring power surging beneath them until, with a thunderous crack, the tabanger split the waters in half all the way from the docks to the shores of Laixfu.

Δ

The front door opened and closed abruptly. "I didn't expect to see you home so early," said Bexhiera.

"I'm taking a leave of absence for however long it takes us to find him."

"I'm so glad to hear that. What did Council have to say?"

"It doesn't matter what they say. Council will have to do without me for a while. I appointed Valus to cover for me. The elders of the board have appointed members from the junior staff to assist as needed. I mean, I just can't believe this. Five days have passed and still not a clue!"

"I know, dear. We just have to trust that they're doing all they can. There are still a few places they haven't searched. Also, Enjevix contacted me earlier today. He said they'll be taking over from Ring Three to give them access to Sky Patrol," said Bexhiera. Her fears had been somewhat alleviated, but she was far from at ease. Jhar'ensky similarly felt hopeful and disquieted.

"So, they've moved our affairs all the way up to Ring One; the best of the best. Anything else?" Jhar'ensky was actually rather disappointed it had taken so long before being passed on to Ring One. After all, he was Council Principal.

"They're going to the search the immediate surrounding districts, from Khalterzhan to Zenlan."

"That's a an awfully wide range."

"I don't care if they search the whole tzierhan as long as they find him."

Mr. Regalis lowered his head mumbling something inaudible before joining Mrs. Regalis on the turujo. She leaned her head on his shoulder.

"I'm sure we'll hear some good news soon. All we can do his hope for the best right?"

"We'll do more than that," said Mr. Regalis. He promptly stood and walked into his study.

π

The tabanger whizzed along pulling them ever closer to the mainland which was getting clearer in view. What Apeay saw was both amazing and surreal. A city of daylight coming from both Heyliun in the sky and the reflective polished stone buildings, evenly spaced and intricately placed along the coast-line.

In a flash, Jenshii curved the tabanger's course before abruptly cutting off the fanxi core, as waves from underneath the slashing tabanger splashed the shore. "Here we are, Dokun Sector, Laixfu!" Jenshii exclaimed. She seemed to be more than enthusiastic about transporting people to and from the main-land; which was probably why she'd been assigned to do so.

"Thank you, my lady," Haru said with a bow and tip of the hat. Apeay awkwardly mimicked the gesture.

"See you in a while," said Jenshii, who wasted no time bolt-ing her way back towards the capsyint docks, and was soon out of sight.

"Mmmm mmmph, just smell those fresh baked poppels. Gets my mouth all worked up. Let's get some breakfast, kiddo."

"I'm not that hungry," said Apeay

"You sure? Cause your stomachs been singing a different song since we got here….oh…" Haru noticed that one of Apeay's eyes were leaking. "Hey there kid it's gonna be alright. I al-ready gave you my word I'm taking you back for sure. It's just my circuit only goes one way. It's a double one sided loop. We'll be back to Estellar in a few days, I promise." Apeay feigned a smile.

"That's a better look, my guy. Now, how about a bite to eat?" Haru walked over to the makeshift stand at the corner of the square. He reached deep in his black velvety bag to shell out some empty bottles. The man behind the stand inspected the bottles and nodded his head. Then he handed Haru a basket of poppels, honey-nuts and a bottle of winchu juice.

"That's crazy, man."

"What are you talking about?"

"You gave him a couple empty bottles and he gave us all this in return. That should cost at least ten ellure."

"I gave him plenty. Whatever an ellure is, we don't have need for it round here in the boundless life." Apeay wasn't sure what that meant. But he decided to save any further questions for after satiating his appetite.

After their morning meal, Apeay and Haru walked six squares over and eight squares up through the busy streets to the gensico shop. The door made a snapping sound as they walked in. Apeay looked over the edges of the door to see what caused it. He didn't see anything out of the ordinary until he looked out the door window. The square was empty, and he didn't see anyone outside.

"Where'd everyone go?" asked Apeay

"They're handling their business, like we're doing."

There was someone hollering from the rear of the shop.

"What, the new ension benders aren't fast enough for you, you old traveling fool?!"

"At least I'm still goin' about." Haru hollered back.

The voice became a shape, then an outline of a body, transforming into a whisker-faced old man.

"Apeay this is my friend Ghilael Alishenz, from the first. We traveled the waters over the lands, nearly everywhere until he gave it up for a more *settled*-existence one might say." Ghilael looked refined and slightly older than Haru. In his eyes, there was a brilliant glimmer that spoke to having seen more than one could remember. The top part of his garment was covered in a black dust that sparkled at random when he came into the light. In his left hand, he was holding some type of instrument for measuring.

"Good morning sir." Apeay remembered to be polite using "sirs" and "ma'ams" as he had been taught.

"Oh, no need for that. Thank you, but my hairs are grey enough. Being in one place long enough will do that to a person. Well, Haru, you don't seem to be doing so bad." Ghilael went over to a shelf and observed that the three-piece device was spinning moderately about a cubic sphere. "Let me guess. Since the last time I saw you, you've put on close to 186 trillion reels on that capsyint of yours. That means you're just about due for new H-rods, yes?"

"That'd be right on the mark. You know best, my fella."

How could he know that? Apeay was fascinated by Ghilael's genius.

"My friend here needs some work done too."

Apeay retrieved the model glineer from his back pocket and handed it to Ghilael.

"This is an easy fix. Be right back," said Ghilael.

He retrieved the essential items for Haru, and by the time he returned Apeay's glineer was in mint condition. In actuality it was better, because it could now fly like the real ones. Ghilael demonstrated it for Apeay. "Just push this button on top and use this navigation pad to control it."

"Wow, how'd you do all that so fast?" asked Apeay.

"I thought to myself, what's the best way to fix a glineer for Apeay?"

"And?"

"And, what?" asked Ghilael in return.

"You have to pardon my young friend here. He's fresh in," said Haru. "By the way, Ghilael, you said you had some juicy news about the late festival so, cough, it, up."

"But how?" Apeay repeated.

"Don't worry, I'll tell ya how he fixed it on the way out, but for now, I need to hear some of these festive details, my friend."

Ghilael nodded and filled Haru in on the latest in Laixfu hearsay as Apeay perused the shop, fascinated by the wondrous devices that moved on their own without a power source, as far as he could tell.

The other two spent a while catching up, sharing stories and recent happenings, before Haru eventually caught up to describing how he found Apeay.

"You don't say." Ghilael leaned back stroking his whiskers. "I can't recall the last time something like that happened. Don't know if it ever has."

"It's like it's all new," said Haru "Well, we aren't getting any younger. Better get going."

"Sounds good. It's about time you let me get back to my work."

"You don't work. You just tinker and gossip all day. You forget I know you."

The two went on bickering until they eventually gave up their foolishness and waved goodbye to each other.

Apeay and Haru left the shop and continued their stroll through Laixfu. In an instant, the people who were previously out of view, reappeared.

There was much to take in about central Dokun. Each square was crammed with color, bursting with sound which seemed to originate from wherever there was movement without further explanation. The atmosphere was the antithesis of the polished-to-a-shine, "no nonsense" manner of central Estellar. There were street dancers on almost every corner performing the most energized routines Apeay had ever seen. They danced to the melodies of various skilled musicians, whose melodies and rhythms sent waves through the city that could be seen like mists of color in the sky. There were also traveling illusionists who kept the people amused with sleigh-of-hand trickery. The two of them came upon a small crowd gathering around one such illusionist, whose show had just begun.

"This should be good," said Haru as he and Apeay pulled up on the performance.

"Who's ready for a spectacular feat by the Mysterious Zenowic?" The crowd cheered on the man in the flowy purple robe. "I'm holding in my hand an ordinary ball. Please, you two gentlemen come forward and see for yourself." Two men from the audience stepped onto the limestone stage. They were looking and feeling around the ball like well-trained inspectors. Then, they returned to the audience with their certificate of authenticity. "Prepare to be amazed as you witness the unthinkable."

In one hand, the Mysterious Zenowic held the ball as the other waved over the top. The ball began to float up, above, and around his head before coming to rest back in his hand. And with another wave of the hand the ball faded away into nothing before their eyes. There were "oohs" and "ahs" mixed with cheers from the crowd.

"Hey!" Apeay shouted. "I can do illusions, too." All eyes including the Mysterious Zenowic's, were now focused on the novice performer.

"What can you do besides waste my time?" Zenowic was clearly annoyed by this preposterous interruption.

"Look!" Apeay said, yanking his ornament and flinging it high in the air. Just as before, the ornament spun and shone as brightly as Heyliun. However this time, Apeay had control over its movement as he drew it back to himself with the wave of his hand. The crowd gasped, as did the Mysterious Zenowic. A person from the crowd shouted, "Is he another one?"

Haru grabbed Apeay by the hand.

"Some tricks are meant to be kept to yourself, kiddo. Let's go." He hurried Apeay down the road away from the crowd. Apeay was bewildered.

"Why are we running?" he asked.

"You still...want to see...the palace right?" Haru gasped between breaths.

"Yes, I do."

"Alright...we have to get there before the gateway closes."

"Haru, was that you? What are you up to now?" said Zenowic, calling after them.

Apeay looked over his shoulder. Oddly enough, they hadn't put much distance between themselves and the crowd. But though the crowd wasn't running or chasing after them, he could feel their eyes still on him. Haru looked over at Apeay. "Will you stop looking back? You're slowing us down!"

"Right. Sorry," said Apeay

"Don't be sorry. Just keep running."

Eventually, they made it to the edge of the last square. The street ran into an open field that stretched towards the foot hills. It was lush with newly growing plant life. Halfway across Haru signaled them to stop.

"Ok...*phew*...we're here."

Apeay looked around in anticipation, and saw nothing. *Was this a joke?*

"This isn't a palace? We're out in the middle of nowhere."

"Sure. We're out in the middle of nowhere. You're right, in a way, except that this nowhere, is actually somewhere. And saying there's no palace, now that's just flat out wrong, my friend. Try looking up."

Apeay looked up towards the center of Tenzha Valley, where the massive inverted pyramid hovered loftily in the clouds. Its appearance was that of translucent gold, made visible by its aura that appeared to rotate. Heyliuns rays refracted off the pyramids surface in all colors of the spectrum. Under these conditions, it was hard to tell whether it was an illusion or not that the pyramid was revolving north to east, to the south, and to the west.

"Ah, the welcoming party," said Haru.

Apeay lowered his gaze just in time to get acquainted with a hard fist.

Wap!

Apeay stumbled backwards, hitting the ground.

"You want in to the palace, you go through me," said a hostile boy to Apeay. He was about Apeay's age, but boasted well-defined muscles.

Apeay was shaken, but managed to rise to his feet. He was more surprised than hurt. There was no one but him and Haru when they arrived. This place Haru brought him to continued catching him off guard. Rubbing his aching cheek, he looked to Haru for advice. "What's he want? What am I supposed to do?"

"Put up your hands, kid... and fight!"

Δ

I think there's something you're not telling me. If it's for my own good, then never mind. Sit with me for a while. Maybe, there's something I will tell you.

Knock, knock.

Two solid firm raps on the door had Jhar'ensky up in a rush.

"Hold on." Mr. Regalis said, ripping off his smock. He was oiling his old search and rescue devices from when he served as a Legionnaire Guard. For Jhar'ensky, it was a short career. He never made it to becoming a nikashiro like his father had hoped, for he was passionate about bureaucracy .

Jhar'ensky peered out the looking glass. *Yes.* On the other side was the person he was hoping to see.

"Honey, Zennite Thorel is here. She must've found out something. I knew she'd come through."

Rionazen Thorel was zennite over the five Rings of Legionnaires, making her one of the most influential, and powerful people in Estellar. Her dynamic presence, coupled with quick-wittedness and striking good looks caused her to stand out wherever she went. She rose to the number one position with unwavering resolve. Thorel previously held the rank of nikashiro, which she achieved three cycles earlier than the average career Legionnaire. She achieved this after testing with the highest marks, and passing the physical assessment at level diamond.

Rionazen personally attributed her accolades to receiving wise counsel during her early cycles on guard. But above all, it was her deep involvement and genuine care for the common people of Estellar that separated her from the other candidates. And the people could see it. They would say, "She soars above to keep watch for those below." Therefore, when the time came to run for zennite, she won the vote by a favorable landslide filling the position left vacant for several cycles by the former zennite. She was also a former, fellow Legionnaire Guard alongside Jhar'ensky, making her a personal friend of the family.

"Come in Rionazen. Please, have a seat with us in the expanse room. Would you like something to drink?"

"No, I'm fine."

"How have you been?" said Mrs. Regalis as she came down the steps.

"I'm well. The real question is how are you two holding up?"

"We're as good as we can be."

"I can only imagine...Well, we have a lead. Rionazen unfastened her Legionnaire-issued satchel and pulled out a tablet along with session programs with Apeay's name emblazed on each one. "Earlier, we found this in the southwest quadrant of the canals. We think he may be somewhere in that area."

Jhar'ensky shook his head. "The canals? How did he even get there? He can't operate a mynersha," he said huffing, nervously pacing the floor.

Bexhiera patted Jhar'ensky on the shoulder. "That kid is smart. I think he'll be alright."

Jhar'ensky gasped, "How can you be so cavalier about it?"

"Think about where he attends session. There's a mynvad station with an express to the old northern border. I believe he's been taking it for a while now."

"You've known about this the whole time and didn't say anything?"

"You know I wouldn't have kept something like that a secret. Look, last cycle, I found a voucher for an express ride back from the Zenlan district under his faja. I figured it was something he'd picked up off the ground while on the way back from session. But, after hearing this, and seeing how he seems to always come back late from 'playing with friends' every end of phase, I'm now sure that he was the one who purchased the voucher. He probably uses his lunch funds to purchase the discounted round trip. That's something for a nine-cycle child to do. Yes, I'm stressed out, too, but Apeay's going to be alright.

I know it. Now, Rionazen, is there anything else we need to know about?"

"Yes, there is. But I'm not sure who needs to tell who what this time. One moment..." Rionazen activated her map, displaying it in the middle of the room. She pointed to the area where they were searching. "This is the exact location where we found his tablet. Over here is where we tracked him to, on the other side of the ruins. Which for some reason only took him a jhenta to cross. That is, if our scanners aren't malfunctioning. From there the trail goes cold."

"The other side...by the old capsyint lines," said Jhar'-ensky. "It's not like he got a voucher and took one out of the region."

"Of course not," replied Rionazen. "Those lines went inactive ages ago."

ΩΩ

"Four one three."

"Transmit, your excellency."

"Return to the canals in three ahkmeres. Come alone."

"Accepted..."

CHAPTER 4

Wap, Wap. Thud.

Another two blows to the face, and Apeay was down again.

"Are you serious? You think we let just anyone into the Imperial Palace?" said his aggressor. The young man posed himself in a fighting stance as Apeay steadied himself and rose to his feet.

"Get out of my way!" Apeay shouted. But the young man didn't change his position or demeanor. Apeay then attempted to juke him the way the boys on the metsvar team do when going for the goal. But his moves were no match for this level of skill. In less than a jhenta, his opponent leapt up high, spinning, catching Apeay in the chest with a kick that sent him flying. He landed hard on his back. "Ungh!"

"You're pathetic," said the boy to Apeay as he marched away. Apeay was starting to lose hope in his dream of making it into the palace. Haru walked over and stooped over him while he lay face up. He was staring up towards a beautiful place that was guarded by a *demon child.*

"What's going on here, kid?" said Haru. "Earlier today you told me you wanted to see the palace. Now, seems to me, all you wanna do is take a nap. How am I supposed to get you home if you're gonna spend all your time sleeping?"

Apeay thought to himself. *First this boy beats on me. Now, this man makes fun of me. Stupid, funny-hat-wearing man. He just brought me here to make me look stupid? I'm going into that palace, then I'm throwing his weird, dumb hat on the ground and stomping on it, and then I'm going home.*

His "spark," as Bexhiera put it, was fully aflame. It was exploding. Apeay leapt to his feet and charged at the other boy as fast as lighting. Alerted by the sudden rush, the boy whipped around, meeting Apeay, yet again, square in the face with his fist. However, Apeay's gaze was unwavering, and his eyes remained focused on the boy. He balled up his hand into a fist of his own. It made a laser line to the lower left side of his opponents chin. The hit landed with such force that it lifted the other boy off his feet before he fell down. Apeay wasn't sure if it was over or not, but he was about to make sure. Before he could, Haru stepped in between them.

"Looks like you're not the only one who likes to take naps," said Haru.

Just then, there was another voice making itself heard nearby.

"And if he knocked out any of Yuli's teeth, I'm holding you responsible. You should've contacted me before this foolishness played out. Things could've got dangerous."

"I'm pretty sure he wasn't going to go all out."

"As if you would know."

Apeay was startled by this newcomer's sudden appearance. Beforehand, there was no one in sight for sannos and sannos. And how did he get so close without being heard? He was a giant of a person, standing at least one if not two shawaras above Haru. His shoulders were wide and powerful. Everything about him was strong. His face, an older version of Yuli's, with a deep scar that ran from one cheek across the bridge of his nose to the other. In his gaze was a fire as fierce and menacing as a wild gihan. He wore no shirt, only a silver breastplate. His black pants were loose, but held snug to his waist by a single white cord. His forearms were wrapped in silver jewel-studded gauntlets.

"C'mon now, Jahlije. You know all too well how these things go," Haru said. The muscular man shot a look at Haru that shook him.

"*Ahem*...Besides," Haru continued, clearing his throat, "I brought this young man a long way to get his feet wet. No harm. By tomorrow we'll be on our way to Silver Lake."

Jahlije grunted something that no one could make out. Then, he knelt down where Yuli was resting. Jahlije opened his hand. In it was a small mound of turquoise powder that he put under Yuli's nose. In an instant, Yuli was fully revived and up on his feet. Without warning, Jahlije turned to Apeay and grabbed him up by his collar so that their eyes met.

"Put me down!" Apeay cried, wrestling to break free of the beast's mighty grip.

"Be still!" Jahlije's overpowered voice silenced the entire land. Apeay froze like a chirka being carried by its mother, as Jahlije stood silently, observing his prey. After what felt like an eternity, he returned Apeay to the ground and said, "Follow me." Apeay turned to Haru, looking for confirmation.

"Why you looking at me? You heard the man." The three of them trailed behind Jahlije along the Passage of Ardeluxhia. The floral arrangement leading to the center of the Imperial Valley was intricate and elegant. It was obvious that many ahk-meres of devotion were put into the upkeep of the valley.

After a two-reel trek they reached the center.
"Wait here," Jahlije said. He took a few more steps ahead of them to the absolute center
point. On the ground beneath his feet was a series of inter-woven palladium circles emblazed on the valley floor. He lifted his head and belted out a deep chant.

"Yesheng...Shengmain...Maingxos!"

The interwoven circles began to glow, changing in hue to crystalized cerulean. The inferior surface of the palace became lit as the sky as it cascaded, spiraling down in a series of stair-ways. Apeay gazed in awe at the grand entrance.

"Well, I'll be! With the available technology we developed, you Imperials are still using all these steps? There should be a law against that," said Haru.

Jahlije cared not for his criticism, replying with some of his own. "A little over 17,000 stairs is hardly a climb, at least for us."

"More like 17,711 stairs if I remember right."

"No matter, you could use the exercise," he said, smacking the pudge above Haru's waist. "Now, let's begin with....."

Before Jahlije could finish with the formalities, Apeay interrupted, "Me first," and took off on a mad dash up the infinite stairway.

"I thought you were his chaperone."

"If that were the case, he wouldn't be here in the first place," said Haru. "What ya gonna do with a boy like that? You know, no matter what we say, he won't be stopped."

Ξ

"Three one four, honorable Zennite."

"Transmit."

"Yes, we're certain. The tracks stop here."

"Sequence retrace perimeter area. There may be something we've overlooked," said Rionazen.

"Accepted." Will do, Um....Three one four."

"Transmit. And, what is it now?" Thorel was becoming annoyed with the constant plina correspondence. She wanted results, not a chronicle of their activities.

"Yeh...uh...can this kid fly at all?"

"No. Not that any of us are aware of. Now, if you have plans on moving past metashiro, I suggest you stop with the nonsense updates, and get back to the search."

"Accepted."

Can Apeay fly? Mrs. Regalis pondered while listening in on the transmission between Zennite Thorel and a metashiro of Ring One.

After another ahkmere they called it off. Yet another disappointing night.

Thorel stood to her feet. "My friends, please try to rest for now. I have every available ground patrol searching the area while my guys keep an eye out from the sky. We even have teams scouting the border of Alizan, if he did make it that far. For now, good evening, I'll see you tomorrow."

Thorel withdrew herself from the house on the quiet hill. With solemn nod, Jhar'ensky gently closed the door behind her.

Δ

"Woah....." Apeay's mouth hung open as he panted, regaining his breath. He was the first to make it to the corridor at the top of the stairs, fixing his eyes on the majesty before him.

The ceiling was high and beveled on each edge. Carved in the ceiling were faces of mighty land, sea, and sky creatures.

The walls lining the corridor were mirrored, giving the impression of an infinite glass hallway. Yet as impressive as all of this was, Apeay had become fixated on the grandest of statues boldly displayed at the end of the corridor. It seemed to be "guarding" the entrance to the inner sanctum. It spiraled upwards from the golden glass floor, eclipsing the sky above. The delignos; an ancient monstrosity in the form of a fang-toothed, six-winged monster made of clear crystal. Its eyes were like fire that pierced one to their inner most being. The claws of the delignos appeared to be wet from the markings, but razor-sharp to the touch.

Out of its stomach stood the figure of a man made of onyx. The details of his face expressed a look of triumph. The man's hands were fashioned like sabers, pointing up and out. He was speckled all over with sapphires, emeralds, rubies, amethysts and diamonds. Apeay tiptoed closer for a better look.

Inscribed at its base were these words: *Great Phenomenon of the Desolate Stratus*. Apeay had no idea what the enigmatic shibboleth meant . And there was more writing underneath, but much smaller and inscribed in diamond. Apeay read, *BE FREE.*

"Child, do not take another step!" Jahlije yelled. He'd finally caught up with the unmannered miscreant. "You will not go about the palace unescorted."

"Relax 'super guardian' he's not hurting anything," said a somewhat familiar voice from the other end of the corridor. "Besides, he's too cute of a kid to yell at like that."

Apeay lowered his head to hide his face. "Jenshii?"

"The one and only," she replied.

"I thought you worked on the river?"

"I do. And, from time to time, I'm tasked as a Six Hands of the Guard instructor at the palace. I taught young Yuli there the 'Dance of the Flying Hewlix.' From the way he sent you flying on your back, I'd say he learned very well."

Can these people turn invisible? I didn't see her anywhere, like I didn't see Jahlije before he showed up. "You were watching us?"

"Yep. I was out arranging some of the flowers on a hill nearby. Yeah, they keep this lady busy. I'm the best at just about everything. Haven't met anyone who can match me yet. Know what I'm saying, kid?"

"You talk too much," Jahlije scowled. "This way, boy." Jahlije retrieved a twelve-slotted key from the pouch hanging at his waist and gave it a brief inspection before inserting it in a cutout in the base of the monument. The colossal statue separated from itself, the part of it that was the man turned to face, and rise above the delignos which folded its wings backwards, creating an invisible wall for them to pass through.

To anyone seeing the inner courtyard for the first time, they might suggest that the corridor was a mere a visual appetizer when compared to the grandiose of what was to follow.

Workings of brilliant marble and diamond formed an adjacent angled pathway. The contrasting pattern of the pathway gave it an appearance as if it went on forever. At its end, it met up with twelve transparent alabaster steps leading up to the main floor. At the top of the steps, two solid turquois gihans, aligned in an infinite radius stood watch on the left and on the right. Wherever one walked, they watched, their eye always on them. Succeeding them was a procession of dancing opal goddesses, the first were fixed in a twirl, the ones after appearing as if shadows of the first, crouching and gathering flowers from the tzierhan. The last row nearest the center was the completion of the composite illusion, rising up, holding their heads high, floating above the floor. The span of the courtyard was vast, approximately one reel in all directions. Looking up, one could stare straight into the cosmos. Flashes of polychromatic light temporarily revealed the presence of an invisible ceiling 11 reels above them.

Below, on one side of the courtyard, Apeay could see young boys and girls dressed in similar fashion to Yuli. They were tumbling and climbing walls. Others sparring, some empty-handed and others with weapons of bamboo and hemp rope. On the other side of the courtyard the atmosphere was relaxed, but highly focused. The youth there were using shape alignment in ways that Apeay hadn't yet been taught for their formations were living art.

"How do you like the palace?" said Haru

Apeay didn't hear Haru over his own elation at being there. He simply wanted to absorb it all.

Ding...ding...ding...

Three harmonic bells rang in rising sevenths. Near the middle of the courtyard, between the goddess statues, a crystal red curtain drew open. Everyone in the courtyard took to one knee; everyone except Apeay. He was in his own world, with his eyes studying the upper limits of the palace. He began to daydream of what may come next, until a strong grip on his shoulder brought him back to the present.

"Show respect. You are in the presence of Emperor and Empress Xahlahi," Jahlije said in a low voice.

The emperor and empress wore robes of silk interwoven with precious metals, fashioned from the ambience of the palace. The face of the emperor was stoic, his figure robust, while the empress had an air of gentle benevolence about her.

"You there," the emperor said, pointing his finger at Apeay from his lofty throne.

"Me?" said Apeay.

"Yes you. Why are you standing?"

All eyes were on Apeay awaiting an explanation. "Cause I was watching the lights," he said pointing upwards.

The emperor burst into laughter. "So, we have a new-comer to Laixfu. Excellent. Jahlije."

"Yes, your excellency?"

"Please, show our visitor around. And, prepare him for this evening's festivities."

"Right away," Jahlije said with a bow.

"Don't forget to have the chef prepare him a special meal," said the empress. "He's an exceptional guest."

"Understood. Come with me, boy," said Jahlije.

"That's right you've only seen this part," said Jenshii to Apeay. "There's a lot more to see around the palace. It's almost endless. I'll show you."

"You're staying here," said Jahlije

"Whatever. You don't know how to be fun. That makes you a boring tour guide. So, I'm coming with," Jenshii said, putting her foot down.

"No!" said Jahlije, pointing a resolute finger between her eyes. "You're staying here with Haru to make sure he doesn't try to 'enhance' anything like he did last time. And, that's final."

"You're still going on about that? It wasn't even my idea," said Haru.

Jenshii swatted his hand away from her face "See Jahlije, he's not even thinking about it."

Jahlije stood resolute, crossing his arms. Jenshii shook her head, exasperated. "You know, sometimes you take your task too seriously...way too seriously.

Jahlije leaned forward, and speaking in a low voice, said, "Imagine what could happen if I didn't. Being too carefree can be costly if you remember."

"That was another lifetime. Let it go. I'll see ya later. See you this evening, Apeay," she said, as she and Haru rejoined the throng in the courtyard.

Jahlije escorted Apeay down the adjacent corridor. He led him through numerous picturesque passageways accented by carvings within the walls, adorned with precious gemstones. Each one led to either a room of study, observation or rest. As they proceeded, Jahlije went on and on about the chronicle of the Laixfu Empire and some Bianzu legend. *Jenshii was right*, Apeay thought. Jahlije's monotone recitation of Laixfu's history made him feel like he was back in an obligatory analysis session at Estellar Prime. He wished that he could go back to the inner courtyard, where it seemed more interesting things were happening.

Along the way as Jahlije continued his spiel, they passed by HeylanLaejzo's Essence, the Living Garden of the Palace. Looking through the crystal wall, Apeay took in the ambience of the garden. The verdant plant life within was in tune with their presence. For each step they took, a fruit flower would blossom and another would close. Wherever they stood, the trees produced luxuriant leaves.

And then, a familiar symbol above the entrance caught Apeay's eye.

Apeay shouted, "Jahlije, look!"

"What is it?!" Jahlije looked around for the present danger, but none was there. What did this kid want him to notice?

"That's Hydrophena prime from the Book of Ascension," said Apeay pointing to the symbol.

Jahlije lowered his guard, now trying to understand Apeay's enthusiasm with a simple picture. "Hydrophena? What does that mean? What's a Book of Ascension?"

"It's the book of universal order, guiding us along the road to perfection."

Apeay's answer was confusing to Jahlije. He shrugged his shoulders and continued on.

After the grand tour was over, they passed by a crack in the wall, a sliver leading to a long corridor that stretched down an unlit section of the palace. Apeay stopped to peer into the space in between. Was it his imagination or was something whispering to him from the shadows? It gave him the chills. "Where does that go?"

Jahlije looked to where he was gazing and told him, "Nowhere. It's empty space." Apeay peered deeper into the darkness. "Come now!" Jahlije commanded. "Your room has been prepared."

Apeay shook himself out of his trance, "Oh, okay," He followed Jahlije to a room of rest where his meal was prepared for him.

"Eat, then get rest. You will need it." Apeay wasn't sure, but the thought he saw Jahlije smirking as he left him be.

The room was filled with an appetizing aroma. Without delay, Apeay helped himself to all three plates on the glass table. The running around, exploring, and climbing an endless stairway finally caught up with him, and he yawned. Apeay laid down on the soft bed that was next to the table for a well-deserved nap.

Boom, boom, boom boom...

Apeay was awakened by the sound of deep drumming. The door to his room flew open. A silhouetted, muscular figure stood at the entrance.

"Put these on for the festival," said Jahlije.

He tossed Apeay an outfit similar but more decorative than the one Yuli wore, its edges trimmed with silver.

"Do not take long. The festival will begin soon."

After he changed into his new outfit, Jahlije led Apeay down another corridor that took them to a wide, elevated space beyond the courtyard.

"If you are you, time will be," Jahlije said to him before disappearing into the shadows.

Apeay wasn't sure what that riddle was supposed to mean as he stood, waiting in small, poorly lit area for reasons unknown. *Where was everyone?* Suddenly, a large gateway behind him slammed shut as the lights flashed on. Apeay found himself in an unfathomably large arena. There had to be well over half a million spectators all around. From the top of the center balcony the emperor made his announcement,

"This evening our guest Apeay will duel with the Xhalian Royal Guardian and his gihan, Sehktu!"

A loud roar echoed from below. Apeay's heart was pounding. He felt sick to his stomach as the palladium cage emerged from the floor.

"This can't be," Apeay said, trembling in fear.

Jahlije made his entrance, riding on the back of a ferocious beast. He made his way to the center, where Apeay awaited in terror.

"Time to fight again, kid."

Apeay peered over his shoulder, making sure not to take his eyes off the nightmare in front of him. Haru gave him a cheery wave. Apeay was too caught up in what was to come to assess the anger he felt towards Haru at the moment.

"You can beat him my guy. He's not so tough. Take him down with all you've got!" Jenshii shouted, sitting next to the charlatan, Haru with Yuli seated on the other side, sporting a menacing smile.

The empress rose to her feet, raising one hand in the air. "Let the Dance of Delignos Fury begin!"

The palace reverberated with cheers. Apeay felt the same chill come over him as he did in his escape from the abandoned canal. Alone, once again.

CHAPTER 5

Rroooar!

The gihan raised up on its hind legs, then crashed to the ground with a powerful stomp. Apeay had seen enough.

"I have to get out of here." Apeay ran frantically towards the large golden gates. He banged on them screaming, "Let me out, let me out here!"

The ground beneath his feet trembled and quaked. Pressing his back against the gateway, he turned to witness Jahlije riding the gihan in full stride. The attack was imminent, and there was nowhere for him to hide. In desperation, Apeay began to scamper around the arena in every direction. But, as fast as he darted away, his pursuers changed their direction, keeping up with his every move. They were closing in on him fast. While galloping on the back of the beast towards Apeay, Jahlije extended his tree trunk-like arm. The blow intended to topple Apeay missed, as he ducked and ran off in the opposite direction. The gihan stopped and spun around at Jahlije's command. They caught up with Apeay's position in a matter of jhentas. Before he could run off again the gihan took a swipe at his side. Its claws ripped across Apeay's left arm.

"Nothing more than a scratch. Lucky you."

"A scratch?" Apeay was alarmed by Jahlije's reasoning. He wasn't going to let that monster "scratch" him again. How could this be happening to him? Why would someone put him in a place like this? He was just a child up against an elite adult warrior and ferocious beast. Still, Apeay had to survive. As the gihan turned to face him, he poked it in one of its eyes. It began thrashing about in pain, which caused Jahlije to fall off. Some of the crowd began to laugh at the spectacle. Others were taunting Apeay for what appeared to be cowardice. Jahlije was infuriated. After regaining control of the beast, he continued his pursuit with more hostility than before.

"You are not you! Not the one. You will not be you!" Jahlije then uttered a command with a kick of his heel to the side of Sehktu. "Astiox!"

The gihan thrust its front claws into the gravel floor, bucking Jahlije high into the air. Jahlije somersaulted twice, coming straight down with one foot extended, destined for Apeay's head.

Apeay's eyes widened, as he awaited his end.

∞

High above the lush field the cool breeze whispered. The star warmed the pool where she rested, singing her song to the forest:

"When two are one,

renew life again,

power of desire

eternal star within,

Serene state of mind is might my love...."

∞

Apeay's feet were frozen. He knew, standing there like an idol meant certain death. But he couldn't get his petrified body to respond.

"Still gotta get you home, kid!"

He heard that trickster of a man shouting over the crowd. *Home.* The thought of getting back home broke him free of his paralysis. As if it were an ingrained reflex, Apeay took one step forward with his right foot and raised both his arms above his head. The ornament around his neck glowed, the light within took the form of blue lighting, encompassing him but an instant before Jahlije could complete his attack.

"Arrgh!" Jahlije's body locked up momentarily from the shock before colliding with the coliseum floor. But as quickly as he fell, he got back up. He glanced down at his smoking foot and laughed.

"Ha! Now, we will do real battle. It will take much more than a light show to beat me, for I have experience with this type of pain." Jahlije put his hand to his mouth and whistled.

The gihan that Apeay had almost forgot about leapt over Jahlije toward him. Apeay instantly leaped twelve shawaras upwards and sixteen backwards, avoiding the creature. The crowd applauded in astonishment. He as well was astounded by his extraordinary athleticism.

"Did I really just do that?" he said aloud, his body radiant with power.

Observing this feat, Jahlije mounted his gihan. "*Now* he's starting to remember..." The beast scraped its claws across the ground, anxious to charge. However, Jahlije didn't give the command for an attack. Instead, he tapped on one of the jewels on his gauntlet. The arena floor began to shake. The gravel faded away, and the floor was now barren, covered in a cool liquid. Apeay had trouble keeping his balance on this slippery surface. Then, at once, the open grounds morphed into a complex labyrinth of crystal mounds reflecting upon other crystals like polished mirrors, amidst a burning vermilion flame emanating from the center. Apeay observed as the deadly duo ducked behind a massive pillar of fire.

To him, this game of "hide and seek" seemed more like a game of "seek the hidden to stay alive." He ran around to the opposite side of the mirror where they hid.

Like a festive magician, they had vanished. And yet, Apeay could sense they were nearby, but where? How could they be moving about so stealthily? Neither the man nor beast was small by any means. Was someone behind him?

Apeay turned around just as Jahlije unleashed a glancing blow, gliding past and back into the maze. Apeay stood dazed, teetering on his feet. The crowd was chanting something he couldn't make out. "Be clear, be awake," Apeay said to himself as he shook his head. To his surprise, a large portion of the crowd seated arena-side, were cheering him on. Apeay dashed here and there, putting on a show when suddenly the rushing sound of swift feet filled his ears, catching him off guard, for he had, for a brief moment, become too caught up in his own actions. The rhythm of the fluttering feet increased in speed, until it became a noise like wind ravaging across an open field. Apeay looked straight ahead into the blistering crystal mound before him to witness Jahlije sprinting headlong in his direction. Because of the crystal mirrors it was impossible to discern the distance from which he came.

Jahlije took three grand handsprings in what Apeay perceived to be a setup for an overhead attack. As the final tumble came as Jahlije leaped off his left foot as expected, to execute something much unexpected. Instead of the flying from above, it was coming straight at him. Jahlije was soaring evenly, not up nor down. His body was straight with toes pointed, as if diving into water from high above. It seemed to Apeay that this warrior's aim was to sever him in half. That he could not, and would not, allow. Beneath Apeay's feet, the cool liquid lit up in a cerulean hue that drew across the floor in line with his line of thought. As Jahlije closed in Apeay was ready to strike from the perfect angle of interception, but then...

Jahlije spoke, "*Zenxjz...*"

And Apeay's body was there. He landed the blow precisely on target, crying out as he felt its impact.

Jahlije's borrowed kick struck hard at the side of Apeay's thigh causing him to suffer a brutal fall to the floor. The wound was burning hot from the strike, and it began to unnerve him. It didn't make any sense. How could he set up a counterattack, only to get hit with his own attack in the place of his opponent? Jahlije was standing where he was, and he in Jahlije's place.

"That's cheating!" Jenshii shouted from the crowd. There were even a few "boo's" here and there among the arena spectators.

Jahlije hollered back, "Don't reprimand me, lady! What is known by all is not cheating." Jenshii shook her head in contempt. Jahlije wasn't concerned in the least by her criticism. He had an important task to accomplish. "He has his own tricks, but I have great instructions." The last of Jahlije's word's echoed as he took several paces backwards, immersing himself in the arena's indecipherable mirage.

Apeay got to his feet, looking vigilantly for his opponent. It was imperative that he find him before he had another chance to catch him by surprise. So much noise. So many twists and turns. With his senses scrambled by the last assault, he considered the best thing to do was to stop running wild, and think about his next move. Apeay pressed his back against one of the large crystal mounds as he listened for the ghosts of the labyrinth.

Fwshh, wshh, wshh...

Apeay heard it now. The gihan was dashing around him. He prepared himself, awaiting the beast to emerge from the shadows.

There it was. The gihan appeared from behind another mound to the left of him. But, where was Jahlije?

"Here, boy!" Jahlije shouted, appearing on his right. Jahlije cocked his leg back as he jumped at Apeay. Apeay attempted another heroic leap. However, this time he slipped on the liquid floor, giving him no chance of escaping. Jahlije's knee caught him square in the stomach, knocking the wind out of him. Apeay went down on all fours.

"No time for fleeing. No time for magic. This is over."

"I'm..." Apeay said, regaining his breath.

"What's that? Speak up before I end this battle."

"I'm going to beat you...bad!" With that, Apeay dug his foot into the ground and shot up with his fist raised. He landed an uppercut that sent Jahlije reeling back.

Before Jahlije could recover, Apeay executed two Dances of the Flying Hewlix that landed squarely in the face of his opponent.

"Yeah! That's my move right there!" Jenshii shouted from the crowd.

Jahlije made a half-hearted attempt to whistle for his gihan. But Apeay gave him no time to make his call, leaping up on his shoulders. With both fists illuminated by the cerulean light within the orb, Apeay delivered one high-speed blow after another until the muscular giant dropped.

The crowd exploded in thunderous cheers.

"Our new champion! Apeay!" shouted the empress from the balcony.

It was surreal. Apeay felt elated as the applause continued to build. He heard a faint voice speaking to him from the floor...

"You...are...you," said Jahlije before passing out.

Up from the ground, a silver-capped diamond capsule appeared. Two arena guards escorted Apeay to the luxziun lift.

"Get in," said El'hese. He stood on the left of Apeay looking down to him with resentment in his eyes.

"What's going on with you sir?" said Apeay

"I'm just glad you won," said El'hese, his expression unchanged.

"I don't believe that."

"Lil' champion, get in the lift. We don't have all day for this."

Not taking his eye off of him, Apeay hopped aboard the hexagonal capsule. El'hese sealed the door behind them. He slid his finger along an overhead panel, and the luxziun shot up abruptly, lifting them from the arena floor to the cascading balcony at the top. The doors opened to a foyer covered in turquoise grass, blanketed by heavy mist.

He was escorted onto the foyer floor, where El'hese ordered him kneel. Apeay did so right away, but not so much at the command of the shifty guardian, but more so to get off his feet.

The drape of ruby threaded curtains atop the steps parted. The emperor and empress made their procession to where Apeay knelt. As he watched them, it appeared as if they were gliding across the floor of the terrace, rather than walking in the conventional manner. He glanced down to see how they performed this spectacle, but the combination of their long robes, blanketed by mist obfuscated his view.

In their presence, he hoped they would provide the answers to all of his questions. Where he was, why he was there, and what all the challenges were about. And most importantly, just who were these people anyway?

"Why is he kneeling like that? He's our guest, not a captive. Bring him a seat," said emperor Xahlahi.

"Right away," said another of the palace guards stationed at the top. From the corner of the room, he retrieved a stout mahogany chair trimmed with onyx. Apeay took his seat and hung his head out of exhaustion.

"Look up child. I want to see your face for myself."

Apeay looked up to the emperor as best he could, still feeling drained from the battle.

"Interesting," said the empress. "Yes, time will be well."

"You fought bravely. We apologize for inconveniencing you like this. We had to see it for ourselves."

"See what?" asked Apeay

"An event; a happening perhaps. But for now, we will have you taken to the shansen," said the emperor. "They will heal your injuries. Take care of yourself, Apeay."

"Yes, be the best dream."

The emperor signaled to the guards as they parted. After they returned to the arena floor, El'hese had two of his orozans lift Apeay onto their shoulders, taking him to the Hall of Shansen-laixi, where the walls were decorated with a vivid wrap-around mural of people walking from a river up to a land lit by Heyliun. There, they laid him down on a cot of floating steam. It felt good on his back. A palace shansen sat down beside him and hovered her hands over his body.

"What are you doing?"

"Just relax. I remember your essence before the battle. Therefore, *yeshnah meixandee* restore," she said.

Apeay felt his aches and pains leaving him. The cut across his arm sealed up. He sat up and looked himself over.

"Thanks. How did you do that?" he asked.

"This was accomplished by the same energy that powered you during your fight," she replied, leaving the room.

"We are both grateful for her gift"

Apeay felt that familiar, strong grip on his shoulder.

"Jahlije!"

"Yes, young champion. I am well." This was the first time Apeay had seen him smile. "Your friend is waiting for you."

"My friend? Hmph."

Jahlije led Apeay to his room where Haru was waiting.

"Hey there, kid. I knew you could do it," said Haru.

"You tricked me!" Apeay cried. "I don't want to fight anymore. I want to go home!" He dove head first into the pillow on the bed, flooding it with tears.

"Oh well now, don't worry kid. We're leaving here first thing in the morning."

"You're lying."

"All true. The emperor's cook made us a big royal breakfast for the trip, too."

Apeay didn't respond. So Haru decided to let him be. Haru knew first-hand how rough these endless journeys could be.

Apeay was mentally exhausted and dozed off.

"Bet you won't jump off the rocker," said Deslao.

Apeay was teetering back and forth on the infamous "titanium rocker of bruises" at Joru Park. He had a knack for keeping his balance, and held the park record for the longest ride without falling off.

"I bet you won't," Seldao seconded.

"You really think I'm afraid to jump?" said Apeay. "I'm not scared."

"Then do it, because there's our capsyint," said Deslao.

"Huh?"

"Should we wake him?" said Seldao.

"It appears we won't have to. Morning, cutie."

Apeay opened his eyes, peering at the bright light dancing off the Xonique River. He was lying on the deck of Jenshii's tabanger, going gently along the wide angle of the river to the docks.

"See, kid, what'd I tell ya?" said Haru "Our departure is at hand."

Apeay lazily eyed the capsyint on the river's edge, then looked back at Haru. "Yep. You slept the entire time while Jahlije carried you like a sack of changa all the way from the palace to the river. I dare say he was even smiling while doing so."

"Your eyes weren't deceiving you. I saw it too. Sometimes I miss that about him," Jenshii sighed, then perked back up to her usual self. "Of course, he could only take you so far before I took over and here, we are. You must be feeling well-rested by now."

"I am," said Apeay.

With the push of the angled lever, Jenshii guided the tabanger alongside the docks. Haru made his signature bow and stepped out of the tabanger. Apeay went to make his imitation of a bow, when Jenshii scooped him up off his feet and gave him a warm hug, "You be well, beloved. We'll be waiting for your return. Take care."

"I will," said Apeay.

"You better keep this one safe, or I'm coming for you, Haru."

"Don't you have some Six Guards of the Flying Rainbow to teach or something?" said Haru.

"Would you prefer to swim across the river, the next time you visit?"

"Yeah, yeah, okay, we'll see ya Jenshii."

"Take care."

"Bye..." Apeay waved as she sped off at full speed, keeping his eyes on her until she disappeared among the river's reflection.

Haru took notice of how Apeay was watching her. "Alright. Let's get a move on. You've got some time before you know what that's about," said Haru.

"What it's about?" Apeay asked.

"See kid, you don't even know what that means. C'mon now."

They boarded the capsyint and Haru took to the controls. "Gotta charge this baby up at Eos."

"I thought we were going to Silver Lake?" said Apeay.

"We are. It's in Eos. Now take your seat, my friend. We're outta here. One more stop to go."

Just one more stop and I'll be home. Apeay was relieved. As they jetted off, the snow-capped mountains diminished into the distant horizon.

Σ

It was early in the morning. Bexhiera was meticulously tending to the vegetation in the nursery. Her hands worked steadily to trim away old stems and constant worries. She watered them as they sat soaking up Heyliuns rays. The light coming into the nursery was as beautiful to her sight as it was agonizing. It had been over a phase since Apeay went missing, and the Legionnaires had no further clues to his whereabouts.

Bexhiera reached into the flower bed and took out one budding zaitson flower. She placed it in a soil-rich vase, and took it inside.

Jhar'ensky was laying on the turujo sound asleep, exhausted from the all-night search with Ring One. They even dared tread on the foreground of the Forbidden Ruins, the ominous place rumored to be haunted by the ghost of a malevolent warrior from ancient times. Such rumors make brave souls jump at the sound of rustling leaves. But, a father in search of his son knows no such fear.

Mrs. Regalis leaned over the turujo where he lie asleep and kissed him gently. "Thank you, my love," she said, taking a seat on the edge in Apeay's favorite place.

CHAPTER 6

"Eos, Eos..." yelled Haru through the talking box. "Everyone bound for Edarah I believe this is your stop. Make your transfers wherever necessary." The capsyint came to rest on the glass platform of Eos.

"Who are you talking to?" asked Apeay

"The passengers."

"There aren't any passengers. It's just us."

"Tell me then, kid, if there aren't any passengers, who are those folks getting off?"

Apeay looked in the direction Haru was pointing. The doors on the rear cabin slid open. More people exited the speeding cabera than he could count. "Where'd they come from?"

"We picked them up in Laixfu. I swear you don't pay attention to nothing. It's all the same, I guess. Now let's get some galvanic juice for my 'vavoosh.'"

As they exited, Apeay examined the character of the people exiting. They were quiet and obviously in a rush as they headed in the opposite direction. "Where are they going?" he asked.

"Edarah. Or, something like that. I don't know. I'm just a delivery boy."

The two walked up a flight of stairs from the platform which led to a long dark hallway. It was lit only by small slits in the ceiling. What seemed to be a simple passageway turned out to be a complex underpass. It reminded Apeay of the canals back home. He lowered his head and sighed. After what could be considered the distance of a full Legionnaire's march, Apeay caught a glimpse of light waving them in the right direction. Upon exiting the passage, he looked about.

Apeay and Haru were standing on the edge of an endless valley. The ground was lush with tall, vibrant green grass. On each high mound stood tall trees, shading the area. Upon sight of the horizon, Apeay felt comforted. He couldn't reason why, but he knew he was closer to home than he'd ever been.

"Now, what do you see there?" said Haru

"That's Silver Lake," replied Apeay

"You sure?"

"Yep, I can tell. It's the way I imagined it. We're here aren't we?"

Haru nodded, "We're somewhere of the like. Now let's get movin'. Got someone I'd like you to meet."

Apeay was suspicious about meeting more people that Haru knew. "Am I gonna get in a fight?"

"Ha. No, not at all. Just getting my liquids and yours and taking you back. I have to go alone. So, I've got someone to look after you while I'm away."

Haru began walking down the winding trail towards the center of the honey dew valley. Apeay followed closely behind, and it wasn't long before they reached the shores of Silver Lake.

"Hello there my lady," said Haru, speaking to the figure that was seated on the shore of the lake. "I see you've kept this place as beautiful as ever."

The woman rose to her feet and moved towards them. Apeay carefully studied her every feature as she got closer.

Her face was radiant like Heyliun, with eyes that glimmered like starlight. Albeit beautiful, her eyes offered her no sight into this place. Her rich, long hair extended down beyond her feet, and even though it was white as snow, Apeay could make out every color of the spectrum dancing between the locks of her hair. She was taller than Haru, but not towering. Her clothing, woven from the fabric of the surrounding valley. She was the image of a living dream. The valley itself seemed to respond to her movements. The wind blew gently across the lake in whichever direction she went; in the depths of the brilliant lake, a light travelled along a looping path to an unseen endpoint, to another, and back again.

Out of the panorama she drifted towards them, until she was face to face with an old friend.

"Is it really you Haru? How long has it been?"

The sound of her voice was soothing to Apeay. He was intrigued. Her words echoed, though she was barely speaking above a whisper.

"I believe there is another essence here, innocent, perhaps a little brash and brave. Who is this you've found today?"

"His name is Apeay," said Haru, "the one and only."

"Apeay...I never knew the name." She placed her hand atop Apeay's head. "Are you exhausted? Did Haru keep you busy at the palace?"

"Just wanted to see what he could do," Haru interjected.

"Did you make him take such a long walk to get there?"

"Gotta keep his legs strong my lady."

"Will you be leaving for the energy orchards?"

"That I am love." Haru took a knee in front of Apeay. "I'll be right back after I fuel up our ride. Then, it's all aboard for home. That alright?"

"Sure," Apeay nodded.

"Alright," said Haru. "Be kind, and stay out of trouble till I get back. See ya real soon kid," he said with a wink, and skipped back up the trail, out of sight.

"Would you like something to eat?" said the lady.

"Of course," said Apeay.

"Should I have known?" The lady smiled on Apeay. "Do you see something like a home on the other side of the lake?"

Apeay cupped his hands on the side of his face and peered across the shimmering lake. "Yeah. I can see it. Is it in there?"

She bowed slightly, giving confirmation. Apeay gave her another quick examination before taking off. His heart began to beat faster, stronger. Apeay had so many questions, but he didn't know where to start, so he chose to ignore the notion and save his questions for after he returned form the other side.

Before he had made it a full sanno away she called to him,

"Find what you need. Tell me where you are when you return."

"Okay!" said Apeay, continuing to sprint along the lakes edge.

The lady kept her eye focused on him during his flight, until he reached the hut on the other side. After she was certain he had made it there safely, she returned to her seat high upon the shores of Silver Lake. "Who's there?" Was someone rustling among the trees a distance behind her? But, as she turned to see, the sensation of any presence faded. Her heart eased and the wind blew calmly over the waters.

In almost no time, Apeay was standing at the entrance of the hut on Silver Lake. The hut was made from the four massive k'tahn trees and three extraordinary nado trees. However, it didn't appear to be "built." Instead, it was as if the four k'tahns grew up around the nado trees at the center, wrapping their needly branches evenly around them. The thicker branches of the k'tahns reached from the top to ground level. All were tightly wrapped except for areas where they grew to an opening like a window. Apeay was astounded by its natural intricacy. He approached the hut carefully. It wasn't that he was afraid, more that he felt as if he should know something about this place. He slow walked it, taking in every detail, every nuance, searching for something to explain why he felt the way he did. Making it to the entrance, he turned around to give one final look across the lake, before pushing on the large cluster of branches that lay angled across the way. The needly branches cascaded backwards, folding inwards. He walked through the foyer and saw a large stone that protruded from the ground. It was sandstone at the bottom where it emerged and had a pure glass surface. Sitting on the stone was a gift.

"Zaitson fruit!" Apeay shouted. His favorite nadian snack. As was his habit, Apeay breathed in the scent of the petals before squeezing out the bluish green juice into his mouth. One would think he was famished if they saw the way he devoured the array of zaitson and poppels. As he gorged on his afternoon snack, a shimmer from underneath the fruit caught his eye. He moved one zaitson aside, uncovering a single golden recording utensil. Emblazed on it was but a single word, *AWAKE*. He figured it must be what the lady left for him to find.

He placed it in the front pouch of his pants, and continued crunching and slurping up the snack. After he was well satiated, he explored the inner workings of the large hut. The interior was like the exterior, all fashioned with branches and leaves. Some of the branches came together to form solid walls, which bore carvings and designs similar to those within the palace. But here there were no precious metals or jewels adorning them. Everything was plain and natural. Apeay continued to explore the other six tiny rooms within the hut. Each one identical, one circular wall full of carvings with a hexagonal sandstone/glass table in the middle.

As he went his way deeper in the last room, he observed a single beam of light coming through the wall in the room at the very back. Getting even closer, he could see there was a small hole in the middle of one of the carvings. It was in the center of the eye of a great delignos that wrapped it's long body around the perimeter of an elaborate mural. Curious as to what made the hole, Apeay leaned forward to see through to the other side. The moment he peered through it, the wall receded into the background. A small cot made of grass and palm leaves rose from beneath the floor. *Perfect,* Apeay thought. *A quick nap before Haru gets back.* As he lay down, he reminded himself, "Tell the Lady what I found when I get back," feeling the writing utensil in his front pouch. "Got it." Apeay let out a deep exhale. It'd been quite some time since he felt comforted.

Please, Haru come back soon. Mom, Dad, my friends, I miss every-
one. He closed his eyes, and was soon fast asleep.

Δ

"I can't do this today," said Jhar'ensky, pushing the dinner plate away from him.

Bexhiera could hardly believe her ears. "You're turning down a juicy flame roast rhidan steak? I know you're stressed, but you have to eat."

"It smells weird."

"I cooked it like usual. I don't know. Let me see. Bexhiera leaned over the plate and took a sniff. "It smells just fine. Wait, hold on." Bexhiera leaned in again and took another smell. "It's not the rhidan, dear. You're smelling the utensils. It might be because of the new solution used the other day. That's the only thing I can think it'd be."

"You say it's the hanip?" Jhar'ensky lifted the split-pronged utensil to his nose, "I think you're right, it has an odor. I'm going to grab another one."

Before Jhar'ensky could make his way to the fotah, the artaghan rang. Mr. Regalis changed course and answered the door. It wasn't who he was expecting, but it didn't matter. At his doorstep were the elite of Ring One: Legionnaire Nikashiro Nepcizyr, accompanied by Optashiro Bozhil, and Enjevix's Metashiro tyro, Aven.

"Sir, I believe we've narrowed down the location of your son. We think he's in the upper tunnels inside the ruins, but we're not sure," said Nepcizyr. "We're awaiting Zennite Thorel to arrive and give the all-clear to break regulations and proceed."

"So, you're wasting time? Everyone contacting everyone but no one making a move? The regulation is not even standard. You all are just being timid. Goodness, what's become of the Legionnaires? Have y'all lost the spirit?" said Jhar'ensky.

"It's a formality, sir. Regulations have changed since your time. It's a new procedure when dealing with the ruins. No Legionnaire enters without a clearance unless it's their patrol. Honestly, they did it because..."

"Yeah, I think I know why. I was sort of *involved* in the affair, " said Jhar'ensky butting in. "But, I don't care about any of that right now. We want our boy back home safe."

"I understand, sir, that's why we're heading at this moment to meet up with Enjevix and the rest of the search team. Thorel should be there as well by the time we arrive. Please do come along."

"We're already there," said Mrs. Regalis approaching the front door.

"Accepted ma'am. You heard her, gentlemen," said Nepcyzir. "Move out."

Rionazen had just arrived as Heyliun was setting. Eerie shadows loomed over the foregrounds of the Forbidden Ruins. The ruins were largely uninhabited, a home only to creatures of the night and overgrown vegetation. Large stones that had toppled from decay obstructed several main pathways, making it a difficult place to navigate; a labyrinth fossilized in time. Up along the jagged path she caught up with Enjevix who was standing in the place to where he and his team narrowed down the search.

"So, what did you find?" said Thorel.

"Along that path," replied Enjevix, pointing to a rocky trail that led to a dark cavern. He stood awaiting further instruction from Zennite Thorel. Enjevix was tense, and sweating so much that the top of his uniform looked damp.

Thorel's keen eyes picked up on his nervous appearance and asked, "Are you alright, Nikashiro Uzani?"

"Yes, of course I am. I'm awaiting your sequence, Zennite."

"Are you joking me? This is a search and retrieve. There's no need for formalities, and...ah, there they are." Thorel shouted out to the Jhar'ensky and Bexhiera as they neared the foregrounds. "This way, my friends!"

"Thank you for your help. I can never repay you," said Jhar'ensky.

"No need. We're like family, it's my pleasure."

Bexhiera looked about the foregrounds then to Enjevix, and a few of his comrades who'd came with them, had the most nervous expressions on their faces.

"Well, are we going to just stand here looking at each other?" said Bexhiera

Before anyone could respond, she brushed past all of them, marching down the trail. To their shame, the search team of Ring One followed behind. Half a sanno ahead they arrived at the cavern. The cavern entrance was fashioned in the image of a cabera with long menacing teeth, threatening all who dared to enter. An ominous light flickered from its eyes.

"It's a ghost," cried one of the lower tier metashiros.

"I don't care what it is. We're going in," said Thorel.

"These new pledges, nothing like us back in the Golden Era," said Jhar'ensky. "My lady." He extended his hand to Bexhiera, helping her maintain balance on the slippery, uneven rocks around the cave. Hand in hand, Jhar'ensky and Bexhiera squeezed through the fangs of the Cabera into a long tunnel. The Legionnaires carefully followed suit, each of them activating their search lights. Once inside, they stood fast, ready for whatever was to come. Then, they heard a noise:

Mmmmph... mmph

Upon hearing the sound, the nervous metashiro froze in his tracks. Thorel took note and changed his sequence on the spot, sending him back to the foregrounds to stand watch as the rest of the search party pressed deeper into the tunnel. The air was thick, ripe with the scent of days gone by. The tunnel walls were much tighter at this depth. Now, in a straight line, they tiptoed down the narrow passage that led them to the belly of the monster and the ghost within.

There the monster appeared in true form. His mighty belly took in deep breath after deep breath, as he lay asleep at their feet.

"Apeay!" Bexhiera exclaimed. She dropped to her knees embracing her son. Apeay awoke from his deep sleep.

"Mom?" said Apeay. He opened his eyes, astonished to see everyone surrounding him..

"Boy, we missed you. So glad to have you back" said Jhar'-ensky, uniting in their embrace.

Apeay felt disoriented. He wasn't sure when or how it had happened, but somehow, he was back.

"Time to go home, son."

After Ring One's designated aeroxia checked him over for injuries any possible sign of infection, they pronounced him medically clear for reentry into Estellar, and left them be. They walked up the brick path to their mynersha. As they hopped in, Apeay took a look back towards the ruins. He reached into his side pocket. It was empty.

"It's gone," said Apeay. *Just a dream?*

Mr. Regalis powered up the deluxe mynersha, and set course for the house on the hill.

CHAPTER 7

Memories of my tomorrow fade away over time. If dreams are forgotten, they were never mine.

Ding, ding, ding!

The violent attack on the artaghan awoke Apeay. He leapt to his feet and dashed to the front door, yanking it open to see who disturbed his rest.

"What is wrong with you?" It was Deslao. He stood impatiently, waiting for Apeay to come to his senses.

"What?" said Apeay

"Get dressed! Do you even realize what time it is? Pre-succession is less than an ahkmere away."

For Apeay, the day of succession almost passed him by. Even though his father had hired an on-call sebah to help him with his studies it seemed not to make a difference. What he did manage to achieve over the cycles was a supreme level of athletic strength, fueled by a notion to protect himself at all times. Apeay spent most of his time under the tutelage of Deslao and even more training on his own. This unbalanced way of life nearly led to him held over for another cycle at Estellar High until, by some miracle, his scholastic spark was rekindled, motivating him to make the final symbol.

"Aw man, I almost forgot."

"How could you forget when your father is Council Principal? He sent me over here to figure out what was taking you so long."

"Give me a jhenta. I'll be ready in plenty of time," said Apeay. He jetted up the steps to his room.

"Ridiculous," Deslao mumbled to himself.

Nine cycles had passed; nine cycles since Apeay was rediscovered in the cabera's cave in the Forbidden Ruins. On that night, on the way home, he told his parents of his journey through the distant lands of Laixfu, and his encounter with the Lady of Silver Lake.

"You dreamed of myths and legends," his father explained to him. "Those places don't exist in real-life." Mr. Regalis was convinced that Apeay had incurred some minor head trauma. Upon making it home, Mrs. Regalis checked him over once more, using advanced tech understood only by the most elite diamond hands. She found no trace, even at nanoscopic levels of illness or infection. Apeay pleaded with them to return to where they found him so he could show them. But Mr. Regalis would hear no more of this delusional talk from Apeay, convinced that it was nothing more than a vivid dream. And the confounded Apeay wasn't sure himself what had actually taken place. Was he right or was his father? As he contemplated his doubts, he thought of a way to reassure himself. "What about this?" he said, as he threw his necklace into the air. As his parents watched alongside him, the ornament fell to the ground where he stood. Whatever energized his charm before had run out; it was just an ordinary necklace. Likewise, his dreams were only dreams, as Jhar'ensky put it. Eventually his father's logic began to make sense to Apeay. This was the real world. Not one of dreams.

"See fella, I'm ready," said Apeay.

"Finally. Thanks to you I have to speed through the beam tunnels to get us there on time." The beam tunnels, the most commonly used mode of travel for their potential speed up the up the top acceleration of a mynersha three times over; a capability Deslao habitually exploited to its maximum.

"You do that anyway."

"Whatever, just come on already."

The two of them sped off in Deslao's new silver-blue mynersha. Deslao's speedy navigation got them to Estellar Superior with a few moments to spare. There was a sign at the entrance pointing out where all the successors were to congregate.

"Where have you been?" a voice shouted from down the hallway; a commanding voice Apeay had known all of his life. Mr. Regalis stood at the end of the hall dressed in decorative attire; a deep purple robe marked with golden tassels at the sleeves, signifying an official. The diamond region emblem sat perfectly centered on his left shoulder, his positional marker exactly on half-jant in the middle of his collar.

"Oh, Apeay was sleeping as usual," said Deslao.

"Thanks, fella. Because, apparently, I don't have a voice," said Apeay.

"You know how you are."

"That's enough from both of you," Mr. Regalis interjected. "Get to the preparation room yesterday."

As ordered, they proceeded to where the rest of the successors were getting ready for the ceremony. There, they met up with the missing link of their mismatched trio.

"Headline: Estellar Superior's fastest runner running late again. How does a man so fast fall so far behind?" Seldao couldn't pass up the opportunity to take a jab at his brother.

"It's not my fault. Somebody had to retrieve 'dream child.' I mean, you don't have a permit to operate a mynersha yet, do you?" said Deslao. "What happened to yours? Oh, that's right. I remember. You scored a perfect on the written test, and then freaked out three times in a row on the course. 'It's not slowing down! It's not slowing down!' The instructor had to shut it off to get him to stop whining. Yeah, you're one to talk."

Seldao's face tightened. "I'm going to Diamond Hall to prepare my speech." He stomped off as Deslao chuckled with satisfaction.

"Why do you do that to him?" Apeay asked, hiding the smirk on his face. He too found the irony of Seldao's situation hilarious, but felt sorry for him as well. "You know he hates to be reminded of that day."

"Well," said Deslao, posing in a nonchalant lean against the wall. "People like my brother need to be reminded that our life's not all about numbers, eloquent speech and calculations. It's about action."

Apeay looked out the window adjacent to the wall, seeing a sea of parents, families, and friends pouring into the field. In a voice barely above a whisper, he said, "I think you're wrong my friend... I think it's both."

After Apeay and Deslao finished adorning themselves in shimmering white, palladium-collared robes, they made their way to the outer gate at the threshold of Maritas Field. There they joined the throng of successors filled with great expectations of life beyond Estellar Superior. While making some minor adjustments to his robe, Apeay felt a nudge at his side. It was Ms. Clesias.

"Hey. See, I made it," said Apeay.

"I never doubted that," said Ms. Clesias. "You're one of the brightest. But, I was wondering if *all* of Apeay is here today," she said with a wink.

Apeay patted himself up and down, confirming his completeness. "Yep, we're all here."

"I wanted to wish you good luck before the ceremony. Life after succession is a big change. It takes courage to become who you are. To make your dreams come true."

"Well, my dreams are unrealistic. So…I don't know. Maybe I'll just travel. See more of the regions beyond Estellar. Find out what I missing."

Ms. Clesias picked up on the unmistakable hint of sadness in his voice.

"You know Apeay, without dreamers like you, many of us would have no place to travel to. Remember that."

"I will."

"Good, now get out there. It's about time."

He looked up at the minerska at the top of the Maritas Field tower. "Very true, Ms. Clesias. See you later. And thank you again."

"See you in the future, Apeay. Take care."

Not long after Ms. Clesias joined her colleagues on the platform, the Succession Ceremony commenced: "Ladies and gentlemen, family and friends, thank you for joining us here today, as honored guest as we celebrate the succession of the Order of 3,797."

The silver gates to Maritas Field swung open. Everyone in attendance applauded the successors as they made their way onto the overlapping grassy field. The caretakers had taken extra measures to ensure all the plant life was arranged in accordance with the foyer alignment for this special day.

The young men and women paraded onto the field, with those who'd made "symbol perfect" in the lead, walking in pairs. The resounding of the cheers struck a chord deep within Apeay.

Apeay scanned the audience, though his lima cap made viewing anything above eye level a challenge. The crowning jewel of the successor's attire, the lima cap, was speckled with gold, angled on top with a wide circular brim that bent downward. Eventually, he located his mother alongside her mother and father Basxhe and Idon who came to support Apeay. Elasai and Mashelo Mangiazj were seated next to her as well. He waved as they waved back to him.

After all successors were in place, Mr. Regalis took to the podium. He paused for a moment to glance in Apeay's direction. His expression was proud and assuring. Taking a deep breath, he returned his focus to the onlookers:

"Today we bear witness to a new order of successors; a new chapter in the lives of brilliant stars. For it is they who will, in time, will replace us as leaders of the shining new era..."

Shining new era...

The words echoed in Apeay's mind. As Jhar'ensky continued his speech, Apeay drifted off into his private ruminations. *Will I shine? Where will my place be in this "new era?"* He tried to imagine his life after this day. He hadn't made any solid plans for himself. In asking for advice, Jhar'ensky and Bexhiera devised a solution, and Apeay out of a sense of gratitude accepted it. During the early nadian season he would spend part-time at the Estellar Centre, doing volunteer work, and the other part of the day training under his father, undertaking errands for Council as an understudy. And if he was still undecided as the season progressed, his father had a plan in place to guarantee his success. He was grateful for the opportunity his placement afforded him however, he wasn't too eager to begin. The thought of such work jaded him. He started to envision another world...

"Stand up Apeay!"

Deslao jolted Apeay back to the present moment. Jhar'-ensky had concluded his speech, leading them into the subsequent Rite of Advancement. As a final symbol of passage each successor took their lima cap and placed it on the ground behind them. Without looking back, they took one step over their caps leaving them where they lay. Jhar'ensky reintroduced them to the people of Estellar.

"Ladies and gentlemen, the Promoted Order of 3,797."

The thunder of thousands of hands applauding went up for a moment, dissipating into the air. It was time to bring the ceremony to a close.

"In closing," said Jhar'ensky, "we will have a few words from this cycle's top successor, Seldao Mangiazj."

Seldao promptly took to the podium. He'd been anxiously waiting for this moment to arrive, but was ready to get on with it.

"Don't get nervous bro!" Deslao shouted out.

Some of the promoted laughed, but Seldao paid them no mind. He was too well prepared and focused to be distracted by his loud-mouth brother.

"For all life is as a shadow until the highest virtue is known. Then the great 'I' will be no more and you will see me." Apeay shook his head in disapproval. The quote was taken, word for word, right out of the Book of Ascension.

He knew it well, for Jhar'ensky had taken it upon himself to have it engraved into the marble in the middle of their portico. "Who will see us? Who will see you? Where is it you will be seen? What will they say when they see us? Will it be said that you were the aeroxia who cured a disease that we call incurable? Or will they say..." said Seldao, changing the aim of his dignified finger, "it was that shototu that improved the quality of life for all of us? For there are no limitations, except those we place in our minds. You are that truth. You are that cure, that inventor, that dreamer. Yes, you are. For you are us. And we are that one. We are life itself renewed, my fellow promoted. Go forward from here and live! Thank you."

Seldao took his bow as the audience rose in applause. The ceremony was complete. Amahda cued the musicians on the platform above. Delightful melodies rained down on the field as the gate between the promoted and onlookers opened. Mrs. Regalis and Basxhe were among the first ones through, and Bexhiera caught up with her promoted son.

"How do you feel now that you're no longer an Estellar High protozen?" asked Bexhiera.

Apeay shrugged his shoulders, "The same I guess."

"Let's catch up with your father. I'm sure he'd like to see you." Bexhiera whisked him by the arm with her to the stage where his father and other members of Council were shaking the hands of countless promoted, plus their family and friends.

"Look who I found trying to sneak off into the setting Heyliun," Bexhiera said to Jhar'ensky who was absorbed in his official celebratory manors.

"Why, hey there! I mean, come up here with me. I'm proud of you, son. You're on your way to greatness. Everyone, please introduce yourselves. Apeay will be joining our establishment this historical nadian season. He may even take part in the founding of the new sioleh."

Here dad goes with the Council talk again. Better get through with this so I can meet up with the crew. Apeay put on his usual, 'I could care less about this', fake smile as he shook hands with the Council members, starting with Jhar'ensky's best friend, Valus, who appeared a bit startled by Apeay.

"Well, well, Jhar'ensky, your boy has grown so...big. He just about took my hand off with that handshake. What are you feeding him?"

Jhar'ensky laughed patting Valus on the back, "You know how it is for the young guys. They all want to be some type of super warrior, a lot like us when we were their age." The rest of the present members were lined up in order of seniority. And everyone had something to say to the son of the Council Principal.

The receiving line seemed like it took forever, and all the while Apeay wondered if she was still there. He knew she had to leave soon for an appointment that she'd mentioned to him. But it was all the same, he supposed. He would be meeting her, along with the twins, later that evening.

"Well now my brilliant promoted, how would you like to spend the rest of the day?" said Jhar'ensky.

"To be honest Dad, I want to go to the Ciradxha Azje Izos. Deslao, Seldao, and pretty much all of the promoted are going. It's like a final farewell."

"A final farewell," Bexhiera laughed. "You make it sound like you and your order is going to vanish from the tzierhan after the Ciradxha."

To vanish, Apeay thought to himself. *Just a dream.* Talking about vanishing or anything akin to it took him to a world he often thought of, but could never be.

Jhar'ensky took note of Apeay's distant countenance.

"Apeay, I thought you wanted to spend the day at Lexitova Park? It's opening day of the Glineer Games. Remember?" said Jhar'ensky.

"Most of the time, I would love to. But not today."

"Really?" said Jhar'ensky raising one eyebrow.

"Of course, dear," said Bexhiera. "Fun with friends and chasing Zaleah Ryshirix around all evening."

"That's not why Mom," said Apeay, feeling embarrassed.

"Really, my child? You've been quite the cosmic enthusiast since she came to Estellar…"

One cool evening, three cycles ago, Apeay was wandering up the stream that runs along the south east trail of Khalter-zhan. The wind carried him along the way until he arrived at the hidden straw-tuft mound where back in the day, he and the twins threw honey-nuts at unsuspecting travelers. However, on that evening there was another. Up on the mound a young lady stood posed like a goddess. Her body, a balance of sleek-ness and muscularity, which kept her posture gracefully up-right. She was standing with one hand over the brim of her brow, like the captain of a grand vessel. Her other hand rested firm on her hip. Her thick, wavy, Heyliun-kissed hair blew softly in the breeze. Overall, she appeared to be one with the enchanted night sky.

Beside her, Apeay took note of a contraption he was un-familiar with. Hesitant to speak, and not wanting to interrupt whatever experience he was now a part of, tiptoed into her unfocused periphery. Her right arm lowered to her side, and her eyes met Apeay's gaze. He found her to remarkably attractive, but hid it behind a nonchalant face. She looked back at him plainly. After an awkward moment, she returned to her deistic duty. Apeay was determined to find out what secret knowledge this one was obtaining.

"What do you see?" said Apeay

"Nothing...What do you see?" she replied.

Is she being sarcastic or acting bothered to get me to leave? Apeay wondered. To the south of Estellar loomed an overcast sky. Heavy, drooping clouds along the southern horizon were a sure sign of oncoming rainfall. Apeay wondered if she was training to be climate shototu.

"I'm waiting for the first sign of moon glimmer," her voice said, rushing to fill the void.

"Is that a real thing or are you making it up?"

"It's real, fella. It's the residual glow of the oncoming star before it arrives. The initial light highlights the treetops, and all the seas glisten like silver. That's when the Hewlix star aligns itself with Tzierhan. Through my shotatron I can see it clearly."

"So, you come up here every night to watch it or something?"

"It happens only once every three cycles. In my home region the people of the 'old ways', steeped in mystic rituals, celebrate this night in the zaitson fields where they drink and chant songs that tell stories of ancient warriors fighting celestial battles. I can see from here that this region has a group like the ones we have back home, preparing for the Carajah's Dance of Renewal. It's a tradition of the Aberan sect."

Apeay looked behind towards the distant field and pondered why she knew so much about that of which he knew nothing. He had only heard of these "mystics" but had never once encountered them, at least to his knowledge, and had no inclination to. *Perhaps she's one of them*, he thought. "Do you dance too?" he asked, more curious than before.

"So many questions you have stranger. And no, I don't dance. I'm a star enthusiast, not a mystic. But I suppose mysticism has a sort of charm worth studying too. She turned away from him and peered through the shotatron.

"Mind if I take a look?"

"It's not time yet. Besides that... I don't know you." A smile spread across her face. She could hardly contain her delight while toying with the stranger.

"Well, my name is Apeay, and I live up the way from here. Been here all my life. I've never seen you around, so how about you?" Apeay said, eager to hear her reply.

"Well then, hello, Apeay I'm Zaleah. My family and I, we just moved here from Djhalho. It's nice to meet you."

"Zaleah...that's a cool name."

"Yeah, I think so too." She took a moment to look him over again, then gestured with her head. "Sure, I'll let you look." Apeay shot up the hill with laser speed. At the top, he stood before her like a gladiator.

"Wow, that was fast," said Zaleah.

"I train a little, here and there. Nothing major," said Apeay.

Zaleah took notice of a crystal cord around his neck. She slid her finger underneath and lifted it from under his top. "That's a nice necklace."

"It's an ornament. I've had all my life. It glowed bright blue on the inside before it broke."

"I see. Well, it looks good on you... it matches your eyes."

Apeay quickly changed the subject. "So, are you going to show me how this works?"

Zaleah tilted her head, eying Apeay. His sudden haste negated her compliment, and caught her off guard. However, she chose to overlook his uncouthness, simply replying, "Sure." She placed the shotatron in front of him. "First, open the front port and adjust both glass levels to match your specific vision alignment. Do you know your personal 'far extent'?"

"I'm not sure. I know I pass the vision test with a 233-plus every time." Apeay was proud to let her know that fact.

"That's impressive. Makes it easy to adjust. Just use the levers to go full in."

Apeay hesitated to make a move. He was intimidated by the complexity of the gadget.

"It's okay, you won't break it," said Zaleah. "Just move them to the rear and press the apex button. This will open up the front so you can match it to the rear and the shotatron is set for you." He set the view as she instructed. Through word and charade, she guided him through the set up. "Now, open the back portal and look."

Apeay looked through to see a framework of stars sewn on the great cloth of space. "Where is it?"

"Give it time. It's happening now." She counted down in a melody: "Ten we begin again...Nine, eight, beyond the borders of space...Seven, six, five, four, you're the love our heart beats for... Three, two, one, welcome Hewlix Star, the lost twin of Heyliun."

At first, there was only a flicker, of what became a full star, shining brilliantly overhead. Apeay felt his heart beat strong, melting to the scenery before his eyes. He couldn't understand what this emotion was that was taking him captive. Though it was merely a distant star, he could almost hear it call to him like a whisper in his mind: *I will love you forever.*

Apeay shook his head as if to free himself from the emotion as he backed away from the contraption. He turned from Zaleah, staring intently at the stream flowing between the trail.

"Told ya it was amazing," said Zaleah.

Apeay took hold of himself and responded plainly. "Don't you wanna take a look before it fades away?"

"Of course I do. Thank you for being considerate." She adjusted the shotatron to her vision and took in the view for a moment.

Off in the remote expanse of the trails ends they could hear chants echoing into the night:

"Nadjha'rejhing majha...Nah'lai mehling nadha...Nadjha rejhing majha...nadha nahdee, nadha nadha..."

After several moments, the chanting ceased as the glimmer faded into the night. As Zaleah packed up her belongings, she thought of a marvelous way to keep in touch with her newfound galactic protégé.

"You know, I can show you more of our universe if you like. We can meet out here each Oros eve. That sound good?" said Zaleah. Apeay didn't want to appear too eager, so he responded with a nonchalant, "That's cool."

"Okay then, see you next Oros."

They spent the remainder of the nadian season together on nights like that. As his knowledge of cosmos grew during his exclusive sessions outside of Estellar Superior, over time they became close friends and more. To Apeay it seemed as if there could be no other closer to him than she. It was one time in his life when a dream came true.

"Okay son. I understand," said Jhar'ensky. "Be safe and enjoy your evening."

"I will, Father," said Apeay

"Promise me."

"I promise. It's just a Ciradxha. I'm not going anywhere after that. Okay?"

"Alright then. Just, don't be out too late. Remember, we're having the mid-early meal with guests tomorrow."

"Yes, Father."

After bidding adieu to all present, Apeay was off to the Ciradxha Azje Isos.

"On my way people. See you soon, Zaleah."

CHAPTER 8

"This way all you tough guys. Who among you is the true diamond warrior? Which one of you thinks he has what it takes to win the grand prize? Come test your might. Who will contend with the explosive, the mighty, the all-powerful Brovo Ademi?! Surely, there must at least be one worthy opponent among you. Show, and prove to everyone that you have what it takes to win!"

Cardidge Filzox, the announcer, promoter and co-owner of the Brovo Ademi Show was eager to lure another victim into the ring with the promise of a life-changing fortune, upon completion of a not-so-simple task. Defeat the invulnerable Brovo Ademi in a head to head match. Brovo, one of many great pros from the far region of Tazjoha, home to the tallest people of Tzierhan was a spectacle of a man among them, standing nearly eight shawaras tall. His body of pure muscle, weighed nearly as much as a gihan. Brovo's frame was so large that his luxury mynersha had to be rebuilt to accommodate his size.

As it stood, he was the undefeated grappler of the eastern pros in weight his class. Brovo was well known for letting his opponents beat on him as they pleased. None of their attacks gave him a hard time nor did much damage to him. Once that reality sank into the mind of a would-be adversary, they could do nothing but feel impending doom. Despite his size, Brovo never got tired or out of breath. For these reasons, he was one of the most intimidating opponents one could ask for. Challenger after challenger even those that seemed to be on par with his strength couldn't last against him. After they were good and worn out from attacking with no avail, Brovo would simply slam them all over the ring until they fell unconscious.

This was but one of three major attractions at the Ciradxha Azje Isos.

Music from the center vlexcer cascaded up and down, trickling like a mist through the entire park. A small choir sang along with the mesmerizing melodies, each harmonizing in perfect unison. Flashing lights of every shape, color and size highlighted the omnipresent art imitating life in one event so grand that it took up the entire expanse of Joru Park.

Apeay took in the vivid sights amid the park as he strolled, searching for his friends. But wasn't sure where to start. One thing he did know was that searching on an empty stomach made it hard to focus on anything else. Fortunately, there was a *kuro-kuro* stand close by. He made his way to the back of the line, while keeping his eyes peeled for his cosmic lover.

"Look at this guy, getting ready to stuff his face without us."

The smartest of the smart-mouths had found him.

"People get hungry, Deslao," said Apeay. "Maybe looking for a fool in a crowd of fools wore me out. Ever think about it like that?" To Deslao's annoyance, laughter like crackling fire rang out behind him. Seldao had made himself known.

"See, bro, I told you he'd be here," said Seldao. "A simple calculation of comings and goings make it easy for me to find anyone. Seldao *is* Estellar Superior's brightest." This level of arrogance was too much, even for Deslao.

"You get a symbol perfect on the final parallel, give a speech and now you think you know it all. Whatever," said Deslao. "And whatever you get Apeay, get it to go. The main attraction is about to start."

"I know this, my man. I can't make this line go any faster," said Apeay.

"If we weren't out scouring the park for you I'd have enough ellure travel to the tzierhan for a whole cycle."

"Oh, stop it, bro, we don't have time for that," said Seldao

"Time for what?" Apeay asked.

"His pride is hurt because everyone laughed when Brovo called him a scared jzellen after he turned down the challenge. He's been talking about going back to 'set things right' ever since. If it wasn't for me he'd still be back there making a fool of himself."

"Don't mock me, bro. Today isn't that day. But when it is, you'll see. I'm gonna set things right soon enough," said Deslao.

After an endless wait, Apeay reached the front of the line.

"What'll it be fella?"

The man running the stand was an odd one. He had a long mustache that would have looked normal, except for the fact that one side was almost twice as long as the other. His face was frozen in an indecipherable expression. It was hard to tell if he was smirking, or scowling.

"I'll take a double kuro-kuro with a double hapah and two rengi juice please," said Apeay.

"Kuro-kuro hapah caňa, rengi maxjio meĭ, astohzhing!" the man hollered to his assistant in the back. "Okay now, that'll be you two plus three, kid."

"What was that? Three plus a...I didn't get the last part."

"You heard me. Pay the two, two-o'-three, step to the side, and wait for your order. I got a line here. Next!"

The odd-faced man waved Apeay aside as his assistant came forward with his food. "Here you are, and there you go," said the assistant.

"Thank you."

"Sheesh Apeay, I didn't know you were pregnant," said Seldao, upon seeing how much food he'd ordered.

"What's that supposed to mean?"

Pointing out the bulging sack Apeay was carrying Seldao answered, "You ordered a ridiculous amount of food is what I mean. You're like a pregnant woman eating for two."

"Less talking and more walking folks," said Deslao. "For our very own Estellar Superior's brightest, is not so bright after all. Bro, who else likes that smelly dish that he ordered?"

"A lot of people do."

"If it's not in a tablet, he can't seem to grasp it. Just think, she's already here."

"You saw her?" said Apeay. He was as anxious as could be.

"Yeah, I ran into her when we first arrived. She's at Vlexcer One, waiting on us.

"Oh, Zaleah. I see now," said Seldao.

"I'm so proud of you bro. It only took you jhentas instead of ahkmeres for the common sense to kick in. They grow up so fast nowadays," Deslao teased.

The back and forth between the brothers was background noise to Apeay. He was more concerned with catching up with Zaleah. Without notifying Team Squabble, he took off in an even-paced run. This prompted Deslao to do the same, for he wouldn't allow himself to be outpaced.

"Now we're running?" said Seldao.

"Yeah, we are. So keep up, nerd boy."

Seldao would've liked to retort however, keeping up with his athletic brother and the newly athletic Apeay was hard enough. He decided his breath was better spent keeping himself conscious. After jetting and juking around several corners of the park they made it to Vlexcer One. They arrived with only a few moments to spare.

"Look around, look around, look," Apeay said under his breath. His head moved about mimicking a bojo looking for a pimen to come out the ground.

"There she is," said Apeay. From such a distance, he could tell by the way she swayed her head to the sound of the Ciradxha.

"Zaleah!" he called out.

Twelve rows up from where they stood, she turned in a half pirouette, replying with a brilliant smile. Apeay wasted no time getting up the stairs to where she was seated. The twins shadowed his movement.

"Hey there," said Apeay.

"Hey to you. I thought you might have skipped out on me," said Zaleah.

"Never that. It took me all afternoon to get away from my parents. My father just had to show off his promoted son to all thirty-four of the Seventh Council. Besides, I made a stop. Here, something for you," said Apeay as he retrieved the contents of the sack.

"Kuro-kuro, my favorite. Where'd you get it from?"

"The kuro-kuro stand on the other side of the park."

"Isn't that something? I've been all over this park and didn't see one. Thanks, cool guy."

"No problem, anytime you..." He was caught off guard as Zaleah kissed him mid speech. Apeay smirked.

"The things we do for love," said Deslao

"Man, shut up. I don't see you with anyone," said Apeay.

"I don't have time for that. I have to train to get on with Svarnax Fight Force. I'm already stronger, and a lot more skilled than most of the pros. I'm gonna be a somebody. Then, all the ladies will make time for me."

"They don't want your ugly face," said Seldao.

"If I'm ugly, then you're ugly, stupid."

Zaleah laughed at their back and forth slights. "You guys should probably take your seats. This man was kind enough to hold them for us."

"Ah, it was nothing my pretty lady," said the man. He winked at Apeay, who glared back at him. "Oh, you must be her fella. Don't take no offense. I say that to all the women."

"Thank you," said Zaleah.

"Welcome," said the man with a nod of his head.

The four of them settled into their seats. In an instant, the house lights went out. One light remained, illuminating the center of Vlexcer One. Performers sprang from beneath the ruddy sand-covered ground in various flips and tumbles to the rolling rhythm of the atabau. All twenty-two of them continued somersaulting about as flames shot up round the center of Vlexer One. The smallest of them, a boy no older than nine cycles, began climbing a rope to the top of the 90 shawara high platform using only his arms. Then with his arms out to his sides the boy suspended himself upside down holding two silver ropes dangling from the mini-platform. It was an extraordinary feat unto itself which had Apeay, like many of the spectators, on the edge of his seat.

The boy exhaled deeply, letting his eyes travel below to where, in the middle of the fire, an enormous, clear 144,000 dero tank filled with water rose up from the floor. Three whistles sound-ed, and the boy who was holding on at the top let go with a spin. The audience gasped as he spun like a drebil towards the tank. With perfect form, he broke the surface of the water with minimal splash. The boy swam to the surface and waved all around to the spectators, assuring them all was well. Cheers and applause rose up from the stands.

"I could've done that," Deslao snorted.

"A belly-flop from that high up would be very painful," said Seldao. He had his brother on that one and Deslao knew it. Diving was the one activity that Seldao was, in fact, better at. For some reason, Deslao couldn't grasp the technique.

"Yeah, you're definitely not a diver," said Apeay, chiming in.

The young boy climbed out the water, walked closer to the audience and bowed. Zaleah studied him then looked at Apeay then studied him again.

"He sort of looks like you," said Zaleah

"Like me?" said Deslao.

"No. Like Apeay."

Apeay squinted his eyes, trying to see the resemblance. "I don't see it," he said.

"Just look at him," she said. "Besides his look, it's the way he is. Look at the relaxed way he's smiling. You look the same way when you smile. Very nonchalant. And, his eyes have that unusual glow like yours. It's sort of freaky."

Deslao leaned over to his brother and spoke quietly, "Apeay better watch it. She'll be talking about making babies in a jhenta."

"I heard that," said Zaleah.

"Looking out for my fella miss."

The rhythm of the atabau sped up. The performers went into their next act. They were using each other to climb like a perpetual ladder. As one climbed to the top of the human tower another would flip off through a ring of fire. It was amazing to see twenty-one people holding themselves together using sheer strength and balance. With each successive performance the feats became more daring and complex. At one point they were throwing blades and catching them as the flipped. The act had the people in the front rows ducking for their lives, though none of the blades went that far for the performers had perfect timing. For the final act, the audience was asked to pay close attention as the performers catapulted each other into the air. They swung back and forth on cords of multicolored fire. In unison they all let go of the cords and tumbled into mid-air. As they did so, the fires on the ground and on the cords flickered and flashed, and performers disappeared.

Everyone in attendance rose to their feet for a standing ovation.

"How do you think they did that?" said Apeay

"It's just a trick," said Deslao. "Flashing lights, vapors, and mirrors. Simple magic."

The single light that shone at the beginning returned to the center of Vlexcer One. There all twenty-two of the performers reappeared as the round of applause continued. One by one, they waved adieu as they went beneath the floor. When the last one was out of sight, the house lights came.

"Wow, that was amazing," said Zaleah.

"Yeah, that was pretty awesome," said Apeay. "Well, I'd better get going."

"Already? It's so early."

"I promised my folks I'd make it to the mid-early meal tomorrow. And, I don't wake up too early as it is. If I stay out late..."

"We know, and you *know* I know," said Deslao.

"Well, have a good night. I'll see you on the trail, same place same time, right? Maybe we go somewhere else after that?" said Zaleah "Or we could meet at the lake. Follow the river all the way out of this region, just to see where it goes." Apeay pulled her to him. "Sure, my lady. Just say the word and I'll be there."

"Cool, my guy."

He gave her a kiss as they parted ways.

"See ya round man," said Seldao.

"Don't get caught up," said Deslao.

"Yeah, okay. Later fellas."

Apeay strolled off into the twilight, leaving Joru Park. He went up the path that took him directly to the house on the hill. As he walked to the mynvad station, his thoughts lingered on the magical evening, and the breathtaking performance.

He felt fortunate to be there, again.

CHAPTER 9

Who am I now? Is this my future? Will I go on to see? Yes, we will go on our way to be me.

Three cycles ago:

Palladus Hall had a rich history, steeped in periods of contentious debates. This day was another to be added to that history.

"I guess I'd expect that from you because you're a selfish bastard! That's why it's so hard for you to understand that it's not just us! Our region is doing well yes, that is true. But, for how long? We will only continue to remain ahead if the regions we deal with are on equal if not at least one grade below our status level! Just look at how much we've grown since providing essential aid to the region of Djhalho. We've expanded too far to ignore the fact that if the regions that provide us necessary resources we need to progress become broken, and unable to produce, we of Estellar will indeed one day lose our prosperity and possibly our way as well."

"Your thinking is flawed. This is us, once again, spreading ourselves too thin. So, if you think it's selfish of us to ensure we protect our own before leaping into what could be our undoing, then maybe you shouldn't be on this board."

"Is that your reasoning?"

"Yes, and I'm sure many of us agree. We have maintained a high quality of life thus far, because we have focused on what is local, and not that which is outside our reach."

"I'm well aware of what our efforts have done for us."

"Then why are you so resolute to send us into a contract that holds the potential to take us off the diamond course? Speaking of Djhalho, we actually overspent our resources to rescue that failed region, all too soon after recovering from our own economic inadequacies. Or did you forget what happens when funding goes awry because of an incompetent proposal? It put a loophole in our law, that nearly cost us everything!" Olaru looked away from the main floor, and up to the second tier, where the senior council members sat. With his hands, he pleaded. With his eyes, he scolded. "Have we became so foolish that we'd blindly turn ourselves over to an outside committee, led by authorities whom we know little about, because we fear we'll be left behind? I refuse to show support for any contract that would allow for the people within our region to be cheated yet again!"

Jhar'ensky rang the closing bell.

"Thank you, Councilman Olaru, for your input. The time for deliberation is now over, though I would like to say that whether we unify or not, I promise you those days are long behind us. We were all fooled by a schemer who abused his authoritative rights, the reason why we changed to a more open, less private format. And now, the loophole doesn't exist. Zennite Thorel, do the Legionnaires hold any major objections to this unification, and do we have your support to proceed?"

"There are no objections," said Thorel. "You have Legionnaire support to proceed."

"Thank you. We are at mark bronze already, being the last region to come to a decision. I will also say, that I agree with Councilman Hiljherde. Where will we be, let's say in another twenty or so cycles from now, if we don't make a minor sacrifice for the sake of a better future? And, if it's any comfort to those who might be unsure of where we stand within this contract, know that our region will remain Status Diamond One, keeping Estellar as the head region. Now, Council, it' s time to take count. All in favor, display the symbol, all opposed, reverse the symbol."

In favor: 89 Opposed: 55

After endless phases of deliberation, in late sharapixel of the cycle 3,794, Council concluded to laterally unite Estellar with surrounding regions, promising long-term, optimal progress for all. Estellar, therefore became part of Zenlaitazan, a vast domain encompassing the entire landmass of Tzierhan, 400 million square reels total, combining all regions under the authority of Command. Filling the role of Command was a man by the name of Affi'hado, the eldest of the Tazjohan Council members. Ambassadors from Estellar Council and the Councils of both Alizan and Sohexiah, uniformly agreed that Affi'hado was the wisest and most suitable to fulfill the role, as he had already established peaceful working relations be-tween them and their neighboring regions. Among the Legionnaires of Estellar, Nikashiro Uzani was promoted to the rank of zenshiro, filling the vacancy left by the former zenshiro's resignation, making him the commander of all five rings of Legionnaires, superseded in authority only by Zennite Thorel under the direction of Command.

ζ

Present cycle:

"Three one four, Ring One, all clear on the horizon. What's your standing Ring Two?"

"Three one four, Ring Two, clear as the ocean view."

This wasn't what Apeay imagined when his father said to him, *"Son, you'll be working under me and Council guidance, beginning this nadian season. In time you will be eligible for election to the board. But first, we'll get you acclimated."*

Acclimated? I'm all the way in, Apeay thought. Jhar'-ensky decided that, with his guidance, Apeay would make an expedient rise to the rank of a tier-two optashiro, as well as build an outstanding resume, guaranteeing him an early induction into Council just as he had when he became a Council ledger. In due time, he'd pass on the reigns of Principal from father to son. Therefore, after only a few phases post succession ceremony, Apeay took the diamond pledge into the Legionnaire flight academy. Once training began, it didn't take him long to learn all the rules and regulations. And surprisingly, piloting came naturally to him. After the first four sessions, he was piloting a glineer with ease as if he had been doing it for ages. Due to his advanced skill, with special dispensation by Enjevix, Apeay made the patrol link by late nadian. However, he was not permitted to patrol on his own for he was only a first-tier metashiro.

A second-tier optashiro of Enjevix's choosing led the way as Apeay trailed behind in his custom equipped glineer.

Outwardly each glineer appeared the same: An outer coat of brightly polished armor that shined like silver, having six magnetic, unattached wings, allowing for uninhibited motion in the six angles of three-dimensional navigation. This technological feature enables the pilot to spontaneously change their direction with the flick of a switch. On the inside, the controls are custom-made to fit to each pilot's unique adaptation to flight without compromising the essentials of flight or the basic design. Apeay's glineer, set up in "configuration two" to his liking, complimented his relaxed style of piloting.

While patrolling under the supervision of his optashiro, the report screen of his glineer lit up, signaling a transmission would soon follow.

"Three one four, day patrol teams Ring One and Two, sequence air out and dismissal," said Enjevix. The only permissible reply came in from each optashiro. "Accepted."

Apeay was relieved to hear the issued sequence. The repetitive patrols were taking their toll on his body. The force of the glineer changing directions was a heavy load for even the most seasoned pilots to bear. He followed closely behind his lead as they coasted their regal glineers into the proper bay. The moment the speedy vehicle was secured in its bay, Apeay sprang out, readying himself to leave.

"Slow it up junior!" one of the optashiros shouted. "We're not done with the final outs for the day, which include the retrace. We all know who your father is, but don't think you'll be receiving any special treatment from me. Now, let's get it done."

"Accepted, ishiro," said Apeay, responding appropriately out of respect for a superior Legionnaire. He ran through the retrace with his optashiro, remembering to include every last detail of what was seen and heard throughout the patrol from the parks to the lakes, main region rivers and trails.

Trails...

That's when it hit him.

She was waiting for him at the trail. It was the last time for a long while they would have time to spend together. Zaleah was leaving early for Ajina Delta, where she would continue her studies in cosmic order and advanced healing. He didn't have time to waste. As soon as he was dismissed, he headed for the exit.

"Whoa, whoa, whoa! Since when do we stroll out in uniform?" said the optashiro.

"Only in emergency evacuation, ishiro," Apeay replied.

"Then I can assume you know what you need to do."

"Yes, ishiro."

"Alright then."

Apeay quickly made his way to the secure area to change his attire. Once dressed in his civilian clothing, he decided to sneak out the back way to minimize the risk of being further slowed down by the optashiro. He sped off in his mynersha, saying goodbye to his duty in the breeze. He went about the region for a moment, gathering his thoughts. It was one of those days when he questioned everything he was doing with his life. He appreciated the fact that his parents had provided him with his own place and mynersha to get around. But, to him, it seemed like going around and around was all he was doing. Apeay was lost in thought before it came back to him. He still had to make his way to the trail.

Apeay arrived at the hidden mound on the trail just in time to see Zaleah packing up. He leapt out of the mynersha without shutting the door, and ran up to the mound where she sat.

"You're late. I thought you said you'd remember," said Zaleah.

"I did. The patrols went a little longer than usual today. Then I sort of got lost for a second. Can you forgive a fella?"

Zaleah flipped her braids up out of her face as she rose to her feet. She looked him in his eyes and saw the truth. "Sure... Are you doing alright?"

"Yeah. I'm just a little tired."

"Is that all?"

"Nothing else to it. The glineers wear a man out."

"Okay. But you missed out, my guy."

"On what?" asked Apeay.

"You must have a lot on your mind.

"I might."

"Don't you remember? It happens three days before the alignment."

"Ah, that's right, the southern glow," said Apeay. He was now even more disappointed that he'd taken so long to arrive. "The stars of that in appear in our southern hemisphere are visible below Heyliun before it sets."

"That's right. And, now that Heyliun is almost set, they can't be seen that way."

"True..." Apeay looked toward the sky, seeing if there was still a chance to catch a waning glow. *Nope. I definitely missed it. Next time.*

"You can still catch the Hewlix alignment in three days you know."

"Yep..." he said, his eyes still focused on the horizon.

Zaleah sat her belongings down, and leaned her head on his shoulder.

"I wish I could be here to watch it with you. It won't be the same without you…You know what I really wish?"

"What's that?" said Apeay.

"I wish you'd come with me."

"I know, you keep saying that. I mean it sounds great, but I can't. I have my duties here. I don't even know what I'd do if I did."

"That's *exactly* why you should come with me. Discover what you don't know. Maybe things would be better if you do."

"Like do what you do? No, I'm doing my thing. And what do you mean by better?"

"I just saying that maybe if you left Estellar, you'd find something that you really enjoy, and find your own way."

Does she think I'm helpless? "I've already pledged. I found my way."

"But you don't really like what you do. You even said so yourself that being a metashiro is like being stuck in Estellar Prime. If you transfer to the Sohexiah, you can arrange for an early, one cycle served, dismissal and keep all the benefits."

"No. I'm not doing it like that. I can't just abandon my duties. And it'll be half a cycle before I can request for a transfer. You know, this metashiro rank won't last long. I'm already on the patrol link. Soon I'll progress through tiers two, then to three to optashiro and then…"

"And then what, Apeay? You'll just progress and progress until you're in your father's position, debating the day away about how much ellure spent here, what construction goes there, who's the next up for election?"

"What's wrong with that?" said Apeay

"That's not what I'm saying. And it's no disrespect to your father. He's a good man. What I'm saying is it's not you. You're not like him in that respect. You're not like many people. That's what I like about you. I just want you to be happy. I think you're settling because you don't know what else to do."

"Maybe. But I don't feel like I'm missing out on much either." Apeay examined the ground as if the answer would spring up like a wild flower. He didn't like the idea of their too soon separation, but hid it behind a stone cold expression.

"How about you stay here for another three days, and we can watch the alignment together? We'll have a little more time and a better time than today with me running late. And you'll be able to watch me fly along with Ring One, as we make way for the new sioleh."

"*Another* one of those things? As if the region needs a new one. I would love to say yes, but the Ajina director said we have to be there by tomorrow if we don't want to be put on hold for a cycle," said Zaleah.

"Oh. Guess you have to go then. By the way, the sioleh's are one of the greatest innovations of our era. They multiply the magnitude of wave energy drawn out from Heyliun's light more than a thousand times over. And with the new align-ment, we will be sharing our energy field with our less efficient neigh-boring regions. It's almost a necessity."

"Yeah, that's what they say. To me it sounds like an excuse for more progress without majority consent."

"If it's in the interest of the majority, Council deems it consent. You know that."

Zaleah shrugged her shoulders. "I hope you're right. So how'd you end up in this fly along?"

"Yours truly, was chosen second out of the ninety newly inducted pilots to be one of three escorts as Ring One is given 'sequence decimation', thanks to my recent flight scores."

"Way to go, Apeay. Maybe I don't have to worry about you. What's the sequence 'decimation' assigned to? What are they demolishing?"

"The ruins. Council agreed that it was an eye sore because it doesn't match the progression of the modern era. That's where we come in. We clear it out for the new sioleh. The rest of the foregrounds, realigned for living space."

"I see…How sad."

"What's sad about it?"

"The Forbidden Ruins, forbidden only to those who cling to the foolish superstitions. A work of art dating back to a time that no one remembers. Because no one knows when or where it came from, they say it's dangerous closing our eyes to the possibility that it may be valuable to the enrichment of our lives. Sorry, my love. You'll always have my support, but that's something I don't care to witness."

"What about Council's last decree that it was bad for the overall health of the unified regions? People who go there come out infected. They've even pinpointed it as the cause of the juvenile fatigue."

"It sounds like made up nonsense to me. Besides, I've heard quite the opposite from a few aeroxia protozens. They say that it's our progress that's affecting the children. That we've been too careless with what we've created. I'm sure you think the same even if you won't admit it. And infected with what? A supposed disease no one has any real proof of? Archeleon, they call it? If that's the case, how come *you* didn't get infected? You were found there after going missing for two phases."

"The aeroxia said I was lucky that the Archeleon effects didn't take over my mind or I might have been caught in a delusion," Apeay replied.

"And, you believed him? I think he was trying to scare you from going back there. Have you ever heard of an infection causing that to happen to anyone else?"

Apeay had never thought about it until now. He was the only one he knew that had been recovered from Ruins, except for one other person.

"You've heard of Perinzel Shallhir, the former zennite of Estellar?" asked Apeay.

"The name's not familiar to me. Who is he?"

"More like who was he. He's dead now. He was found in the ruins by the former zenshiro's elite diamond patrol. Bloody scars covered his body from head to toe, while he lay on the ground foaming at the mouth. The Legionnaires' lead aeroxia recorded that his heart had already stopped beating eventhough his mouth was still mumbling things like, "He has no eyes, there is no place," over and over before his body solidified. When they reviewed his body, they said he was dead long before they reached him, as if he died from the inside out."

Zaleah snickered.

"How is that funny?"

"I remember now. I read that report. If you ask me, he sort of had it coming. That man was one of the most corrupt zennites in all Estellar history. His entire campaign for zennite was a sham. He was making secret deals with industrial firms from other regions that nearly brought Estellar to impoverishment, while he delegated resources needed for public developments like the Centre into his own private storage. And he was the one who first declared the ruins "forbidden" and "dangerous." Seems ironic that that's where they found him, don't you think?"

"Yeah, I see your point. But it doesn't change the fact that something terrible happened to him in that place. And I have my duties. I'm now a shining member of the Legionnaires, sworn to protect our diamond progression."

"Nah," said Zaleah "You were shining from the day I met you. But I believe, you live unaware of it. That's something else I don't care to witness." She tiptoed to a kiss. "I left the shotatron there for you. If you change your mind about staying here, you know where I am. Find your heart my friend. I love you."

The thick, suffocating air muffled Apeay's reply. "Love you."

He stood statue-like on the mound, his eyes watching her go along the trail to her mynersha. He reached down to pick up the shotatron, and sighed. Another dream had come and gone. He steadied himself before sauntering back to his own mynersha.

"How are we today?" Startled, Apeay turned quickly to see who had snuck up behind him. "You really don't have to tell me. I've been here for a while," said Seldao. "She's right about one thing. Who you are is something other than a Legionnaire. Even I know that."

"Were you spying on us? You were hiding behind the bushes, weren't you? That's not cool man," said Apeay

"I wasn't spying. I was laying down studying. I was here before Zaleah showed up."

"Then how come you didn't say anything?"

"I didn't feel the need to announce myself. It would've interrupted my studies. See, I'm finishing work on my entrance strategics, and my ears just pick up things."

That was another peculiarity about Seldao. Wherever a secret was being told, or private plans were being discussed, you could be sure Seldao was somewhere close by, blending in with the scenery.

"Oh, that's right you'll be leaving soon too. For Fu'Shijehan?"

"Alpha Fu'Shijehan to be correct."

"Okay. But you know, I still can't believe you turned down Ajina. You used to say that you were destined for Ajina after you were invited there to give your delivery."

"I know. But that was back when I was a kid. I'd rather go somewhere that concentrates on my specified interest, instead of its own dignified reputation."

"That makes sense. Dang, it seems everyone's headed away."

"Well, it won't be so soon for me," Seldao said, observing Apeay's melancholy face. "Don't let it get you down. I'll be there to watch you fly my friend. After it's over we can meet up with my bro and have one last get together before I go."

"Deslao won't be there with you?"

"I don't know. Nobody does with him these days. He spends all his time training with Svarnax Fight Force for his first pro fight."

"He's already a pro? How did that happen?"

"I'll tell you how. During a training session, he walked right into the arena and challenged the first pro he saw. And, you'll never guess who."

"Don't tell me it was ol' boy from the park?"

"Yes. None other than Brovo Ademi. You know he's had it out for him ever since he teased him in front of the crowd."

"Brovo? Deslao took on Brovo? No way! That fella's not a man, he's more like a real-life monster. You're telling me he fought that Brovo?!"

"Fought him? He absolutely *destroyed* him. Brovo must've really got under his skin. Deslao came right at him with a flurry of attacks, knocking him out in record time. So, they signed him right there on the spot." Apeay's jaw dropped. "Some type of unbelievable, ain't it'?" said Seldao

"That's some talent he's got."

"Sure is… But now about you fella. Are you doing okay?"

"Thanks for asking, but I'm alright. I'm heading back to my place. Gonna call it a day. I can give you a ride if you'd like," said Apeay.

"I appreciate it, but I'm staying here for a while. Deslao's coming pick me up soon. Maybe I can convince 'super fighter' to forego a day of training to watch you soar the skies."

"I doubt it."

"Me too, but you never know. Take care, my friend. And cheer up. You can always go visit her. Ajina Delta is only a region away," said Seldao. Though he was used to seeing Apeay being distant at times, this was different, and it concerned him.

"You're right. Thanks again. I'll see you in a few."

"Likewise, my friend."

The two parted ways, much as they parted in thought.

Thank you, Seldao. Thank you for reminding me she won't be there, again...

CHAPTER 10

"Shototu Ju-Makana. You're one of the few people who disagree with Council, saying that their actions today are self-serving and outright wrong. Is that correct?"

Ju-Makana was quickly losing popularity with Council, as well as his colleagues. He had aligned himself with the naturalist group that had long protested against the construction of the new sioleh, as he expressed to the interviewer during the live report.

"Yep, that's correct. This is a terrible decision for more than one reason. The data I've collected from my research shows that we may be destroying 'sacred ground' to put it figuratively. And, I'll tell you what else, Averand, the other shototus that gave their report to Council don't have the collective experience between the lot of them to equal my own. I've been researching tri-alpha resonance and its effects before most of them were born. Sure, there are reports and rumors surrounding the ruins, but I'm not here for that. I'm here to state facts and they are this: Every three cycles, the Hewlix alignment sends out alpha radiation into our atmosphere. By comparing the radiation to the normal resonance of visible light, I've deduced that they cause a temporary, minor influx of toxicity in the waters flowing through the canals, due to the depth alignment of their location. 'No big deal' is what my colleagues say, because it's toxin-free where it meets with our mainstream that flows into the personal well springs.

"However, what goes ignored is the routing of the canals. Halfway through, they pass under the backside of the ruins. Right there where they meet is where I began my research. By testing the reaction of reverse alpha waves from my ferro-metrona, I discovered an unknown element that radiates from below the ruins. I call it "trilaixis." "Tri," for it shares all the properties of original tri alpha waves in their unaltered state, "laixis" for the mythical goddess Lai that purified the waters of the lost empire of Xeno. I firmly believe that this element is responsible for the perpetual purity of the waters within our region. It has this effect like it's causing the toxins to 'vanish' in a way that we don't understand. And, for that reason, we must not do this thing."

"A place that causes disease is suddenly purifying our waters? That seems like a far stretch, shototu," said sahresh Averand, the top voice of hearsay in the Estellar Region, a sahresh known for livening up her broadcasts with controversial gossip.

"It's a studied fact," said Ju-Makana

"Then what about the test the other shototus ran after your discovery? I was told that not one of them came up with anything close to your results. Some are even saying you're a shototu who's past his time, an old fool with too many high-tech tools."

Ju-Makana could tell by the catty grin on her face that she enjoyed being yet another ridiculer of his work. He waved it off.

"Preposterous," he said. "None of those young buffoons knows what it means to do a thorough investigation. And, if you ask me, a few of them took certain favors to report whatever Council wanted to hear. So there! You can put that in your silly report, too! Now, if you'll excuse me, I'm with them folk in this region who got some sense."

"What's that mean?"

Without another remark he brushed past Estellar's face of gossip, scurried past the Legionnaires grasp, and joined the group linked arm-in-arm on the foreground.

"Fair people of Estellar, please remove yourselves from the target area. You are trespassing on private property, which is scheduled for decimation. REMOVE YOURSELVES FROM THE AREA IMMEDIATELY!"

The repeated instructions blared from the loudspeakers. But the people ignored the orders from Enjevix, while he led Ring One in flight above. The group refused to budge in protest of Council's decision. Among them were people of similar mind to shototu Ju-Makana, who believed destroying the ruins was a grave mistake. For some, the ruins had aesthetic value. These people admired its rustic beauty and sought to preserve it as a landmark. Others were mystics who regarded the ruins as hallowed ground. Each one, for their own individual reasons, stood unified against the decimation sequence.

Apeay viewed the commotion below as he circled around, flying in Enjevix's shadow.

Apeay awoke that morning to Heyliun's light striking his room. As he stirred himself, the light glazed over his ornament which was hanging on the end of his faja. He hadn't worn his silver pendant in almost three cycles. But on that morning, he remembered what Zaleah said to him when they first met. He decided to wear it for her. It was against code to wear it in uniform, so Apeay hid it beneath the first layer of his gear as he suited up to fly in the ceremony.

Apeay took several deep breaths. His heart was beating rapidly to the ticking of his glineer's mechanisms. With his keen vision, he began to identify the people standing in protest. He identified Ju-Makana next to some of the performers from the Ciradxha del Izos next to others he didn't know, along with a few more familiar faces. Some of them he knew from Estellar Superior. Some were former Legionnaires and former Council members he met through his father. And there was Ms. Clesias.

What's she doing down there? Apeay felt his stomach beginning to turn. And he was trapped in the cockpit of a high-speed glineer, which could only make things worse.

"Four One Three, Enjevix..."

"Transmit, your excellency."

The center display of Enjevix's glineer activated only to display a figure standing in the shadows. Out of the shadows the grim voice spoke, **"Begin sequence ruin decimation immediately!"**

"Your Excellency, if you wish, I will issue a final warning and..."

"I DO NOT WISH! DO NOT ATTEMPT TO DELAY MY SEQUENCE ANY FURTHER! For I wish this; begin decimation on the far side, away from the unsightly mob at once. That will be their final warning. If they remain unmoved, then they will have the imperfection they desire. LEVEL THE ENTIRE THING!"

Enjevix, a seasoned Legionnaire accustomed to respecting superior authority solemnly, replied, "Accepted, your excellency." His display went blank. "Three one four, Ring One."

"Transmit."

"Direct Command sequence; begin decimation from mark twelve to six on target area."

"Accepted."

"Accepted, but you don't think that's being a little too rash?" said Aven.

"It's an official sequence, and I expect full compliance not your opinions."

"Accepted and understood. But we're going to take it slow, right? We're not murderers."

"I am fully aware of what our duties are! Once they see us ascend, they'll clear out. It will take us 15 zahmens to approach their position while our ground team pushes them out. They'll be off the foregrounds by the time we reach the target area," said Enjevix. "Stay off the transmit, and prepare for ascension!"

Apeay flew alongside. He began to fear for those on the foreground below. *Is this what we're doing now? All of them are in danger.*

On the other side of the Forbidden Ruins, the onlookers including Council watched as the Legionnaires began their climb towards the distant heavens, preparing to descend in a fury.

"What the hell do they think they're doing?!" Jhar'ensky exclaimed. "We haven't yet cleared the protestors from the foregrounds. And decimation isn't to begin until one more spin. This is supposed to be a festive event, not a massacre. If we allow this to happen, Council reputation will be synonymous with dung."

"Well, we can't let that happen," said Valus, approaching them from the rear.

"Where have you been? We could use some help from the head of the affairs department to sort this out."

"That's what I've been trying to do. But this supersedes my range of intervention, which can only mean one thing."

"And what is that?" Jhar'ensky waited to hear him say what he dreaded, but knew to be true.

"That sequence must've come from the top without our knowledge."

"What is going on with this Command lately? If this sequence was his doing, then he's once again overstepped his limits of authority. You know, I keep asking myself why we showed symbol to agree to this unification. Looking back, I believe we should've given it more thought."

"We did it for equal efficiency across the regions, remember?"

"Whatever the case may be, I must issue a repeal to the original sequence issued to Ring One and stop this." Jhar'ensky reached to tap his plina, but was stopped short.

"It won't do any good. I've already tried," said Zennite Thorel. Her timing couldn't be more seamless if she tried. "My communication to Enjevix and all of Ring One was cut off before I could issue the repeal."

She looked up to the skies where the proud glineer pilots lifted their vessels to the heights of terror, thinking to herself,

He was such a kind old man. Or at least I thought he was. My successful career was made possible by the wisdom he shared with me. Could it be that all of it was a lie?

"Alright, men let's prevent a massacre before it's too late."

"But if we can't communicate with them, how are we supposed to stop them?" said Valus

"I have it covered," said Thorel. "I transmitted sequence 'delay' to Ring Two patrol. They should arrive in a jhenta and use their close range transmit to break through whatever's jamming my signal. And, as you may have guessed, our excellent Command is the one responsible."

"Are you sure that will work?" said Valus.

"Let's just say I did my homework."

"And what if he issues the same sequence to Ring Two?" said Jhar'ensky.

"I took that into consideration and had their long-range transmit disabled after issuing the sequence. I'm zennite, after all. Now, let's help organize the ground team and get the protesters to safety."

"Uzani," said Apeay

"Proper format!" said Enjevix

"Three one four, Ishiro Uzani.

"Transmit."

"Are we really going to commence with sequence decimation with those people down there?"

"Yes, we are. We have our sequence. Lock it up, and don't question me." There was a brief silence, but not the silence Enjevix wanted to hear. "Do you understand?"

"Yes...I mean, accepted."

"Three one four, Ring One," said Enjevix

"Transmit," said Ring One in unison.

"Once we reach the outer realm, we will be in position to carry out the sequence as planned. There will be no deviation from the final sequence. Is that understood?"

Ring One replied, "Accepted."

Everyone, that is, except Apeay.

"Three one four, Ishiro Uzani," said one legionnaire.

"Transmit."

"It appears our route is being blocked."

"By who?"

"I believe it's Ring Two patrol."

"Three one four, Ring Two."

"Transmit," said Ring Two.

"This is Zenshiro Uzani. Clear the route."

"Sequence rejected, ishiro. We have our sequence set by Zennite Thorel. You'll have to wait. Our apologies, ishiro," said nikashiro Bokshan of Ring Two.

Meanwhile, on the grounds below, Ring Five was having little success detaining the protesters. They transmitted "back-up" to Ring Three.

"What are you staring at?" asked Deslao, who noticed his brother gazing intently upon the ruins.

"I thought I saw something out there like a flicker, or a flash among those large stones," Seldao replied. He couldn't help but feel as if something was calling to him.

"Stones, rocks, overgrown vegetation. It's nothing."

"Maybe, but that's what makes it fascinating, don't ya think? Those people are willing to risk their freedom and perhaps their lives to protect it. Makes me curious. What will we learn today? Will the region be torn apart? Are those people mystics, saviors, or simply mad? Only time will tell." His silliness was too much for his brother.

"I'm leaving, bro. I can't believe I let you talk me out of training to come here."

"Don't be like that. We're here for Apeay. Besides, I'm checking it out."

"You'd better not."

"I have to. I need to get a better look."

"You're determined to be as stupid as you can be today. Is that it? They're detaining anyone who goes near there, and you want to get right in the middle of it. How stupid!"

"Don't you want to know why? What's really going on here?"

"No, I don't!"

"Well, I do. And you know me, bro. Stupid as they come. Later." Seldao took off down the hill from where they stood towards certain disaster. Deslao was livid. Not only was he missing training, but he was now chasing behind his irrational brother. After all, he was their protector. And his brother knew it.

"Three one four, Aven," said Enjevix

"Transmit."

"Sequence formation break, over speed, non-lethal clear, reform to original formation in the tail."

"Accepted."

The complex sequence was like basic flight to Aven. He could clear Ring Two with ease, and catch up to join the descent to decimation before it began. Aven's capabilities were unmatched.

Aven, the number one glineer pilot, held his title with pride. At one time he went so far as to bet Enjevix he could clip the stem of a zaitson fruit without damaging the fruit itself. Enjevix took him up on the bet, and lost. Enjevix said it was the most amazing feat he'd ever seen a pilot pull off in his entire time as Legionnaire.

"Three one four, Ishiro Uzani ," said Apeay.

"Transmit."

"Requesting sequence stop Aven."

Enjevix was fed up with Apeay's ludicrous requests. "What the...?! Look. I'd better not hear anything more from you for the day. One more transmit from you and..."

Apeay didn't bother listening to Enjevix any further. He broke formation in pursuit of Aven.

"Three one four, Enjevix," said Aven.

"Transmit."

"It appears I've picked up a tail."

"I know, I know! Damn it!"

"What do you want me to do?"

"Don't hurt the young fool. Sequence disable propulsion. Get him out the sky now!"

"Accepted."

Faster and faster Aven went. His glineer, modified to accelerate at a rate that would render the average pilot unconscious, made it easy for him to pull away from Apeay. Before completely out of view, his glineer spun one-eighty, heading straight for Apeay.

"Three, one, four, Apeay," said Aven

"Transmit?" said Apeay.

"You should learn to stay on your level. Good luck."

CHAPTER 11

"Stop! I said Stop!"

A legionnaire from Ring Five was in pursuit of the Mangiazj twins. Or, more accurately, he was pursuing one of them. The other, grudgingly along for the ride, mumbled curses under his breath.

Seldao had made his way past the ruin's foregrounds and those guarding it, while Deslao did all he could to keep up with his brother's spontaneous curiosity, curiosity which struck Seldao with yet another idea. He figured since he was already well into the ruins, he might as well take a peek inside one of the elongated caverns. He assured himself he wouldn't get caught if he was quick about it.

"Zoom, zoom, bro!" Seldao shouted back to Deslao.

"I swear you'd better not be headed where I think!" said Deslao. *Of course,* he thought. *I do all the planning, driving, strategizing . Obviously, I'm the one with good sense. And, him? He has whatever was left over at birth.*

But it was too late to stop Seldao. He bent a quick corner and went inside the extensive cave. Deslao, not far behind, joined his brother who was already deep within the shadowy cavern. Their pursuer, however, was losing ground; his protective gear was weighing him down, and he was now several sannos away.

"Are you seeing this?!" Seldao exclaimed as he continued his mad dash. While he scurried through the narrow tunnels and caverns, he noticed every detail etched into the remnants of a world past. Strange markings and symbols aligned in combinations unaccustomed to their modern era covered the walls. "We should've come here instead of spending all those cycles on the trails." Seldao's ability to talk, and more so, shout without getting winded was incredible in the worst way to Deslao. This outlandish feat from his brother had him second guessing as to which one of them was the true athlete.

"Just look at these stone carvings! They're amazing! Who did this? And what's...that?" Seldao came to a stop in front of one of the stone carvings on the wall. "Those symbols are rare ancients... they resemble the first three of the..."

"Let's get out of here, bro!" said Deslao as he caught up, giving him a sharp blow to his arm. "You hear me? The legionnaire's catching up to us, fool. He's already at the entrance. We gotta go!"

"Relax, bro. I hear you, okay?" Seldao rubbed his aching arm. "Man, you do hit hard," Seldao poised to take off again.

"Wait," said Deslao, "what was that?" Something about the ground felt wrong to him.

"What? Make up your mind. Are we leaving or not?"

"Don't move... It's the ground. I think..."

Before the legionnaire could capture his prey, the clay beneath the twins' feet gave way. He quickly assessed what he had witnessed, and slowed to a shuffle as a terrifying sound filled his ears. The gurgling roar prompted him to lie down, crawling to the spot where the two once stood. Close to the edge, he saw the monster below. A raging waterfall went on for a hundred sannos, or maybe more. Who could tell when peering into the endless abyss? He reached for his transmitter, but it was useless. What could he do for them besides locate their family and console them when he returned, he supposed. The Mangiazj twins were gone.

On the foreground Rionazen, was leading Ring Five in a strategic sweep that was making headway. But they needed to push harder if they were to clear the protestors from the foregrounds before Ring One inevitably resumed sequence decimation. "Make sure to keep a tight flank on the rear. No stragglers left behind! Keep pushing the line!"

In the sky above, Enjevix was successful in directing most of Ring One around Ring Two patrol. He was counting on Aven to finish dealing with their problem, and clear the remainder from their path, for once they began their descent there would be little anyone could do to stop them from carrying out the sequence.

"We almost have full clear," said Thorel. "They've reached peak."

"Not all of them," said one of Ring Three. "Check that out." Thorel lowered her gaze to the spectacle unfolding below the main attraction above; two flashes of silver riding the horizon, heading straight for one another.

"Three, one, four, Apeay," said Aven.

"Transmit."

"See you on the ground."

Aven, still two reels away from Apeay, opened the lower cutters on his glineer and locked his configuration on the upper propulsion device atop Apeay's glineer. All he had to do was clip off the top like a stem on a fruit, and Apeay would go coasting down the ground, for a rough, but survivable landing. After that, back to dealing with Ring Two.

"Oh man, what am I doing?" Apeay said aloud. His fervor for protecting the protestors became swallowed up by self-doubt and trepidation. "I can't take him on. Even if I could, I'm going to be detained. I messed up this time. Father is going to be so disappointed."

"**YOU FOOL!**"

The powerful voice jolted Apeay deeper into his nightmare. A shadowed image materialized on the center screen of his glineer. There was a brief moment of daunting silence.

"Now, I see. A mystical creation indeed...You will not stop perfection! Who do you think you are to stop me boy?!"

Apeay's eyes widened. If there is something he could never forget, it was that unnatural voice that haunted him as a child. *But, how is that possible, from all those years ago?* he thought.

"Who are you?" he asked

"I AM COMMAND, DIRECT, SUPREME AUTHORITY OVER ESTELLAR, AND ALL OF ZENLAITAZAN! Those who go against Perfection must be done away with. To go against the will of Perfection is to suffer this fate. Therefore, your synthetic life will be no more!"

The screen in Apeay's glineer went blank.

"Four one three, Aven!"

"Transmit, Command."

"Sequence terminate the defector."

"Command, I am proceeding with sequence disable propulsion under Zenshiro Enjevix. Apeay is not an enemy. He's a comrade."

Without regard for Aven's commentary, Command proceeded to caution Aven. "Perhaps then, I will issue this sequence to legionnaires who know how to follow protocol on your behalf as well. Am I understood?"

"Yes, Command, I understand full well. I'm the number one pilot. What you don't understand is that being number one is more than just being the fastest or the best sky fighter. It's about knowing how to carry yourself as the best. And, if I follow through with that sequence, I will no longer be the best. Sequence rejected!"

"Is that so? You think you can defy my authority and live? Very well. YOU TOO WILL BE NO MORE!

Aven steered his glineer off the path towards Apeay, and pulled alongside him. "Three one four, Apeay."

"Transmit, ishiro," said Apeay.

"Don't worry about me. I'm no longer coming for you, but something much worse is. You have to get out of Estellar, right now. I'll provide cover for you. This Command, he's not the proper ruler we thought him to be. I think he might even be a madman. Escape this place, and find somewhere to hide until I can give an account on our behalf."

"What about you?"

"Me? No one can touch me up here. You'll be long gone by the time I get done distracting everyone. Take the reverse path to the west of Estellar. Fly stratus high, at full speed. Now, find the third cord in from the door beneath your control panel and snip its connection. It will disable the ESSA and make you nearly undetectable. Now go! As your superior, that is my sequence to you."

"Accepted, ishiro...Thank you." Apeay did as Aven instructed. After some nervous fumbling, he found the cord, sniped it, and bolted away, disappearing into the clouds.

"Four one three, Ring One!"

"Transmit, Command," Ring One replied in unison.

"Aven, like that traitor, Apeay, has defected, and gone rogue. They are to be executed immediately! Any noncompliance will be regarded likewise."

"Three one four, your excellency," Enjevix responded. "On what grounds do you bring these accusations?"

"Willful disobedience, unreasonable non-compliance with malicious intent and treason! They are to be brought down and done away with to ensure order is maintained on Tzierhan."

"I don't believe this, your excellency." Enjevix refused to believe that his long-time pupil and friend was capable of treason.

"He was given a sequence from you, was he not?"

"That he was."

"To do what?!"

Enjevix hesitated for a moment. He let out a deep breath with a slow response. "...To take Apeay out of the sky."

"Apeay, yes he is a problem for us."

"Your excellency, I sent Aven to deal with him. Why are you calling my number one a traitor?"

"Why? Take a look for yourself. Your number one is aiding his escape. Watch and see for yourself."

Enjevix's display switched to an onboard view from Aven's cockpit. He watched along as Aven steered his glineer away from Apeay, with Apeay speeding towards the outer realm among the clouds. "Your excellency, Aven's not against us, he's...well, he's doing things his way. It can hardly be called treason."

"You're trying to make a suggestion to me? Have you forgot who I am to you?"

"No, I have not."

"Good, because *you know* where I stand. Apeay, Aven, sequence capture or kill. ANY NONCOMPLIANCE WILL BE REGARDED AS TREASON! IS THAT UNDERSTOOD?!"

"Yes, your excellency." Enjevix's screen went blank.

"Three one four, Ring One," said Enjevix.

"Transmit," replied Ring One.

"Postpone sequence decimation. Superseding sequence per Command."

Hesitantly, the call was answered by all. "Accepted."

"May the firmaments forgive us."

Δ

"Wow, that is wild. You said you're from Estellar, right?"

Zaleah made a conscious effort to forget ever since she left. Being accepted into Ajina "the prestigious gem" of the Sohexiah, the neighboring region of Estellar was a rare honor that only a handful of the promoted qualified for. Every amenity one could wish for was there, providing the best experience for all. Despite its luxurious façade, Ajina maintained the most rigorous therapy curriculum. Therefore, Zaleah did her best not to remember the place she was from. Not there. Not the nadian when she met him. She did not wish to feel heartache, reflec-ting on the times spent with Apeay. But today, making report universal, a story of who was not to be remembered, unfolded on the glowing screen.

"Yes, I am. Why do ask?"

"See for yourself," said LaLa'ila.

From the ionix cylinder: "I'm here, corresponding live from the Forbidden Ruins of Estellar. What was considered to be a day of celebration and new beginnings has taken a tragic turn for the worse. It began with a riot on the foregrounds where protestors took a violent stance against the construction of the much needed enhanced sioleh, which has the potential to not only add to, but double if not triple the energy required to support the ever expanding unified regions. And, as if that were not enough trouble for one day, we've now learned that two Legionnaire pilots, names Apeay Regalis and

Aven Nikay, turned rogue as they began to attack their fellow comrades."

"Oh no…Apeay," Zaleah whispered, clutching her chest.

"Both pilots are being pursued by the Legionnaires under the sequence 'capture or kill.' We'll have more details later as the story develops."

"Woah. A wild mob and two insane pilots. No wonder you don't talk about that place." LaLa'ila seemed to be entertained by the report.

"He's not insane," Zaleah said in a whisper.

"You say something?"

"I said he's not insane."

"I beg to differ," said LaLa'ila

"You don't know anything about him. Shut your mouth!" Zaleah was now screaming in Apeay's defense.

LaLa'ila was shaken by Zaleah's furious retort, and threw up her hands in surrender. "Okay, so he's not. You must know him or something."

"Yes, I do. We're… we're good friends."

"He's your lover, huh?"

Zaleah didn't respond.

"I'm sorry for being insensitive. It's Averand reporting after all. Never know what to believe with that one."

Zaleah fell to her knees in tears. "Why did you stay? Why didn't you come with me? None of this would've happened. I just know it."

LaLa'ila knelt beside her. "I'm so sorry. I'll turn this off if you want me to."

"No, you can leave it on. I want to know what's happening."

"You're going to trust the scandalous Averand D'velamoix to keep you updated? Good luck with that. You'd have a better chance of getting the real story from the local gossip circles."

"You're right," said Zaleah, springing up off the floor. She opened up the storage wall in their quarters.

"What are you doing?" asked LaLa'ila

"I'll be back before the primary induction," said Zaleah, not wasting a moment more. In a whirlwind of commotion, she stuffed a large bag full of various containers, and marched out of the room.

θ

In the atmosphere between Tzierhan and space, Aven was putting on a beautiful display of unmatched talent. He sent every rival glineer coasting to the ground, before they had a chance to lock on to his position. To Aven, this was an effortless exercise, not combat.

"Three one four, Aven," said Enjevix.

"Transmit, old timer."

"Old timer?"

"You heard me. You're too old and too far removed from real-life experience to keep up with me. Keep this going and there won't be enough of Ring One left to carry out the original sequence. That I can guarantee," said Aven.

"I'm issuing you a final sequence. Land and surrender."

"Sequence rejected."

"I'm trying to help you. Stop being arrogant, and land."

"No. You're helping yourself. This is about you securing your title. Me? I'm helping Apeay and everyone else the best I can. Apeay may be confused and out of line, but the sequence issued to me in response was more out of line than anything I've ever heard. What's worse is you know it and won't do anything about it. Actually, I'm disgusted with you right now. So, do me a favor; stay off my transmit and let me continue doing the right thing in keeping all of us safe."

The transmit went silent. Aven's words cut Enjevix deep. He was one of the first Legionnaires he'd personally taken under his wing in his patrol squad. The first he poured his knowledge into, teaching all the virtues of duty, honor, and justice. And now those virtues that had matured in Aven, were slapping him in the face. Enjevix backed off his thruster, staring out of his cockpit viewer at the anarchy of the skies around him as he ingested the painful awareness that his protégé fed to him. *I can't let them hunt down my number one. I'm calling this off.*

Enjevix reached for his transmit a moment too late. Before he could repeal the sequence to Ring One Aven's glineer was struck from behind. It was only by chance that he'd been struck by another pilot. The pilot was supporting Enjevix's main team when Aven flew past his line of fire.

"Three one four, Apeay," said Aven.

"Transmit," said Apeay.

"I've been hit. I won't be able to cover your escape route anymore. You should be nearing the southwest border. As soon as you cross over, land, and flee on foot."

"Alright. And, thanks again."

Unknown to Apeay, Aven's kind advice would be the last words he spoke. One final shot ripped through Aven's cockpit before he could eject, killing him instantly. Spectators from the ground below gasped and hollered at the sight of the fastest glineer ever made exploding into a million shiny pieces of scrap.

Upon seeing the tragedy, Enjevix wept. The realization of what he'd helped come to pass was too much to bear. It was a clear sign that his time as a Legionnaire was over.

"Three one four, Ring One, Ring Two," said Enjevix.

"Transmit," Rings One and Two replied.

"I am no longer your zenshiro. Effective immediately, I'm removing myself from duty and will no longer aid you in the pursuit of Apeay. In doing so, I can no longer issue you any further sequences. Before I end this transmit, I would like to say this: I do not recommend that you continue in this pursuit. We just lost a good Legionnaire, and probably the best pilot that has ever defended the skies of our great region. Today, I forgot what it meant to be a Legionnaire and we all paid dearly for my short-sightedness. I hope all of you remember what it truly means to be virtuous. No good can come from a unit where unity does not exist. Transmit complete." Enjevix powered down his glineer, and coasted to the ground below. There were a few others that followed suit and did likewise, while the rest remained in the air, flying about in uncertainty.

"Three one four, Ring One, Ring Two," said Nepcyzir.

"Transmit," Rings One and Two replied.

Out of all five rings Nepcyzir Gahalihn was the senior nikashiro, next in line to Enjevix and undeniably anxious to make his debut as the surrogate zenshiro. "I am now in charge and the original and secondary sequences will stand. Those of you who have abandoned your position will be dealt with in accordance to the high-level command set by Command."

The newly established zenshiro's transmit was met with an array of responses from the compliant, to foul-mouthed commentary unbefitting of a distinguished Legionnaire. The excessive bickering and commotion brought the entire sequence to a standstill. By this time many of the pilots were on the ground. Some were even fleeing the site altogether. Each time a glineer touched down, cheers went up from the detained protestors. The pilots who remained in the air scrambled to locate Apeay.

However, there was no trace of his signal on their ESSA. He was saved by the number one's noble act, for he was already beyond the boarder of Estellar.

Δ

Apeay's glineer came to rest on the edge of a forest plain where he made his escape. On the edge of the woods two eyes were peering. They'd been watching this flying thing come into view and land. They were spying on Apeay as he covered his glineer with large branches and leaves. His head was spinning with worry, thinking about the mess he created back at the ruins. After he was sure that his glineer was properly camouflaged from eyes above, he continued his escape on foot. Apeay dashed through the trees around stumps and roots. Apeay's stampede was the thumping of his heart. But why did it sound like he had two hearts? Had someone found him? That couldn't be. There was no way anyone could have caught up so fast. His pursuer was on his heels, determined not to let him get away.

"Will you stop running? And tell me...what's happening to you?"

CHAPTER 12

I wasn't expecting to see you. Fortunately, we always have a place for guests.

Frothing crystal waters raged on, crashing down and through several bends and corners as overwhelming currents hurled him downstream.

Deslao shook his head, regaining consciousness through gasps for air. The events leading up to now, came to mind. Now fully aware, he thrashed about attempting to control his movements, and locate his brother.

"Seldao! Seldao!" Deslao repeatedly shouted, hoping he'd hear a response. *Where did he go? Did the current pull him further down?* He dove below, looking in every direction. He went under as long as his lungs would allow before resurfacing. He began to fear the worst. Deslao swam to the river's edge to regain his strength, before making another attempt to rescue his brother. He dragged himself onto the shore, momentarily at rest. His head was bowed as he breathed heavily. He took one last deep breath as he readied himself to go back in.

"You are going nowhere." The deep voice rumbling behind Deslao startled him, almost causing him into fall back into the river. But, there was no need to worry, because something snagged him up by his feet. He was bewildered, dangling upside down from a vine attached to one of the trees near the river's edge. A large figure wrapped in a dark cloak approached him from behind the tree line.

"Now we have two," said the large figure.

"Two? You say two?" said Deslao. "You've seen my brother? Where's Seldao?"

"Seldao? So that is a name for him...over there." The large figure pointed upstream. Deslao followed his aim to see his brother passed out, sleeping on the ground. He was relieved to see Seldao alive and well, which made him quite irritated with the man in front of him for detaining him.

"You better let me down right now! And what did you do to my bro?!"

The man didn't acknowledge his request, or even the fact that he was speaking. Instead, he began to rummage about the sack tied around his cloak.

"I know you heard me! When I get myself loose I'm gonna make you hurt for holding me up!"

The man continued to ignore his outburst as he pulled a small cube like object out of his satchel. The cube was almost transparent and shone, displaying various gemstones trapped within it. The man walked over to Deslao and held the cube up to his face.

"What's that? What are you doing?!" said Deslao.

The brilliant cube split in two forming two separate but attached prisms. A faint teal vapor emitted from its core, which rendered Deslao unconscious. The man put his hand to Deslao's mouth.

"You are strong. Unaffected you two are," said the man. "How fortunate for you. How fortunate for us…"

Δ

Zaleah threw her arms around Apeay. She embraced him with every molecule of her being, but couldn't feel him. His mind was neither with her, nor where he had come from.

"Apeay," said Zaleah as she looked him in the eyes.

"What do you want?"

"What do I want? I want to know what's going on. Are you ok? Did you get hurt? You know. The usual things a person wants to know when they care about someone."

"I'm fine. It's whatever it is, it was."

"Just like that?"

"Yeah. But, hold on, how did you find me? Was I easy to spot?"

"No, not really. I was headed to the local capsyint port until something caught my eye. I saw a small flicker of light traveling high above the lake. I could hardly make it out because of the forest. But it gave off just enough light for me to follow it to edge of the field. By then I could tell it was a glineer. I followed it, hoping whoever was piloting could give me some answers. When it touched down, I hurried to meet them, and it was you. I could hardly believe it, especially after that report."

"So, you found me," said Apeay. "If you saw the report like you said, then you know I'm in trouble."

"I'm just glad you're alright." Looking into his eyes, she saw fear. His hands were trembling. Apeay looked so wrecked from worry that it scared her. "What happened back there? Why are they after you?"

He paced back and forth, shaking his head as Zaleah anxiously awaited his account. After letting out a deep breath, he told her of his grave mistake.

"What didn't I do that wasn't wrong? I disobeyed a direct sequence. I called myself trying to save the people."

"The people? What people are you talking about?"

"The protestors. They were standing on the ruins' foregrounds in protest of its destruction. Our Ring was going to murder them. They would've been killed."

"So, you're a hero!" Zaleah was delighted. "That's impressive, my guy. I knew you were special."

"You're right I'm especially stupid. Don't you get it? Once the Legionnaires catch wind of where I fled to, they'll hunt me down. I'll be detained with punitive measures taken against me that not even my father, the Council Principal, can get me out of.

Zaleah lifted her head looking skyward. As she pondered, she stroked her chin as if she were a sage old man. "I have an idea. Let's go back to Estellar," she said.

"Are you crazy? There is no safe haven from them. I know. I've spent all of the later nadian patrolling with them. There's no place to hide."

"I have a question. Did they end up destroying the ruins?"

"From what I heard on the open transmit, no. They abandoned the sequence."

"Then, there is...we'll hide in the ruins."

"The ruins again. I'm sick of talking about them. The ruins are ruining my life!"

"Don't say that. Say what is the best of you, and you'll make it through. Think about it. It works. That would be the last place they would think to look for you. We can hide there until we reach your father. Then, he can go talk to Council on your behalf and straighten things out."

Apeay didn't share her optimistic perspective. On the contrary, he was offended that she persisted in throwing her proposal in his face after he dismissed it.

"WE WILL NOT!" Apeay shouted.

"Why not?" asked Zaleah. "What's wrong with you?" It was the look on his face more than his reply that concerned her.

She'd never seen him so angry. The scowl on his face appeared as if he were born with it.

At that moment, Apeay spoke coldly. "I should've let them die."

Zaleah was shocked. "I can't believe you just said that."

"Really? Then you tell me, where are the people I saved? They're at home. That's where they are. At home, enjoying a meal, watching reports, celebrating their victory while I'm out running for my life."

"They wouldn't be celebrating if it wasn't for you. Doing the right thing doesn't always mean you'll be appreciated or thanked. So don't expect to be. Just know in your heart, you did what was right. Getting upset only makes things worse."

Apeay was disgusted with her rationalization, but could find no reason to argue with it either. "Alright, we'll go back. Go hide out for a while. Then, the first chance we get, we go to my father and Council and disclose what Command did, how he deliberately issued a sequence for murder, and have him brought down. And, if Council does nothing, I'll do it myself."

"You'll do what?"

"I'll take him out. I'll kill Command!"

"Hold on Apeay," said Zaleah. "I hear what you're saying, but you're not going to solve anything like that. Relax your mind."

"Relax?! He wants me dead! So, the same goes for him!"

"I understand, my love, but listen, please. I understand how it might make you feel that way. But you have to think about where that's going to get you. You're upset, but now is not a time for rash decisions. We have to come up with a plan if we're going to make it."

"Maybe you're right. But I will find him." Apeay, coming to terms with his dilemma, regained his usual disposition. "I'll hide in your storage until we arrive."

"You think they're patrolling the interregional border?" Zaleah asked.

"I know they are. And I'm not cargo you want to be caught with. They won't check your storage if they don't suspect you, so act normal. When we get there, take the beam to the canal's four main open chambers, and listen for my directions. They'll be on enazjhei seven, so keep away from any beam heading directly towards the foreground area. As a matter of fact, take the express beam to the west side of Zenlan. Exit the beam and head northeast until you reach the river's end."

"Got it."

Apeay looked over at where he hid his glineer one last time, making sure he didn't forget anything, or anything that was worth remembering. "Let's go."

"Don't worry. I'll get us there safe. And, knock if you need to get out to... ya know, relieve yourself. I'll pull off somewhere out the way."

"Yeah, I got cha."

"Yeah, you do."

As planned, Apeay hid himself in the storage of Zaleah's mynersha. She covered him with the fanzuay blanket she took from her faja.

"Hey, Apeay, I packed something special for you when we get there."

"Oh, yeah?"

"Of course. It's your favorite."

"Thanks, I appreciate it."

"Command won't get to you today my love. You're gonna be just fine," said Zaleah as she sealed him in.

Δ

Grey and black, grey and silver, then grey and black again went the long panels making up the walls of the examination quarters. Mixed workings of white marble, onyx and polished palladium gathered from the depths of the old quarries were gathered here to make this a sturdy, suffocating house of accusations.

"Where does Council sit on disciplinary actions against infraction 1, 'willful disobedience' and infraction 2 'abandonment'?"

"We suggest half of single status demotion up to and not to extend beyond dismissal for initiates of first-tier meta-shiros. An eleven phase period of half status demotion for rank optashiro and above. Extra task without salary until next phase for all found guilty of the accusations."

"That's outrageous!" Nepcyzir screamed from the other side of Palladus Hall as he leapt out of his seat. "You're going easy on them because your son is one of them! On top of that, he's the one who started all the trouble, and everyone knows it!"

An unsettling commotion broke out among the members of Council and the Legionnaires.

"Order! Order! Everyone stay calm! Look, no one is going easy on anyone!" Jhar'ensky shouted. "The entire ordeal is suspicious."

"We know they disobeyed," said Valus. "But the sequences from Command were, in themselves, questionable, to say the least."

"As a Legionnaire of the most distinguished order, it's not our job to question," said Nepcyzir. "Our job is to accept and execute!"

Nepcyzir was determined to prove himself worthy of his newly inherited position. He felt as if he had spent far too many cycles in Enjevix's shadow, and voiced it on several occasions during the promotion finales.

"Then accept this," said Zennite Thorel, who had heard enough from the high-strung chief. "Sit down, and keep your mouth shut."

Publicly shamed, he acknowledged her request and took his seat, in the physical sense. In his mind he was strangling her for humiliating him.

With Thorel tightening up Nepcizyr, the bickering among the members ceased.

It was Thorel who called for a predetermination hearing immediately after the disaster at the ruins. She decided it best if it were held promptly before anyone else, including Command, could weigh in on the matter. Thorel did so to expedite the process so she could get back to her original mission.

"Now if that's all from Council, without any further outbursts, I will sum up this hearing. We will strongly and most respectfully consider Council's assessment. As the presiding authority, I will deviate no more than one measure above or below. For those found in good standing, one measure below; for those found otherwise, one measure above. That is all. Legionnaires ranking from optashiro tier one and below, you are dismissed. Council will now resume control of the floor."

"Thank you," said Jhar'ensky. "There will be no further deliberation on any other matters at this time. This meeting is adjourned."

The guards at the entrance pushed the heavy doors open, making way for both parties to retreat to Palladus Garden.

Jhar'ensky stood slowly, gathering himself. He felt a hand rest on his shoulder.

"How you holding up, my guy?" said Valus.

"Honestly, I don't know how I feel. This is like déjà vu but worse."

"Jhar'ensky," said Thorel approaching his bench, "may I have a word with you?"

"Of course. Valus, I'll get with you in a moment," said Jhar'ensky.

"Sure. I'll be outside when you're done."

After Thorel was sure that the two of them were far enough away from the crowd, she revealed her true reason for the speedy pre-determination and asked Jhar'ensky to keep the matter a secret.

"You're telling me there's a conspiracy within Council and the Legionnaires and that Command is the one pulling the strings? I should've known this by now."

"This mystery group is sneaky," said Thorel. "They keep themselves so well hidden that I feel like I'm chasing a ghost."

Jhar'ensky looked over to the courtyard where the members of Council were gathered together with the high-ranking Legionnaires. He felt uneased in many ways, as he recalled a conversation from long ago when he was a junior member of Council. He huffed, and turned his attention back to Thorel. "Please, continue."

"I stumbled across a transmit coming from one of the private sections in this hall from two cycles ago. I was testing a new L.N. scanner, when I picked up their wave alignment. The conversation that followed clearly identified Council involvement. Since then I've gathered over about twenty recorded transmits confirming their conspiracy. The only thing is I can't determine who's on them. As you'd expect, they speak in coded language and go to great lengths to mask their voices."

"None of this makes a lick of sense. We're on the verge of restoring harmonic balance to the region, and now all of this is surfacing."

"I know, it's frustrating. But we'll get through this. It'll be like the old days on guard when I gave you the heads-up on who was and who was not Council when you forgot."

"You always were the sharpest Legionnaire guard. I wasn't surprised when you made zennite. You could see danger from reels away while keeping track of everyone around you," said Jhar'ensky.

"That I did with some help from my friends..." said Thorel. They were caught in a nostalgic moment of an era past, but passed by as Thorel asked her fellow former guard, "Has Apeay contacted you yet? It's alright if you've kept it secret. I'd rather it be that way."

"No... Not at all," said Jhar'ensky. It was apparent he was upset, but his professionalism kept his countenance neutral. "I should've known better. He wasn't ready for this."

"Don't blame yourself. Trust me, none of us were ready for yesterday with the mob and that final sequence from Command. That's why we need to locate him immediately. He's key to my plan. His testament, along with that of Enjevix and a few others, should be all we need to get Affi'hado thrown out. Agreeing to unify the regions under his directive was surely a mistake that must be repealed."

"I agree, but why does Apeay need to be involved? You have plenty of recorded transmits."

"I do however, most of them I can't use because of how I obtained them. Council would throw them out. The few I can use are the ones that were sent through my channels, don't contain enough incriminating evidence. They were clever not to send too many that way. They got wise to me shortly after I started recording them. That's when I started tapping into channels that I wasn't authorized to monitor."

"Really? How'd you get clearance? You need at least a secondary clearance to obtain those channels."

"Well, I could've had Council grant me that right under a 'Zennite Special Permissions' clause. But that would've alerted whoever's involved that I was still recording them. So, I reached out to someone for help; someone who's apparently doing the same. Someone who knows about high-level clearances, and how to work around them. Someone who trusts you."

Jhar'ensky smirked with a name in mind, going back to the Golden Era. "That old man never stopped looking."

"Exactly. Now, for the safety of Apeay, we need to find him before he's found by the Legionnaires, or any Council member, for that matter. There's no telling who and how many may be part of the conspiracy. It's likely there are some who still might carry out the terrible sequence issued by Command."

"You make a good point. That I will not allow!" Jhar'ensky mulled it over for a moment. "My son... his girlfriend attends Ajina Delta. He always talks about going to visit on his 'off phase.' Knowing him, that's where he went."

"An out of region trip. Just what I was hoping for," said Thorel.

"But, how are we going to get the all-seeing, ever elusive Command to Palladus Hall?"

"Apeay," said Thorel. "From what I've gathered, Command has taken a peculiar interest in him. I'm sure once we find him, Command will come to us."

"What makes you believe that? My son is only a metashiro. He has no pull with the Legionnaires and is far from being accepted into Council. He poses no threat."

"I thought you might say that. So, I brought this." Rionazen pulled a small cube out of her pouch and tapped on one of its sides. "This was recorded right after the incident. Just listen."

The recording played from the cube:

"...time that was wasted! Though it will be redeemed in an eternity when our path is made clear. So find Apeay, if he indeed exists, and bring him before me."

"Yes, your excellency," replied a masked voice. "Yes, accepted. I've already sent out the "diamond seeker." Did he not help lead us to him before?"

"That incompetent lackey. You mean, did he not fail before? One that does not exist being found is complete failure. One that is not is never found. Now, a mere fairytale has plagued every piece of this region; my region, my Tzierhan! I will destroy this myth, this legend that even you now hold on to, before this imperfection corrupts our great cause. Show me an Apeay, and I'll show you no one."

The masked voice replied, "As you wish, your excellency. I have it covered. All will be diamond."

"You better have, or I will take the diamond out of you. The time of perfection is upon us. Now, tell me..."

The cube cut out.

"That's all I was able to record on that transmit. They switch the wave alignment every 35 jhentas. By the time I tapped into the new wave, their transmit had already ended."

Jhar'ensky nodded solemnly. "I will appoint a provisional Principal. We're leaving for Ajina right now."

CHAPTER 13

Traffic at the Estellar/Sohexiah border was at a standstill. The Legionnaire border guards were performing checks on each vehicle passing through. Little by little, Zaleah crept closer to the border, where she was stopped by one of the guards.

"I.D., and state your business."

Zaleah handed her I.D. over to the metashiro guard and replied, "I'm on visitation."

"Who are you visiting?"

"My mother."

The guard looked her over, then checked her I.D. front and back. "It says here you're a student at Ajina Delta. If I'm not mistaken, their session starts this phase. But you came all the way back to Estellar just for a visit?"

"Yeah, and?"

The guard looked over his sequenced protocol, before giving her the order, "Lady, power down your vehicle and step out."

"For what?"

"I need to check this vehicle before I let you pass through. Make sure there are no fugitives in tow."

Zaleah's heart skipped a beat, but she did well not to show it. Instead, she put on an indignant front. "I'm not a fugitive, I'm a citizen of this region. And as a citizen, I don't have to surrender my vehicle to you. That's against the civilian bylaws."

"Lady, this is an emergency sequence; it supersedes the civilian bylaws."

"I'm staying right here."

The Legionnaire guard unslung his neutranevex and took aim, "Power down and get out, now!"

"What's going on over there?" said another guard approaching the vehicle. The rank insignia on his collar denoted symbol "senior guard, tier three", the optashiro in charge.

"Ishiro, she's refusing to exit the vehicle for a search."

The senior leaned on the vehicle asking Zaleah, "Is that so?"

Not now. This can't be real. Once the guards identified her cargo, it was over. At the very least, she and Apeay would be detained, at worst, Apeay would be executed upon recognition. Zaleah thought hard and it came to her quick. They were Legionnaires true, but still ordinary people underneath their uniforms. That's what she'd play to.

"I'm sorry, sir, but my mother is really sick and I'm all she has. I came back to check up on her before my session begins." She poured all the heartache she could into her eyes as she pleaded with the legionnaire, channeling her emotions for the secret cargo she was protecting into welling tears.

"Ah, she's just emotional. Typical. Shoulder your weapon, let her through."

"But, Ishiro..."

The senior raised his hand, silencing the metashiro. "I said let her through. We have more important things at hand. Lady, I'm going to let you slide this time, but don't ever give another guard backtalk again. Do you understand?"

"Yes sir, I do."

"*My* mother passed away three cycles ago. Not a day goes by that I don't miss her. You take good care of your mother."

"I will, thank you." Zaleah pulled away, feeling as if a heavy weight had lifted off her chest. She crossed into Estellar, and took the express beam tunnel for the northmost district of Zenlan. In about five ahkmeres, the mynersha came to rest. She parked in the place Apeay spoke of before. Zaleah hopped out and opened the storage compartment.

Apeay squinted as the setting twilight reflecting on the waters hit his face. He looked around to make sure they were alone before leaping out to stretch his cramped body. "Thanks, my lady. Good job back there."

"I told you no worries. And, wow, look at you."

"What about me?"

"These canals, they're massive, a little creepy too. I can't believe you walked through these by yourself when you were a kid."

"I didn't pay it any mind. They were more like a second home when I wanted to be to myself," said Apeay. "And your mynersha is good where it is. Trust me. We never patrol this section of the canals. It's like it doesn't exist to Council."

"What do you mean?" said Zaleah

"One day, it occurred to me that we never checked this subpar area. When I asked my optashiro why we didn't, he told me that Council agreed that there was no need to, that patrolling this section would slow down our 'strategic efficiency', which is perfect for us. Even with an emergency sequence, they don't have a team put together for this location."

"That's good to know, but weren't we supposed to hide out in the ruins?"

"We are. Look up on that hill."

"Which one?"

"That one right there, where the river meets the canals."

Zaleah looked up to the hill Apeay was pointing to. There were large smooth stones, some in the shape of cylinders and others that looked like broken stairs and jagged walls ornamenting the hilltops. "That's right I passed by large fields of broken stones on the way here. They're part of it, right?"

"Of course. In essence, we're at the ruins' backdoor."

"Ha. Only the most exclusive guests get to use the rear entrance," said Zaleah. "Will you escort me, kind sir, into the palace? For, I have no one to take me to the royal dance."

"Don't be stupid, Zaleah. This isn't a game. Let's just get up there and find a place to hide."

Zaleah sighed. " I was hoping it'd make you smile. You've been frowned up since we got here. Everything's alright."

"Whatever, Ajina girl with a perfect Ajina life. How about I just go find my father alone and get this over with. I really didn't want to camp out here anyway."

Until now, Zaleah had been tolerant of Apeay's moaning. She'd had enough of his adversarial attitude. "You know you're really messed up Apeay. Whatever trouble you're in, I'm in it right alongside you. I just gave up my perfect Ajina life' for your sake, because I care that much about you. And you keep talking to me like I'm dirt. You don't do that to someone who has your back. If we get caught, I'll be charged with aiding a fugitive. A risk I'm willing to take, because I care. Maybe I care too much for someone who doesn't."

Apeay said nothing. He only glanced at her and looked away. He knew she was right. But was still too bitter for words.

"Apeay?" said Zaleah.

"Yeah, I heard you," said Apeay. "Sorry, it's been a long day... I appreciate your help."

His dry retort was a sure sign that he was worn out from worry. Zaleah massaged his shoulders as she looked him in the eyes." Are you ready to go on?"

"I'm ready. I'm fine. We'll stick with the plan. Wait until tomorrow to make our move. Hopefully no one recognizes this uniform." Apeay looked down, examining himself.

"Don't need to worry about that. I picked up something for you along the way." Zaleah reached into her bag and pulled out a dark grey two-piece garment. The top was hooded, and aside from the silver, braided rope that held it together, it was the most ordinary clothing one could hope for.

"I wondered what you stopped for back in Sohexiah." Apeay discarded his uniform and slipped into the casual outfit. "It's a perfect fit. Thanks."

"I know. I'm the best."

After Apeay hid his uniform in the storage compartment, the two of them made their way up the hill. "Here," said Apeay, extending his hand to help Zaleah climb over the stones piled on top of each other.

"Thanks." Zaleah planted her feet on the soft, marshy ground. But what was this she felt as she stood on the uneven terrain?

Zzzmmm, zzzmmm...

It started as a subtle vibration, then grew into a quake, until *shkuhm!,* after a violent shudder, the shaking ceased.

The fog that rested over the entirety of the ruins lifted from the ground, gathering together in the air above. It was an unsettling sight. Zaleah stood fixated on the abnormal fog. It was growing larger by the jhenta as it gathered together in the late evening sky.

"How strange," said Zaleah.

"Right. Strange enough to attract Legionnaire attention."

From there they took a long, silent stroll towards the center of the ruins where the broken stones became larger stones, then even larger stones with overgrowth dangling like natural garnishing. They were deep enough in, that it'd be extremely difficult to find them, even if Zaleah's mynersha was spotted.

As for Apeay he was still in the process of collecting himself. His stomach still had a tightness to it. Just being back in the ruins gave him an awful feeling he couldn't shake. The harder he tried, the more he remembered why it was that he couldn't. Under his shuffling feet, the leaves rustled and twigs cracked loud enough to cover his murmur, "I *hate* this place."

Soon, they found themselves standing in front of a cave covered by drooping vines. Apeay pushed the curtain of vines to the side and took a peek inside. He didn't see nor hear anything that looked like it would cause harm. And the extra concealment provided by the vines made it an adequate hideout.

"This will do."

They stooped under the overhanging, verdant vines that covered the entrance, and took refuge behind an immense boulder buried within. Apeay sat down, leaning against the dusty wall. His eyes remained concentrated on the entrance to their hideout. Zaleah took her place next to him, resting her head on his chest.

Apeay's breaths were shallow and quick. "Apeay, were fine. Like you said, they'll never look for us here. Try to get some rest for when we make our next move."

"He nodded and rested his eyes. He no longer appeared to be anxious, merely withdrawn. With a gentle caress she pulled herself closer. A deep, paining exhale flowed out of him, and she felt it. She felt it as if it were her own.

Φ

Splsshh

"Who...*cough*...who did that?!" Deslao sprang up onto his feet, coughing up the water splashed on his face. The large man who greeted him stood next to him, holding a sizable skin for carrying liquids.

"You are awake."

"You're getting your butt whooped."

"I'll ignore that. More important things there are. You and your bothersome brother are with us now," said the large man.

"Seldao, where is he?"

"That name again? That really is his name?"

"Of course it is. Look man, you're starting to piss me off."

"That's fine by me. But you need to prepare yourself."

Deslao looked around to find himself high upon a hill in the middle of nowhere, surrounded by a dusty field blanketed with fog and mist. The mist glowed like a fading rainbow but not from any light in the sky. Deslao set his eyes to peer deep within the river. He was astounded that he didn't notice it when he was still within its tow. At the bottom, there were what appeared to be gleaming jewels or polished metals, producing random sparks of light, causing the river to shimmer like silver.

"Goodness, you didn't have to drown the young fella. A simple nudge would've done it." Deslao looked to his left to see another stranger approaching. The man was stout with a glint of cleverness in his eyes. He carried a satchel in one hand, and some type of unfamiliar device in the other.

"Time to go," said the large man.

Deslao compared the two as they stood side by side. The large man did not seem to be as old as the other stranger. Sizing up his physique, it was apparent that he was built for the type of action Deslao was accustomed to. "I said let's go!" said the large stranger, pointing towards the distant horizon. The northern sky was radiant. But, the eastern sky was ominously overcast. Between the two was where he was directing them to travel.

"Bro!" Seldao came running up from the bottom of the hill. "Bro, bro, that was crazy, right? Like, where are we? And this guy right here," he said, acknowledging the large man, "he's insanely strong. He pulled me out that river with just one hand."

"Really?" said Deslao. "Wait, if you remember all that, then why were you passed out when I showed up?"

"Oh that? Don't know if you've noticed, but he's not all that conversational. He said he didn't like my babbling, so he made me sleep to put it nicely."

"He choked you out, didn't he?"

"More or less."

"Seems about right," said Deslao. Then he turned to the large man. "You better not put your hands on him again, or something's gonna happen to you. We clear on that?"

The large man didn't bother to acknowledge Deslao's warning. "The reunion is over. Follow me."

"Follow you for what?!" Deslao shouted.

The man stared intently at Deslao's for a moment. It was as if he was searching for something within his eyes. The man's glare irritated Deslao as he took it as a challenge, and stared right back. Within the rings of Svarnax, he faced many men whom most would run from. But as Deslao saw it, they were but steps to reach a new level of combat. There was no need to view this man any differently.

Stepping aside, without further concern, the large man stooped down to rip up a handful of dry grass on the hill where they stood.

"You must help us find Apeay."

"Apeay? You? No, and I'm done, we're out of here," said Deslao putting his hand on Seldao's shoulder.

"You must come with us!"

"Is 'no' a confusing word for you?" The man didn't respond, unmoved by Deslao's cynical remark. "Man, look here, we only so happened to meet because of Apeay and this idiot's need to put his nose in places it doesn't belong. I don't know how you know Apeay, or what this is all about, but we're not involved."

"You don't understand." The large man opened his hand. "Do you see these blades of grass?"

"Grass is grass, and you're a *fihgazz*. What are you, a nature guide?"

"How true grass is grass, you smart-mouth fool. However, the grass that grows on this hill can only grow here, because it is this hill these blades came from. You and your brother are the blades of grass. Apeay is the hill. If we don't find him, you and your 'bro' will be no more."

"Nothing like a good old-fashioned, spooky riddle to motivate a person," said the other stranger.

"I didn't ask for your input."

"I'm just saying, there's a difference between informing a person and scaring a person with cryptic riddles. Hell, you threw me off ripping up that grass. I don't know who's more mysterious now, you, or that crazy lady by the pond?"

"A lady?" said Deslao.

"Ignore that," said the large man. "All you need to know is that this is a matter of the survival of everyone. How far along are we now? If you two think you know more than all of us, tell me.

Deslao looked around them. Seldao did likewise. There was nothing familiar about the scenery. Hill upon hill stretched across the plains with only the river that brought them here flowing between. Deslao was certain the man was ridiculing them and wouldn't tolerate it. "Shouldn't you know oh wise one? Why don't you tear up some more grass and throw it in the air and tell us?"

The large man burst out laughing. "Like I thought, you have no idea like the rest of us. A major problem indeed. There are none left who know how far along we are among our land. Yet, you speak to me with contempt like you know."

"Something's not right bro," Seldao whispered to Deslao. "We should be in, or about, Estellar, right? But this Tzierhan is topographically askew for Estellar, or the bordering regions."

"And why don't you know where we are?" Seldao finished, raising his voice.

"You are a poor listener. We know where, as do you, but not when. We, the seventh of an unknown origin. With you and Apeay, we will restore our land and knowledge," said the large man. "As long as you're with us, Apeay will appear. So, I say to you again: Follow me…"

The twins looked at each other and nodded in silent agreement, acknowledging their shared mistrust for the strangers. But they decided to go along with them until they figured out their true motive.

Seldao nodded to Deslao, who nodded back silently conveying to his brother, *'Just say the word and I'm on it!'*

"Ok big fella. It's your show," said Deslao.

The large man and his accomplice walked down the hill along the path of the river as the twins trailed behind.

∞

Deep in the belly of the cave, they rested. The luxuriant overgrowth hanging over the entrance, completed the darkness within. That was until a light awakened Apeay. He found himself surrounded by a hundred or more people singing in one voice. He reached over to awaken Zaleah, but she was gone. Not only was she absent, but the cave they took refuge in was full of light that shone from the center of the choir. A young lady with dazzling white hair and eyes of diamond stepped forward from behind the others, and took Apeay by the hand. While continuing to hum the melody, she walked him to the back wall of the cave. It was breathing, as if it were alive. Every khodah of the wall was covered in ancient symbols. The singing guide placed his hand on the wall as she spoke to him.

"Tell me, Apeay, what did you find? Don't you remember?"

"Remember what?"

"Who you are...You can't sleep forever..." The woman faded back into the choir as they sang their surreal melody: "Nahdeeah nahdee...nahdeeah......."

Apeay laid down again and awoke again. This time, awakened by a light that crept into the cave through a hole in the ceiling. Apeay leaned over and kissed Zaleah atop her forehead, awakening her as well.

"Hey babe, you still awake?" said Zaleah.

"Yeah, something like that," said Apeay. "We're going back there. We're going back."

"Already?" She stretched her arms, yawning. "I thought we were waiting till tomorrow? But going at night does make more sense. I'll activate the mynersha on silent mode."

"No need. What I'm talking about is here. Help me, Zaleah. Help me find it!" Apeay jumped to his feet and began scouring the wall that the woman in his dream led him to. He searched frantically, as if he were running out of time.

"What are you looking for?"

"A door, a gateway, something. It's in this cave."

Apeay's sudden enthusiasm over the walls of a dingy cave caused Zaleah to wonder if the stress he was dealing with had brought him to the brink of a mental snap. "Relax, Apeay. One more day and your troubles are over. One more day and everything comes to light. You're good, fella.

"Light," said Apeay. "You're right. It's bright for the middle of the night. I couldn't sleep because of that light." He looked upon the brilliant starlight beaming through the ceiling, remembering that it occurs once every three cycles on this Oros night. "It's the night of the Hewlix Star."

"True. But, what does that have to do with anything?"

Apeay traced the ray of light to its end. The light rested on a small stone that protruded from the wall. He could faintly make out a carving that looked like seven wheels in one. He placed his hand on the stone and pushed. The stone didn't budge. Apeay pushed on it again, harder this time. He was certain this was what he was looking for. However, no matter how hard he tried, the stone remained unmoved. Apeay was torn. His disappointment was obvious. He stood before the wall shaking his head in disbelief. Zaleah was aggrieved to see him in such a state.

"It's okay. You're alright, my guy, " said Zaleah, as she put her arms around him. "Come, lay with me." She placed her hand on his heart. "What's this?" she said, rubbing at the center of his chest. "No wonder I can't feel you." Zaleah traced her fingers up and around Apeay's neck, revealing his ornament to the sky. "It still matches your eyes."

At that moment, a peculiar phenomenon transpired. The starlight that shone through the ceiling bent towards the ornament. The sight of it was perplexing. Zaleah was astounded. It gave Apeay an idea.

"Let me do this," said Apeay. He took the ornament from around his neck and held it in the air, moving it side to side. Wherever he moved it the light followed. He then took the ornament and placed it directly in front of the image on the stone. The ornament began to glow from within in the way it did when he was young. The blue flame had returned as before, dancing within the sphere. He could hardly believe his eyes. Not only was it glowing, but it began to spin about rapidly, forcing Apeay to let go.

"All this time I thought you made up that story about your ornament to impress me," said Zaleah. "What is it doing?"

"I don't know. I never did. But it's working!" The ornament began to drill its way into the center circle. A brilliant light burst forth, enveloping them as the cave began to shake violently. The walls around them began to realign. Some of the stones were tumbling both upwards and downwards as the walls continued to quake. "Get down!" Apeay threw himself on top of Zaleah, shielding her from the fluctuating stones. Spaces between the stones opened up to more spaces between them, while the air shuddered with audible vibrations.

After a few more moments, the vibrations stopped. What was once a cave was now a newly furbished portico. Apeay took Zaleah by the hand helping her to her feet.

"Are you alright?"

"Yes, I'm fine," said Zaleah.

As they took a step through the doorway, they looked upon a sky that was both bright and dimmed by a haze. For reels upon reels tall tapered cliffs lowered into the hills that leveled out becoming a barren land with a shimmering river flowing in between; the river stretched from the land beneath them to the distant horizon. Behind them, what was once ruins now appeared to be some type of abandoned fortress. It had high walls on six sides, spread far apart in all directions with walls laid in between that stooped low. The stones of the dusty walls were deep cerulean swirled with emerald. Sweet, pungent aromas filled the air. Upon second glance it seemed to be a district unto itself. On each of the six sides of the colossal building were two smaller buildings in perfect alignment with each side. By observation, one might approximate the entire layout to be eight or nine reels around.

"Woah...what is this place?" said Zaleah. She was taken by its impeccably symmetrical aesthetic beauty.

Looking about, they could see several pathways leading to different entrances identical to the one before them. Each path made of the same stones of this fortress. The deep cerulean-emerald stones twisted through the hills below, where the path was wide at the top in a tighter swirl at each entrance. Zaleah clasped Apeay's hand. To her, they were emissaries in a new land. Apeay smiled. In his mind, they were unexpected guest in a world he once knew. At least that's what he thought. However, the landscape was a bit off. The more he took, in the more his smile began to fade. For this was a land of familiar anonymities.

Ω

"There's someone here to see you."

"Could you ask them to state their business? I'm behind in all my entries, I have to catch up before I leave."

Bexhiera's assistant, Aserleita, was stunned by Bexhiera's response. She was usually more eloquent, speaking with pleasantries when there was a visitor. "As you can see, there's a lot of material for me to review and I'd rather not be disturbed for the moment. So, if it's not urgent, have them leave a note."

"Of course," said Aserleita.

Bexhiera had been using that pretext as a cover. Jhar'ensky pleaded with her to come with him and Thorel as they went in search of Apeay. But, she declined saying, "I'd only slow you down. And I have a million things to get done here. Besides, if we're both gone, who will be home if he happens to show up?" Jhar'ensky agreed, and told her to contact him if anything changed.

After nearly collapsing from worry after the festival gone awry, Bexhiera headed to the Centre. But she hadn't come to work, rather to put her work before her eyes to distract her from her anxieties. She glanced over aeroxia entries from the Centre archives. All information regarding each case of juvenile fatigue lay on her sakxhama stand. Included with them were authorized journals from shototus working alongside their department who supported certain undesirable theories as the majority of Council saw it. Together they formed a joint research team that worked tirelessly to discover a cure for the mysterious disease that continued to plague now almost half the children of Estellar. But today, she found it difficult to concentrate. Her mind went back and forth between her research and her son. *What am I sensing?* She couldn't help but feel as if someone was constantly looking over her shoulder, though she knew not from where. Perhaps it was merely her imagination from feeling stressed out.

"Here's the note they left."

"Thank you," said Bexhiera. She glanced upon the note her assistant gave her and read, *"I'm hungry. Make me some zaiti soup."*

"What? ...Yes, I get it!" Bexhiera arose and dashed down the hall, catching up with her assistant. "Aserleita, who gave you this?! Where are they?"

"He already left. He left so fast I didn't even have time to ask his name. But I do remember the way he was built. What a body! I mean he was well built, like an elite Legionnaire combatant. If only I could've seen his face. That big, droopy hood he wore made it hard to make out. Fancy outfit, too. He was something to see."

Bexhiera ran further down the hall and out the main door. There were so many people milling about outside that it was hard to make out the person she was looking for. She came back for a moment to give her assistant some final instructions.

"Aserleita, I'm taking leave for the day. Deliver these to Aroi Nadjinh. I've illuminated some strategic pathways that I think he'll find interesting." She hurriedly shoved the documents into her assistants hands and headed home.

CHAPTER 14

"Slow down, man. I can't keep up!" said Deslao.

"I know you can. Stop holding back," said the large man. It was true Deslao was holding back for the sake of his brother. But how this man knew it was beyond him.

"Well this is killing me," said the small man.

"I don't care to hear it," said the large man.

"Look man, not all of us are freaks of nature like you. My legs are getting stiffer than a pappo tree." The small man began to hobble until he broke down on the side of the foothills.

"Everyone stop!" said the large man. He marched over and hovered over the small man. "You know like I how important this is. And yet you sit there. We don't have time for your weakness."

"Weak? You're an idiot. Going all fast to who knows where. We don't even know where uh...uh...what's his name?"

"Apeay," said the large man.

"Yeah, this Apeay is gonna show up."

"Yes we do. Along the outer brink of the Xeno highlands."

"Like that narrows it down. The outer highlands are about a 55 relah stretch. Real accurate, fella."

"I'm no fool. We're headed to the highest hills. That's how you scout."

"I have a better idea," said the small man. "How about we break for a moment and get some ideas a-flowin, and tell these two what that crazy old lady had to say. Maybe they can make better sense of it."

"First thing I'd like to know is who you two really are. Or, maybe you'd like me to beat it out of you," said Deslao.

The large man squared up to Deslao.

"I don't recommend that," said the small man. Xendsvar is the lead protector of our village. No one, and I mean no one, or thing that has ever entered by the riverway, made it past his watch. Now, for me, I'm just a man that keeps everything up and running. An 'exceptional thinker,' as the people say. And the name's Hanjiah. So I wonder how is it that you two don't know this. I mean, we're sort of famous to everyone around this part of the world. Even outsiders of Xeno have heard of us." Hanjiah waited for one of them to acknowledge his claim, but the two only stared at him with skepticism. "Hmm...anyway, like I said, the lady living by the pond told us of him. Would you care to expound on it, my friend?"

"Great, I love a good story," said Seldao.

"This is more than a story," said Xendsvar.

"It's all the same to me," said Seldao. "What's the word, man?" Seldao was on edge, waiting to hear what the man had to say. He too was tired of the aimless wandering, and considered that the man's words might give them some direction.

Xendsvar sat down nobly upon a broken stone. "Here, we are simple people. We work hard to maintain our well-being. But lately, all our efforts to sustain life seem to be in vain. Our crops fail more than they yield enough for us to live on, for rain is scarce.

"It began around nine thousand cycles ago when the first generation discovered death and began to pass on. A kind-hearted child named, Heylan from the 'land of the gods' gave them a new idea; a new way to grow the flowering fruit to make them stronger and wiser, extending their life span. For many it was deliverance. But to the offspring of the second, it seemed unnatural, so they sought another way. The others remained curious, so they listened to what he had to say. For three-thousand cycles they were guided by his voice, and did as he instructed.

"From the beginning, after only the first phase, the new fruit blossomed. The method worked exactly as he foretold. The old people found their strength and their youth restored. Many of them became wiser, obtaining knowledge they never knew before. The boy spent another three-thousand cycles watching them improve, until he was sure they'd became 'whole.' Satisfied with the results, the young traveler parted ways never to return to Xeno. Because of this, no one passed here before their two-hundred thirty cycles. Then they say around nine-hundred cycles after his departure, the nature of our land began to change. They noticed the weakening of the crops with each passing cycle. Each generations that came afterwards, not as energetic as the previous. At first, no one thought too much of this until the land changed again eighty one cycles ago, when a permanent haze engulfed the horizon, cutting off the purity of the rain from the firmaments. Over time all waters became toxic or stale, making them hardly suitable for nourishment. But many have let this go on without care, enjoying our newfound improvements."

Xendsvar turned his gaze towards Hanjiah, who replied,

"Don't start with that right now. Don't even go there. Just tell em what they need to know so we can get goin'."

Xendsvar eyed Hanjiah a bit longer. He respected Hanjiah, but didn't care for his overly pragmatic way of thinking. "We of the Cabjha, and even a few skeptics like this fool, agreed that something had to be done besides leaving our fate to chance or other strangers, no matter how great they may be. In a desparate attempt to find a solution I sought out a guide."

"We, together, sought guidance," said Hanjiah.

"If you weren't the only one I trusted to keep their mouth quiet, I would've asked someone else.

"Through word, we were told of an old woman living by a pond in the valley on the remote outskirts of Xeno. We were told she was the oldest living among us, though we could not fathom the length of her years. We traveled there, the two of us alone, to keep matters quiet as possible. The woman spotted us from a distance and began to hide herself among the trees, as if she did not want to be bothered. So I called out to her, telling her our reason for seeking her out. The failing harvest of our zaitson flowers. Something about that must've troubled her, because she wasted no time in welcoming us into her hut. Once inside, she revealed her hidden knowledge to us.

Breaking her silence, she said this to us: "Do you know we live from beyond ancient times? Beyond time of a future or past in a land that is no more, only to be again? Did you see a place no one knows from where to go or return? For this land was once beautiful and full of life. Fruit was abundant. Fruit trees sprang up for those who wished it. At that time people could go wherever they pleased. If it was in mind, it was so. If it was not in mind, it was not. There was no discord or strife. Everyone lived to days without end. Now, no one remains except those of us that live here."

"Nope. No way," said Deslao. "You're telling us that we're in a land where people lived forever? And, now these people are gone? You're either messed up in the head or a bad liar, because I'm not buying it."

"I'm not finished."

"Whatever. Continue."

"The people thrived in a land of perpetual regeneration until the great cataclysm tore the sky in half. A monster blazed through the sky faster than light and sent every star crashing to the ground. All stars were forgotten. All but one star fell to the ground. When the monster saw that one remained it opened its mouth and swallowed it. But the star did not die."

"What happened to it?" said Seldao.

"I'm getting to that. No more interruptions from anyone!" Xendsvar readjusted his posture once again. "The monster began to thrash about the sky in pain. The scorching heat from the star was too much for it to handle. The monster spat the star out and flew past it into the void created by the cataclysm, never to be seen again. She says our land came out of that void. Therefore, only one that lived before the void has the power to restore our land.

"She said, 'His name is Apeay. He will bring the forgotten back, the land to health and all to come. You will find him when the other two find you. They will come from just over the hills to you in Xeno. Two men, young in age, that share one face.' Therefore, it was more than chance we found you so far away from the mainland. I myself, did not understand the meaning, it was more of a feeling. All of this, *feels* familiar to me. Before knowing where to look, I sensed you'd be somewhere near the river, before you arrived."

"Wow...that's unbelievable," said Seldao.

"What I thought," said Deslao. "Unbelievable."

"What do you mean?"

"I figured it out. These two are some type of covert Legionnaires and they're looking for Apeay for some other reason. I'm right, aren't I?" said Deslao to Xendsvar. "My brother may be gullible, but I'm not. You made up that story hoping we had some info for you. Xeno, the imaginary land. Man, get that nonsense out of here. We're still in Estellar. Aren't we, big fella?"

"Whoo-whee, this one is something," said Hanjiah. "This land is Xeno, has been since I can remember. You must've hit your head somewhere in that river."

"You know my brother my not understand much of tzierhan positioning, but he's right; Xeno is a myth. No shototu ever found a trace of evidence proving its hypothesized existence," said Seldao.

Hanjiah reached out and pinched a fold of skin on Seldao's arm.

"Ouch, what is wrong with you?!"

"Did that feel like a hypothesis to you? Hmm? And, what's a shototu? You know, it's you two that have me worried. Estellar, Legionnaires, swimming in dangerous rivers for no reason, wearing funny clothes. Maybe you have something to tell us for a change?"

Xendsvar leaned forward, as did Hanjiah, awaiting their reply. Seldao looked to his brother for direction.

Deslao leaned over and spoke quietly in Seldao's ear, "Go ahead, tell them. Even if this is a trick, maybe they'll let us go after they see that we don't know where he is."

"Alright," said Seldao. He then told the two strange men where they were from, and how he and his brother arrived in the land of Xeno.

Δ

"She's already gone."

"Did she say where she was going?"

"No, she just left. Didn't say a word, after that report. My guess she left for Estellar.

"Really?" said Thorel.

LaLa'ila nodded. "Yes. We were watching the report on that festival that went crazy." Jhar'ensky lowered his head and sighed. It was a great embarrassment to Council. One that only time could erase. "When she heard the bad report on Apeay, she lost it; packed her bag and left without even saying bye."

At that moment, the plina on Jhar'ensky's collar alerted him. "Connected this is Principal Regalis."

"Hey...hey, dear where are you?" Bexhiera sounded out of breath.

"I'm still at Ajina Delta. We're talking with Zaleah's roommate. I believe..."

"Come back home. Apeay's here. He contacted me not that long ago. I'm going to meet him right now."

"We're on our way." Jhar'ensky double tapped his plina dismissing the connection, and turned to LaLa'ila. "Thank you, kind lady. We appreciate your help. And now, we must take our leave. Good luck here at Ajina Delta. It's a great place to learn." He gave a nod to Thorel, and the two of them exited the room.

"You must have a good reason for cutting the interview short," said Thorel.

"We no longer have need for it. Apeay's come home. It was just a matter of time."

"Excellent, though I am a little disappointed."

"And why is that? Is it because you didn't get a chance to use your mastery of analysis to solve this mystery?"

"No... But the taverns."

"What?" Jhar'ensky shook his head. "Are you serious?"

"Yeah. You know the northern districts of Sohexiah have the best taverns, and we don't even have time for *one* beverage. Looks like it's time for sequence, 'flash grab.'"

"You may be Zennite Thorel to everyone else, but inside you're still the 'Speedy Tho-tho' I remember."

"We never change, do we?"

"Perhaps not," said Jhar'ensky. "Though, life does change. I mean, look at me. Bexhiera and I never imagined we'd have a family. Then one day it was there, staring us in the face. He changed everything that day. Sure, I posted a declaration on the Legionnaire board for a found child. But, I knew the truth. He was on our doorstep as a gift for us. Tell me, Rionazen, have you ever considered getting..."

She quickly dismissed where he was going. "My duty is my lifelong mate. No, I haven't considered anything since the day he disappeared."

"My apologies I didn't realize you still thought about him."

"It's not like that. I would just rather stay in the moment. Who knows? Maybe, once we bring some stability back to Council, I'll have more time to pursue other things. But for now, it's this. And every jhenta counts."

"True... Tell you what, let's head back, meet up with my wife and son, then come back to celebrate while we sort things out. It'll be on me."

"I have no objections to that. Sequence 'good times' accepted."

Jhar'ensky and Thorel returned to the stately glinzoxe, Estellar bound.

Φ

The wind whispered without any beckoning to come or go, to stay or to leave, breathing on a land so vague that one could get lost before they started going.

"It's not right. Nothing about this is right." He was convinced. "Why is it so different?"

Zaleah began to make her way down the hill.

"Where are you going?"

"Somewhere besides here. We're in the middle of nowhere. I say we get to somewhere."

"This is all wrong," said Apeay. "It shouldn't look like this."

"How should it look?"

"It's hard to explain. But not like this. Look around, it looks dead. Remember the first nadian we spent together? I told you about that dream that seemed more than a dream I had when I was young. The one you teased me about?"

"I didn't tease you about it."

"You do remember what you said?"

"Man, all I said was, 'Maybe you should doze off in another cave.' It was my way of showing support."

"Then you giggled like something was funny."

"Apeay, I wasn't teasing ya. I thought it was cute. It made me like you even more." Apeay paid no mind to her elucidation, and continued to look onwards. "Hey man, even you said that you weren't sure what really happened to you."

"Well I'm sure now. Whisked away to another land, while in the same place, but this time, it's different."

"Different how?" asked Zaleah.

"This setting doesn't seem lively; like someone set fire to the land." Indeed, the land looked parched and drab. The still air that blew from the east almost burned for lack of moisture. Where a hill stood, lied jagged rocks, some covered in wilted overgrowth, piled below at its foot, welcoming travelers with hazardous, uneven ground. Plants seldom grew among the rocky soil, except for the few covered in thorns, alongside a shaded patch of rotting fruit. The haze of the sky engulfed all else. From the dark side of the sky to the light, all was haze; a blanket hiding a faint blue glow. Apeay closed his eyes as he contemplated a reasonable explanation.

"Maybe he never took me this far," said Apeay.

"Who's that?" Zaleah asked.

"Haru."

"You're saying it like I know him. Who is he?"

"The man who picked me up in his capsyint and took me to the palace. Remember?"

"Not really."

"Whatever, I'll explain later. We need to head towards that light. That's either Dokun or maybe it's the palace, now that I think about it." Apeay nodded. He was sure of it. "You're about to see something magnificent like nothing you've ever seen before. You ready?"

"I've been ready."

"Trust me," Apeay grinned. "C'mon." Without warning he scooped Zaleah up over his shoulder, bolting down the spiraled path through the foothill.

"In a rush?"

"Maybe. Hold tight."

Apeay sprinted so quick that it was if they teleported the bottom, where the jagged valley greeted the high hills. Apeay set Zaleah down on the pathway. The path ran a course weaving in between each hilltop.

"Look at this," said Zaleah. She was kneeling before a row of wilting flowers. Apeay looked alongside her.

"Dead stems," said Apeay.

"Yes, dead zaitson fruit stems. You can tell it doesn't rain much here. I can almost taste the aridness with my mouth."

Apeay knelt down beside, her observing the dwindling flowers. "Yeah, these look bad. What a waste of zaitson."

"Your favorite too. Well, at least you're covered for today," she said tapping at the side of her backpack."

The two rose to their feet and continued to follow the path along the valley floor. The entire path resembled that at the beginning to the left and to the right for reels and reels on end, lifeless zaitson stems bowed in sorrow. For an unknown time they walked the lifeless trail among slits of ethereal light and formidable shadows. On several occasions, Zaleah turned to look behind them, feeling they were being followed. Apeay, on the other hand, seemed not to sense any danger, but could see the apprehension in her behavior.

"What's the matter?" Apeay asked.

"I feels like someone's behind us, but I don't see anyone."

"It's probably just the newness."

"Newness?"

"This place is new to you so, you're uncomfortable. That's all. Let's keep going, I think I see the source of the light."

As the last curtain of shadows lifted, they reached a clearing at the end of the valley. It was still late enough at night to be ahead of the dawn when they arrived at the source of the light they saw from the distant hilltops. However, it was not to Apeay's expectation or liking.

"I don't get it. Why is this here?!"

They stood at the edge of a tall dry grassy field. Torches marked the perimeter for at least 21 reels around. Surrounding the field were rows of wooden planks. On one section rested a large bronze cart, with enough space to carry fifty individuals, ornamented with the face of a cabera protruding as a relief at the head. Far beyond that, to where the twilight-to-night sky touched the horizon, an elaborate cluster of grass woven huts sat in the middle of a distant field. It looked to be quite a large village, a panorama out of an archaic template.

Zaleah studied the village among its natural surroundings. "Little huts in the middle of fire fields."

"People riding up on cabera wheels," said Apeay. "Hazy in the eyes, sleepy as we know."

"In the missing diamond land of Xeno," they said in unison. They were citing a verse from a popular children's rhyme passed on from eras long ago.

"It's impossible," said Zaleah. "There's no way. It's only a legend. A land that vanished ten thousand cycles back through the ages. It's not even possible."

"No. I think it is. *That's* why it's different."

"Explain it then?"

"Explain it? What is there to explain?"

"How we got here. Explain how we made an incredible 10 to 11,000 cycle jump into a nonexistent past."

"Not sure. We just did. And I accept it as so."

"Well, I can't just accept it so easily. I want to know what really happened. That's me."

"I know...Well maybe it had something to do with the starlight that entered the ruins and my ornament. Remember when you were explaining the Hewlix alignment to me? You said the light always reaches us from the past; that we were literally looking at a time that does not exist?"

"But that's describing *light* going forward into the future from the past."

"What if it's not just limited to light? And what if it can go both forward and backward? Our ratio of time to space doesn't hold constant when the object in question does not hold constant in speed to the direction of distance it's travelling, for time is an illusion of our senses."

"You get that from Seldao?"

"I got that from I don't know where. I just know things like that."

"Impressive."

Apeay grabbed Zaleah by the hand, venturing into the tall, grassy field. They were making their way towards the village. However, not long before they could make it halfway across the two reel trek, several people appeared out of nowhere surrounding them. Each was dressed in clothing woven from the grass which had made it easy for them to blend in with the field. All were brandishing some fashion of an edged weapon.

"Gxos gxos, sheng!" one of them shouted.

"Gxos gxos, sheng!" Now, there appeared to be a young woman advancing with the first line. Apeay looked around for an exit. But, the three other groups created a tight, overlapping enclosure.

From the advancing line, the young woman pointed her weapon at them. "Give the answer before I give you death."

Δ

"Apeay?" Bexhiera rushed into the house, throwing her belongings on the floor. "Apeay where are you?! It's okay, no one's here but me." Bexhiera dashed around their estate. "Your father will be here soon. You're safe, my son."

From the window she could see the nursery door ajar. Bexhiera went out the back of the house. As she got closer to the entrance, she saw a figure of a man standing in the doorway. All the plant life surrounding the man had wilted. A vermilion aura silhouetting him made it difficult to see his face.

"Apeay?"

"There is no Apeay. Not at all, your highness ..."

CHAPTER 15

You're going too far... Oh well... It's not like it's the first time.

"Say something Apeay," said Zaleah "I thought you knew these people."

Apeay was halfway listening. He was more focused on the weapon inches away from his face. "These people are different. I don't know what they want." He turned towards the woman who was impatiently awaiting their answer. "Astiox! Does that work?"

"No! Therefore..." She advanced several paces beyond the first line. Edging forward, her eyes began to widen as she looked upon Apeay's face. Then trembling, she spoke as she dropped her weapon, bowing to Apeay. "Forgive me, Magnificent One. I didn't recognize you. I've never seen you return from your work with another person." She eyed Zaleah up and down, then returned her focus to Apeay. And, your new look is...different. You cut your hair?" The woman rubbed Apeay's head while embracing him with a kiss, much to his and Zaleah's shock. "Wow, soft lips too." The feminine guardian turned to the rest of them, shouting, "He has returned to perfect us all!"

"It's you! Yes! Look, he has returned!" the others began to shout. Each one lowered their weapon and bowed.

"What is going on?" said Zaleah.

Apeay whispered in her ear, "I have no idea. Just glad they're bowing and not interested in killing us anymore. I'm going to try something." To the kneeling group he said, "Stand and take us to the village."

"Right away, Magnificent One," said the woman. The woman was slightly taller than Apeay. Her appearance was slender and ruddy. Her eyes were as beautiful as they were fierce, showing she was not as young and tender a flower as she appeared to be. Upon looking into Apeay's eyes she smiled a smile to make any fellow her helpless prey. "You'll be pleased to know we've begun construction of the first restoration center ahead of schedule. All will be diamond. All will be perfected."

The rest joined her in chanting, "All will be diamond. The symbol is perfect. For we dream not as a fool, but forge the shining world by our hands."

A lady with long braided hair retrieved a short, spiraled tube with four holes bored through the center out of her burgundy satchel. She took a deep breath and blew into the smallest of the four holes. It produced a harmony that started out low, and rose three octaves. It could be heard for reel upon reel. The chain of carts sitting on the wooden planks began to move. The mechanical cabera came to them, stopping on the edge of the field.

"Your transport awaits, Magnificent One."

The four stayed their course alongside the river. But they had made little progress in finding Apeay. Deslao, still in disbelief, contented that the other two were still not completely honest about their motives. Part of him was honestly hoping they were liars, just to get the chance to whoop Xendsvar.

While they made their way, quarreling with one another, the sound of a whistle dancing in a three-part harmony entered their ears.

"Did y'all hear that?" Deslao asked.

"Pay it no mind," said Xendsvar.

"Why? Is it an alarm? Something else you hiding from us?"

"No. It simply does not concern us."

"Just tell him!" Hanjiah hollered. "This is why you stay out by the river. No sense of communication. Sheesh!"

Xendsvar scowled as he informed them as to what they were hearing. "It's a call to the village. The 'Magnificent One' has returned. It does not concern us because the wise lady was specific: 'Return to the village only upon finding Apeay.' An instruction that suits me well. I'm tired of answering the call. I don't favor the 'Magnificent', even with all the *wondrous* things he brought us, as some say."

"You don't care for him at all," said Hanjiah. Xendsvar scoffed at his remark.

"Why would I?!" he shouted. He looked angrily at Hanjiah. Both of his fists were clenched so tightly that his nails drew blood from the palms of his hands. His body was quaking as if he were a mountain about to erupt. "You dare go far with me?"

"I'd like to know what kind of wonders he's talking about," interrupted Seldao.

"Nothing more than junk, that this follower of unnatural works turned into more junk."

"We used some of that 'junk' to get out here," said Hanjiah.

"I despise the Nvekbarah's Ascent. It's making us weak!"

"It saved us time, fool."

"For you, yes." I can out run the worthless thing. *That* was a certified fact.

Seldao stepped between the two bickering men. "We're looking for my friend, not debating philosophy. And the more I think about it, we're going the wrong way. We fell from above and went downstream, where you found us."

"That's the part that has us vexed," said Hanjiah. "We told you already. There's no waterfall at the beginning of the river, only a double-sided fall at the end. It's mysterious because it flows backwards from the mouth of the Eostrezan Sea."

"Not what you said last time," Seldao said, recalling their earlier encounter. "You said you saved us from the river of the Silver Mirror."

"That's a moniker we gave it on account that its surface is completely reflective; shimmering like none other. The real marvel was finding you two alive."

"I can swim. What's surprising about that?" said Deslao

"You swam in cursed water," said Xendsvar.

"Cursed?"

"He means it's toxic," said Hanjiah. "Like we said before, our water sources are scarce. Most of it gets caught in the haze. What little doesn't, we collect before it stales. Any of the rains that fall on the rivers, lakes or the sea instantly turn toxic. Anyone unfortunate enough to fall in, dies within a few zahmens. The toxins kill them from the inside out."

"Curious," said Seldao. "I'd like to hear more. What does it do to them?"

"It gives them a living nightmare is what it does, starting with the nerves. The person begins to panic, while their mind is thrown into a delusionary state. While the nerve damage causes their heart and lungs to seize up, they begin to imagine strange things. After that, they start babbling about whatever it is they think they're seeing. Once that sets in, there is no hope for them. They go on like that until the end. According to our village healer, they're actually dead several moments before they stop babbling like some sort of phantom being."

Seldao mulled it over for a moment. "When was the first incident?"

Hanjiah glanced over at Xendsvar. "I'm not sure. It's been going on for a while now. Only the survivor of the first is immune to the river's toxin."

"The first?"

"Yeah, the first generation," Hanjiah replied. "She's..."

"Let me guess, the old swamp lady," Deslao interjected.

"It's a pond almost a small lake, actually. Not a swamp. And yes, you're correct, 'clever *fihgazz*.' Her lifespan is inexplicably long. I'd like to think that it's because of all the enhanced fruit they had available to them before bad times hit us. But, if that were so, she wouldn't be the only one left. Not like it matters anyway."

Outwardly, Seldao was calm. However, inwardly his mind was ablaze as it mind raced from one end of the universe to the other, calling to mind the conversation he overheard between Apeay and Zaleah back at the trails. "Where does this river reach its end?"

"There in the unlit zone," Xendsvar said, pointing to the range of high, mountainous hills a great distance away. The limited light from the evening sky gave the high hills a bizarre look as if they weren't associated with the surrounding environment.

"Care to take me there?"

"I thought 'this' was the right place." Deslao side-eyed his brother. "Or are you second guessing your own calculations?"

"Not at all. I recalculated. And now I'm sure of it. He will be either here or there. So, we'll split up. Xendsvar can guide me while you two wait here."

"Here we go again with another of your brilliant deductions."

"Which turn out to be right most of the time."

Xendsvar stepped in between them. "Enough talking. We will do so, for the journey to the Temple of Fuxirajhe, 'Pedestal of the Cabjha', is farther than it appears."

"That's where the river ends, isn't it?" said Seldao.

"Not quite ends, but there it is," Xendsvar replied.

"Good. That will be our plan of action." Without hesitation, Seldao began walking towards the high hills.

"Hold on. We'll travel by zabanghir up the river." Xendsvar nodded to Hanjiah. "Keep your eyes open."

"Don't worry, we will." Hanjiah retrieved a chunk of dried pimen meat from his pouch and took a bite. "Would you like a piece, young man?"

"I'm not hungry," replied Delao.

"Look at your brother go. It's like he knows something," said Hanjiah.

"He always thinks he knows," said Deslao. "One day his head's gonna get stuck while walking through a door."

"I can't say, but your brother might be on to something." Hanjiah looked up towards the distant hills. "No one, except for the Cabjha make visits to the temple."

"So, you've never been there?"

"No, not ever. It's not a place that holds value for me, or Xeno in this era. The temple is ancient. It's construction began back in the first generation, thousands of cycles ago. We don't know what prompted them, but like Xendsvar, the Cabjha believe the ritual of "temple visitation" is the right way to live to appease the gods."

"The gods? We're on that again?"

"I didn't come up with it. It's superstitious jabber to me. Anyway, the first generation laid the foundation and framework for the temple. Then the second continued and passed it on to the third. The third generation was close to completing the building, but never found the last elemental alignment structure needed to complete it; the 'Aurujha Mobius,' they called it, though I couldn't say what that means because the structure looks solid enough to me."

"I don't care how it looks. It sounds like all they believe in is wasting time. Who would spend all those cycles, living and dying building something, only to say 'forget it, we're done'?"

"Oh, they searched for this mysterious element up until the end of the sixth generation, when they lost the knowledge of what they were searching for. Then, about six-thousand cycles later he shows up; the one who changed everything. The Magnificent One. He brought unseen, unheard-of, contraptions with him. Right then and there, most lost interest in anything to do with mystic ways. He also denounced the temple, calling it a 'relic of fools'. So even if anyone cared to find lost element to solve the mystery of the temple, they'd be too afraid to try it under the Magnificent One's watch. That's why no one bothers to go there, except Xendsvar and his mystical associates of the Cabjha to practice their 'secret magic'. A bunch of nonsense to me."

Deslao looked in the direction his brother and Xendsvar were travelling. Hanjiah placed his hand on his shoulder.

"Don't worry. Your brother's fine. Xendsvar may be a mystic, but he's no one to toy with. He'll keep him safe."

Deslao shrugged it off. "I'm not worried." It was obvious he was concerned, while trying to hide his feelings. He was worried that there may be trouble ahead. Deslao felt he couldn't afford to sit by idly. He had to find out firsthand all there was to know about the situation they were in. "I want to see the village."

"I don't know if that's a good idea. The Magnificent One is back, and he's not fond of unidentified newcomers showing up."

"That doesn't matter to me. I want to see him. Introduce me to him, like you introduced yourself and "big angry" to us. Either way, I'm going."

Hanjiah shook his head. "Fine. I'll introduce you, and hope he doesn't rip my head for it, then we're coming right back. We can't miss your friend if he shows up."

"Yeah, *if* he shows up. If you're that concerned, stay here. I'm pretty good at navigating myself."

"I'm going with you, but I'm done walking for the day. It should be fully charged by now." Hanjiah pulled out from his bag a small, spiraled tube with one solid hole drilled through the center. When he blew into it, the tube made a low-pitched whistle. "Step to the side, youngster. I aimed its landing point where you're standing."

Deslao saw nothing initially. From a ways back in the distance from where they came he heard bojos making their signature warning call. The uniformly spherical object that had caused the disturbance was heading their way until the large multi-angled cart hovered overhead. As Deslao gave way, the cart came to rest in front of them.

"Hop in. Time to fly."

Δ

The door to the home on the hill was partly open, and the air was still.

Mr. Regalis slowly pushed open the door. "Apeay? Bexhiera, dear?" Did he miss something in her transmit? Was this not where she told him they would be? "This isn't the time for jokes you two. No time for surprise games either. Come out, so we can straighten things out."

'Silence'

"Did she give any indication that they were in danger?" asked Thorel.

"No. She said all was well, that Apeay was here waiting with her."

"Then they contacted me," said another voice from inside. He made his presence known as he entered the main room.

"Valus? What are you doing here? And why are you shouldering a Legionnaire's neutranevex?" asked Jhar'ensky.

"Apparently Bexhiera got a hold of me right after she contacted you. She said something wasn't right, and to tell Apeay to run. After that her plina link cut off, so I came as quickly as I could, ready for anything. But when I arrived, no one was here. I've been waiting for someone to return since then."

"If that's the way you felt, you should've, at the least, asked for the accompany of a few Legionnaires with you. You're an important member of Council now; your combat days are long past," said Thorel.

"I know. Sometimes though, I wish it was still like it used to be back in the old days when I was more than just Council's pet analysist."

"This is a different age. We're in an entirely different echelon," said Jhar'ensky. "The Head of Council Affairs, who does diligence on behalf of the security of the people is a cherished gem in our modern society."

"I guess you speak true. Ah, and one more thing, " Valus said solemnly. "I couldn't have brought help if I wanted to."

Rionazen and Jhar'ensky leaned forward, intently awaiting his explanation. "Everything has changed due to Council's acceptance of an 'absolute resolve.'"

"Impossible!" Jhar'ensky shouted. "How could they make such a gesture? I've been away and gave no authorization on any such action."

"I don't know how to put it in strict, council affair terms except full-on mutiny. In a manner of speaking, you've been unofficially superseded...Command, along with Heylan Command, have completely taken over. All of Council is at the mercy of their will."

"Heylan, like the fabled god Heylan? What kind of mockery has Affi'hado created?! Under the articles of unification, we were charged with following the directives of Command. And those directives are balanced by countermeasures and safeguards. He can't just go off and contrive a new juris-prudence out of his imagination!"

"Of course not. It's not a dictatorship."

"So then, how did it happen? Did everyone lose sense all at once?!"

"Your guess is as good as mine. It's as if they were planning on him giving the resolve and fell in line accordingly. I say we get to Palladus Hall promptly. With us three, we should be able to close this matter before they go too far."

"And what about my family?! This whole affair it's...too much! It's too much..." Jhar'ensky felt broken. Everything he knew was fleeing him through circumstances beyond his control. He knelt down on the linen chair with his eyes closed, hoping to hear an answer.

Thorel knelt beside him, placing her arm around him. "I'm sure they're safe. Apeay's smart. Anyone who can hide from five teams of Legionnaires for this long will be alright. And, I told those who report directly to me, if in fact they still do, not to turn him over to anyone but me." Though she empathized, she maintained focus on the urgent matter ahead. "We need to get to that hall, and show a strong face."

Jhar'ensky took a deep breath and rose to his feet. "Valus."

"Yes, my friend?"

"Prime the glinzoxe. I'll be right back." Jhar'ensky walked up to the second level while Thorel and Valus boarded the multi passenger transport. He returned wearing his outdated armor and carrying a "Golden Era"-style neutranevex.

"Now you too?" said Thorel. "We're going here to find answers, not start a war."

"I know, Tho. But I'm damn sure not going to let us get caught off guard again. I'm ready for whatever else this Command throws our way... Sequence, 'Let's finish this!'"

"I can't argue that. Accepted."

The glinzoxe levitated to the heights of the stratus and took off. Thorel leaned back in her seat, looking out at the shrinking ground below. She couldn't help to think that she had missed something, but felt strongly that all the unknowns would be known, sooner than later. In the meantime, she kept her uncertainties to herself.

Ω

I remember when you fed me, rocked me to sleep and mended my wounds. For what did you do these things?

The silver rope that kept her tied to the nursery fountain loosened. The home on the hill was quiet, but for two pairs of footsteps moving silently about. One leading as the other followed.

"Didn't you say this Apeay would be with them?"

The other nodded, unable to speak. Ultrafine cords of pure crystal bound her mouth shut.

"So you lie, while the old emperor yet again tries to defy my great order set from the beginning; the perfect alignment of all that is."

Her eyes looked upon this image of a man with sorrow.

"You will witness as I bring the brightest day to Estellar and the unified regions beyond. Then when this boy you dream of is no more, you will see your error. You will know that I have created an everlasting paradise with what is real. The reality of diamond perfection from my great command!"

CHAPTER 16

Their cart glided over the soft metal tracks with ease. The soft rails were warmed by Heyliun which charged them, powering the mighty beast. As they went further away from the northern border, the curvature of the great field split apart, making a clearing. Then, going beyond the fields and into the subtle lower flatland, the village and many of its hidden features could be seen in detail. The grass huts were more than grass. The grass itself was coated in some type of clear substance, held together by polished metal. The advanced application of metalworking, coupled with the highly sophisticated architecture each hut exhibited, suggested that these people knew more about technology than they had originally thought.

The woman riding next to Apeay was studying him and his anonymous guest. Her eyes went back and forth from one to the other.

"Who is this new, strange servant you bring?" asked the woman.

Zaleah was shocked that she would assume her a servant of Apeay. *'A strange servant?!'* She wouldn't let the notion go unchecked. "I'm his friend."

The woman was perplexed; Apeay took notice and re-affirmed Zaleah's position. "Yes, she is a friend."

"His friend?" The woman studied her with more intent, then turned to Apeay. "You have friends now? That's different. What's your friend's name?"

"Her name is..."

"I'm LaLa'ila," said Zaleah, cutting him off. "And who are you?"

"Xenzashii, the first lady. It's no secret you know." She looked upon Apeay with apparent admiration. "I will bathe you before taking you to see our progression."

"I must advise against taking that action," said Zaleah.

"Oh? You do not wish him to be clean from the filth of his travels? My Magnificent One always gets his cleaning. It's his will."

"I could use a bath," Apeay said with a smirk. "Ow!" Apeay turned towards Zaleah to see what jabbed his side, only to see her smirking with the glint of menace in her eyes.

"What's the matter?" asked Xenzashii.

"He is suffering from pains," said Zaleah "As his advisor, I suggest that we avoid his bath for now. It may cause the pains to accelerate."

"You said you were a friend."

Zaleah postured herself uprightly. "I'm both friend and advisor. He comes to me for advice about many important things."

The mysterious woman's words perplexed Xenzashii. She rubbed Apeay's shoulder as she asked, "Is that true?"

"Uh...yes, it is," said Apeay.

"Wow, why didn't you tell me about it? And for you to give advice to the Magnificent One , you must be like a..."

"Yes, I am like a god, a goddess to be correct. Remember that before making any further suggestions concerning the Magnificent One."

Apeay's face went blank before feigning a smile. Zaleah did likewise. Then the two shared their eccentric look with Xenzashii, making her feel somewhat awkward. She couldn't help but sense that something was off. But, for the sake of her delight in having *her* Magnificent One back, she pushed the notion aside.

Just outside the village gates, the cart came to rest next to an elongated marble walkway. It was roughly three times the length of the cart.

Xenzashii waved her hand over a small gemstone embedded in the cart's framework, and the bronze cart separated into two halves receding from the walkway. She gave a slight bow towards Apeay.

"Please, come see the progress we have made, my great one. The people are following your directives as stated. And Hanjiah's team has begun to lay the groundwork for the region between in accordance with your plan." Apeay wasted no time getting into character, seeking answers to the mystery of this enigmatic land.

"Yes, show me now. If it is to my liking, there will be rewards for all."

"And for me?" asked Xenzashii

"Whatever you desire will be granted."

"Finally, it will be real this time."

Apeay kept his composure, though he wasn't sure what she meant. "Yes, it will be real; very real this time."

Zaleah swooped in between them. "Excuse me, Xenzashii, I need a to have a word with the Magnificent One. We'll be right back."

"But of course, goddess LaLa'ila. We'll be waiting."

Zaleah strutted off away from the welcoming party as Apeay stood still.

"Where are you going?" asked Apeay.

"I need to talk to you in private. Please come along!" Her tone of voice was demanding.

Apeay grew impatient with her constant request. Getting to the bottom of this matter was all that concerned him. "How about we discuss whatever it is later? We need to see what they've done for us."

"What they've done for you," said Zaleah. "I'm only your advisor. Maybe that's *all* I've ever been."

At that, Apeay knew what was bothering her. "My advisor is calling for an emergency Council meeting. We'll return in a jhenta." He caught up with Zaleah. The two went around the corner, behind one of the huts, putting a suitable distance between them and the others.

"Say it," said Apeay.

"Say what?" said Zaleah.

"I'll just go back if you're going to keep this up."

Apeay knew her well. Zaleah was one of the most self-assured people he knew. She did not believe in showing weakness. Therefore he'd wait patiently to hear her dignified reply.

"Did you come here to find answers, or are you looking for something else?" asked Zaleah.

"We came here for answers. This is the fastest way to. And, no, I'm not looking for someone else. Okay?"

"I didn't say someone. I said something."

"Either way, I can tell because you're acting funny. And what's with the fake name? Who's LaLa'ila?"

"She's my roommate at Ajina. I wasn't giving those goons my real name. You should do the same, and keep your real name a secret."

"That's easy. They did that for me. So, for now, I think we can trust them."

"Trust them? We don't know them. And you don't know her. For all we know, this could be a trap. What if she had gave you that bath and the others were there waiting to jump out and kill you? Did you think that one through?"

"If they were going to kill us, they would've already tried. Look, I know what you're thinking. Sure, she's cute. But you're my babe. That makes you the most beautiful of all."

"So you think she's pretty? Sure you don't want to see this thing they've done so you can see some other things with your secret girlfriend?"

"Come here..." Apeay grabbed Zaleah by the arm, drawing her to him. While kissing her, he gently stroked the back of her neck. "It's just you, Zaleah. Trust me. But I need answers. This is far from normal for either of us. We have to play along until we know the deal."

"It's the way she looks at you. It's like she's expecting you to take her as yours. It's hard for me to play along if that's what is expected of the 'Magnificent One.'"

"I understand. I can be nice to her without...you know. If she has a thing going with whoever it is they think I am, I can't just shun her. People would get suspicious."

"Well...I see your point. But no one is giving you a bath but me."

"Okay, but you better not jab me in the side again."

"Sorry, I panicked."

Apeay nodded. "Alright, my lady."

They concluded their private meeting, and rejoined the group that awaited them.

"Did we do something wrong?" asked Xenzashii.

"No, we're good," said Zaleah. "I forgot to brief the Magnificent One about his future travels. His busy schedule is hard to keep up with. Therefore his time here will be limited."

"Exactly," said Apeay. "So, where is it?"

"The perfection is this way," said Xenzashii.

She led them deeper into the village until they reached the center, where a group of men and women were occupied with an elaborate construction. Some of them, looking over tablets, working out the intricate details of the structure, while others were going back and forth carrying materials and tools.

"What do we have here?" said Apeay. He went up to one of the people holding a tablet and demanded, "Hand that to me."

Without hesitating, they did as commanded. "Yes, Magnificent One."

Apeay looked over the text within the tablet. He recognized all the symbols inscribed on the tablet. How could he not? Some, in fact, he knew from the Book of Ascension. The others he learned in session at Estellar Prime. However, the symbols were arranged in an indecipherable order; impossible to interpret. The equations which followed the symbols didn't correlate with what each symbol should stand for. Apeay was confounded. The more he looked over the document, the more confusing it became. What were they building? What was this foundation that lay before him? Apeay turned the tablet over, looking for more clues. On the underside of the tablet, there was but one image. Upon sight, Apeay discovered what it was they were building. But he needed to be certain.

Holding up the image to the man he took the tablet from, Apeay inquired, "What is this?"

A puzzled look came upon the man's face, but not for too long. He smirked as he shook his finger at Apeay. "Ah, you test me, Magnificent One. It is the xhilheolleh, the infinite energy magnifier. An invention of your unlimited wisdom, which we will make real."

Zaleah was standing but a few paces back from Apeay, and close enough to hear the man's reply. To make sure she wasn't imagining things, she asked of the man, "Could you repeat the name of this structure? But this time, say it slowly."

"Why? Who are you?" asked the man.

"She is goddess LaLa'ila, my advisor," said Apeay. "Do as she asks of you."

"Yes, right away. No problem, your excellency. My apologies." The man lowered his head towards Zaleah. "It's the xhilh...heolh... leh; the great energy magnifier. Like you said, 'A child will not have to dream, when all they need is before them.'"

A cosmic explosion of knowledge set off in Apeay's mind.

As a child, Apeay spent many nights playing games by the fire. He remembered the various conversations his mother and father had about all the activities in Estellar and the outer regions. When Mother would talk about the Centre, it was always the same; children not sleeping well, children fatigued. And those that did sleep regularly, had little deep sleep. Apeay was one of a handful who didn't exhibit any of these symptoms. In fact, if he had symptoms, they were quite the opposite. For this reason, his mother never discussed this aspect of him at the Centre. The second lead, Diamond Hand Aeroxia Nzhil, took interest in cases like Apeay's, and made it his business to probe to the point of near intrusion, something his mother wouldn't tolerate.

There was one conversation in particular he would never forget. It took place the evening of the first day he discovered the canals:

"This day completely drained my energy," Bexhiera said as she leaned over on the turujo. "It took us with rotating staff a full 21 ahkmeres to help rest this girl. The fatigue is making her delusional. I felt so bad for her."

Jhar'ensky sat upright, loosening his collar. "Delusional, how?" he asked.

"The girl didn't want help. Her parents were at a loss. They said they had to force her to breathe the remedy in, because she refused to do it on her own. She's been so long without adequate rest, that she likes it now. The girl stumbles all over the place and tells her parents, 'I don't have to dream. Everything is shining gold.' And the siolehs, she laughed, gleefully saying to us, "they're all shining diamonds."

"Well, they do have a bright polish over the emerald."

"Jhar'ensky stop. It isn't funny."

"I didn't say it was. I'm saying, it's how they look."

"Well, speaking of the siolehs, how safe are they?"

"The siolehs? Are you serious? We've never had any malfunctions, so if you're fearing the worst, I can assure you we make certain they are kept under strict regulation. The chance of a meltdown is just about nil."

"That's not what I'm asking," said Bexhiera.

"Alright then, what particular danger are you referring to?"

"It's hard to explain, but it is a theory. We've ran tests on children from both here and the surrounding regions, and it seems that those who live the furthest away from Estellar, which boasts the largest and most powerful siolehs, are not experiencing these symptoms to the degree that the children within Estellar exhibit."

"My dear, that could be the result of any number of things. Am I supposed to go to Council and suggest that we impede the progress of our region based off speculation?"

"So you don't believe me?"

"No, that's not it at all. In fact, you could be on to something. However, without any real proof, your theory would be severely scrutinized and dismissed. I know these people. If you were to find evidence to support your theory afterwards, they would be inclined to ignore your request for a hearing. Not even a Council Principal can force a hearing if the request is turned down by the majority." Bexhiera took a deep sigh, shaking her head. "I'm not saying that you should stop your testing. I mean, where would we be without you and the aeroxia division? Estellar is forever grateful for everything your group has done to restore our region to its former health and beauty."

Bexhiera nodded. "Thank you."

"In the meantime for cases like the one you encountered today, are there any better treatments? Something stronger, perhaps, to give her rest?"

"No, not without endangering her health. Unfortunately, she's one that will have to outgrow it like the rest. In a few more cycles she'll be resting normally."

"Indeed she will. It's a shame though. But, I'm sure you will soon have this thing figured out."

"I hope so. Until then, the best cure we have to offer is time itself."

"Time...now that's something I wish I had more of, especially when people opt to waste mine."

"Ha, everyone wastes your time when you're in a hurry, dear," said Bexhiera.

"I was in no hurry to get anywhere today." Bexhiera raised an eyebrow, knowing her mate's disposition all too well. He couldn't hide himself from her. "Well, maybe I was. Today was just filled with assembly after assembly. Deliberations were being dragged out over petty squabbles. Then, after the last assembly, Valus said he wanted to show me something exclusive. I told him it would have to wait for another day, but he insisted, saying he knew the meeting place of the eldest Council. It sounded intriguing, so I gave in. He then takes me all the way to the north, where we get out of his mynersha for a walk along the outer path to the canals. Mind you, we're still in our Council attire, which means I'm wearing my hard-toe drapels, most unfit for a long stroll. Then, halfway down, after my feet feel like they're going to fall apart, he says, 'I forgot the way. We'll have to find it some other time.'"

"Oh, don't let that bother you," said Bexhiera. "He probably did, and wants to make sure he knows for when he does show you."

Jhar'ensky didn't change his position. "Waste of time."

"Apeay."

"Yes, Mom?"

"Pack the games away. It's time for sleep."

"Your excellency...Magnificent One...did I speak out of turn?"

"What? No. I was contemplating how to improve its overall efficiency before you interrupted my thoughts!"

"My apologies."

Clearly, Apeay was lost in thought. He had many questions to ask. But first, there was one question he wanted answered the most. However, he considered that asking too many questions especially those he, or the Magnificent One should know might blow their cover. Therefore, he devised a way to ask without asking. "I'm sure you're setting this up the way I requested without altering its operation."

"Yes, that we are," said one of the overseers.

"Run it by me so I know that you have not deviated from my plans."

"Accepted. First we get the longest part over with, routing the waters of the river. And you were right. The nature of the river does not interfere with its functioning. We route the waters, lining the base of the flow propeller with them. After that, it's a simple matter of following the encoded guidelines to complete the 1-5-21 inverse frame with a palladium seal. The power transport, we attach to the frame before completing the outer shield. Also, thank you, Magnificent One, for the extra carbozhian. It gave us enough materials to complete a miniature working version of the xhilheolleh. We hope it's alright. We used some of your stored power to initiate it."

"My power?"

"What else is there? It's the only power we have to initiate any device in the land. Whoever thought there could be a way to store vast amounts of energy within gemstones."

"Do you have them here?" Apeay asked.

"Yes, right over there in that container." He pointed to out a palladium chest fused into the framework of the foundation. "These, too, are ready for you to energize."

Apeay walked up to the chest and studied its exterior. The smooth black surface made it hard to make out the writing lining the visible five faces of the chest. Symbols both familiar and unfamiliar were mixed in between the inscriptions. On all four corners of the front were the faces of a cabera, a gihan, a sea nulia, and a man. Then, as Apeay crept closer, leaning over the top to read, something unexpected happened. The ornament around his neck detached itself from the cord and fixed itself in place in a small concave opening in the center. It was as if the chest drew the ornament into itself. The lid sprung wide open, revealing a mixture of sapphires, emeralds, rubies, amethysts, and diamonds sitting in a gold and palladium wire basket within.

Being caught by surprise almost broke Apeay out of his assumed character. "Za...LaLa'ila, come look at this," said Apeay. Now, more than ever, he was convinced that his childhood experience of being whisked away to the land of Laixfu was more than just some vivid dream. Zaleah came up, and gazed into the chest alongside him.

"It's beautiful. There must be at least a hundred million ellure's worth of jewels in here," said Zaleah.

"Maybe, but don't say that to them. They probably don't know what an ellure is. Know what I mean?"

"Yes, true on that one."

The man with them couldn't understand why the Magnificent One had opened the chest that he had formerly sealed shut, with strict instructions, not to open it until the xhilheolleh was complete. "Are you planning to energize the jewels ahead of schedule?"

Apeay's instantly jumped back into character with a callous response. "Of course not. Are you saying I'm some sort of idiot? This is *my* design, not yours!"

"I'm sorry, I didn't mean it like that. I was just curious as to why you opened it."

Apeay decided it would be best to cut short any further interactions with this man for the time being. "Don't be concerned with what I do. You concentrate on your task."

"Understood, Magnificent One."

"Good. We will be leaving now. Update us on your progress when we return."

"I hear and accept. All will be diamond."

Apeay stepped forward and closed the lid. The ornament reattached itself to the crystal cord on his neck as quickly as it had left.

Before taking their leave, Apeay had another question for the man running the site. "You said you built a functional miniature model."

"Yes, would you like to see it?"

"I would. Where is it?"

"At XiaPrazju. For all the children to see and believe, just as you instructed."

"Right. You've done well."

Apeay had to think fast. He had no clue as to where Xia-Prazju was, but being the "Magnificent One, the people of the land would expect him to." But how could he find this place without appearing clueless? He looked around him and came up with an idea upon locating his most faithful servant.

"Xenzashii," said Apeay.

"Yes, my magnificent," she replied.

"Goddess LaLa'ila and I are heading to XiaPrazju soon, and I want them ready for our arrival. So, we need you to go ahead of us to prepare them."

"My pleasure, but why is she staying behind."

"She...has more to see concerning the village progression. Also, have them prepare a meal. I'm hungry from our journey."

Xenzashii froze, staring at the Magnificent One. It was as if she was sizing him up before turning to his advisor for guidance. "Goddess LaLa'ila, is this another symptom of his pains?"

"What symptom are you talking about?" asked Zaleah.

"The hunger. The Magnificent One doesn't eat."

Zaleah glanced at Apeay. He nodded to her, urging her to come up with an explanation.

"Yes, you are very observant. I'd expect nothing less from his first. It's true, the pain he's experienced lately has caused him to develop a very large appetite. Now, he requires almost constant nourishment."

Xenzashii gawked at Apeay. "You weren't gonna tell me? You know if you would've said something, I'd already have a meal on deck for you."

"It's alright," said Apeay. "Just have a meal ready for us when we arrive at XiaPrazju. Make sure they make enough for everyone, including yourself."

"I will. Thank you."

Xenzashii did as directed, making her way south beyond the center of the village.

"Good work, babe," Apeay said to Zaleah.

"You know I've got you covered."

"Yep. And now the trick is, how does the 'Magnificent One' follow someone in secret, in a place where everyone knows him?"

"He doesn't. The mysterious goddess that no one knows does and comes back for him."

"I see. Just be careful. And, be like a shadow; always there, but barely noticeable."

"I know how to be sneaky." Zaleah looked south watching Xenzashii's figure shrinking into the village backdrop. "She's just now far enough away for me to follow without being seen."

"Okay I'll be around here when you get back. Hopefully I will learn all I need to from the people here."

"Yes, and maybe you can figure out a way to get us back home."

"Yeah, that too."

Zaleah made her way south along the same path Xenzashii traveled, while sticking to the sides of the buildings among the villagers. As Apeay walked back towards the foundation the villagers were working on, he felt a warm sensation about his chest. Looking down, he noticed his ornament was not only glowing but radiating heat that made it uncomfortable to wear. He snatched the ornament from around his neck, and another peculiar thing happened. The light from the ornament shot straight into the sky going northwest, towards the center of the haze in the atmosphere above. Every villager nearby stopped their work to view the amazing phenomenon. Not desiring more attention than the Magnificent One was already receiving, Apeay hid the ornament beneath his hooded top as he said to the villagers, "Carry on with your work. I'm testing something."

They did as he said. All but one, who was running towards him.

"Hey! Finally found you!"

"Deslao?"

"Yeah. Why are you looking at me like that?"

"For one, what are you doing here? How did you get here?"

"That's a story for a headache later," said Deslao. "We've been looking for you. My brother and I, and these two strange guys that said, 'We must find Apeay.'"

"Okay, one thing I have to tell you," said Apeay. "Don't use my real name. Don't mention it at all. And what strange guys are you talking about? Where's Seldao?"

"So you have no idea who they are? Yeah, I thought something was funny about all this. One of them is over there." Deslao pointed to Hanjiah, who was still in the process of securing the nvekbarah.

"When he comes to greet me, follow my lead. You'll see what I mean."

Not a moment later, Hanjiah walked up on the two of them in the center of the village square. He bowed deeply before Apeay. But as he stood upright, he couldn't help but think that something was off with his appearance.

"Magnificent One…eh, you're uh…"

"What's the matter?!" Apeay's harsh tone succeeded in thwarting Hanjiah's suspicion.

"Sorry, it has been quite some time since you've honored us with your presence. And this fellow here with me, his name's Deslao. I didn't mean to bother you by bringing a stranger along, but I thought he might be of good use for the progression of Xeno. It could be a benefit for us to show him ways to help our advancements in this great village. And if it's alright, we'll be on our way to attend to a small matter."

Deslao's eyes widened. It was apparent he was about to speak. Apeay covertly shook his head at him, hinting for him to remain silent. Deslao secretly nodded back in agreement.

"What is this small matter you speak of?" said Apeay

"It's no big deal. I have some maintenance work that requires an extra hand. So like I said, I believe he has the necessary skill to assist me."

Apeay turned his back on them as he thought it over. He needed to get Deslao somewhere alone. At any other time, he would have had to make up an excuse. However, in this place, it was all but a matter of knowing who he was.

"He will not be assisting you any longer. He is to stay here for questioning while you go about your work."

"But, your excellency, I really need his help with this one. If you could..."

"This is not up for debate! And tell me, is this man alone or are there others?"

Hanjiah sighed with a slight bow. "Yes, Magnificent One, there's another. His brother is with Xendsvar. I hate to be the one to tell you, but, they're on their way to the Temple of Fushirajhe."

"In that case, your maintenance work will have to wait. You are to bring them to me at once. I will hear nothing else but your acceptance."

"Then it is so," said Hanjiah. "They will be with me when I return." As Hanjiah walked past Deslao, he whispered to him under his breath, "Keep quiet about the Apeay business. Don't know how the Magnificent One will react." Within a few jhentas, Hanjiah was in the air.

"Okay, what's the game, Apeay? What is it?" said Deslao

"What game?"

"All of this. We came here because of you. No, because my brother wanted to see you fly along with a group of people, that you said, from your own mouth, at the beginning of nadian season, that you had no interest in joining. Then somehow, we all end up here in some fake, made up land where you run everything."

"It's not how it looks. I'm just as confused as you are."

"Yeah, that's what you say but your little cohort, you claim ya don't know, who just took off to go retrieve my bro, didn't seem confused at all. By the way, he said not to mention Apeay to you before he left. So, how I see it, this is all some twisted game and you're at the center of it."

"I wish it was. At least I'd know what was going on. Deslao raised a skeptical eyebrow to Apeay. "I'm for real, man. I've never met that guy. I only know how to act because they gave me that title, 'The Magnificent One,' a few moments after they about killed me and Zaleah."

"Zaleah's here too?"

"Yes. She just left to follow some woman who thinks I'm her lover, or something, We don't know at all what's happening. So, how about you help us figure this thing out instead of assuming you know what's up?"

Deslao paced back and forth in front of Apeay. He knew Apeay wasn't a liar. If anything, Apeay was almost too honest.

"Alright, we'll wait," said Deslao. "And while we're waiting, you're gonna tell me everything, from when you hopped in that glineer, until the point where we met here."

"Thank you. I thought you'd never ask..."

CHAPTER 17

It's madness. Take me back to a simpler time, for this is too cold a future.

It was one of the most silent moments. Glinzoxe rides were typically full of ideological debates, relaxed conversation and talks of future provisions. However, on this night it was all anxious worry floating loftily hundreds of shawaras in the misty sky. Overcast clouds parted ways for mist that hung heavily like gaudy drapery blocking the stars from view, while each distinguished member of the diamond civilization stared intently at the region below, considering their next move.

The beam tunnels, usually filled with mynershas traveling back and forth throughout the region were devoid of traffic; random spheres of misty light signaled an occasional traveler immersed in an atmosphere saturated with trepidation. On the streets below, they viewed a great number of patrols marching in unfamiliar patterns.

"Thorel, is it my imagination or have the Legionnaires adapted a new patrol sequence?" Mr. Regalis asked.

"That isn't the march of Legionnaires," Thorel replied. "It's the march of an entirely different regime."

Palladus Hall was nearly in sight when they were met with two unexpected escorts.

"You're on an unauthorized route. Follow us or be eliminated." On their display was one of the glineer pilots, whom Jhar'ensky immediately recognized. He was one of many who took the Pledge of Diamond Excellence alongside Apeay under Council's witness during the early nadian season.

"How dare you issue sequence to a zennite!" said Jhar'-ensky. "You're metashiro Kentili Kejhii, are you not?"

"You are imperfect! I am Delignos 55 of Heylan Command. You will follow me and Delignos 54 to the proper landing zone, or be eliminated!"

"Understood," said Thorel through the transmit. "Take us to the landing zone."

"Perfection is law!" The display went blank.

"I'm shocked," said Jhar'ensky.

"Don't be. I know what you're thinking, but we're not in a position to put up a fight. This is a defensive transport built for defensive measures. Taking on two glineers? Unwise. That'd be us signing our own death tablet."

Jhar'ensky pounded his fist hard against the wall, "Heylan Command! I've had enough of this nonsense!" He peered out at the rear lights of the glineers they were that powerless to go against. "They must've been plotting this for more cycles than even you were aware of. I've been thinking this through ever since we left. Where did I miss it? How did they coordinate this takeover without me noticing a single thing?!"

"I'm more concerned about *what* they're planning next than the *how*," said Thorel. "Because if I'm right, the how will be answered the moment we enter Palladus Hall. And Valus, who was it that suggested the 'absolutist resolve'?"

"Nepcizyr did," said Valus.

"There's our first problem. Nepcizyr is provisional zenshiro, not zennite. He has no authority to cross the lines of both Legionnaire and Council. But somehow he did."

"I know. I spoke out against it, Thorel. Everyone knew it was wrong, but no one had the courage to speak up, except for me. The next thing I know, they tell me I've been removed from my position and threatened to take my life just for speaking against him. Almost half of Council followed along without a rebuttal, as if they were awaiting him to give the command. That's when a few others started to speak up, but they met their end. Some didn't know what to do and stayed, accepting whatever was to come. The rest of us fled Palladus hall. I'm not proud of it, but I fled with them. I ran for my life."

"So we're all giving into tyranny without a fight? How weak we've become!" Jhar'ensky hunched forward in his seat, mulling over the drastic situation in his mind. "It's a resolve, no matter what level of resolve it is. It's not a sequence nor is it an agreed upon motion to prompt a fixed sequence. Therefore, it can't be used to simply restructure the entire organization anyway an individual sees fit. They unlawfully broke the statutes that we abide by," said Jhar'ensky.

"I know that. But, the people, our fellow Council trapped within that building are too terrified to consider that truth. What are we going to do about them?"

"Talk reason," said Thorel. "Obviously they're going along because of fear. We will make our statement, and convince them otherwise. We have to convince them to resist."

On the ground another member of the newly contrived Heyliun Command was directing them to their landing point. As the glinzoxe came to rest, a fleet of ground forces surrounded them with their neutranevex's all aimed at the transport.

"I suggest both of you leave your neutranevex in the glinzoxe," said Thorel. "We don't want to look like we're ready for action until the time is right."

"I'd rather keep mine at the ready," said Jhar'ensky.

"And I'd rather you stay alive. You're the one most capable of helping me persuade the misguided members of Council to go against Command."

Jhar'ensky gave it a quick thought, grudgingly agreeing. "Alright, we'll leave them here, hidden and at the ready."

"Now you're thinking. I was going to suggest the control panel slide out."

"I know a better place. If they search this transport, that would be the first place they'd look. So, we hide them in the one place that makes the least sense."

"Behind the thruster tanks," said Valus.

"Exactly. One misfire there and the entire transport goes up in flames."

"Good, do it quickly," said Thorel. "It looks like they're getting anxious."

"Thorel...THOREL!"

A stout, dignified man paced back and forth before the established regime. All stood tall, proudly, arranged in precise order in the garden of the marble Palladus courtyard. Their uniforms were not ocean-blue and silver-lined as they would be in accordance with the Legionnaire format. Instead, they were gloss black, each one with its own varied streaks of one, two, or three gemstones running through them.

But the one who paced, his steps were firm with a youthfulness not seen from him since his days as a metashiro. Nepcizyr took one final step, and the ground quaked as he turned his shoulders square to the nose of the glinzoxe. His uniform was like none other in the regime, being a living armor of diamond-coated onyx. His body was one with it. Nepcizyr's forearms were adorned with compressed palladium, diamond-studded gauntlets. Flares of polychromatic light zipped around Nepcizyr at lightning speed.

"Come out that we may talk of the power of perfection! The power that only the loyal know of; the power the cosigners to betrayal will kneel to!" Nepcizyr stomped his foot, sending out a shockwave that violently shook glinzoxe. "The next time I will send you and all aboard into the pits of the tzierhan."

"Are we ready?" asked Thorel.

"Yes. Neutranevex secure. Open the hatch," said Jhar'-ensky.

The hatch to the glinzoxe rotated open. One by one, each one exited as the outlet passed by them.

Stepping out of the glinzoxe, they breathed in the super-fluous pomp and glory that suffocated the air about the garden. Before them, Nepcizyr stood splitting two rows of three large regiments of followers. Behind them the gates to Palladus Hall flung open as a cutting gust of wind forced its way through. Nothing but silence followed the raging wind. After a silent moment of undisturbed tension, Nepcizyr turned towards the gates. With his back to them, in utter disregard for their presence, he addressed his most hated nemesis.

"You were so sure of yourself. 'Sit. Be quiet.' You thought I sat because of the presumptuous Thorel? Far from the truth, little zennite. We were too close to our greatest achievement for me to care. And thank you for all your hard work. We couldn't have done it without you." said Nepcizyr as he turned to greet a supporter of their cause.

"Without who?" asked Valus.

"Don't try and con me like you did them. When he told me the plan, I knew exactly what his excellency meant when he said, 'My dokinja one is securing the empress.' An odd way to put it I thought, but it's all the same in the end, I guess...It's time for you to stop with the act. You've proved yourself worthy to receive the gift of diamond-engineered perfection. Only the lead affairs officer could track her location so quickly. And you brought them here as promised. Good work."

"Is it as I think? Thorel asked. "It is, isn't it, Valus?"

Valus lowered his head, then looked up towards the sky. "There's really no other way. I'm sorry, Thorel, but once you see his perfect plan, that it's the only path to an everlasting power great enough to be shared with all, then you'll understand that there is no fighting this."

"It's always there staring you in the face," Jhar'ensky said subtly, caught off guard by the words of his longtime friend.

"I knew it from the start. Ever since the great hearing of the Golden Era I knew something about you was off," said Thorel. "It's been you the whole time. Then today at the house. Why would you be there? How long were you there, hiding, keeping silent listening to us while we searched the house?"

"Believe it or not, I had just arrived not moments before you," said Valus. "Too bad your boy wasn't with you. Then we would've had everything we needed."

Jhar'ensky was vexed by this current revelation. "So then, if we had known their location, had we said it out loud, would you have used your neutranevex on us?"

"Not completely," said Valus.

"What does that mean? Answer me!"

"Only if needed. And I would never use it on full power against you. You know that. I was only going to knock you out for a little while if you didn't go along. But once I realized you didn't know his whereabouts, the request had to wait until a more opportune time. And that time is now. At least we have one person he wants. And, my friend, all you have to do is comply, and there will be a place for you, too."

"Friend? That's what I used to think you were. I don't want a place in this. To think I made a pact of kinship with you. That if anything were to happen to my family, you'd be the one to look after them like you did for me over the cycles. Well, being the performer that you are, you won't mind if I put on a demonstration," said Jhar'ensky, before dashing in front of Valus with a left cross, laying him out on the ground.

Nepcizyr laughed. "Ouch. He should've seen that coming. Lucky for him, we're the everlasting order." Nepcizyr stepped forward, reaching down to grab the hand of an unconscious Valus. "Your gift: *Zhimhonextiox Vallax gxostiox!*"

A gaseous vapor, sparkling like diamonds, went out from the crystal-lined opening at the top of Nepcizyr's gauntlet, vanishing into the body of Valus. Valus' eyes opened at once as he levitated to his feet. His Council attire rematerialized into a two-piece work of living diamond-coated onyx at one with his body, like the armor of Nepcyzir.

Before their eyes, Valus reverted to his youth, appearing as he did during his time as a Legionnaire. "It's amazing. I feel nothing. No pains in my body, almost like it's not there. The ride made me thirsty, and now I no longer have the urge for a drink."

"Was that technology, or some type of magic you used on him?" asked Jhar'ensky.

"Enough questions," said Nepcizyr. *"Gihan marxos heppe mingxan oct!"*

Gihan Patrol replied, "Gihan accepts this perfection."

"Follow us into the hall this instant for the new deliberation, where he's waiting. Try to run and I'll end you." Nepcizyr gestured with the swipe of his hand through the air. *"Yishing-mingxah!"*

Rows of Gihan Patrol faced in unison towards the outer gates. To the rhythm of their own march, they went in three abreast. In the lead was Nepcizyr in all of his splendor, feeling the great power and recognition that was due him, surging through his being.

"Why so much with the mystic tongue?" Jhar'ensky whispered to Rionazen.

"I don't know. There's no way they learned it from them either. Most mystics detest our Legionnaire-backed Council, even more so since we agreed to the Unified Leadership of Command, Unification of the Regions. And, from what I see here," Rionazen looked to her right and to the left, "these former Legionnaires have equal vitriol for the mystics as well. Nonetheless, we're going to put a stop to this tyrant here and now."

"You know that for sure, eh?"

"Yep, it's like a good dream I have."

"Oh, don't you worry, Honorable Zennite. Your career isn't over yet," said Valus, proudly strolling alongside Nepcizyr in full bravado.

"I don't speak with schemers. I have nothing to say to you."

"It's not a scheme, you nosy binnal. Our region was falling out of step with the ultimate plan. It's a good thing Command came along and regained control when he did, or we would be lost. This is the true future! The real perfected future! We'll be living with no more worries about resources running out, or people living with disease. No more death. We will flourish in a state of constant perfection."

"Perfection is the dream of mad men. Life is a matter of both ups and downs; for there to be life, there must be an end of all things. And in the future I advise you to watch your tongue in reference to me."

"Or what? Please don't bore me with any empty threats. If you think to end my life over a smitten ego, then let me inform you, I cannot be killed by a non-diamond like you. Not in this state. Soon the rightfully selected will be everlasting, just as we have become. Give up your resistance to the truth, come to things the right way, and you'll have a chance for an upgrade as well."

"Quiet, Valus that is for Command to decide," said Nepcizyr.

As they approached the inner hall, a second violent gust of wind thrust the heavy palladium doors open. A mighty voice called to them from within the main hall.

"Come in, so I may share this knowledge with you. Sit beside me, become one with perfection! Pledge loyalty to direction of Command, the Perfected One!"

Φ

Downstream, a gentle current carried them along the river. The air was slightly misted by whiffs of sharp poison, for the haze was heavy this day. Old, rotting trees stooped pointing the way ahead as the shadows increased. As they floated closer to their destination, Deslao noticed a strange phenomenon. The river seemed to be flowing in two directions from where it entered the base, being swallowed alive by the vast hollowed out cabera's head, and spit back out at equal time and speed. It was a perplexing sight that, when coupled with the bleak, haunting landscape of the region's borders, gave off an aura of divine desolation.

"It's been many cycles," said Xendsvar.

"What do you mean?" asked Seldao.

Xendsvar pushed the zabanghir aside the river bank with a long stick, where they stood at the bottom of a tall spiral stairway. "When we get to the top, I will show you the truth of this place. Many have forgotten and thrown out the ceremony at this temple, where we offered sacrifice that gave us the purity we desperately needed."

"A sacrifice? Like to a god?"

"Yes, the first of the balanced firmament, god Heylan-lexjheos and goddess Laeoxia. At one time, all did the same. But most are idiots now, listening to the 'Magnificent One', and following his methods that we, the Cabjah, reject. Because so many of our people no longer believe, the gods closed their eyelids over the skies and our waters became cursed."

"I don't want to call you a liar, but where I'm from, we don't sacrifice to any gods and our water is just fine so, I'm having a hard time believing you on that."

"You will see when I make the offer of life. We will drink from the waters that pour from the river of the gods."

"Sure, but you're taking the first drink."

They began their ascent up the long spiral staircase. As they rose higher it became evident to Seldao why Xendsvar agreed to go with him. It gave them a great vantage point to view further beyond the hills where they met. But if that was the case, then why didn't Xendsvar choose this location in the first place?

"Xendsvar."

"What?"

"If you were looking for us and Apeay the whole time, how come you didn't start here?"

"It was a feeling. And, I needed flowers."

"What are you talking about?"

"When we found you in the river, I was nearby collecting what I could find of the fading flowers that grow in the wild. Only wild flowers can be used in the ceremony. They are from the land, we are from the land. So, they are as they have been both before now and after."

"I have no idea what that means."

"I know," said Xendsvar. He gave a slight bow as they reached the zenith of the stairway pointing to the crossing into the temple. "This way."

Seldao looked about him as they took the half-reel trek towards the entrance. The hazy horizon silhouetted the massive temple with a bright aura. With each step, he observed the stones on the left and right of him going up and out in equal proportions of infinity. The outward angles of the building were a perfect inversion of the stones on the ground, causing the opening of the portico to appear to be without end. To Seldao, this was the ingenious work of shototus rather than that of the Cabjha. Upon reaching the entrance, a sweet aroma overwhelmed his senses.

Looking up, he noticed three symbols carved in strategic order on the mantle: hydrophena in the middle, with heliox left, inverted right, and quashiraz right, inverted left, producing a patsy equation, for the inversions made it only a theory and not solvable by any known strategic means. Could it be that these mystics knew more about *strategics* than he did? But Xendsvar couldn't keep up with his basic knowledge along the way, so it didn't seem likely. Maybe if he could talk to that lady by the pond himself, she could provide a sound explanation.

"Aren't you going in? Why do you stand there like that?"

"Can you confine the expanding sphere to the hydroxic axis?" asked Seldao. He was hoping to be astounded by a flash of strategic brilliance from Xendsvar that would explain an ageless mystery. However, he would have no such luck.

"You murmur foolish talk like Hanjiah. It means nothing to me."

"How disappointing. But it's interesting as well, for other reasons. Yes, big fella, I'm walking in. And I have more questions for you."

"What kind of questions?"

"Okay to start, what's with this 'Magnificent One' and why do you hate him so much? From what I've seen, he seems to do a lot to improve your land. A progressive thinker like me."

"Progressive? Hmph! He is unnatural, a tyrant and a liar. Unlike the others, there is nothing that I and the Cabjha want from him. He brought his wonders and seduced my twin into following his path. Never does he come through on his promise to her."

"You have a sister?"

"No..." Xendsvar hesitated to speak any further, for it was not a pleasant subject for him. But he saw no harm in telling one such as Seldao. "Not a sister, a twin. Her name is Xenzashii. We're the exact same cycle in age. Both her and I were discovered as abandoned children. She was found in the north beyond Xeno, I in the south. We were brought together by the wandering Cabjha mystics, whom I stayed loyal to, swearing an oath to protect my twin with my life. She, on the other hand, never took to their ways. One day, she became entranced by this, Heylan, as some people call him in blaspheme of the true gods, for his supposed miraculous devices. One day, I will find a way to deal with that perverter, and she will be free from his spell."

"A twin of fate, I see...Well, if you feel that way, why haven't you done something already? Don't tell Deslao, but between you and me, I don't believe he'd stand a chance in a fight with you. You're monstrously strong, and quite nimble for your size."

"If it was that easy, I would've done something long ago. That man is also powerful in a way that breaks the laws of nature. Many cycles ago, when I was a young man like yourself, I witnessed his true face and the terror of his power. A man in league with him, who now that I recall dressed strange like you and your brother, that man questioned the Magnificent One's ideals to the point of rebellion.

"The Magnificent One became furious, his eyes turned pitch black upon hearing his subordinate speak against what he called his 'golden gateway to the diamond infinity.' Enraged, he grabbed the man by the collar and threw him into the river, splitting it in half like a flash of lightning until his body reached the mouth of the Eostrezan Sea where he sank to his inescapable doom. At the moment, his back was turned to me, so I thought it best to attack him while off guard; an error in my judgment. Without thought, I lunged my blade towards his back, but before I could blink, he spun around faster than light snapping the blade in half. The wind from his swift movement was so powerful, it knocked me to my knees. He gripped my throat, asking me if I wanted to swim upstream as well. I may not have survived if not for Xenzashii's intervention. She begged him to spare my life. He did so, on one condition. That I and the Cabjha would not interfere with his affairs. And upon my acceptance of terms, as lead protector of the riverway, I alone would live there outside of the village. So now, you tell me what is so great about the Magnificent One?"

"When you put it like that, I understand why you're so adamant about this mission."

"You think that's what this is, a mission? That means your mind is like the unlearned. You think of life in terms of passing events because you don't understand that there is only one moment, that happens again and again. Now with our divine nature out of balance, there will soon be nothing left. A desolate moment with no time to know it." Xendsvar pushed Seldao aside, entering the portico of the temple. "You were so ready to find this place and now that we're here you aren't ready to learn the truth."

"Take it easy, I'm right behind you. See? I'm walking in." Seldao trailed closely as Xendsvar led him from the portico towards the center. Seldao looked about and marveled at the interior stone work. It was the reverse pattern of the outer stones of the courtyard. They were arranged in the order from the infinite to a finite point at the center. Engraved in the ceiling, floors and walls were symbols and symbol alignments he'd never seen before. Some of them were even outlined in silver, white gold, or palladium.

"This is a strange place for a group that doesn't believe in progression to meet up."

"We come here in obedience with what is above progression. You will sit over there, while I sit opposite in the reverse position," said Xendsvar, denoting a symbol on the floor.

"What if I don't? If I sit crooked, will the gods not like me?"

"Mock me all you want, but mock this ceremony and I may not find you useful anymore."

"It was a joke, fella. You should learn to laugh more. It's good for ya."

By looking at Xendsvar's face, it was obvious he found no amusement in his jesting, so he put it to rest.

Xendsvar opened his satchel and took out the wild zaitson flowers, placing them in a golden six-sided bowl in the center that had two small concave cutouts on the interior, on opposite sides. The bowl was fixed in place above an opening in the floor, wherein the end of the river could be heard flowing in and out of the foundation temple beneath them.

"Do as I do. After I give merit, the ceremony will begin. You must chant as I chant, the same words at the same time in the same tone." Xendsvar closed his eyes and spoke. "Laeoxia, Heylanlexjheos, great gods of the eternal essence, hear us and accept our offering that we may know life in balance with the nature of your wisdom:

"*Nadjhaah... orah, zilzehni-ajhenah... Nadjhaah... orah, zilzehni-ajhenh...*"

Seldao, being skeptical about anything involving mysticism, held silent as he watched Xendsvar chant on. He didn't know what this man expected to happen. He also did not wish to make a fool of himself.

"Feel free to join in at any time. The ceremony takes at least two, and I am but one man."

"I don't know," said Seldao. "This isn't my thing. I feel awkward just watching you. It's weird to me."

Xendsvar shook his head and stood slowly. He kept his back turned away from Seldao. "Is it too much to ask? I can tell you are an advanced thinker like Hanjiah, so to you, I'm slow. You believe I lack understanding."

"I never said that."

"You don't have to. I can tell. Everything I say is a joke to you. We might as well go back outside and scout. I'll continue this, with someone who appreciates the gods' gifts at some other time."

"Look, I just don't get it. It's like fairytales to me."

"I see. When you told me of your land, Estellar, is that correct?"

"That's what it's called."

"I thought of your Estellar, as a fairytale. That you were making up some wild story to convince me that you were of no use. But, when I considered that you and your brother did not die from the curse after being immersed in the river for longer than anyone has, I chose to believe you. What led you to come this way in the first place?"

"Finding Apeay, like we're supposed to be doing."

"Maybe, to find Apeay and the truth of the ceremony as well. When you stood outside, what were you looking at so intently? There was something intriguing you. Join in with me. Perhaps you'll find what you're looking for."

Seldao thought it over. He was, in fact, already walking among a land that should not exist, and yet there he was.

"Fine…I'll join in."

Xendsvar nodded and sat again opposite Seldao chanting, *"Nadjhaah...orah, zilzehni-ajhen..."*

Seldao did likewise, and in unison they chanted,

"Nadjhaah... orah, zilzehni-ajhenah... Nadjhaah... orah, zil-zehni-ajhenah..."

The reverberation of the chanting rose into the high ceilings, vibrating through the passageways and upper tunnels of the corridor. Suddenly, there was a breeze from all six sides blowing through the center, cooling the air above and heating the air below. The breeze spun tighter and faster as they continued the chant. At that moment, the flowers in the bowl burst into bright flames instantly turning to ash that slipped through the slots into the water below. A whooshing sound could now be heard over their chanting. From where the ash of the flowers fell, steam shot up into the air, into ducts in the ceiling.

"The gods are pleased," said Xendsvar. "Look upwards." Out of the upper tunnels on each side, a small current of water poured onto the temple floor. "Come drink the best waters of Xeno. Renew your strength with the waters of the gods."

At this point, Seldao couldn't think of any reason not to trust the man. He cupped his hands under one of the small cascades and drank. "This is amazing. The water is cool and tastes pure. Where I'm from, there are things we have to do to our water to get it like this. And you're right. I feel great! That's some technique you Cabjha came up with. I'll figure it out in time."

"The technique, as you say, was given to us by the gods. I doubt any person could understand their ways. You should be thankful there was enough zaitson for today's drink. Most days, there are not."

"Well, I am very thankful for you sharing this with me, but I will figure out how it works. Now, shall we scout?"

"That is why we are here."

Before exiting, Seldao put his head underneath one of the currents as it died down. The flowing of the waters ceased as they left the temple center through the same portico as they entered. Outside the sky was dark. Twilight and night shook hands and passed on the responsibility of the sky from one to another. Seldao looked up and saw a star that fell towards their direction.

"Hey, hey!" the star was shouting at them. "We have to put the show on hold for a while."

"Why are you here?!" Xendsvar shouted back. "Where is the one that was with you? Where is his brother?"

Seldao seconded his concern. "Yeah, where *is* Deslao?"

Hanjiah landed the vehicle on the grounds of the courtyard. "I tried to tell him, but he was very stubborn. He wouldn't listen to me and insisted that I take him to the village, where we ran into none other than the Magnificent One, who is fixed on not letting him assist us any longer. He also demanded that I bring you, and you with me to see him right away."

"That's not happening," said Xendsvar.

"Come on, man. Do you want to risk upsetting him? We just have to see him, say hello. After that, we go back to what we were doing," said Hanjiah.

"When we get there, I will talk. You seem not to be able to keep your mouth shut about other people's whereabouts. Who knows what else you'll tell him?"

"Pardon me for wanting to keep my life. You and your damn Cabjha seem to think the gods won't let you get killed. I'm not playing that game."

"I don't know. They do make some pretty fine water," said Seldao.

"Oh great he pulled the water trick on you, too?"

"You've participated in the ceremony?"

"Heck no. This is the closest I've ever been to this place. People talk about it though. Anyway, get in. I'm not trying to be caught by him out here."

Xendsvar nodded to Seldao. The two of them hopped aboard with Hanjiah, and took off for the village of Xeno.

CHAPTER 18

Ever so ardently, the elated Xenzashii skipped along the path. She was overcome with exuberant emotion as it had been more than a cycle since she last saw him. Now that the waiting was over, she began to imagine their life together, letting her conscious thoughts slip into daydreams. But her fantasy would be short-lived, as her senses had alerted her that she was not alone on this road. Using an old mystic trick she'd picked up from her caretakers, she made herself one with her surroundings, awaiting her pursuer to appear.

The footsteps slowed. She watched her turn left, right, to the rear and front again. This was definitely the one who was following her.

"Why are you spying on me?"

The lady turned to see but a shadow of a tree behind her. "You disappeared. That was sneaky."

"*I'm* being sneaky?" said Xenzashii as she emerged from the shadows making herself visible to the goddess. "Inside the village you were hidden among the commotion. But out here, anything more than a bvoljhio in flight alerts me. So, what are you doing, Goddess Lai? Does the Magnificent One not trust me anymore? Or is it you?"

Between their fixed gaze, the northern wind cut down the path to XiaPrazju. Her once pleasant face became as menacing as it was when she appeared to them in the fields. She was not letting anyone come between her and what was rightfully hers, no matter who they may be.

"He may come to you for advice, but in the end, he has chosen me to reign with him in the eternal bliss of pure perfection. You must know that. My love has shared so much with me. He's spent more time together with me than anyone, even you. I bet you don't even know his secret name."

"A secret name?" Zaleah couldn't fathom what Xenzashii meant by a secret name. But for the fact that she was confusing Apeay with another she had no knowledge of made her curious. She figured she'd trick Xenzashii into telling.

"The goddess knows everything, it's you who does not. So, show me that you know."

But, the astute Xenzashii, saw right through her trap. "You really don't know do you? Well, I'm not telling. If he hasn't told you, he must have a reason for it. You see, I care for him more than anyone. You can't replace that, and you won't replace me."

Fire burned within Zaleah. Xenzashii couldn't possibly fathom how much Zaleah wished to correct her; to tell her the truth of it all that Apeay was of her world and that the one she held in mind wasn't him. But there was still too much to find out.

"I'm not here to replace anyone. I simply wanted to follow you for myself to ensure you were doing as told. I advise and guide him, so I must be sure that his wishes are carried out. There would be no grand design without my wisdom. Did you think of that?"

Xenzashii pondered her words for a moment. "I guess didn't. As long as you consider me, I will. And..." Xenzashii let out a deep sigh, "it's just hard for me. He used to come so frequently. I would see him every phase, then the phases became further stretched apart until I started thinking he'd never come back. It's been almost two cycles. Where does he go? And this time, he returns with you, a goddess equal to him in wisdom and authority. Where do I fit into that? Will it be real for me this time, or will he leave me again? If you are his guide, then could you be sure to guide his heart towards me? I've done everything he's asked. All I want is to be with him, help him create his grand vision, the perfection of our world."

Zaleah was at a loss for words. The anger in Xenzashii's eyes had vanished into yearning and sadness. She felt for Xenzashii, but could not convey it nor did she understand why she felt it so deeply within herself. She had to switch subjects and quickly, lest she slip up and say anything that could give herself away. Zaleah averted her eyes around Xenzashii and pointed down the path. "How much further is it this way?

Please lead the way, and I will bring him here. Everything he does must stay on schedule with his routine. I believe he's fell behind leading to delays in his plan, and maybe that's why you haven't seen him in so long. I won't let that happen again."

"Really?"

"Of course. I am a goddess, after all."

"Thank you. Actually, we're here. XiaPrazju's been modified by the structural team to fit in with the grand design." Xenzashii made her way to the edge of the path where clusters of shrubbery were lined like Legionnaires at attention. She pushed her way through the overgrowth into a small unobstructed clearing at the center, where an opening revealed a descending stairwell.

Zaleah peered down into the opening, then back at Xenzashii.

"Is this for real?"

"Yes. We hid it so the Cabjha wouldn't burn it down."

"The Cabjha?" Zaleah wasn't sure what she meant. Then she remembered that there was a possibility that she should.

"Those stubborn mystics are stuck in the past. They're always doing something to try to sabotage my love's plans. But why? Who doesn't want a better future? You're his advisor, so what should we do? How do we stop them?"

"Ah, yes the Cabjha. I would suggest talking to them. Try to explain what it is, as it is beneficial for the future of everyone."

"It's hard to explain things to that group, because they're mostly morons."

"Don't say that about them. They're still people."

"Well, they are kind. And, they actually do a lot of good. But they don't know how to change with the times."

Now fully embracing her role as advisor and goddess to Xenzashii, she said, "They may be afraid. A lot of people are afraid of change. It's quite natural. Give them time. Allow them to see his works come to fruition and be patient. They may come around."

"If you think that's what's best, I'll try...This way, goddess Lai."

"After you."

The shaft went deep into the tzierhan. At the bottom of the stairway was a silver trimmed, dark crystal door. Xenzashii placed both of her hands on a small diamond in the center chanting in a singular tone, "*Mei'Rahjzeming jhaxejho hapnia-xhe.*" The doorway split apart, sliding open.

Zaleah had no idea why Xenzashii chanted like a mystic after ridiculing them for their ways, unless there was some other ancient language the people of the Xeno spoke that she never heard of. In all of her time studying the cosmos, it was only on the nights of the Hewlix Festival when that she heard the illuminated chants of the Aberan, some of whom were travelers and street entertainers. So, was her mockery intentional or something else? But there would be no reason for

Xenzashii to put on such an act for her. And in what way did the chanting enable the doors to open for them? The more she found out, the stranger things became. Therefore, her sense of urgency to uncover the mystery that would put them on their way was doubly intensified.

Past the entryway, they came across two guards standing watch on both sides. "Hey, Xenzashii, who ya got there with you?"

"Goddess LaLa'ila, counselor to the Magnificent One. She's here on his behalf to inspect our progress. He's returned, you know."

"Oh yeah, we know all about that. Even heard he was strutting with a different sort of gemstone on the side." He glanced over at the other guard who silently chuckling to himself. "I mean, he brought another traveler with him this time."

"You already knew?"

"You know how Hanjiah's team is with current events. Some say he brought a helper. But we thought something else."

"Well, then," said Xenzashii, "we'll be on our way to the main hypzerxhe. The miniature xhilheolleh is still there on display, right?"

"Yep, still in its place. How about you?" The guard smiled at his own reply, while the other guard snickered.

Xenzashii leaned forward, putting her face close to his, as she spoke in a low, calm voice. "Pay attention. You're a nice-sized man, with some nice-sized arms and shoulders about him. I've seen you around. You come into the village on import days, protecting the valuables, helping us fight off renegades. Most of the village women praise you for your strength and duty to our future perfection. But you see, I don't care about your subpar obligation. You think you're strong? I grew up training with my twin, who's a lot stronger than you. He made sure that by the time of our fifteenth cycle, I could survive all-out head-to-head combat with him. Tell me, would you like to enter the Compass of Nahlriax with him, or just me for leveling?"

The guard stared down and away as he shook his head.

"I didn't think so." Xenzashii glared at the other guard, who quickly looked away. "Now, apologize to goddess LaLa'ila for your embarrassing behavior."

"I apologize, goddess..."

"Call me goddess Lai. It seems that's all your small minds can handle to remember," said Zaleah. "You guards should be ashamed of yourselves for mocking her like that. She's been a big help to the Magnificent One and me since we arrived. We're grateful for her service. Maybe I should tell him of your conduct, and see how long you last in Xeno."

Nothing in all the tzierhan struck absolute fear in the hearts of Xeno's inhabitants like the mere thought of upsetting the Magnificent One. "I apologize, I didn't mean any of it," the guard said, not looking away from every detail on the ground beneath him.

"Sorry for letting these *baglagzh*-heads for hold you up, wasting precious time. Now, down this hall is the main hypzerxhe. If I'm right this is the day the lead zhebxhila instructs all ranges at once on cycle formation. Everyone should be there."

"Thank you, but about what you just said."

"About what?" replied Xenzashii.

"Fighting off the renegades," said Zaleah. "Is that who you thought we were when you encountered us?"

"Yes, and I apologize for the mix up. Their attacks have become more frequent after some of our own, mainly a large sect of the Cabjah joined up with mystics and bandits from other lands. But now that he's back, they won't last long. He promised he'd put an end to them and their meddling when he returned. Under your guidance, I'm sure he'll make good on his words."

Her words troubled Zaleah. The thought of "ending" a group of people was not something she wanted to be associated with. However, under her guise as the goddess she kept her reply vague. "As he will."

Xenzashii nodded in agreement. "That's enough of the unpleasant reports. It's time to show you what we've done. The model is straight ahead."

As surely as she spoke, it was the day of fused knowing. All subject matter crossed barriers under the wise instruction of lead zhebxhila, Martazumen. On this special day, the learning period extended well into the night, after the children were given a period of rest and play to prepare them for the extensive lessons.

Xenzashii wasted no time getting down to business as they approached the hypzerxhe packed full with children and young people, learning all they could with the hope that they would soon be chosen to participate in the new development of Xeno. She marched to the middle of the room and hollered, "Martazumen! Greetings everyone. I don't mean to slow you down but we have a very important guest among us. Please, welcome Goddess LaLa'ila, who has come on behalf of our recently returned Magnificent One."

"Well Xenzashii, I have no objection to the welcoming or the presence of one on behalf of the Magnificent, but you could stand some tact in your manner of grasping our attention," said Martazumen.

"I got, didn't I?"

"Indeed, in your own annoying way. And you are goddess...LaLa'ila, I presume? Welcome to Xiaprazju. What is your connection to the Magnificent One?"

"I'm his advisor. This is my first journey to Xeno with him. I usually stay back, keeping watch for the others who come to me. But with him achieving so much in such a short time, I thought it best to come along and see that he was doing so in proper order." Outwardly, Zaleah was a pillar of confidence as she disclosed her backstory to the unknowing audience. She even impressed herself in coming up with such an explanation so expediently.

"Is this so, Xenzashii?"

Xenzashii confirmed her backstory. "Yes, the Magnificent One told me himself."

"Then *that* is the secret to his knowledge. His own goddess to enlighten his mind. Goddess LaLa'ila, in your visit, will you enlighten us as well? Maybe share with us a little of the wisdom that you've given him?" Martazumen looked longingly into the eyes of the goddess, as did many others in that room, searching for an answer that they knew not the question to.

"In time," said Zaleah. *What am I thinking? In time? In time, they'll figure this out if I can't show them something greater than whatever it is they've already seen. Oh yes, the xhilheolleh.* "But first, I must ask you to show me something...Show me the functioning xhilheolleh. I would like to see it functioning for myself."

"Yes, your own demonstration. I did make word that they would. Martazumen!" Xenzashii shouted.

"I am not one of your field lackeys, nor am I slow. I was on it the moment she spoke. And for you goddess, please sit here in our most comfortable seat and look towards the center display. Everyone, listen well. We are taking a slight pause in the lesson for our special guest. She has requested a demonstration of our progress, and we will oblige. Goddess LaLa'ila, without further hesitation, we present the xhilheolleh, the great energy convertor. Now everyone, remember to keep your distance. Do not touch anything."

Two other zhebxhilas standing near the center lifted the drapery covering the device. There it occupied a space on a much smaller scale than what Zaleah was used to seeing within Estellar. Looking at the stout triple cut emerald model from this angle, it seemed to her as if it was incomplete in a way she couldn't understand. Next, they walked to the wall and stood equal distance from the center. Each of them took out a small cubed object and simultaneously pushed them into a cutout on the left and right of them. A panel on the lower side of the wall opened, allowing the most shimmering water Zaleah had ever seen to flow in as another panel in the base opened. It entered and gradually filled the reservoir around the onyx base, activating the miniature model. A familiar humming noise came from the model.

"Now we will give it a task, to show how much power this little marvel can produce. The lift over there is weighed down with a full load of onyx boulders. Even with using a triple easy-pull wheel, it would require the strength of a hundred men or twenty ahrvadigxa pulling at the same time to lift it to the surface. But with this..."

The other two zhebxhilas took out six quartz from their satchel and aligned them at the straight-angle between the xhilheolleh and the lift. They then took two other matching ruby-like gems, placing one in a cutout on the lift and the other on an attached alignment in front of the miniature xhilheolleh,

"Using not even a fraction of its potential power, the lift goes up at once."

The heavy palladium-coated lift shot up 60 shawaras to the surface. Everyone was amazed, though many had seen this once before.

"Who would think that one individual alone could master the inconceivable wisdom of this goddess?"

And, as the goddess looked about her, a peculiarity caught her eye. The eyes of the young children seemed dim as if a fog was over them.

At that moment one of the children shouted out, "I want a diamond statue at my hut too!"

"Vertriljzheo, quiet down. You said that last time. Shining child, you still have your gemstones confused."

"But zhebxhila..."

"Relax, child. We'll spend the last part of lesson focused on tzierhan gem types to help you along the way."

Zaleah examined the children further, and noticed many were exclusively focused on the xhilheolleh rather than the transport fixed in place, hovering at the surface.

"Thank you, Martazumen. That will be all for now," said Zaleah.

"You're very welcome."

He nodded to the other two zhebxhila. Slowly they eased back the alignment and the giant transport gently descended back to the underground compartment. As they closed the panels the water was removed from the base as if it flowed back into the wall. However, the impossibility of that physical feat must've meant it was draining somewhere below.

But, Zaleah had something else, other than the observable mechanics of the xhilheolleh on her mind. "Martazumen, do they always stare like that?"

"Stare? Who staring? Were the children staring at you in some type of way?"

"No, that's not what I mean. While we were watching the demonstration, I noticed many of them were focused only on the xhilheolleh. I want to know if that fixation is normal or not."

"If it is a fixation, I wouldn't know. We only know what he showed us. And, apparently that knowledge came from you."

"Not all of it." Zaleah, now realizing how much influence she held, made what was in her mind, a whimsical suggestion. "However, regarding the water, perhaps he's not using the recommended type for the xhilheolleh."

"You know, I thought it was odd, when they told me that this made use of the river water. I was under the assumption that the toxins in the water might take a toll on the mechanics in due time. Am I right, goddess Lai?"

Zaleah didn't know what to say. She had only mentioned the water as a part of a ploy. Now, the warning they gave, along with the extra protective measures, made sense. Just thinking that she considered scooping up some of the water for drink as it flowed into the base, while unaware of its toxic nature, made her feel lightheaded. She concealed her face, pretending to rub her eyes, inhaling deeply through her nostrils and out of her mouth to keep from passing out.

"He doesn't make mistakes," said Xenzashii. "I'm sure if it was going to be a problem, he would've said so. He's bringing the perfect future."

"Be careful, Xenzashii. Love is also blind," said Martazumen.

Xenzashii waved off his remark. "Are you satisfied Lai? Is it time to bring him?"

Playing her part, Zaleah assured Martazumen she would do her duty as a goddess. "I'll have a talk with my protégé, the Magnificent One, to make certain he's following my recommendations. Water should be pure."

Martazumen bowed. "We appreciate your wisdom. Thank you, Goddess Lai."

"Let's head back, Xenzashii. He's waiting."

"My pleasure... Martazumen, don't think I'm just some ignorant field soldier. I know the future when I see it. And have someone prepare a meal for the Magnificent One. Don't ask why, just do it."

Δ

"See what I'm saying? There's never been anything right since that night or that first day. I don't even know anymore. It seems my whole life has been jumping from one place to another. I don't even know who my real parents are. I was just found on a doorstep on some stupid cold night. Who does that to a baby? And now this."

"What are you talking about?"

"This is the second time that I can't get back to where I'm not even sure I belong. And, do you know why?"

"Good grief...why, Apeay?"

"Because there's no capsyints in Xeno. Not one! On top of that, my necklace is acting crazy again. And what if I *do* go back? I'm a fugitive, man!

"Alight, stop, stop all of that," said Deslao. "What the hell does that have to do with how you got here?"

"I already told you, fella!"

"Stop yelling. Some of the people are starting to check us out. You need to relax your mind; calm down. You didn't tell me anything that made sense. All you told me was that some man yelled at you from a box in your glineer. You got scared, so you ran off with Zaleah and hid in a cave where some lights from the cosmos made the stones turn into Xeno."

"You made that sound messed up."

"I didn't have to. Look, this is how you say what happened. This is how me and my bro got here: I chased Seldao because he was running like a fool around the foregrounds. So, a legionnaire started chasing us. Then, his ridiculous *fihgazz* ran into a cave on the foregrounds where he and I fell through a soft spot on the ground, down a waterfall into the river that's right over there. That's how we got to this Xeno place."

"You think that makes more sense than my story? You fell through a hole into an ancient place that not one person in the entire world knew about. You think that doesn't sound just as messed up as my story?"

"It still took me less time to get to it."

"And you're still an idiot. Why don't you go fall into fire somewhere?"

"Dang Apeay, what's the matter with you? We're all stuck in this...whatever this is until we figure it out. This ain't like you. Look, fella, you just sent that man back to get my bro, who's off at some cult temple with another person we hardly know that's been out looking for you. I'm not there to look out for him right now. Right now, I'm looking out for you. So come on, man! Get right! When they get back, we're going to see some woman who lives in a swamp who's gonna tell us why you're a hill we have to climb to get back to Estellar. And then we're going back!"

At first it was muffled, but soon it was clear. Whatever mood had overtaken him dissipated as he broke character, laughing out loud among the villagers. "Now *that*, sounds messed up for sure. I'm sorry, my guy. I wish I could explain it all. But, no one was there with me the first time. It's cool."

"Are you cool?" Deslao asked.

"Like a nadian night breeze...So, you met a lady who lives in a swamp?"

"Naw. We learned about her from a big fella named Xendsvar. He's the cult leader my brother took off with. He's a big, mean son of a..." Deslao peered over Apeay's shoulder into a remote alleyway going out from the heart of the village.

Apeay turned his head to see what had arrested Deslao's attention. The alleyway was empty, but for a few baskets of dried straw. "What are you looking at?"

"I don't know, man. I thought I saw someone."

"It was probably a bojo. Anyway, Zaleah should be on her way back. And when your brother gets here, we have to keep his big mouth shut."

"You know I know better than anyone. I might just punch him in the face for running off again. That'll keep him quiet."

"It's only because you care."

"Man if you weren't my friend, I'd swell your face too. I'm not soft like you."

"How am I soft?"

"You never realized, but I'd be out there some nights, seeing you and Zaleah sitting up on that mound with your head all curled up in her lap like a baby."

"What is up with you two? You know you and your brother would make good infiltrators. What else have you seen us do?"

"Not that, man! Ha-ha. I don't spy on anyone. I go out to the trails to train in private, and some nights you so happen to be there," said Deslao.

"Whatever. Let's head down this path a little ways until we're outside of the village. We'll meet up with Zaleah and be just far enough away to see Seldao arrive without him seeing us first."

"That makes sense. We do this, my fella."

Deslao and Apeay made their way down the path leading to Xiaprazju. Behind them, the villagers continued their work for the future, focused on improving and renewing the land. All moving here and there, but none out through the remote alleyway which moved on its own.

The straw in the baskets rustled as the winds whispered, "I see you. I see two. All together. What will we do?"

CHAPTER 19

If a choir had been present to sing a glorious song, the blood of the dead would transform into the flowers of rhashidhel, for the splendor was beautiful beyond terror.

Splashes of crimson gave a reverse sense of life to the formerly lifeless palladium and black panels lining the walls. All were kneeling, except for those laying out lifelessly prostrate. Those who knelt before Heylan declared as one, "Hail the Great Command. The Magnificent One is he. By the light of Heylan perfection has come. Hail the Great Command, for we are one with perfection!"

Above, on the very platform from which Jhar'ensky oversaw countless assemblies, there was one radiating with power. He stood tall, wearing a dark electric-cobalt, palladium lined top with a shrouding hood. The garment itself was a testament to the perfection of power with supporting alignments forged into its main seam, holding it firm in both a liquid and crystal state. A single crystal cord hung from the side, tying into his dark cobalt pants, where it intertwined with a sphere. Wrapping around his feet, reaching up to the shins he wore interwoven ribbons of polished palladium. With his back turned to his throng of subordinates, he lifted his right hand high towards the ceiling, clenching his fist, lifting his very being up a shawara.

"*XIAMNEHZOXNIAN, Zhimhonex*, **PERFECTION!**... *Zeppnarhazean mingxan octzje!*" A raging wind came from out from his being lifting the man's chest skyward. The wind crashed into the crystal shatraxia which crowned the central hall, shattering it to dust. In the atmosphere four colossal, violent cyclones materialized, merging with one another, to form a cloudy crystal haze. Out of the haze, violent electrical storms produced lightning of all colors, shooting straight up, higher into the sky. At their peak, they combined into one massive bolt that spun round in the mist. But it wasn't actually spinning, it was falling, like water down a drain. When the bolt reached the center of the haze it shot down towards Palladus Hall.

Jhar'ensky's eyes widened as he braced for impact. Rionazen did likewise, with one hand clutching the railing around the stands, and the other clinging to Mr. Regalis' coat sleeves.

Precisely before the unavoidable impact, the galvanic bolt dispersed itself into four separate bolts of scarlet, cobalt, emerald, and gold, striking the four empty corners which but a moment ago supported the shatraxia. There was a great quake. The temperature inside the hall skyrocketed, before winds from the outside spun about, bursting through the doors with a chilling icy breeze. At that moment, Palladus Hall transmuted before their eyes. No more was the lackluster gallery for monotonous debate. Every wall, both inside and out, formed a brilliant monument of gold, capped off by polychromatic light. Once a cubed hall, now a massive, translucent pyramid three times the size of the former building.

The spectacle was amazing as it was terrifying, urging more adoration from his devotees.

"Hail the Great Command, he makes all as new!"

The one resting loftily above lowered back onto a new surface of transparent lapis tinted diamond. Turning about, ready to give word to his loyal followers, he looked up towards the light moving in a shatraxia pattern, and removed the hood from his head to allow more light to strike his face. Lowering his head his countenance was a mystery to all. In his eyes was a void, but to Jhar'ensky the rest was unmistakably familiar.

"What?! Affi'hado...Command...is Apeay? Apeay, what happened to you? Where's Bexhiera?"

"SILENCE! This is my domain. No longer yours to rule in ignorance, nor will it ever be again. For I have returned the perfection. Soon it will be diamond again. It is my task to correct your countless errors from the highest realms to the lowest." The void in his eyes, materialized into a pair of diamond-like irises as he singled out Jhar'ensky. **"You did nothing to help then, nothing now, and if I had not come back to set things right, you never would have. You let those mystics come into my most cherished region, and create**

imperfections against the diamond law. I expected more from the emperor. Imperfect indeed!"

"Apeay, what is this?"

Rionazen tapped her friend on his shoulder, "Jhar'esnky, you have to accept it. He's not your lost son. Even if he was he'd be hard to get back now. Look at him, at his clothing; it's metallic as silver but flows like water. He has diamond eyes that have a look of rage that I've never seen in your son. Apeay was never like that. His gaze is distant, as if he's looking right through us. Besides, his hair is long, and tied in locks. I think he's even a few cycles older than Apeay. A look-alike, but not your son. But it is strange. How *does* he have Apeay's face?"

"I've heard enough about this fabled Apeay! I know all of all within every region. There is no one I don't know. Therefore Apeay is a mystical, manufactured imperfection to be located and wiped clear from this place."

Jhar'ensky could not believe his eyes or ears. Murmurs and whispers went up among those gathered within the hall but out of dread they kept their voices low, for this one had already obtained their respect, admiration and fearful reverence.

"I left you to do as I instructed for merely an instant, and what do I find when I return? A COUNCIL OF IDIOTS TRADING IN THE PERFECT LAW FOR IDEALS OF A NON-EXISTENT NATURALITY! There is no naturality! I know because I saw it come into form. I know where your im-

perfect thinking was contrived; dreams of the ignorant mystics and the fools who listen to them. But soon, mystic ways will be destroyed. I've spared their imperfection for far too long!"

"If I may ask, Command, what is this imperfection you speak of?" asked Thorel. "You talk down on the mystics, but I hear your followers and just now, even you speaking in their language. How can you take from their culture and at the same time be against them?"

"You speak the very essence of what I mean by imperfect thinking. You have it backwards. We speak the highest level of Bianzu Directive. What they speak is a perverted, blasphemous mockery; an imagined duplicate of the real. All the while they engage in inane riots and rebellions!"

Rionazen responded in a tone as if she were counseling a tyro. "I understand you not liking the riots. No one did. I was there when it happened, all those times of unrest, some of it extreme resulting in needless casualties. But that was back then. Today, they've become an essential part of the day-to-day life in our region. If anything, it's you who's the imperfect one. So much secrecy from your followers, betrayals, chaos and pointless killings. How is that supposed to bring perfection? You're shoving your deranged dream down our throats, is what you're doing. Our Tzierhan may be imperfect, as you say. But that's what makes it grand. There's room to improve. It gives us a chance to grow together, to learn together. If you ask me, that is perfection as it should be. You'll destroy the lives of our people if you continue this way. They'll be crushed under your supposed perfect rule."

Thorel hoped that her words would inspire a few others to speak up. However, all remained silent, obedient to the will of Command.

"No. You dream. I remain awake for all cycles. You know nothing! I, and only I kept all alive to this very day from the first. You were nothing but ignorant children of unintelligent speech who couldn't even feed yourselves when I first found you. Everything you know was given to you. But it seems to me that now under your own advanced and greatly flawed forgery of order, cosmic positioning, and social existence, you think you know something. YOU ARE IGNORANT TO TALK TO ME OF PERFECTION WHEN YOU'VE ABANDONED THE VERY FOUNDATION OF IT'S BEING! So much power, and energy from my own essence it took to create this. You can't even fathom what I had to endure to ensure the Tzierhan would have the chance to flourish, to become the shining gem that it is."

"You think that gives you the right to decide the fate of everyone? How can you be so arrogant to think that you can dictate the future for all?" said Thorel.

"Because..." Command stepped down from the platform to stand directly in front of Rionazen, **"there wouldn't be a**

future for anyone if not for me. Your lack of gratitude for what I've accomplished shows me how little you know as you attempt to delay what can't be stopped. For that alone, I would end your very existence if it weren't for your role to play."

"Roleplay alongside a maniac and his mad regime? You don't know me at all, if you think I'm joining forces with your illegitimate Heylan Command. I don't care how powerful you may be, I'll go out fighting before taking a knee to your rule. Everyone listen to me!"

Before she could utter another word, the crystal cord bound to the diamond rope on Command's uniform unhinged and spun about, shooting directly towards Thorel. They wrapped around her face faster than she could react. The ornament attached to the other end of the cord gagged her, releasing a vapor of diamond light from its core, rendering her unconscious.

"**How wrong you are**. You don't know how much I've admired your fighting spirit from the first. Yes, I know you well, my empress. It's who you were meant to be from the beginning. We'll finally be back where we belong."

Jhar'ensky rushed to Thorel, who lay unconscious on the diamond floor. He tried hard to remove the cord from around her face, but the harder he pulled, the tighter it became as it began to burn his fingers. As he yanked his hand away, he noticed that the ornament had something etched in its center.

Leaning in for a better look, he read the faded lettering in the middle of the ornament:

DREAM OF ZJVXENOZB

"Dream of... Zjvxenozb? That's not what this should say." Looking up at the apparition of his lost son, Jhar'ensky pleaded, "Please, my son, if you were upset with me, you could have told me. But this has to stop! Look what you've done."

"First you annoy me with your incompetence. Now you mock me to the point of fury! I, am, Heylan Command. The one you speak of is a fantasy conjured by ludicrous mystics in an attempt to destroy the flawless design. When I find this false manifestation of a being, I will destroy it! And since you speak of this ghost to me without regard for my being, you will be as one yourself."

The ball dislodged from Thorel's mouth and hovered above Jhar'ensky's head, glowing in various gemstone hues out from its vermillion core. At this gesture, he finally realized the truth. Though he felt every bit of Apeay coming from him, this outraged man was not his son. He was not Apeay.

Command stretched his hand out in alignment with the ornament. **"An imperfect emperor has no place in the return to perfection. No place in my realm! You, and the ignorant ones like you will be no more."**

"I don't think so. We're not all so easy to intimidate as your corrupt Council and these disgraceful, so-called Legionnaires," said Enjevix marching into the inner deliberation hall with his neutranevex trained on Command. Following behind came a throng of the formerly dismissed Legionnaires, along with Legionnaires withdrawn from service from the neighboring regions. Also, there were those from the previous Golden Era, together with the Xenadin and Aberan mystics, and Shototu Ju-Makana at his side to form a small regiment.

"A pathetic sight you all are to my eye. Enjevix, my "diamond seeker", who should be with us in perfection, has instead turned his weapon against me? Is this why you haven't captured this mythical being? Did their enchantments persuade you to join them in their insurgence?"

"I was wrong! It was a mistake to think you were for right. You never believed in a proper and descent future for all. I knew it on that day, when I saw you for the monster you are. All he wanted to do was help and you sent an order of death upon him. Then, you had my best legionnaire and friend killed for protecting him. I could not be a part of that future anymore no matter how perfect it may be. And he's real. Very real. Don't expect me to do any seeking for you anymore. Instead of searching for Apeay, I've been putting together a team of my own. Besides, even if I did know his whereabouts, I wouldn't tell you."

"I should've known. You've always been hesitant to carry out your tasks; too concerned with what is fleeting over what is eternal. And I see my chosen shototu has chosen to remain in imperfection as well."

"I choose to think for myself, thank you very much, you damn crazy fool," said Ju-Makana.

"I'm crazy? You reject immortality and call *me* crazy? To think, you could've helped me alter the very fabric of existence beyond the Tzierhan like you wanted to so long ago. We could've perfected the entirety of the cosmos. But now you will perish, along with rest."

"No, he chose right as did I. To stand against you and your twisted dream!" said Enjevix as he dialed his aim squarely between Command's eyes.

"If that's the future you desire...Here it is." Command stretched arms wide as if to welcome what he knew was to come.

"Jhar'ensky hit the floor!" Enjevix shouted before sending three rapid hytradilihan rays from the neutravenex straight towards the head of Command. Enjevix was nothing short of a flawless aeroxia, removing an infection with precision when holding a neutranevex. Command, however, would not be upstaged.

With the slightest glance, Command reversed the hytradilihan rays, bending backwards from his face, into the unknown center of the ornament. With another glance, Command repositioned the ornament to sit directly above Enjevix's head.

"There are no mistakes." Command opened his hand in alignment with the ornament and it became like golden fire. A searing flame went out from the fire to the top of Enjevix head, incinerating his flesh so fast that his body became as one of light.

Perhaps it was his strong Legionnaire's spirit that allowed him to briefly remain intact. But his body of light began to fade as he turned towards Jhar'ensky and spoke, "Here, between the realms, I can see it all. Apeay, your Apeay, he's alive. He's the same child that doesn't like coming home right away, and so much more. He's a noble dream. That's why Command can never destroy him. He's an anomaly that can undo his supposed perfection. That's why he fears his existence..."

"Enough!" With a wave of his hand, a strong gust of wind dispersed the remaining light into nothingness. ***"Gihan, Delignos, Nulia, yesh hepnianox xhioranzhe gxos astiox!"***

All of Heyliun Command: "We accept this perfection!"

In rows of two they marched out of Palladus Hall while Command gave further instructions to his dokinja two, Nepcizyr.

The marching unit passed by Jhar'ensky, who was seated by Thorel. He attempted to revive her from her deep sleep, but she could not be awakened. The spell of Heylan had trapped her essence trapped in a realm he couldn't speak to.

"Just grab her and run. We'll cover you," said one of the Legionnaires who remained loyal to the former Council.

"I'm on it," said Jhar'ensky. "Is this everyone?"

"We're half those of who remain. The others are securing whatever armory and vehicles they can find. We're not letting them go through with this."

"What is it? What's his aim?"

"Eternal life, so he believes," said Ju-Makana. "An eternal life no one will know exists. It's all contained within hidden designs for our region. Thorel discovered them during one of her investigations."

"I wonder why she never told me."

"She probably didn't know who to tell at the time. And there was something else she discovered. A complex model of our universe and a double pyramid device in a container that once belonged to Perinzel Shallhir. The symbol arrangements were too complex for her to decipher, so she generated copies and sent them to me. After deducing the alignment in reference to the setup of the region, I discovered an existence above and below. The one we find ourselves in is like an altered continuation of the tzierhan below. And it's been around longer than time itself. Only, not in a physical way."

"Then in what way?"

"It's a mirrored existence in the space between time. It's part of our past that exists in a place that no longer exists in our present."

"I don't understand."

"In all my time as a shototu I thought I knew all there was to know about existence, just to find out that it was only a small door leading to more than any advanced strategics or multi-shape symbol alignment could teach me. The symbols don't lie. It exists. And when he activates the last sioleh, the energy conversion will shatter through the space between, pulling that space to a close; the space vital for movement in all places at all moments."

"So, what does that all mean?"

"There'll be no movement and no time to know it. For his *eternity* to work, he has to keep time from moving forward. He knows that immortality is not enough when ya got time. Because where there's time, there's entropy. He's ending time to create the perfection of nothing."

"It's a good thing we didn't finish the last sioleh."

"But he did. When I read through the hidden logs, I found that it was an early construction with the foundation laid in Estellar many cycles ago. With all that time, it's likely it was completed. He didn't want the ruins gone to build the sioleh. We wanted them gone to reveal it!"

Jhar'ensky's eyes widened. "So it's already completed?"

"Yes, he did it all with or without us. We're merely tools of progress to him, and nothing more."

"Then we were all fooled from the start. The constant push for improvement to the unification and division of the people within our region, it was all him. I see that now. But his face, it's my son's face. How? I don't get it!"

Ju-Makana observed Jhar'ensky slipping into a state of shock. He had to snap him out of it.

Ju-Makana shouted, "Hey man, if we don't take action right now, you're never going to see your actual son or Bexhiera again! You hear me Jhar'ensky?!"

Jhar'ensky shook his head, snapping out of his daze.

"Indeed, my friend," said Jhar'ensky. He knelt down to retrieve the still unconscious Rionazen Thorel. "Alright, I've got her. Let's go." Oddly enough, Jhar'ensky felt a change come over him as he struggled to get to his feet. He was not a weak man by any means. Even in full armor he could manage to outmaneuver many of the younger Legionnaires. "What has she been eating? It's like lifting a boulder." His legs were hard to move. He felt as if he was trying to force his way through a swamp of waist high clay. No matter how hard he tried, he couldn't break free from his position.

"FOOLS! Your limited knowledge blinds you! Each person is a place unto themselves with energy unseen. And I've concentrated yours three times over. All of you are fixed on the spot where you stand. As for my empress..."

Winds from every direction rushed in, lifting Rionazen away from Jhar'ensky, into the arms of Command. **"She goes where I go. Perhaps some of you still have a chance to**

repent and be perfected at my great return to the highest. But in your state of delusion, I doubt it. I will see you never again."

Light from within the ornament engulfed Command on all sides, morphing into a flaming double pyramid with a highly polished blue-silver vehicle in the middle. In a flash, the fiery apparition vanished then reappeared, flying overhead of the marching men, torching the skies.

"What now?" said Jhar'ensky. "There's no one left who can stop him."

"Ha. He told me all I needed to know. Bokshan, toss me your neutranevex. It will seem a great deal weightier than usual, so give it a good heave," said Ju-Makana.

"You don't have to tell me. I've been fighting just to keep the right side of my body up straight since he did whatever he did to us. Here you go." Bokshan unslung his neutranevex and put all his might into tossing it over. Ju-Makana was brought to the ground under the weight of it as he caught it in mid-air.

"Ungh, man that hurt."

"Are you alright?" Bokshan asked.

"Yeah, I'm fine. Just old. So, you want to play with graviton, Mr. Command? We'll see whose knowledge is perfect today. Jhar'ensky, it ain't over yet."

∞

"Fire! My hut is on fire!" Flames shot up the villager's hut as the people around gasped, running to their aid. The fire came out of nowhere and it was spreading fast, leading many to believe it was yet another of the Cabjha's attempts to abolish the works of the Magnificent One.

"Those mystics are at it again!" one shouted.

"I swear we're better off without them. They do nothing but complain. Where is their progress?" said another. "It's a good thing he came back when he did. He'll deal with them."

"Yes, he will. But, where did he go?"

They had only made it a short distance outside the village when they saw the smoke rising. Apeay gazed at the embers flickering in the air, unsure whether to stay hidden or investigate the matter.

"What do you think it is?" said Apeay.

"It's a fire. Can't you hear all that screaming and hollering?" Deslao replied.

"I'm asking, what do you think happened?"

"It doesn't matter, we're not in it, we're good. Just keep your eyes on the sky for that floaty thing carrying my bro. That's all I care about right now...speaking of which, look!" The rotating vehicle was on a steady descent, heading their way. "Help me get their attention. Hey, Seldao! Seldao!"

"Stop, Deslao. We want them to land in the village first."

"Naw, man. I'm not letting my bro get burned up in a wild-fire. Seldao! Over here!"

"Who are you yelling at?" a voice asked from behind. Des-lao turned around to see another familiar face along with a new beauty.

"Zaleah and… a lovely friend?" Deslao said with a grin. "So, Apeay wasn't lying after all."

"Who are you? And who's Apeay?" asked Xenzashii, doing her best to play off the fact that Deslao was using their real names. Up until now, they had an unspoiled cover and couldn't risk Deslao blowing it for them.

"He's new to Xeno, and in a bit of shock with the recent wildfire," said Apeay as he nudged Deslao. "It's making him a bit delusional."

"I agree," said Zaleah. "We should return him to the village and help his people." In her eyes Deslao could see she was urg-ing him to follow her lead. However, Deslao was not interested in putting on a ruse. All he wanted was for him and his brother to return to Estellar.

"I'm not doing that, Zaleah. We've found him, so we're out of here."

From above, seated in the low hovering nvekbarah, Seldao looked toward the village to see who was shouting his name. In every direction, the people of the village were running back and forth, carrying large buckets of sand to dump over the hut to suffocate the flames, but none that called out to him.

"Did you hear that?" said Seldao.

"No," said Hanjiah.

"I heard it," said Xendsvar. "It came from over there, just beyond the village."

Looking in the direction of Xendsvar's gaze, he spotted them, while Hanjiah kept watch on the commotion below.

"I thought you Cabjha were done with all the sabotage after the last encounter."

"Why are you blaming us for the fire when any careless person could've caused it?! When we make a vow, we stick to it. We have a code, you know."

Hanjiah gently guided the nvekbarah around the pillars of smoke to where the call had come from.

"That's good to know, because the one hollering at us is standing right next the Magnificent One himself."

"The Magnificent One?" said Seldao as he looked at the man Hanjiah spoke of. "I see…"

Xendsvar observed him as well, "Yes, the Magnificent One, it would seem." He didn't waste time waiting for the nvekbarah to land. While still several shawaras above, Xendsvar leaped out, abruptly crashing onto the ground, intruding on the four standing below. It was so sudden that the four of them stopped their chatter.

"Are you angry or surprised that I'm not out by the river-way?" said Xendsvar "No surprise that you, Xenzashii, found your way to his, like a lost pet."

"Xendsvar, stop it! I asked him to spare you once before. Why would you test him again?" said Xenzashii.

"I test him, because I don't know him."

"I am the Magnificent One. Leave us now!"

"I don't think so! You look like him. That is true. At first glance, I thought you were him. But, there is one problem. The Magnificent One is an unnatural being. So much so, that even his scent is strange. He smells like metal burning in a furnace. You..." Xendsvar inhaled deeply as he stood above Apeay. "You smell like flesh and blood. And your eyes are nowhere near as raging as his. Xenzashii, if you weren't so wildly captivated, so desperate for him to return, you'd have noticed as well. You better tell me who you truly are before I take my revenge for all of his perversions through you."

"Really now?" a voice spoke from among the trees on the right side of the path. "Did you already forget why I sent you out?"

"Who's there?" said Xendsvar.

"First, answer the question." The voice was now coming from the trees on the left side of the path. Who is he? Did I send the wrong person or are you really so entrapped by your anger that it has blinded you?"

Taking what was said into consideration, Xendsvar looked him over again.

"You are… Apeay?"

Deslao felt exasperated. "Yes, he's Apeay. By the gods you swear by, he's Apeay! I'm here, my brother's here. Now, what do we need to do to get home?!"

"Apeay!" Seldao hurried over to join the crew after the nvekbarah came to rest. "Or perhaps the Magnificent One? You know, I've read about anomalies like this. But they were only in theory. I'll need to borrow a sample of your hair when we get back to Estellar."

"How could you do that to me?!" Xenzashii screamed. "I was so happy. Why?" Tears poured from her eyes as she looked upon the image of her heart's desire.

"Young lady, do you think it's the end?" Out of the trees on the path came an elderly woman. Her appearance was one of preserved beauty. Even though she appeared to be old, she did not look as if she was aging. She walked with a slowness that comes with seeing life for many cycles. "You'll be just fine. All things will be made new again."

"No, I won't be. He's never coming back for me." Xenzashii glared at Apeay with sorrow. "That's why she's with you. You two have been playing me the whole time. Fine. I don't need anyone!" Xenzashii took off running away from the village, away from all of it.

"Please, Xendsvar, go after her. Trust me, she will be fine. We need her, but right now she needs you. Xenzashii is just as important to this as everyone present," said the elder woman.

"You're asking me to bring her back after the pain they just caused her? He may not be the Magnificent One, but his image is too much like him for me! Why didn't you tell me when we came to you?" said Xendsvar.

"If I did, would you have gone out in search of him?"

Xendsvar, now understanding her reasoning for keeping it hidden from him, exhaled heavily. "Not likely."

"It's not their fault. All of this is part of the restoration. How many do the Cabjha require for a full ceremony?"

"Six. Why do you care?"

"To make you consider something, perhaps. Something you forgot. And right now, we have five and she makes six."

"We have six here."

"You can't include him," said the elder woman, pointing at Apeay. "His role is different. Why is it always so hard after the next to remember?"

Xendsvar looked upon Apeay with disgust and shook his head. "There are more of the Cabjha that I'm sure would be willing to fill in."

"That may be, but they are not of the essence of you and Xenzashii. I have only met you once before. Now, have I told a lie somewhere? Will you not help with the restoration?"

Xendsvar considered her words carefully, and thought it best to stay the course. "It is only because your words have been true so far, that I will return with her. After this is done, I will take her away from this place."

"Thank you, our most royal guardian. I promise I will help you find a better place for both her and yourself."

"Hold on now," said Hanjiah. "I don't believe in none of that Cabjha trickery, and I ain't going into that temple."

"It's not a temple," said Seldao. "It's some type of purification apparatus. The water that came out of that place was amazing. It was purer than the refined waters from the Estellar canals."

"As it should be," said the elder woman. "Your explanation of the place is funny."

"Why? That's what it is."

The elder woman laughed. "Why is it always a new name? 'temple', 'apparatus.' Was the water really that good?"

"Yes, it was fantastic."

"He drank it up like a fool," said Hanjiah.

Indifferent about what Hanjiah had to say, the elder lady sauntered over to a large fir resting at the side of the trail. Leaning back a bit, she looked up to the drooping branches, scratching her chin like an old man with whiskers. "Young lady, where were you at the beginning of this place?"

"We're from Estellar," said Zaleah.

"That's not the meaning. When this was the place you saw, where were you?"

"If you're asking how we got here, I'm not sure. We were in a cave, then the cave became a place somewhere over in those hills."

"Yeah, after I woke up from a strange dream," said Apeay.

"Should I have known?"

"What'd you say?"

"Will you take us to the place from which you came?"

"No, lady, he can't," said Deslao. "We're supposed to be going back to Estellar, not going more places. I'm tired of all this riddle-talk. If you're the one who sent for us, we've completed the task. They found us, we found Apeay. We go home."

"If I were you, I'd listen to the one who sent for me."

Deslao sighed. "Why not? If that's what it takes to get back, then yeah, I'm listening."

"With all present, we travel to that place. Be it a temple, or apparatus you will find it there."

The entire time since the elder woman appeared, Apeay had been studying her every feature. Nothing about her face or appearance was familiar to him. Even her voice was unfamiliar. However, he felt a strong connection with her.

"Have we met before? A long time ago?" asked Apeay

The elder woman smiled ever so faintly. "There's no such thing as a 'time ago.' Either you know a person, or you do not.

One that always sleeps, faced with one that never has. I wonder, will he ever come to rest?"

Apeay shook his head. "I'm starting to agree with you Deslao. Her riddles are making my head spin."

"Why should I speak different? As you say, you don't know me. But you will. Take us to the place from where you came, Apeay, and everyone will return home."

Apeay looked at the nvekbarah resting on the ground. It seemed to be a less complicated vehicle than the glineers he was accustomed to. After taking a closer look, he was sure he'd be able to figure out how to operate it with some guidance.

"Is there a starter on this or do we use the wind?" Apeay asked.

"Its operation is all a matter of vibration," said Hanjiah. Pulling out a small slotted spiraled tube, Hanjiah said to Apeay, "This is all you need. It's just a matter of matching pitch with elevation. How good are your lungs?"

"That won't be necessary," said the elder woman. "Did you really forget?"

"What do you mean forget? It's the only thing big enough for us to travel in."

"This part of you I miss. The wonder, the innocence…" The lady took time to observe a bewildered Apeay standing there, before proceeding. "Are there any shapes you haven't seen before? You must remember." The lady approached Apeay, snatching the ornament dangling from his neck.

"Woah, lady. Give that back."

"It's funny, this thing. I thought it might burn me, but here I hold it in my hand. Perhaps it's broken. Is that what's going on here? No, I think not." The elder woman tossed the ornament back to Apeay. "Take us there, Apeay. Bring everyone, Xenzashii, Xendsvar, bring us all. You know what to do. Look above you."

Apeay looked up at the haze in the sky above, but could not, for his sake, understand why she instructed him to do so. The haze was all there was and nothing more. It was a strange haze resting low, stretched out over the horizon in four different directions. It seemed to be the largest at the top, shrinking to almost nothing at the center below. "All at the center below," he said to himself. And then he knew. Somehow, without knowing how, he knew exactly what to do. Apeay took his ornament and tossed it up over their heads in alignment with the center of the haze. The ornament froze in midair, spinning about.

As the ornament spun, Apeay stretched out his hand in alignment and shouted out loud, *"Zhyeshiax onex vihvoxozh maingxozhi!"*

Cerulean light emitted from the ornament in twelve symmetrical directions, half going upwards the others down.

"Nothing less than amazing. All the stories you told me about your childhood. It's all true," said Zaleah. "But when did you become a mystic?"

"He's not a mystic, but a star speaking a language he once knew before he was born. As the twin stars draw near, he remembers more of what he forgot, and becomes more of who he is, than who he is now," said the elder woman.

"Everyone come close," said Apeay. As he looked over his shoulder to see where everyone was, he noticed that Deslao's eyes were fixed intently on the floating spectacle above them. "Deslao, what's up with you?

"I was hoping nothing strange was gonna happen, because I've been scared of that thing since we were kids. How close are those lights going to get to us?"

"It's alright man," said Apeay. "I think I've got this now."

"You think? You better know."

Deslao was one of three fixated among them. Hanjiah was studying the angles between the beams of light. Even though they never fully formed, what was missing intrigued him, and then he understood. What was a light show to most, to Hanjiah was symbol alignment at its finest. "A nvekbarah materialized from the elemental remnants of the first cosmic alignment."

"Just what I was thinking," said Seldao.

"I really don't know what it is," said Apeay "But I'm know how to control it. Lady, how did *you* know I could do this?"

The woman looked away from him towards the village where the fire raged on. "Do I forget with the rest?" Then she waved her hand saying, *"Seh'ah jhevaxonique."* A windy mist blew over the area putting out the fire. "Now, will we spend forever in this spot or will you take us?" said the elder woman.

"Yeah, Apeay, how about giving me a ride?" said Zaleah. She squeezed Apeay round his waist. "C'mon, my guy, let's go. Make it work."

Lifting his arms, Apeay spun them in opposing directions. The light became greater, enveloping them all within the invisible design. Then, with a movement of his hand, lit by the ornament, the luminous vehicle took them away on a path of light bound for the Temple of Fushirajhe.

CHAPTER 20

If only my life were as long as my heart is big, I would live forever with you.

From the time they were young, he protected them. On some occasions, when they went to foreign lands to scout, it was their ability to remain hidden that kept them alive. Therefore, he had learned how to be stealthy despite his size. A skill he implemented to sneak up on one he trained, for she was a bit faster than he, and he didn't want for her to run off a second time.

It burdened him to see her in this state. There was not a day that passed without him feeling that he should've been stronger or somehow faster on the day of his banishment to the outskirts of Xeno. Thinking that if he had been able so somehow overpower the Magnificent One, he could've shown her the right path. Now this he had to deal with; his utter failure to protect Xenzashii at all times. It was the sacred vow he kept for their caretakers, who died from the curse of the river. Words would not come to his mouth, as he watched her weep atop a large stone in the open field.

But a few jhentas later, Xenzashii stopped crying and sat herself upright on the stone almost becoming one with its still nature. Xendsvar kept watch in silence, still pondering what to say to the one he failed.

"Leave me alone."

"When did you see me?"

"You can't be serious." She wiped her face clean. "You taught me how to navigate and seek with all my senses, and you didn't bathe today. Your Cabjha mischief must be more important to you than smelling decent."

"I almost want to say, 'Alright, if that's what you wish.' Then leave you here and walk off. But, I'm a man of dedication and loyalty. Maybe it's something you can't understand while you accuse me of mischief... I did the best I could."

Xenzashii kept her place, unmoved atop the stone. "Loyalty...loyalty is foolish. What good does it do a person? You hear time and time again that next time is the last time you say goodbye. Then they just say goodbye again. And if that's not enough they tease you by coming back, but not at all."

"Xenzashii, please, that man you hold on to is no good. Can't you see that now? He made so many promises, and where is he? Is he here to fix all the problems his so-called progress has made for us? Our people are beginning to turn on each other for a chance to participate in his perverse fantasy, while the land is dying, and not one of his wonders has ever fixed that."

Xenzashii turned herself about atop the stone to face away from him, staring off into space.

"You can't stay here forever."

"Yes, I can. I'll build a hut over there and scavenge enough to eat. There are plenty of wild bvoljhio running around."

"But for how long? The bvoljhio are fading like the flowers. When the zaitson disappear, they will too. Another problem your Magnificent One has created."

"Shut up! He's going to make things better when he returns. I know he will. He just has to…he has to come back. Why would he leave me?" As best she tried, it was impossible for her to hold back her tears.

Xendsvar climbed atop the stone and sat down, placing his arm around her. "I didn't mean to upset you. But, you were taken captive by someone who never truly cared for you. That's what bothers me. Ever since we lost our caretakers, all I've ever wanted is for you to be safe and happy. I never wanted you to feel that hurt again. Even now, I wish to keep you away from any further pain. But we may have to help their group back there to restore our land."

"What are you talking about?" Xenzashii asked.

"The elder woman needs our help both mine and yours. And they will be there."

"Forget it. I can't. I won't help them after how they tricked me. He looks too much like him for me."

"My feelings are no different. The woman was sneaky to hide that detail from me, knowing I wouldn't help if I knew. But now I think different." Xendsvar fixed his gaze on the haze resting hundreds of shawaras above them. "I almost *know* different. There were two young men that came before him, who told us a strange story of how they came to be in this place. I would've called them liars, except for the strangest thing of all. We found them in the river and neither was affected by its curse. Every word the elder woman said was true, saying we would find Apeay when we found the two that share one face. But still, it's odd because you found him before us. How did that happen?"

"It was like any other day; our patrol was on its usual rounds, when a light in the distance caught our eye. It came from the temple's direction, so at first we thought it was Cabjha magic. But then I realized that all of you Cabjha had already returned from your magic practice."

"It's not magic. We'd appreciate it if you'd stop calling it that."

"Whatever it is that you mystics do. Everyone except for us was back within the village borders so, we thought it may be more bandits from the northern land spying on us. We went out into the fields for a closer look, and we spotted them. At first they were just standing around. We couldn't tell what they were after. Then when they tried to cross the fields leading to the village, we surrounded them in an ambush."

"Stop right there. Whenever have you known the Magnificent One to come by way of the temple or the fields?"

"Never. He usually comes by way of the Eostrezan Sea. And he didn't have a vehicle either. He was on foot."

"Exactly. Nothing like the Magnificent One we know. And how did he seem when ambushed?"

"Now that I think about it, he looked confused. He didn't even give the correct keyword when prompted. The only thing that saved them…"

"Was how he looked." Xendsvar nodded his head. "I see now. All that deceit was to save their lives. They didn't mean any harm. This Apeay may be as clueless as we are."

"Then why is he here?"

"I don't know. Maybe after we complete the full ritual all will be revealed."

"*We*? You think I'm going to participate in a ritual? You know I don't do those. I've never believed in that mystic stuff. Now I get it. The Cabjha ways are all you care about."

"Not at all. I came here to see about you, Xenzashii. I care about you. There is no ritual more important to me than your wellbeing. The request is from the elder woman. She believes there is something special about our 'essence' as she put it."

"That makes me no more interested than I was before. Special or not, it's still a trick."

"Maybe it is."

"Hold on. *You*, the most devout mystic of them all, are finally admitting that you and your crew go up to the hills to do nothing more than put on an act?"

"Listen, our rituals are celestial instructions passed down from the gods that guided the first generation. None of us know how they work, but we do as inscribed within the walls of the temple and the results are constant. But this time I say maybe, because I've studied all the ancient insignia about the temple, and there is not one mention of 'essence' or its significance in any ritual. Not even in the *zinjrahajzhi* flowering insignia, the final ritual, is there word. So I agree, it is an odd request. For our Cabjha principle is, 'ritual is ritual, a being is a being, none greater or less but an equal balance of life.'"

"Then why do you trust her?"

"I don't trust her. I believe her; it's a feeling. But I'm not letting my guard down. Any sign of trouble, I will put a stop to it all. Apeay, the elder woman, everything. I'll keep us safe."

Xenzashii leaned her head back and huffed to the sky, "*Jheldazho baglagzh.*" Then stretching her hands skywards, like a vhihanxex upon awaking, she leapt off the large marble stone. Xendsvar sat watching while Xenzashii bobbed around, stretching and twisting, holding her limbs in various positions. "Well, are you going to sit on that stone all day?"

"Ah, I see you have come to the understanding of this matter," he said as he too leapt off the stone.

"That's not it. I just think it's time we deal with this together, whether it's a trick or not. I let myself get so wrapped up in his progression fantasy that I thought it would bring to me that which I forgot to cherish. Forgive me," said Xenzashii as she kissed Xendsvar.

Xendsvar, pleasantly surprised, simply replied, "Both of us are stubborn in our own ways."

"Yes, and you're still slower than me."

"Speed doesn't matter when you're not aware of your surroundings. If you were, you would've noticed the pair of vahpilligen about to wrap around your legs."

"What?" startled Xenzashii looked down at the ground to see nothing more than clay rising towards her face. But the clay wasn't rising, she was falling. She'd been tripped by her mischievous partner, who ran ahead, sprinting through the hidden pathway.

"Since you're faster, you should be able to catch up. Ha!"

"You so can't stand to lose a foot race that you resort to cheating! I hope you feel quick today, because I'm right behind you!" said Xenzashii, springing to her feet, bounding effortlessly over fallen branches and stones along the hidden path. In no time, she was upon her lifelong mate, making faces as she passed by him.

Above them, a streak of electric blue split the haze in two. Xenzashii to Xendsvar, who'd already observed this anomaly.

The two followed the falling star, sprinting along the secret path to the temple.

Ω

It was hard for Thorel to tell if she was dreaming or not when she came to. Every region that was, or had ever been was spinning about her as he carried her along. Above his head the ornament glowed brightly, sending fiery light up and down in twelve symmetrical directions. Though the fire encompassed them it did not burn. But how was this happening? What was it that she was seeing in this incomplete pattern between the flashes of light? It was unusual for her nerves to be rattled, but this was no ordinary sight. It was like she was trapped in another world with, and by someone determined to destroy the one she lived to protect. Anxiously, she clasped her hands together. But what was this strange feeling? Where was the warmth of her body? Her hands felt like smooth crystal. She touched the side of her neck to see if she was, in fact, alive or not. In doing so, she felt a hum like that of an electrical current going through her. Sensing its movement through her body, she realized that she was no longer made of flesh and blood. Her body had become like that of Nepcizyr and Valus.

"Why are you doing this? What's wrong with my body?"

"Your former body was wrong; it was aging. But it won't anymore. You're in a state of eternal youth, the flawless empress at my side with a perfected body better than any aeroxia treatment ever could give to you."

"You can't do this to me. I didn't ask for your perfection. I don't want it. No one does."

"Perfection does not care what you want. It just is. It is absolute, even beyond me. I am one with it and I am its messenger. You should consider yourself lucky to have been chosen. Through the covenant between you and I, all will be perfected and those who refuse our blessing will vanish forever. You will absorb the immortal code from the former empress at the rise of the final sioleh and we will give birth to the pure everlasting order."

Thorel leapt out of his arms attempting to jump out of the inexplicable vehicle carrying them above the marching Team Gihan, only to be knocked back by its invisible barrier.

"Don't do that again! How could you be so ungrateful after receiving the most prestigious place in the eternal? Are you so blind like he was that you would abandon it? Maybe you were better off dying with him. Maybe I was wrong if that is all you are; an ungrateful heir to power beyond the expanse of infinity, clinging to the ghost of an incompetent mystic of melody. Pathetic behavior for royalty like yourself. That's something I won't tolerate. You are the chosen empress, the twin Star of Heylan Command as you were destined to be. So act like it."

For Thorel, something about those words stuck. Under her breath she whispered, "Heylan Command...Heylan...look into the star of Heylan and see your perfection..." It was then that the sinister reality of her former lover's fate came to her. Until now, she had wrestled with her imagination, over and over in her mind, since the day of his disappearance. If it was something she had done, something she had said, was there another waiting on him, or had he simply left to get away from it all? At one time, Thorel considered leaving her duties behind to join him in his travels throughout the regions. A fleeting dream that never came to be.

"You...you killed him. You killed him! I didn't know whether to be angry with him or myself, and it was you all along! It was always you right from the start. You were so kind. How did you become so cruel? Or was this always you?" Her heart was torn between hatred and sorrow. All the cycles she carried the weight of bitterness, not knowing who to blame. Now she saw it was this man, or some twisted apparition of a man. Lowering her head, Thorel looked between the spaces of indifferent horizons to those below marching proudly to their perfect undoing. She felt like crying, but her "perfected" body seemed to be incapable of producing tears. Instead, her eyes turned void.

"I kill no one. They either are without flaws or they do not exist. This is why you know nothing of life and death. An actual perpetual state of uninterrupted bliss is some-

thing you can't comprehend. But you will in full, when the eternal comes into you."

Physically, she was his captive. However, in her essence, the fire known as her authentic "Speedy Tho-tho" self was lit, awaiting the first chance to escape his clutches and help the others take down his mad regime named Heylan Command. But as for this man, Heylan, he was a mysterious power that couldn't be taken lightly. She couldn't afford to make another halfhearted attempt to flee. She'd have to be decisive, precise, and act when he least expected. For now, she would have to wait.

They came to rest on the foregrounds of the ruins, locked in position between the three rows of two Team Gihan as Team Delignos ripped through beyond the stratosphere.

The fiery light surrounding them unfolded, retracing its origin to the ornament floating above them. He lifted his hand, calling it back to him, returning it to his side. With a loud cry, he called into being the final phase of his grand design.

"Zjehy xenian yeshing! Marxhilhil oniex Xeno **PER-FECTION!"**

A violent quake rattled the grounds, creating a deep, wide rift splitting between. As the caves and all the stones of the ruins tumbled into the rift, a massive structure unlike any other rose to the surface. It was a sioleh at least three times the size of the already massive energy converters spread through-out all the regions. Unlike the others, this sioleh's tower was made of pure diamond instead of emerald. At its base, surging waves of water poured in from a source within the lower part of the canals.

"Now it is. *Gxos shiinex vexhianzen axivahenzei*!"

Thorel felt as if she'd been seized by an apparition. A strong, invisible force gripped her body as she found herself floating towards the center of the sioleh that had produced a multi-angled prism of light. Within the prism, the figure of a person materialized.

"Bexhiera!" cried Thorel as the prism swallowed her being.

"Rionazen!" Bexhiera exclaimed, embracing her. As she did, she couldn't help but notice the unusual hardness about Thorel's body. "Rionazen, are you wearing armor under those clothes? And you look so young! How did you..."

"This wasn't my doing. He changed me against my will. He killed my former lover, Alcardazj...he's destroying everything. Oh my, I just realized."

"What is it?"

Thorel thought it through. What had happened to Jhar'-ensky? Did this raging cabera destroy him as well? There was no way of knowing. But, she couldn't say that to the already troubled mother of the one who should be with her. Speaking of which...

"Where is Apeay? I thought he was with you?"

"I believe my son is here, but lost," said Bexhiera looking painstakingly upon the man in power on the edge of the foregrounds.

Thorel followed her gaze and shook her head.

"Bexhiera, this man only looks alike, I know…"

"I raised him. I've known him all his life. You may not understand, but that enraged man out there is every bit as pure of heart as Apeay. As he brought me to this place, he told me his entire reason for his course of action, and I heard him. Though he didn't say it, I could tell, on the inside, he was hurting. In his voice was agony; the voice of someone worn out from losing more than could be gained. I can only guess that something, or someone pushed him over the edge of his sanity, because it was odd. On the way here, for the whole ride, he spoke to me as if I were someone else he knew from somewhere else, though he still acknowledged me in a way that a son would. I called him by his name, and he scolded me for it. But who else would he be to me? My senses tell me that it's him. What happened during the festival? Did the Legionnaires push him too far? Is that what made him so angry? What happened to my son?" Bexhiera began to weep.

Rionazen clasped Bexhiera's hands. "We don't know just yet, we were still looking for him. And I know you're hurting bad right now, and want to see your son again, but that man out there…I'm afraid he's not Apeay; not one bit. We'll find…"

"No, no...Just take a look at his mannerisms. Watch him while he paces back and forth; he moves like him. No one, not even a skilled performer, can imitate another person to that level."

Thorel, not wanting to antagonize Bexhiera, artfully sided with her wishful thinking.

"Then who am I to judge a mother's intuition?" said Thorel "If you believe it's so, then perhaps there's a chance to talk him out of this. Because according to Ju-Makana, his pure intentions will be the end of everything."

"I don't believe that."

"Believe it or not, Ju-Makana is a prodigy among geniuses; someone whose warnings shouldn't be taken lightly. And... what's he doing?"

Looking out from the prism they watched him levitate over the rift as he gave final instructions to his army.

Command hovered over to the prism at the center of the sioleh. "You will survive only to see it once and never be again, your highness. That I promise and apologize for. Perfection is its own eternal reward." His eyes were ablaze with a desolate glow while speaking with Bexhiera.

"Would it hurt to call me 'Mother' again? Just once before you go too far, could you do that? I don't know what happened to you my son. But you don't have to go this way. We loved you from the first day. It was the perfect day when we found you Apeay."

"NO! There is no Apeay! Would it hurt you to call me by my name, or did you forget? That false imperfection you slander me with will be destroyed with the last of your reminiscent hopes! The failed former emperor, the mystics, and all the royal guard have always been against me. Therefore, once I confine the expanding sphere only she and the chosen few will remain..."

"Why, what was it? Did we do something wrong? I'm sorry if we couldn't protect you..." Bexhiera was saddened, crying aloud. "You said one day you'd show us another place better than the one before. Wasn't that always your lifelong dream?"

"I don't dream. I actualize!"

Rionazen consoled the grieved Bexhiera. There was nothing left for him to explain. The time of perfected eternity called to him. As he began his descent to the base of the enormous sioleh he, spoke one last time to her. "Thanks for taking me into your care. But, I didn't need your protection. I needed you to speak up for me back then when I tried to show you better. Now, it's too late. Goodbye, Mother...**I am Zjvxenozb.**"

Though his words puzzled Bexhiera, she felt she should've known what he meant.

Zjvxenozb looked below at the waters swirling about, through the center of the grand sioleh. Touching down at its base, it gave one last look at the two trapped within the prism. To the cadence of his hand gestures, the ornament at his side aligned itself with the doubled golden pyramid in his hand. The strange technology morphed the ornament into multiple spheres aligning themselves up, down, forwards, backwards, in and out, and beyond the alignment of the sioleh as the base of the unwrapped itself, allowing him to pass through...

Chapter 21

"Finally, we're here. Why does this thing have to spin?"

"Are you alright? You don't look too well."

"I think so...nope, get out of my way!"

The light retracted back to the ornament. They arrived at the temple with only moments to spare before Seldao reeled over to the edge of the high hill, heaving up everything within him.

"Dang bro, I swear you can't handle anything going faster than a mirah," said Deslao.

While his stomach settled, Seldao observed the plant life on the west side of the temple. Bojo were fleeing to the skies, as the overgrowth shook from one side to another.

"Hey guys, I think we were followed."

"Is that what you think?" said the elder woman.

"Come see for yourself. Someone or something is headed right for us."

"It's Xenzashii and Xendsvar," said Apeay.

"How do you know?" said Seldao "I don't see anybody."

"I don't know; it's more like a feeling."

"The ambience is becoming aware of itself. This happens again," said the elder woman.

"Ambience, you said that before," said Deslao.

"I sure did. The connection is growing ever stronger by the moment.

"So are you going to tell us what it's about?"

"Why would I explain when you will know?"

"Because when someone asks for someone else's help they…wait…" Deslao adopted a fighting stance. His eyes were focused on the edge of hill in front of them. Within a jhenta two figures leaped up, somersaulting onto the walkway.

"Look, I don't know which one of you puked, but you're lucky I have fast reflexes. I almost stepped in that nastiness."

"But you didn't, so it doesn't matter," said Xendsvar. He observed Deslao, who seemed to be ready for combat. "Why are you standing like that?"

"I don't know. Maybe the ambience made me do it."

"See, that right there is why I never come to this temple," said Hanjiah. "It makes people crazy."

"Is it less crazy to remember tomorrow or sane to forget an era past?" said the elder woman.

"As far as I'm concerned, lady, your concept of sanity don't count. Now how about we get this thing started since all of us are here."

"I'm sorry, Xenzashii," said Zaleah stepping forward.

"It's alright," said Xenzashii. "You did what you had to. I get it."

"You do?"

"Sure, you had to survive. He's not my type anyway. Lying to save his life, that's like a coward, unlike your friend over there," she said, acknowledging Deslao.

"I already know, I'm that guy," said Deslao.

"Oh, I'm a coward now? I thought I was magnificent." said Apeay. "Everyone follow the walkway to the entrance. Seldao, Hanjiah, it's up to you to formulate the proper alignments. I'll be leaving you now."

"I'm coming with you," said Zaleah.

"No. Not this time. Where I go, I must go alone. Everyone **do as I say, and be quick about it! Here, take this with you.**" Apeay removed the ornament from his neck, holding it outstretched. "Deslao, this is now for you to protect. When you reach the center, you and Xendsvar will secure this in its place."

"But..."

"Right now, I'm being drawn to a place beneath here. I don't know why, but I must go. Outside of me, you two are the only ones strong enough to handle its true gravity. **Now, take the ornament!**"

Deslao was hesitant. The thought of handling that ominous object worried him. "Fella, I don't know about that."

From the way Deslao was eyeing the ornament, Apeay knew what had him spooked. "I get it now my fella, don't worry. I'm giving you this for our common use."

Xenzashii detected a bit of uncertainty in Deslao's voice as well. "Don't tell me you're scared. I thought you were that guy."

Deslao glanced over at Xenzashii then back at Apeay, "Of course I am. Give me that!" He snatched the ornament out of Apeay's hand. The ornament itself began to emit light like a vapor that engulfed Deslao's wrists. The light around his arms solidified into translucent golden gauntlets. Xendsvar gasped as his arms were now wrapped in similar fashion. Deslao sighed in relief. "I wasn't expecting that. Yes, my fella, it's safe with me."

"More Cabjha tricks going here, I see," said Hanjiah.

Looking at his forearms, still caught up in awe, Xendsvar refuted the accusation. "This is not of the Cabjha." Xendsvar held up both his arms, displaying the detail of their structure to Hanjiah. "There is no ceremony to manifest a wonder like this."

Leaning her head on his shoulders, Zaleah clasped her hands around his waist.

Apeay knew what she was thinking. But, he couldn't let an emotion hold him up and broke himself free from her hold. "There is nowhere I go that you are not. You'll always be with me."

"He speaks true," said the elder woman. "You two are inseparable. But for now, he must go where he will, with only the ambience that speaks to his essence to guide him."

"And what about us?" said Hanjiah.

"You will be guided the same."

Seldao had removed himself from the group and was standing at the temple's center entrance. From there he could still hear their conversation. He meditated on the elder lady's words as he studied the patsy equation engraved over the entrance of the portico. *"You will be guided the same..."*

"Oh sure, my essence will show me the way," said Hanjiah "Tell me when's that going to happen?"

"How about now?" said the elder woman.

From the entrance, Seldao shouted, "Hanjiah have you seen this?"

"Seen what, an entryway? Yeah, I've seen plenty of those in my lifetime," he hollered back.

"Come here and look, man!"

"Ok, I'll look. But I'm warning you, and you," he said to the elder woman, "if I don't see anything worth seeing, I'm leaving all of you here with your silly mystic babble. Don't get me wrong, the light show was great. And that magic sleeve trick, I've never seen anything like it. But there's only so much trickery I can take in a day."

"That's alright. You'll do what you want to," said the elder woman.

Hanjiah walked up as Seldao was attempting to decipher the intricate symbols over the door. "What is it?"

"This is a symbol equation, right?" said Seldao.

Hanjiah looked it over for a bit and shook his head, "It's fake. Look, kid, there's no way for this to exist, which is why the Cabjha don't know anything."

"Why do you say it's fake?"

"Just look at it. Multiple symbol materialization can't exist at the same time and occupy the same place. That's physically impossible. That's like saying Xeno exists fixed within another place..."

"Above, below, or in between," said Seldao, completing the thought. "Wasn't that what the Magnificent One put you in charge of? On the ride here, you said it was your task to design the region within the region of Xeno."

"And that's what I've been doing. But this is something else."

"My fella, I'm telling you it's the same. Read the symbols again. Please, my friend."

Hanjiah studied the "fake" equation for a few moments, and stood back from the portico, turning around to view the horizon. He looked along the path of the river from the base of the temple to its end at the Silver Sea. Using his hands, he measured the angles in between the directional sections of Xeno, applying the equation above the portico to each one. It was at that moment his intellect expanded to understand an enigma of a greater universe. "If the axis were to be confined, this place would collapse becoming an entirely different place, but all the same, and no one would know the difference."

"Exactly," said Seldao.

"But how? Even if my calculations are spot on it would take more energy than several exploding stars to produce that type of power."

"Will you not go in now?" said the elder woman approaching the entryway. "We are at that moment. Come along," she said, waiving to the remainder of the group that were still several paces back.

All but Apeay, who had already begun to walk down the spiral stairway, made their way up the path leading to the portico.

"Apeay!" Zaleah shouted. "Where are you going?"

"To be with you!" he shouted back. "To be with everyone. That's what I'm sensing, so please do as we will do. There's **no more time to waste!**" Without further word Apeay, leapt off the spiraled stairway into the river below.

"Now he's beginning to sound like the Magnificent One" said Xendsvar."

"I think your guy might be stressed out," said Xenzashii.

"Why do you say that?" Zaleah asked.

"Your man, Apeay, and the one who was formerly mine, Zjvxenozb, they do more than look alike. In some ways, they're exactly the same. Most of the time, when we were together, he spoke normally in a calm voice. But whenever he got in a mood, especially when angry, his voice got like that."

The elder lady appeared between them, "He's a man living with the ghosts of many lifetimes lived before. When the other half of him transformed, the memories awoke and were given a voice. Apeay is the newest life. And now that he's in close proximity to himself, becoming himself again, it will become more difficult to distinguish the difference between them. But no more explaining. It's time." Zaleah began making her way inside the portico, while Xenzashii stood unmoved. "You too, young lady."

Xenzashii explained herself, "I just wanted to see him off."

"I know. You always do."

"Zjvxenozb? His secret name," said Zaleah. "I can't believe he never told me."

"He should have nothing to tell you for, you've known him so very long," said the elder woman.

Zaleah shook her head. "You talk like you know so much. I've been with him..."

"Ever since you and your mother left Djhalho for Estellar," said the elder woman cutting her off. The lady peered into her eyes. "He can't tell you something he doesn't know. Nor can he be someone he forgot. If you are to be reunited we have work to do. Now will you two please hurry up?"

"Sure, lady."

Θ

"Are you sure you know what you're doing?"

"Don't worry, man. If you get vaporized, I'll tell them you went out fighting."

Jhar'ensky didn't find anything funny about Ju-Makana's remark. It was he who had a neutranevex pointed at him, not the other way around.

"Yes, I know what I'm doing," said Ju-Makana. "This isn't the first time I've reconfigured molecular resonance. It's just the first time I've done so to deal with graviton."

"Oh man!"

"Stop that. You're flinching all over the place. The more you move, the harder it is for me to aim it at the core of the hold point. Now show me that Legionnaire discipline from the days when you actually wore that armor, and stand still."

Jhar'ensky exhaled and took his stance. "Ready."

Ju-Makana, using all of his strength to hold the weighted neutranevex steady, took aim and pulled on the lever. A faint vapor wave flashed from the neutranevex, making a sound like a miniature lightning bolt striking the ground. Instantly, Jhar'-ensky broke free from his fixed position.

"Look at that. It worked. You and Council wanted to kick me off the panel, and I'm here saving your *fihgazz*. I better be made Principal Shototu after today."

"I won't object to that," said Jhar'ensky. "But first, we have a matter of saving our region to take care of. We're not losing this fight. We will not lose Thorel. I will not lose my family to this madness!"

After releasing himself, Ju-Makana proceeded to free the band of men joined with him to put an end to Command.

Now free to move, they quickly assembled outside as directed by Jhar'ensky. From the former Legionnaires, those that were most capable of ground movement were lined up by size giving each one the maximum sight advantage they needed, sending them directly to the ruins by way of the outer canals where they would be hidden from view of Command's Team Delignos. A great number of mystics from the nearby regions agreed to aid the ground team on foot. Pilots, who had managed to obtain training glineers, equipped with minimal strike currents, had their glineers modified by Ju-Makana to do twice the damage, twice as fast to make up for their lack of weaponry. Before taking off, Jhar'ensky ordered them to rise to the highest altitude, well above the normal patrol level, to head east and to the west and regroup at the northeast and northwest, to the rear of the ruins. The remainder, joining the ground team, with him and Ju-Makana in the heavily protected mynderajzens, were briefed on their primary task.

"Team, we will be serving a dual purpose," said Jhar'ensky "Our first task is take their ground force head on. We will be the initial disturbance and, in doing so, we will buy time for the remaining team to rejoin us, catching the opposition off guard. This will give us the advantage, having them surrounded. They will be fighting an outward battle on all sides. We must be victorious for the sake of Estellar and the regions beyond. Our families, our friends, their lives going forward depends on our swift and fierce response to this mad regime. Three one four, onward to the ruins!"

Ω

Two powerful tidal waves of energy swirled upwards and downwards about him as he stood fixed in one position. He observed their movement and counted each time they crossed, waiting for them to reach full oscillation at the perfect moment. After an endless time, all things would be set right. It was the only thing he had been set on since his return to the imperfect land, and soon the argument between the imperfection of life and the will of perfection beyond the cosmos would be amended. For he knew he'd accomplished this in the most authentic world. Not one of myths and legends, but a world forged by his shining hands as he sang in perfect, directive tone.

"Xenteedah ahdan, Xenteedah ahdan, gzhoushing... *Xenteedah ahdan, Xenteedah ahdan, gzhouxenon...* **Hope you've been practicing since our last fight, that is, if you didn't die..."**

CHAPTER 22

Inside the temple, they walked along the main pathway to the center chamber in the inner courtyard. Given that it was his first time inside, Hanjiah studied every angle of every stonework within. It was apparent that whoever was responsible for its design possessed a knowledge of pattern angles that exceeded his own. Symbol alignments covered the walls, alongside pictures and other inscriptions that read like anecdotes. This was a mysterious thing indeed, since he was taught symbol alignment and pattern angles by the former principal xhovadu of Xeno, which at that time it was basic. It was he, Hanjiah that expounded on his teachings. His advanced understanding allowed them to progress rapidly over the twenty seven cycles to follow, which led to the Magnificent One appointing him Principal Xhovadu of Xeno.

To Hanjiah the Temple of Fushirajhe was a design from the future carved out of the past.

"You know I'm curious Xendsvar," said Hanjiah as he spun a fully around, looking up towards the high ceilings. "This is a great deal of advanced technology for a group of mystics to deal with. But without a proper power source, I don't see how you all get anything accomplished. And who taught you how to work this anyway?"

"You still don't understand, my misguided friend. Here we follow the instructions of the gods passed down from the first generation. This is their 'technology' as you put it. Not a cheap imitation, like that of the Magnificent One," said Xendsvar.

"May I offer a suggestion?" The elder woman appeared between them. "Try not to think of this place as anything."

"You always talk like you know so much, but you never give us any solid answers. Why is that?" asked Hanjiah.

"Okay. I'll give you an answer. But you won't understand it. Where you are is in a garden connected to a land that does not exist in this realm."

"Then why do we practice the rituals here if this is not a temple?" said Xendsvar.

"It is a temple, for you. Did I disagree? No. I only told you where you were standing. You're standing in the Garden of HeylanLaejzo. If it is your temple, then that it is as well. The rituals you practice do exactly as you think they do. But, maybe for other reasons than you know."

"So, Xendsvar, you and your crew come up here to grow magic plants. Do you use the magic 'god water' on em' too?"

"Disrespectful!" Xendsvar shouted.

Hanjiah, you are intelligent, but not as wise I think. You didn't understand at all. The vegetation this garden produces doesn't grow here; it manifests in another place. The ambience of that place returns to this place as zep-alignments to form every molecule of water that falls from the sky."

"You're right. I don't get it. Sounds made up."

"Either way, will you two agree that we are here for the same thing?" She looked back and forth between Hanjiah and Xendsvar.

Hanjiah huffed. "Agreed."

Xendsvar nodded his head.

"If you think too hard, you might miss it. If you comply without thinking, you will never understand the internal mystery. And Xendsvar, I assure you, the workings of the Magnificent One are far from a cheap imitation. His knowledge is so great that it pains him. That's why it takes one like Hanjiah, even with his limitations, to absorb his knowledge for the sake of everyone."

Hanjiah was taken aback by her critical appraisal. If he had such great worth, then where was his fault?

"Well, if I'm not all you think I'm supposed to be, then why am I here?"

The elder looked Hanjiah in the eye and said, "It's you that limits yourself because you see only part of yourself. Expand your world beyond your narrow view of what technology is and is not. We're standing in a place beyond modern progress as you will see when you align yourselves for the first and final ritual. You will see it all. You can do that for us, can't you?"

"Lady, I align symbols for material production and gemstones to dynamic angles, not people. You're talking that crazy talk again."

"Is that so? I thought you'd been everywhere and seen everything. Have you not? If I stay any longer, who will greet him?"

"Oh wow, lady, you're the one stirring up this wild adventure. Why don't you arrange us?"

The elder woman smirked. "Once again in three...two... one..."

"Hanjiah," said Seldao, who was standing at the center where he and Xendsvar were before. Deslao, Zaleah and Xenzashii were at his side as he attempted to read the inscription around the center bevel that he hadn't noticed until a moment ago.

"Could you help me decipher this? I've never seen these symbols, but the alignment is familiar. I had to write absolute entry on it for my final parallel on this exact arrangement."

"They made us write one on this, too," said Zaleah. "But don't ask my opinion. My absolute entry was way off. Lucky for me, it wasn't my primary concentration, or I would've failed."

"Well, what are you waiting for?" the elder woman said to Hanjiah.

Hanjiah acknowledged her and he and Xendsvar strolled over to see what the hype was all about. "Okay, let me see." He studied the inscribed symbols which were very familiar to him.

"Kid, how can you call yourself an expert on symbol alignment if you don't know the most basic symbols of all?" Pointing to each one, he called them by name, "Jhesoxhele, hydralpheta, yovhaxahedra. Real basic stuff."

"Of course, the first centered three," said Seldao. "And, pardon me, but where we're from they're known as isojephele, hydrophena and tevanhedra. And the symbols are always listed separately, not attached to each other like these ones. That's why I didn't recognize them."

"Well you do now. You see those directional marks?"

"Yes, they're doubled back and forth."

"Exactly. They're dual, which means these three have to be repeated in two directions, making a total of six reflecting pattern angles. If one goes in with the smaller value going out, the range of possibility is infinite; any type of molecule following this alignment should be able to escape to an infinite, endless direction, even if the molecule is in a bond align..."

Hanjiah was rendered temporarily speechless, realizing why he was there with them. Whether it was a temple of counterfeit magic, apparatus, or advanced technology didn't matter to him anymore. He looked up at the group, taking a quick estimate of their size and back at the symbols. "Xendsvar, I apologize for not taking you and the Cabjha seriously. I guess I was too smart for my own good. And, my lady..." Hanjiah turned back towards the elder woman. However, she was no longer with them. "Well-well, guess she fooled us after all.

Dammit! This equation is useless if we don't know what elements to incorporate."

"Sure we do," said Seldao. "We deciphered the alignment, which leads to the elements."

"I know that, but it's asking for an unknown element to be incorporated. One of them, we may be able to obtain if we're lucky. That sneaky old lady left us here without a clue. It's useless."

"Please, try to stay calm," said Zaleah. "We can figure this out if all of us put our minds together. First, what's the element that you do know?"

"Trilzhazalhin. It's the element most responsible for the formation of zaitson flowers. And this alignment is calling for more than a little. We need at least a bundle of zaitson. Something we won't find around here."

Zaleah removed her satchel from her waist and pulled out a round, stout container. "Maybe this will work?"

"What is it?"

"It's zaiti soup. I packed some for Apeay before we got here. It's his favorite."

"Zaiti soup?"

"That's perfect," said Seldao. "It's made from the vaporized compression of at least 50 zaitson flowers. That's easily more than a bundles worth."

"Vaporized compression, you say?" said Hanjiah.

"Yeah, you people of Xeno don't have that tech. We can speed heat a substance at such a rate that the physical structure changes, but retains all its original properties. There are, in fact, just over 50 flowers in that container in liquid form."

"Talk, talk. Technology heads and their talk. What's next? What else do we need?" asked Xenzashii, who was now pacing back and forth. She was ready to get the ceremony done and over with.

"Give us a jhenta and we'll know," said Seldao. "This isn't so easy to figure out."

"Yes it is," said Xendsvar, who had been silently observing until this moment. Pointing to the inscriptions below "the centered three," he said. "Trying to make sense of these symbols will do you no good."

"Explain. Why not?"

"Because it's a riddle, not an equation. Look around you, look at the walls, the floors and the ceilings," Xendsvar said, acknowledging the engravings directly overhead. "Do you not see the drawings among the symbols? The riddle is the story of our origin passed onto us by the first mystics, written in the mystic language of Xhal."

"Then tell us a story," said Zaleah. "What does it say?"

Xendsvar first pointed to the carvings above them. "Like the last, it was the first, everything perfect but nothing of worth." Then to the carvings below the center, he pointed and read, "Awakened by passions of love and anger, there was a stranger likened to protection, pursued by danger. If not a blue star none would see. Twice they awake, again they will be." He then read the carvings directly under "the centered three": "Out of furious fires, peaceful waters flow in streams; awake Aurujha Mobius, the golden dream."

"The fabled Aurujha Mobius, putting us right back where we started. Lost," said Hanjiah.

"Maybe you should study pictures as much as you study equations." Xendsvar tapped his finger on a carving inter-twined within the symbols. Between the inscriptions was the image of a man standing in water, surrounded by fire. Hanjiah took notice of what Xendsvar was showing him. However, he still didn't fully see it.

"Some sort of man, or is it one of your mystic gods?"

"Look closer."

Hanjiah leaned in closer. "His neck is cut, and he has a hole in his chest!"

Xendsvar laughed from deep within his belly. "For once, we agree. All these cycles, I've come to this temple seeing the same thing. A man with a scarred neck and a hole in his chest. But today, the one I was ready to destroy did a most peculiar thing. He took the scars off his neck and removed the hole from his chest. No, I didn't understand it then. But I do now."

Deslao held up the ornament. "Hey, Hanjiah, it looks like we've found that final piece. The Aurujha Mobius."

"Well, I'll be humbled again," said Hanjiah. "You two fighting beasts have me questioning my own reasoning. And it's *fantastic*! We have everything we need."

"Then let's be quick about this and put all the pieces in place," said Zaleah. "Apeay is waiting on us."

"Yes," said Xenzashii. "Get to it, Hanjiah. Align us."

"Relax kid. I'm not over here setting the pace marks for no reason," said Hanjiah, who in fact had already begun to calculate the alignment configuration.

"Good, then my brother will give us the magic words to speak."

"We will sing an ancient chant, that is *not* magic, in perfect to imperfect tones of sevens. If you are unfamiliar with tones, follow my lead," said Xendsvar. "What Xenzashii has overheard many times is what we, the Cabjha, practice, in hope that one day we would find the missing element that is now in our possession."

"All set," said Hanjiah. "Young man, please take that which you so proudly hold in your hand and place it over the basin at the center. Get a good, firm grip on it, and don't let it go until I say." Deslao moved to the center where the bowl was fixed above the cutout in the floor, anxiously waiting for what was to come. "And, Zaleah, is it?"

"That's right," said Zaleah.

"You see that deep-set, engraved circle around the center basin?"

"Yes."

"It's the core xhilhyden converter."

"The what?"

"It's like a backup. On second thought, it may be the original design. Anyhow, you're going to pour the liquid zaiti into the circle, ever so slowly. If I've read this right, your friend might lose an arm if you do it too quickly."

"Hold on, Hanjiah," said Seldao. "I've went over the symbols again. They equate to something that's on a grand scale beyond our world; a direct cosmic angle alignment to be precise. A feat of that magnitude within these confines? It's not feasible."

"I agree, but like you calculated for yourself, that's what it's stating."

"My bro is strong, but that's on a different level."

"You make a good point. Xendsvar, could you give him a hand. He'll probably need it."

"I'm not weak," said Deslao. "I can hold on to a small ornament."

"An ornament sure, but a star, I don't think so," said Xenzashii.

"Now, what do you know about cosmic angle alignments?" asked Hanjiah.

"It's gets boring guarding the fields at night. How do you think I keep my mind occupied? And think about who was my guy for all this time. Think he didn't teach me anything? Or do you think I can't grasp the advanced concepts he taught you? Like everyone in your crew, you think I'm slow because I'm a field guard."

"I didn't say that."

"No, but you implied it. It's alright. I don't care to be seen as a know-it-all like you."

Xendsvar smiled at her remark and walked up to where Deslao stood. "Open the strand that I may help."

"I've got this, fella," said Deslao.

"What if you don't?" Deslao looked at him with disdain. Xendsvar, being a man of pride himself understood. "Look, proud warrior, if you don't, we will have come here for nothing, and you will never return to your home." Deslao eased his countenance and opened the strand, allowing Xendsvar to take a firm double-handed grip on it as well.

"Great, we're ready," said Hanjiah. "First, I need everyone to look at me. When the last drop of the zaitson is in the cutout, you Xendsvar and Deslao are to let go of the ornament, and take your place. Place alignments are as follows: Seldao you will sit there in the spot marked for west facing northeast; Zaleah, you will sit at the northwest mark facing southwest, Deslao you at the northeast facing southeast; Xenzashii, you there at the southeast facing northeast; Xendsvar, you will be at the southwest mark facing northwest; and I, at the east facing southwest. Go no farther in or out of that exact placement. Now, my lady, you may pour the liquid ever so carefully."

Zaleah opened the container holding the zaiti soup, and began to carefully pour the contents within into the circle.

"Just as I expected," said Hanjiah.

From the inner depths of Apeay's ornament, the blue light within multiplied outwards, forming a circle, then a doubled circle mimicking a sphere about 15 shawaras around. As the liquid gradually filled the groove, the circles began to spin faster, swirling upwards and downwards.

It took all of their might to keep hold of the ornament. Their straining increased with each drop that fell out of the container, until it seemed to be unbearable.

"How much more is in that denjakoz? I feel my grip slipping," said Deslao.

"Be strong," said Xendsvar, who was also holding on with all his might. "We must be as strong as the energy itself." The golden gauntlets on their arms began to vibrate. In an instant, their strength magnified one hundred-thousand times over, allowing them to hold on to the ever-increasing weight of the radiant ornament.

Zaleah tipped the container fully upside down, letting the last drops of zaiti flow into the circle. "Done, it's empty."

"Let it go, fellas!" said Hanjiah.

Xendsvar and Deslao promptly released their hold on the ornament which sunk into the basin and split in half while remaining whole; existing in the higher realm. The ornament had become two untouchable ornaments fixed within two cutouts in the center six-sided basin, and continued to pro-liferate the pattern until it connected with the ceiling in perfect symbol alignment.

"Alright," said Hanjiah, "you know your places, so get to it."

Each of them sat in the designated place marked out for their being. An overwhelming phantasmal aura filled the center chamber. They might have become lost were it was not for the steady concentration of Xendsvar.

"Everyone listen well!" said Xendsvar. His resounding voice snapped the team out of their temporary enchantment. "Repeat these words in the seventh *denzin,* and sing as one for the moment has come."

"Nahdeeah nadee ini, nahdeeah...nahdeeah nadee ini emo-si, nadee renghi mehling, selalu nahdeeah nadee... rejhing majha emosi, nah, nahdeeah..."

He recited the ancient song over and over. One by one, they joined in melody as they memorized the words, echoing his chant. As they repeated the song, the circles of energy expanded further, beyond the confines of the temple into the outer courtyard. Six winds blew from the exact direction that each of them faced, swirling at the center high above them. The winds became one great cyclone that spun so fast it began to lift them off the ground, before crashing through the cutout in the floor into the waters below.

At the bottom where Apeay sat, the waters spun around him and passed through him. His essence merged with the ambience in the waters as if they were one with his body.

"Look, zhebxhila, look!" shouted Vertriljzheo. The day of fused learning had passed. Martazumen, along with the other zhebxhilas, were escorting the children along the path to the village when a most unusual site appeared in the sky. A great light shone in the northern sky, highlighting the night spectacle. The Xondhelan River rose from its resting place, folding on itself three times in a loop with no end around the land of Xeno, as faint images of grand places began to materialize all around.

"The river! It's warping." said Martazumen as he looked in wonder with the others. "Is the work of the goddess?"

"Maybe this will help." A middle-aged woman appeared at his side startling him.

"Who are you?"

"You are Zhebxhila Martazumen of the Xaldanhir people, are you not?"

"Yes, what's happening to our land?"

"Just that. A happening, an event, and nothing more."

"Like the end of our world? Is that what you mean?"

"You asked was this the work of a goddess. So then, why would a goddess bring your end if she came to help?

Take this. Forever keep this in your possession and study it well." The lady handed him a silver tetravhenda that was no bigger than a child's fist. It was a double pyramid, emblazoned with symbols on all sides.

He glanced over the symbols turning it about. "Sure, but what is it? Lady?" As quickly as the woman appeared, she had vanished.

While he attempted to figure out what type of device the lady had bestowed on him, cries of astonishment went up from the villagers and children under his watch. Martazumen looked-ed up to see the river that was folded over on itself, oscillating at high speeds. The haze about the atmosphere was being drawn into a vortex created by the spinning river, until it had completely vanished. The river subsequently reverted back into its original alignment. Water from the sky fell like a heavy downpour. And it was the first time in many cycles, the people of Xeno could see the stars of the universe on a clear night.

Martazumen cupped his hands, collecting a sprinkling of water, and took a sniff." It's fresh! No odors." He lapped up the splash of water in his hands, and felt the good feeling of cool purity wetting his throat. "Goddess Lai, you did it. My people, she did it! Our waters have been made pure." The accompany-ing zhebxhilas and children rejoiced.

A full spectrum of light appeared, lighting their path back to the central village as they strode along, blessed by the cool descending mist.

∞

In this place, he stood alone in one fixed position while the winds around him raged on. The winds felt hot as they swirled about him, going upwards and downwards. In his heart, he felt anxious, but calm. For there was no fear but a readiness for something he didn't know to expect. The waters that engulfed him receded, revealing that he was standing on a solid, reflective crystal. Apeay knelt down, placing his hand on the crystal, gazing upon his image; a most hostile image like his own.

"It's you. Who do you think you are to imitate my existence? On this day... YOU WILL BE NO MORE!"

CHAPTER 23

Now I remember. Now I remember it all. From the beginning, the only one in my way was you.

Command rose up, raising both hands. Never had he been so furious. He was nearing the fulfillment of his ultimate vision. And threatening that vision was this one, a counterfeit being that should not exist.

"Sa'ah, xhe, xhe gxos!"

Winds from every direction of Estellar were drawn to him with such swiftness, that the skies became like a mist created by powerful vortexes. In one crushing motion, he slammed his hands on the ground, directing the winds to the very place he stood, shattering the crystal mirror below.

Apeay gasped. Whirling winds drove him backwards, pinning him to the wall. He breathed rapidly to keep from asphyxiating as the terror of his youth floated up from the other side. The man grabbed Apeay by the face, turning his head from one side to the other, looking him over.

"You're the one they created in an attempt to stop me; an exact replica in my perfect image but flawed. That

makes you a cheap imitation. Your likeness mocks me. Therefore now...you will die."

With all of his strength, Apeay fought hard to free himself from his position. He could hardly breathe, let alone move as the Magnificence of Perfection closed his right hand, drawing in power like fire from an unseen place.

Why? Why do these things happen to me? Apeay wondered. *Is this all my life is? Running from place to place with no place to return to, only to die? He looks just like me and yet he hates my very existence. What did I ever do to him to deserve this? I can't even move to save myself. No way. I just can't. I can't die here...not like this...*

"**NOT LIKE THIS!**" Apeay's shout reverberated through the lower chambers of the temple. The winds that once held him captive dissipated.

"You know you can't end him. You never could and you never will."

Between the two, a young woman appeared, radiant like a star, with the white locks of her hair reflecting polychromatic colors. "If you desire perfection, as you say, choose a better path this time."

"**There is no better path than perfection itself! But you wouldn't understand. You betrayed me the day I realized this.**"

"Was it I who betrayed you, or you who betrayed yourself? Will you continue until there is no more?"

"I have saved us all from eternal death. But you would undo this by helping those mystics along every step of the way. First you teach them to misuse the perfected language by means of malicious tales set against me, to my unawares. Then you deceived me into helping you construct an abomination, before weakening me for endless cycles that sent me into the most desolate place! And now this!" he said, pointing to Apeay. I am too close to fulfilling the Perfected Diamond Law for you to stop me. Move out of my way traitor or be destroyed with him!"

"No one's destroying me!" said Apeay. "Especially not you, the one who ordered death on me, on Aven, and everyone else! You even chased me from everyone I loved, all that I knew when I was just a little boy."

"What do you mean by that? Explain yourself before I end you."

"I was minding my own business, when I got lost in the canals. Then, you showed up and chased me until I was far from home."

The eyes of Command widened, turning void, then back to normal. "So, it really was you. The child who vanished to where I could not."

"Yes, it was me. And, you've got one thing right; today someone will die! That someone is you!"

"Apeay, you must not," said the young woman. "Will you not awake, Apeay? You can make this like never before."

Neither heeded her words. The resolve of their own aim was all that mattered to them; one on a quest to rid the world of its imperfection, the other driven to end the one responsible for bringing so much turmoil to his life.

"**While I handle you, the last of the imperfect world will be handled too!**" He clasped his hands together then drew them apart. "*Meljheding Gihan, Delignos, Nulia: Xenandeadah deljaddah, Xeno astiox!*" Those intrinsic words echoed from deep within his belly outward into the land and skies above.

"Withdraw that directive! How could you just forget their kindness? They devoted themselves to you. How could you do that to them?!" said the young woman.

Apeay shot his gaze between her and his likeness. "What did you do?"

"**The low place no longer suits me. The higher realm draws nearer to me. So, there is no more need for Xeno. As there is no longer a need for you.**"

This charlatan's callousness infuriated Apeay. He raised his fist, and his great opponent did likewise striking at Apeay with a devastating blow. Apeay planted his rear foot, directly countering from the opposite side, hitting Command with a head-jarring blow from the energy he drew from the tzierhan. The cross of their attacks shook the entire planet.

It was unavoidable, they say. The great building of ancient, which long ago stood tall on a Heyliun lit day, began to crumble.

"We have a new diamond sequence. I have heard its call and it is absolute. Delignos one to twenty-one, *Xenandeadah* upwards and south *mingxan oct astiox* obliteration!" Through his new perfected knowledge, Nepcizyr deciphered the location of their great leader, sending those under his authority forward for the final onslaught.

"We accept this perfection!"

"Three one four, Jhar'ensky." Hevzanadi, the former zenshiro pilot, was in the lead as one of the glineer pilots in secret pursuit.

"Transmit," said Jhar'ensky.

"These pilots, they're like nothing I've ever seen before. They're pulling gravitational maneuvers wild enough to kill a man, like it's nothing. We're struggling to stay on their tail. Speaking of which, hold on, I have to pull a turn." Hevzanadi breathed tight as he directed his glineer to shoot upwards. "They're changing their course. But their flight pattern is complete nonsense."

"Keep up with them as best you can. They may be quick but you have the experience. We must take them down, no matter what."

"Accepted, but please understand, they're headed in a direction that's impossible for any glineer to travel. They're on course for the outer exosphere."

"It must be a ruse of some sort. Their glineers would shut down before making it that far out. Stay on them!"

"Understood, we're elevating now in pursuit. Three one four, maintain pursuit, elevate angle 36."

"Accepted," the Legionnaire pilots replied in unison.

In stealth mode, the seasoned pilots altered their altitude alignment while maintaining adequate distance for stealth pursuit. In doing so, they became aware of a phenomenon too bizarre to fathom. In all of his years as a pilot, Hevzanadi had never seen such a thing.

"My god...what is that?!"

"What's going on?" said Jhar'ensky.

"I don't know. This can't be right!"

"Tell me, what's going on up there?"

"The Tzierhan, it's above us! Them and us, we're headed straight for it! Look in the sky can't you see it? Goodness, the sky is getting brighter. But at night?"

Jhar'ensky slammed open the port on the side of the vehicle, leaning out to view the sky, and could hardly believe his eyes. Surely as Hevzanadi spoke, another tzierhan began to appear above the stratosphere. As he continued to examine the horizon, the image became more confounding. Images of grand places manifested all around the region of Estellar and the regions beyond. One their side it was night, with the Hewlix Star reigning supreme over all. On the other side, it was becoming dawn. Jhar'ensky saw a star likened to Heyliun rising over the split horizon. The horizon itself glistened, as if it was blanketed by a sea of crystals spreading out over the atmosphere.

"Yes, I see it. I agree, it's absolutely bizarre. Nevertheless, continue your pursuit no matter where in this collage of space they go. This is..."

"It's already happening! Bring them down before it's too late!" Ju-Makana interjected, taking over the transmit. "Try not to get disoriented as you cross from place to place, realm to realm. It might make you feel ill at first. But don't worry. With all the tavern-hopping you fellas do, you're used to the feeling."

"Who is this?" said Hevzanadi.

"You old dummy, I'm the one that outfitted that glineer you're piloting. I suggest less jibber jabbering and start taking those other guys down."

"Who you calling a dummy?"

"Three one four, maintain focus," said Jhar'ensky, resuming control of the transmit. "He's a little high strung, but I agree, it's time to make a move. All rings strike now!"

"Accepted." Following his lead, each pilot updated their flight sequence to "supreme assault." The battle for the future of Tzierhan had begun.

Tremors shook the land. Deafening explosive shockwaves came one after another. The appearance of shrieking silver apparitions spitting fire out of a twisted sky over the land sent many running in panic, while there were some that stood their ground, preparing to take on whatever might come their way. Among them was a Cabjha elder, declaring their inescapable demise.

"The gods have become furious and sent their caberas to end us! This is the punishment of Xeno for disregarding their ways!"

"Shut up, old man!" said one of the upper tier field guardians. "I'm not letting anyone, man or god, attack this place without consequence. Lexani squad, take to the high hills on the nvekbarahs. May your weapons be sharp and resolve even sharper. Destroy whatever attacks us. Protect the village!"

"We hear and accept."

The majestic walls of the temple were crumbling as the ground beneath shifted and swayed. The light of the ceremony was no more, nor was the ceremony itself. Was this what was promised? Had they chanted to the melody of their end?

Zaleah looked into the cutout below, looking for the source of the disturbance. But, all she could make out were waves of water slamming into the walls and a great, spinning mist. Sounds of agitated shouts filled her ears.

"Lady, what do you see?" asked Xendsvar.

"I can't tell. It sounds like Apeay is in a fight with someone down there. He sounds angry."

"Not anger," said a beautiful young woman who appeared next to them. "He's confused. You have to leave this temple before it collapses."

"Who are you?!" said Xendsvar

"Really now? The ceremony was successful was it not?"

Xendsvar nodded his head. Her words granted him knowledge beyond anything he learned from the Cabjha. "So everyone has their own."

"Sure, but keep that to yourself for now." Outside quickly, this place will not last."

"Understood."

"I don't need anyone tell me that!" said Hanjiah who was running ahead of the group. "Especially not a...who are you, anyway?"

"I'm just keeping your old legs strong. Know that," said the young woman.

"Well, excuse me. Goodness, is this what you Cabjha do? Chant songs, conjure up women, all while creating chaos that has us fleeing for our lives?"

Seldao, who was running as well, looked back towards Deslao. "Bro, doesn't this feel familiar?"

"Too familiar," said Deslao.

As, the last of the group made it out onto the main path, the great walls of Temple Fushirajhe collapsed folding in on itself.

"Apeay! Apeay!" Zaleah shouted in horror. She feared the worse. Both her and Xenzashii ran towards where the entrance once stood.

"Get back, you two!" shouted the young woman. "The delignos is rising!"

Blow for blow, fist for fist, they stood fixed delivering great pain to one another. Driven by the anger and disgust they felt for one another, neither would not submit to the pain itself. They would only continue to increase their attacks with more fury and power. When one crossed the other parried, when the other parried, the first countered again. They were like two contenders of Svarnax, battling for the ultimate prize. And, in this matter of survival, complete destruction of the other was all that mattered.

Dodging Apeay's miscalculated cross, Command leapt backwards on his hands and sprung back feet first with the fire of the perfected star. "**You lose, forever!**" The soles of his heels caught Apeay square in his solar plexus, launching him up through the stones and rubble into the atmosphere above.

The temple grounds exploded, knocking Xenzashii and Zaleah to the ground. He elevated himself from the pits below to stand before them. He looked up to the sky above, searching for the one that should be right above him. Yet there was no trace of him in the atmosphere. Sensing that it was not the end of his existence, he questioned those before him. "**Where did he go?**"

"If you'd clear your mind of this delusion you'd know by now," said the young lady.

Upon seeing the people standing with her, six in total, he reasoned what it was that accounted for her return to youth. **"Laeoxia, you had them go through with that preposterous ceremony didn't you? Well, it's too late. The ambience bends to my will."**

"Not completely. Not without my compliance and you know it. Your misguided followers won't be able to wipe away the ambience of this realm."

"You're determined to fight me to the end."

"I'm determined to keep you free. But you won't remember until it's too late."

Xenzashii shook her head, clearing her vision. "Is it you? Is it really you this time? Yes! Zjvxenozb, you're back like you promised. This place is falling apart. Will you save us? Won't you save me?" Xenzashii grabbed hold of him.

"Xenzashii, to save you..." For a brief moment Zjvxenozb gazed into Xenzashii's eyes as his countenance eased, but not for long. The fire in his eyes returned once more. **"Save you? There is nothing here to save! Only imperfection to destroy! I have chosen the empress and perfected her being.**

Don't interfere!" He shrugged her off his arm. "**Where is Apeay hiding?!**"

"I've had it with you!" He crashed upon him faster than he could respond. This time he had surely caught him off guard. Xendsvar pounced upon him, striking him relentlessly will all his might. "That is the last time you insult her!" he said, continuing to strike at his face. Finally, he had the tyrant of Xeno pinned to the ground.

How did he get so strong, and so much faster, since their last encounter? What had this imitator done to cause such a strange thing to happen? The very thought of it enraged him. "**PERFECTION WILL NOT BE STOPPED BY AN IMPERFECT MYSTIC!**" Reaching with his feet, Command stopped Xendsvar from landing another blow. Grabbing him by the arm, he launched Xendsvar over his head, straight into the broken walls behind them. Quickly, he sprang to his feet, but instantly, was caught off guard yet again.

"How about a pro?" said Deslao as he landed a charging blow so fast it spun the Magnificent One around in his place, putting him down to one knee. "So, you're this magnificent guy causing all the trouble? Dang, you two really do look just alike. Twins like my bro and me. But, you're not such a big deal. "

"Careful," said Laeoxia. "He's calculating your strength to outmatch it. We must stay clear of him until it's new again."

"Lady, please, I can handle him."

"**You are out of line, Deslao!**"

"How do you know my name?"

"Svarnax Fight Force's youngest pro. A would-be replacement for my former guard. But you took to another path. Nonetheless...SIT DOWN!" With only two fingers he struck Deslao in the abdomen, forcing all the air out from his lungs. Deslao slumped over, unconscious.

The indignant Command stood to his feet, resuming his original mission. He looked into the sky above. **"I know you're here. You can't hide for long. Where are you, boy?"**

"Would I be wrong to say that he's right here. You're my Apeay, but different," said Zaleah.

Command froze. Looking upon Zaleah, the diamond irises in his eyes changed to brown with an encompassing silver ring as he said, "I watched you die. How are you here?"

"When did that happen?" Zaleah asked. "What makes you think I'm going to die?" Zaleah reached out, stroking the hardened face of Command. "I'd never leave you, Apeay."

Command came out of his trance. The cold diamond stare returned to his eyes. **"I'm not Apeay. And your life was taken. You shouldn't be here."**

"If you're here, then she's here," said Laeoxia.

Command clenched his fist, **"Since you answered for her, I must assume this is another one of your deceptions. I see I'll have to deal with you again. This time you won't escape. Now, for the first nuisance. WHERE IS APEAY?!**

"RIGHT HERE!" Apeay, engulfed by cerulean light, came zooming down as the other elevated, intensely aglow in vermilion as they clashed midair. Their collision sent another powerful shockwave throughout the land. Together, they went up among the shrinking atmosphere, locked together in combat, flying south beyond the temple, out of sight.

Zaleah ran to the edge of the hill. The air was open and the sky was torn. Faded traces of light showed the way to which they departed. "Apeay...Apeay!" Her shouts would only be heard by those gathered on the hill, for he was too far gone, pushing further and further into a desolate, unknown region.

"Three one four, Principal Jhar'ensky."

It was the worst possible time to be interrupted. Their well-planned arrival on the foregrounds alerted Command's Team Gihan, as expected. Breaking focus for one jhenta could cost one their life when faced with overwhelming opposition. But, even so, he couldn't risk ignoring what may be vital information.

"Transmit, and make it fast!" said Jhar'ensky.

"Yes. We have them locked in strategic exilan angle 1-2-8, but it won't hold," Hevzanadi reported.

"Then change it! You're the great zenshiro of the golden era, are you not?"

"You know I am, youngster, but there's no angle to keep us safe from this new assault."

"More glineers? I thought you had all of them in sight."

"It's not glineers. I don't know what it is. They're too small to track and they're taking everyone out. Us, them, anyone in the sky. It's like they're on no one's side but their own. I have to call the team back for split assault, or we'll lose all of them. Do I have your recognition for sequence: split, shadow cover, and main support?"

Jhar'ensky was never in favor of retreating from anyone. Even when he was young, back in his earliest days on solo duty when he was caught off guard by a group of nine north star bandits who attacked him, he stood his ground despite having an exit route, and beat four of them so bad the other five ran off. But on this day, it wasn't just a matter of him alone. There were many more lives at stake. Back and forth, Jhar'ensky's mind turned wrestling with the proposal. In the end, he came to the conclusion that, if Hevzanadi in all his knowledge as the greatest zenshiro of the golden era thought it best, then he had to agree.

"Recognized. Sequence, split, those in split continue attack in free-form angles, shadow cover, and main support."

"Accepted."

Just as he tapped off the transmit, their vehicle was hit by a neutraxova ray. The armor on their vehicle dispersed most of the destructive radiation away from them. Still, the mynderajzen had taken considerable damage. Another direct hit might break through, leaving Jhar'ensky not a jhenta to hesitate. It was time to implement the last phase of the plan.

"Three one four, teams Three and Four, sequence inward fold and overtake!"

"Accepted."

The two teams that traveled along the outer path to the foregrounds, revealed themselves with a loud battle cry.

"Three one four, Team One, sequence line devastation, secondary sequence, decimate the sioleh."

"Accepted."

Like a lifetime lived over once again, Jhar'ensky was in full stride, leading his team to a strategic victory. Upon viewing the grand diamond sioleh, he shook his head at his own blindness. He could have prevented this all, he thought to himself, if he had only paid closer attention to the dealings within. But he shrugged off the notion as not to lose sight of the current task at hand. Jhar'ensky, studied the oversized sioleh, looking for its weakest points.

"Three one four, Team one, listen on the front west…" Jhar'ensky bit his tongue. What sequence would he issue that would not bring them harm? In the middle of the sioleh, he saw a transparent crystal prism encloser that imprisoned both Thorel and Bexhiera.

"Three one four, transmit was suspended, please repeat," said Team One's nikashiro.

"Repeal secondary sequence. I repeat, repeal secondary sequence!"

"Logic of repeal required."

"Use your eyes and look! Captives are trapped within the sioleh. One Zennite Thorel," Jhar'ensky held the transmitter firmly to maintain his composure as he continued, "and one Bexhiera Regalis."

"Secondary sequence repealed."

Ju-Makana gasped as he looked over Jhar'ensky through the viewport. "What kind of madness is that?! He's got them up there like they're a trophy or something."

"Another unexpected setback. But at least we've found them. It looks like they're alright, thank goodness."

He could see them looking back at him from within the prism. Both waving their hands about, when he heard a voice.

"Jhar'ensky it's me."

"Thorel?... How are you communicating with us? You're not coded to this combat channel."

"She's using her body's new ability to merge with energy wave forms to create a link between her mind and the vehicle's transmitter," Ju-Makana explained.

"Ju-Makana, is that you?" Thorel asked.

"You know it. What can I do for ya?"

"I'm hoping you know a way to get us out of here."

"Sure do, lady. More than likely, he put a magnetic seal on that prism, set to the polar opposite of the sioleh's mechanics. Easy work."

"That's good to know.

Haru peered out through the mynderajzen's viewport to see where they were heading. Up ahead, he caught a view of the sioleh. It was emitting crystal vapors into the air, and above the sea of crystals the image of a translucent gold pyramid appeared. Above that, a third tzierhan manifested.

Jhar'ensky took a deep breath and transmitted a new sequence. "Three one four, Team One."

"Transmit."

"Sequence, cover strike over my vehicle; continue cover strike once we're on foot."

"Accepted," replied Team One.

"On foot?" said Ju-Makana.

"Of course," said Jhar'ensky. "As in, we're going in on foot to get them out. This is a large vehicle which makes it a large target. I can't risk anyone firing near the sioleh."

"Sure and I have two words for you."

"What is that?"

"Principal shototu."

"I already know, just be ready to run when I stop the mynderajzen."

"I believe I'm more ready to run than you are. Just give me the sign."

With the tap of a lever, the doors slid open. In one economical motion, Jhar'ensky leapt out the of vehicle while slinging his neutranevex over his shoulder. Ju-Makana trailed closely behind.

As they stood over Deslao, Seldao reassured everyone, "My bro's alright. He's taken harder hits than that."

Just as he spoke, Deslao regained consciousness and sat upright. Holding his abdomen he said, "Ugh, damn, that hurt bad. I gotta learn that technique."

A large boulder fell over where Xendsvar lay. He was conscious but badly injured. Xenzashii felt compelled to check in on him, deeply moved by his actions. A great emotion came over her as she placed her right hand on his chest in perfect alignment with her left hand resting on the crown of his head. "*Yeshnah... meixandee...* restore."

The cuts and bruises on Xendsvar's body vanished. His fractured ribs mended as his dislocated shoulder went back into place. With his healed arm, Xendsvar caressed Xenzashii's face. "Thank you."

"No, thank you," said Xenzashii. She felt a sweet sensation drawing her into his eyes but was pulled out of it upon hearing cries from the village. Xenzashii walked over to the edge of the high cliff where she could see the turmoil unfolding before her eyes. "I don't understand. What kind of perfection is this?"

"The day he forgot his dream, was the day he forgot everything," said the young woman. "But for now, we wait."

"Wait for what?" asked Zaleah. "And who are you?"

"I only left you for a moment, an etch in the cycle and you already forgot me? Look in my eyes and know the ceremony was a success."

"The old woman? And he called you Laeoxia. You're an actual goddess?"

"You're mistaken, I'm a person, like you. However, I'm entwined with the ambience itself. The ceremony reverted the temporal alignment to nine thousand cycles in the past, returning me to the way I appeared when he and I first arrived."

"This place is being destroyed, while Apeay fights for his life, and you're telling us to sit and wait?"

"Yes, we wait for Apeay while you come to your senses. We all know how Apeay can be. He has a tendency to be a little late in his affairs."

"You're making fun of him?"

Laeoxia laughed. "No, I wouldn't dream of it. Perhaps I'm teasing just a bit." The lady took a seat on the edge of the high hill. "You see, he finally did doze off in another cave. While you stayed by his side like we once did a long, long time ago." Her words mystified Zaleah. When Laeoxia said, *we once did a long, long time ago,* a montage of visions ran through Zaleah's mind. She saw a boy in a field and herself. Then the figure of a person snagging her as the boy chased after.

"Look up and around you."

They turned their attention to the sky above. But there was no sky. Around them three identical tzierhans were closing in. In the shrinking atmosphere, glineers skirmished, going from tzierhan to tzierhan, sending enemy glineers crashing above, below, or in between.

"Laeoxia, if you are not a goddess, as you say, then are they the gods of the air who are at war with us?" asked Xendsvar.

"If that is what you believe, then yes, the gods are always at war. But I suggest this is the doing of everyone that is, or ever will be. We all evolved from the land of the gods. And what you see there, those are physical alignments brought from another place to this place for the purpose of complete annihilation."

"In plain terms, they're glineers, big fella," said Seldao.

"Come again?" said Hanjiah.

"Glineers. Are they still fighting from the festival?" Seldao arched back, taking in the full view and saw it all. "It can't be."

Zaleah looked on as well, confirming his unbelief. "Estellar?"

Seldao paced back and forth on the high hill, looking in between the land below them, above them, and around them. It was only in theory that such a thing was possible. But after these recent experiences, he wasn't one to think so skeptically as to what could or could not be. "If confining the expanding sphere to the hydroxic axis, a new space unseen must come into being. A space outside of space itself, outside of time and matter aligned with the closing center like a mirror reflecting its own image over time," said Seldao.

"My stomach feels better, but now my head's hurting. What's that supposed mean bro?" said Deslao.

"It means there's a new place in time, like a new tzierhan, or even a new cosmos maybe, coming into being in the middle of a collapsed star."

"It's where the invisible alignment hides. It's always right next to us, even though we can't touch it," said Hanjiah. "Well, now I see where he conjured that nvekbarah from. And folks, I suggest we get out of here."

"You're want to leave the people behind?" said Xendsvar.

"The people are fine, they'll fight and survive until it all changes, or collapses into nothingness. Either way, they'll be fine, unlike us involved in the ceremony. We'll be trapped. The little old, young lady here left out the part about us becoming entwined in the invisible alignment."

"I was wondering when you'd figure it out," said Laeoxia.

"I figured it out right before it started. You see I gave the Magnificent One the schematics to create a land "in-between." When I did, I thought of the danger it could pose if someone got it wrong. So I came up with another schematic for a device to counter it. During the ceremony, we were the device. For the device to work, its energy's gotta bind within the collapsing sphere, trapping it there. Wow, I never thought he'd use those schematics like this. He used them incorrectly on purpose. For once I agree with you, Xendsvar. That man is perverse."

"You only agree because it's obvious now."

"Talk about ruining a good moment. Anyway, were gonna do like Apeay did and make us our own vehicle."

"But we don't have a power source," said Seldao.

"Oh yes we do," said Hanjiah, reaching into his pouch. "I figured it hadn't worn out its use and snagged it on our way out." He held the ornament in his hand. "And seeing it for what it is first hand, I'm sure we can get it to work as long as Xendsvar can tell us what to say to it."

"You don't need him to tell you," said Laeoxia. "You have all the ability to do that for yourself."

"But I don't know all that mystic talk like he does."

"There is no longer a ceremony to invoke, only a vehicle to make. That you can make on your own, and when you do, you'll take us everywhere."

"Even if they can, I will not abandon my own people," said Xendsvar.

"Nor will I," said Xenzashii.

Xendsvar joined his partner Xenzashii on the edge, looking over his beloved home. Among the chaos of the village, amidst the fires and quakes, he heard the cries of the young and old. He heard the voices of his fellow Cabjha chanting the "Song of Serenity." Xendsvar's heart was pounding like the atabau. "The people of the village need me."

Laeoxia placed her hand over his heart, "I'm glad you feel that way. But for now, the people are fine and defending themselves. Soon it will be like a dream; today's war made a legend, and you in a new life."

"Laeoxia," said Seldao, "to travel to any place beyond the confining sphere would require a speed unknown to reality itself."

"Then stop trying to know, and feel it. Create for us something to travel in. A vehicle fashioned to your liking."

"That won't work," said Deslao. "The only thing ol' boy can handle is a capsyint. It's the only travel he thinks is safe." He knew that one stung because it was true.

"That works just fine," said Laeoxia. "No matter the vehicle, it will travel to the same place. Together create us a capsyint to take us home."

"How am I supposed to do that? I don't know how to use that "Aruja" ornament thing like Apeay does."

"You will, once you take hold of it. Apeay gave us the ornament to use as we will because he trusts us for who we are."

"And who might that be?" asked Hanjiah.

"We're his friends. We were always his friends, even when he forgot. We need to be there for him, so he knows where he is. Make a way back for him, Seldao."

Seldao took the ornament from Hanjiah's hand. "Sure is a lot of work being Apeay's friend. First you're watching him fly at a festival, the next thing you know, you're figuring out how to save him from himself. I wouldn't have it any other way."

The ornament began pulsating until the light from the center traveled up the veins of Seldao's arm, lighting his blood stream to his heart, then returned to the ornament.

"That's the way," said Seldao. "Hanjiah, guide my eyes to the outer start and endpoints of Xeno."

Hanjiah looked between him and the young woman who simply nodded her head. "One here, at north prime, one there at south, a direct 20 relah, where the horizon drops off and the rest at four equal alignments aligned horizontally and vertically between."

Seldao sat down and drew in the dirt with his finger. He drew out not a calculation, but an image of what he wanted, and stared upon the image for a brief moment. He stood to his feet and held the ornament to the alignment defined by Hanjiah and spoke, "*Zhyeshiax onex capzhiahdan maingxos!*"

A single cerulean ray of light emitted from the ornament, traveling to the outmost points of Xeno, then splitting in two. The other ray traveled downwards towards the tzierhan. Now, like the river had been before, the light became a continuous ribbon folding over on itself three times, as it changed hue from cerulean to amethyst. It extended itself around the land below on all sides, while the other light path above mirrored the one below.

"It's ready," said Seldao.

"Bro, that was something different but, um, I think you were supposed to build some sort of vehicle," said Deslao.

"He did," said Hanjiah. "Some people just can't follow an alignment to its end. Look down the hill behind you."

A translucent onyx capsyint, trimmed in gold, rested on glowing violet rays.

"That's one big cabera," said Hanjiah. "I hope you can handle it."

"I've never navigated one before. Thought you might be able to help me," said Seldao.

"What about Apeay?" asked Zaleah.

"He has his own way of getting where he wants to be. And there is no place he'd rather be than with you. Believe me."

Zaleah looked up towards the shrinking stratosphere as the blue and orange fires jetted back and forth among flashes of exploding silver. "You better not forget this time. And don't be late."

Each of them scurried down the hillside to where the capsyint awaited them. As they neared the brilliant vehicle, the doors slid open. All but the young woman hopped aboard.

"Hey lady, aren't you coming?" said Hanjiah.

"I am already where I need to be," said Laeoxia. "I always am."

"I swear, lady, you're one of the strangest I've ever met. And, something tells me it won't be the last time we cross paths."

"Perhaps."

"Well then, take care of yourself."

The young woman simply nodded to him with a wink, vanishing into the landscape. Hanjiah's eyes widened as the doors of the capsyint slid shut. His heart beat intensely while peering out the viewport.

"That's the way it came to me, too," said Xendsvar. Hanjiah had come to realize what he'd realized some time ago. "The kid there is ready. Show him the way."

"Good, because I've been ready. And don't even think about stopping this capsyint until we're back, bro." said Deslao.

Seldao was too captivated by the simplistic complexity of this technological monster to pay heed to his brother's words. The symbol alignments were broken down into singular angle directions. No matter how far, close, above, below, in or out the destination may be, the desired destination could be navigated to by singular directions attached to the crystal cords at his fingertips. Therefore, the mystery was how to pinpoint a specific location with such a basic navigating device.

"Don't overthink it, kid," said Hanjiah. "Take us there the same way you got here."

"Just like that?" said Zaleah. Everyone on board awaited his explanation.

"Yeah, it's like that. Sort of like looking up at the sky. Not because you don't know what's gonna happen. But, because you do know. You know that soon the star will rise. And when it does, you're gonna ride that starlight right back to where you were before. Do you see?"

The vision Zaleah had prior, came back to her in more detail. This time it was her and a boy standing in the field looking up at the stars, a man grabbing her, the boy chasing them until a falling star struck the field. "I don't know what I see, but I feel it. I think I get it now."

In his mind, Seldao recalled everything prior event up to this point, going all the way back to the first day he and his brother met Apeay.

"Alright people, we're outta here," said Seldao. He pulled on one cord and the capsyint charged up. Hanjiah sat down next to him, keeping an eye on the workings of the mechanical alignments. As the great capsyint continued to grow in power, each of them took to a seat.

In Xenzashii's heart remained a trace of regret. She let out a deep sigh, staring out the upper viewport. Zaleah followed her gaze into the shining devastation of the stratus and moved to a seat beside her.

"It's really not that bad," said Zaleah.

Xenzashii lowered her head, staring Zaleah in the eyes. Her eyes were asking but one question. Zaleah embraced her, comforting her, and whispered in her ear.

"For real?" said Xenzashii.

Zaleah nodded her head in confirmation.

The capsyint whirred, fully charged at its maximum capacity. "Sit tight and hold on everyone. Time to fly!" In a flash, the capsyint bolted away, on course to their new home.

CHAPTER 24

In the expanse above everyone that stood below, the atmospheres of every tzierhan from each age were merging into one. There was nowhere to escape to. The people of Xeno, the entire inferior tzierhan, along with the people of Estellar, Sohexiah, Alizan, Djhalho, and Tazjoha, stood watching in terror as the skies closed in on each other.

Meanwhile, the most exclusive of battles raged on. The supreme ruler would not allow more time to slip by. He would not stand to lose control of his master design.

"You might as well fall. Fall down and yield to the great perfection. Your power is fading, while mine is ENDLESS!"

Apeay had already come to this reality. Indeed, with each exchange, his strength dwindled. He was beginning to have trouble just keeping up with the high-speed movements. They were soaring across the sky so fast that neither he nor Command took notice of the war being waged around them, as the velocity of their speed created supersonic vibrations instantly disintegrating anything in their path. In, out, back and forth, they flew through countless regions, drawing their atmospheres into the gravitational pull of their flight. However, the chaos left in their wake was insignificant to them. Each had but one driving thought. The absolute annihilation of the other.

"Fall to you?! After you made my life a living nightmare?!" Apeay shouted. The insolence of Command's suggestion disgusted Apeay to the core of his being. Enraged, Apeay roared with each swing of his fists, striking Command with seven consecutive blows, the last one sending him headlong through the northern gemstone factory tower. Apeay sped to follow up with another blow.

But as Command shook off the attack he flew into the face of Apeay and scoffed, **"A flurry of punches mean nothing when you lack true power."** Command waved at him beckoning him on in his attack. **"Come try again."**

Command's goading worked. Furious, Apeay found yet untapped strength within him. He tensed ever muscle within his body until his entire being was aglow with tremendous power which he released in an instant.

"*Zenxjz*," said Command.

It was like it was back then, when he fought Jahlije in the palace. The perfect strike to his enemy, landed precisely on target, straight to his own face. Moreover to Apeay's surprise, he stood to his own side grabbing his own wrist while still reeling from the blow. Apeay could not pull back his hand. Command, back in place, gripped his wrist tight. He yanked

Apeay to him and clasped his head with a dauntingly powerful grip.

"If it is a nightmare you say I have created, then I will end it for you!"

Like a falling star, Command drove Apeay towards the tzierhan. To Apeay, it seemed the harder he pulled away the deeper Command's grip dug into his skull. Command had him in a death grip. With his face to the stars above, Apeay impacted the ground with a great thunderous boom, as Command burrowed them deep below the surface. The collision sent a shockwave through the middle tzierhan.

Down through the foregrounds, past the rift, the energy from the twin stars' impact jolted up through the foreground, past the rift., and the diamond sioleh cracked. The multi angled prism holding Bexhiera and Rionazen captive, shattered.

"What was that?" Ju-Makana exclaimed.

Jhar'ensky regained his balance, observing the point of impact. There was a deep crater and rows of fissures around it. One of fissures went straight towards their primary destination. "I don't know, but look up there."

Bexhiera was free, freely floating, holding tight to Rionazen, who had come to the full understanding of her perfected body. They touched down just a step away from where they stood.

"My dear, it's so good to see you!" Jhar'ensky held Bexhiera in a deep embrace. "I'm sorry I let this happen. I shouldn't have let you stay there alone."

"It's alright," said Bexhiera "Apeay, something has happened to him."

"We know. We still can't find him."

"He didn't go far. He's still here."

Jhar'ensky grasped her meaning. "If so, then he still went far. Thorel, how are you flying?"

Rionazen shrugged her shoulders and replied, "It's just like walking. I see what he means by perfection, though I wouldn't call it that. It's like being in an alternate state at all times. I'm both here and there, on Tzierhan but within the ambience of a star, that I can draw to or pull away from."

"Bravo, you caught on fast. But what will we do with you, now that you've ruined his sioleh?" It was Valus accompanied by Nepcizyr amidst a group of Gihan soldiers. They had them surrounded. The Legionnaires, who had provided cover fire to keep them at bay, were struggling to hold back the overwhelming opposition, losing comrades on all sides.

" It wasn't I who damaged it. Something else did that. But what a pleasure," said Rionazen.

"Oh, is it such a pleasure? Are you changing your mind, now that you've experienced some of the advantages of the eternal perfection?" said Valus.

"Not at all. My wish was to see you just one more time. Once more to watch you and all your cohorts go down for good."

Valus cut his eyes to Nepcizyr, then looked back to Thorel and laughed. "I think your newfound abilities are clouding your sense of judgment. We're winning; your team is losing. What a shame. A grand rescue attempt, just to bring us back to where we started."

Jhar'ensky unslung his neutranevex from his shoulder, pressing the muzzle against Valus' forehead. The surrounding Gihan soldiers responded immediately, training their neutra-nevex's on Jhar'ensky. Nepcizyr motioned for them to hold back their assault.

"Go ahead, let them fire," said Jhar'ensky. "This one will be long gone before I go down."

"My old friend, haven't you figured this out?" said Valus. "I can't be killed like this and neither can she, unfortunately. Don't you see what we are now?" Valus stood tall, looking him squarely in the eyes. "I don't see how they ever chose you over me. So dense, lacking the wisdom and the vision needed to bring proper order to our region. But in the end, it's all the same. Order has been restored."

"You're the idiot, Valus," said Bexhiera. "It was our sector that kept you out of that position. When the principal aeroxia asked you about your plans for the new Centre, you waved it aside like it was an inappropriate question. You never expressed any interest in helping any cause outside of anything that wasn't directly linked to your personal concerns. Therefore we unanimously voted against you."

"Yes, and voted your husband in. You thought you could keep all the power unbalanced and unchecked if you kept it at home."

"Just the opposite. We did it for balance."

"Sure you did. And the region about fell apart only three cycles into his illustrious career. What an excellent choice you made."

"That was your doing, along with everyone who conspired alongside you," said Jhar'ensky.

"No, my friend. We did what we had to make certain the course stayed true to its original path. The shortcomings of Estellar were a blasphemous scar on our name. We had nothing to do with them beyond the fact that we took the necessary measures to get this vessel under control and steer it right, without your input. We've made practical, working, functional perfection, one can grasp with their hands, while you whittled your time away strolling in gardens with mystics and caretakers. Their charms must've misled you to give in to ideals that were certain to keep us from achieving its greatest reward."

"Were you ever really my friend? I sought to live my life as a man of honor like I once thought you to be. But now I see. You were just pretending. There's no so-called 'reward' great enough to overlook the needs of the people, to sacrifice the lives of innocent people, just because they don't share a certain ideology. I was elected Principal because I understood that. My biggest mistake was being too caring, too trusting of people like you."

"You don't get it. I saved your life several times. I think it's fair to say I was friendly enough. So if you're going to shoot me, then do it. What's stopping you? Pull the trigger already," Valus taunted. "Can't do it, can you? I mean, after all, you were only a Legionnaire Guard and not a true soldier, so you never had to make any hard decisions then. That's why you couldn't pull the trigger then, and you won't now."

Valus repeatedly tapped his forehead against the neutra-nevex, doing so until the neutranevex went off.

The electrified crackling startled Jhar'ensky. He didn't re-cognize himself pulling the trigger. But to his and most every-one else's surprise, the hytradilihan rays were orbiting about Valus in a whirlwind of light.

"Thank you for the boost of energy. Not that I needed it," said Valus. "Here, try some for yourself!" He struck Jhar'ensky across the face with the back of his hand, expelling the hytra-dilihan rays in all directions. Jhar'ensky flew backwards into Ju-Makana, who was standing several paces behind him, knocking him to the ground with him as he fell.

"Jhar'ensky!" Bexhiera hollered.

"What about me?!" said Ju-Makana "Do you know how heavy a man in armor is? I can't breathe under here!"

Jhar'ensky shook his head. The blow was a mixture of raw power and overwhelming heat. It almost felt like he'd been shot with a hytrin shooter. The side of his face where Valus made contact was singed. After another shake of the head to clear his mind, he rolled himself over, mustering the strength to stand to his feet. "I'm alright."

Ju-Makana huffed as he regained his composure. "Using any type of radiant energy against them is out of the question. Their bodies are in an unbreakable alignment with the stars, giving them the ability to absorb and redistribute enormous amounts of energy as they please. That's where their power is coming from. They're like conduits for cosmic radiation."

"Why didn't you tell me this beforehand?" said Jhar'ensky.

"I just figured it out. Just because I'm a shototu doesn't mean I know everything."

"Then figure out a way to undo it. Nothing is unbreakable."

"Even if he could, he won't have enough time," said Valus. "What do you say, Nepcizyr?"

"I say, our generosity has come to an end," said Nepcizyr. "*Meljheding Gihan vovoshi-jhozhesta astiox*!" The Gihan soldiers present retrained their aim on the encircled four. "And Thorel, since you were foolishly given the gift of eternal perfection, this won't work on you. I'll end you personally!"

"**You will?! ON WHO'S COMMAND?!**" Command hovered, fixed between the shrinking sky and the throng amongst the foregrounds.

Nepcizyr spun around, quickly taking to a knee. "Your excellency, it's clear she has no interest in upholding the diamond law, *your* diamond law. Why should she remain when she is clearly against us?"

"**My diamond law exists on the foundation that my discretion is in alignment with that perfection. She can only be for us, whether she believes it or not, chooses it or not, for it's the choice of perfection. DO NOT QUESTION ME UNLESS YOU WISH TO BE FOUND IMPERFECT YOURSELF! So I say...ungh.**"

Command was in a headlock. Apeay had snuck up to his rear, seizing him without warning.

"You thought it was over? You thought you buried me? **It's far from over!**" Apeay shouted.

They were side by side in a struggle; Apeay to the right and Command to the left. All those present on the foregrounds were stunned. Who was this one to challenge their great leader?

Looking up at the perplexing sight, Bexhiera cried out, "There he is! Apeay, Apeay, we're here!" Bexhiera continued to call out to him, but to no avail. Apeay's focus was on Command.

However, for Rionazen, upon seeing them face to face, she awoke to the truth of this mystery. As her thoughts traveled about, she devised a plan to end the conflict once and for all. Taking advantage of this distraction, she pulled Jhar'ensky, Bexhiera and Ju-Makana close to her. "I apologize in advance for what I'm about to do."

"Don't do it," said Ju-Makana.

"I haven't told you my plan yet, and you're already against it?"

"You don't have to. Ever since I singled out the source of his endless energy, I've been calculating a way to break the alignment. A collapsing star within a collapsing star. It'll ruin his gateway, too. How'd you figure it out?"

"Because I'm one with him. He didn't just change my body, he gave me his knowledge."

"That's why he calls you his "empress"."

"Exactly. I have to do what must be done."

"I don't know if that's safe for any of us, but it's all we have. I just hate that it's you."

"What are you two talking about?" Jhar'ensky asked.

"This isn't a time to worry," said Thorel. "Listen carefully before they get wise to us." Jhar'ensky could tell by her tone, that she was concealing her own unease for their sake. But he didn't interrupt. He nodded to her, then looked away as she continued. "I'm going to create a diversion. When I do, you three head to the mynderajzen. Leave this place quickly. Give a sequence to get everyone as far away from this place as possible."

"I don't understand. We're in the middle of a battle," said Jhar'ensky.

"I do," said Ju-Makana. "This battle will soon be over. Don't worry. We will." He bowed his head and sighed.

"And what about Apeay?" said Bexhiera. "Won't you help him?"

"My dear, that's exactly what I intend to do. He's going to be just fine. I brought him back safe last time, didn't I?"

"That you did," said Jhar'ensky. He clasped Thorel's hands for a brief moment and let her go.

"Don't forget after this is over, you owe me a drink," said Thorel.

"You bet, Speedy Tho-tho," said Jhar'ensky.

Rionazen looked above to the two locked in contest with one another, and elevated her position to meet them in the atmosphere. Perceiving her objective, Valus and Nepcizyr did likewise, while the Gihan ground troops took immediate aim as she approached their great leader. They were no longer concerned with the other three standing on the foregrounds.

"It's now or never," said Ju-Makana.

"I can't" said Bexhiera. "He's our child. I just can't leave him behind."

"My dear, we must go. You can trust Thorel; our son will be fine. Honestly, I don't think we ever had to be worried. Whatever clever strategy she has up her sleeve is going to work out. As long as I've known her, she's never failed to make good on her word." Jhar'ensky looked Bexhiera in her eyes. "We have to go. I have more legionnaires to look after, some whom may require your expertise. Everything's going to be alright."

"Well it won't be if we stay here," said Ju-Makana. "Let's get out of here before they notice us."

Bexhiera looked up to her son in midair as Jhar'ensky pulled her away. The three of them took a path to the side, going the long way around the foregrounds to where the mynderajzen rested.

Meanwhile, in the great shrinking atmosphere, the perfected ones caught up with Apeay and Command.

"Apeay, as your empress, I command you to let him go!" said Thorel.

"This man is a murderer! He can't be allowed to live!" Apeay shouted.

"He is no murderer, only an idealist. His objective is to perfect all as they should be."

"Spoken like my true empress. Do as she says and LET GO!" Command struck Apeay in the face with his right elbow, then his abdomen with his left, forcing Apeay to release his hold. He spun around with fist raised, ready to strike Apeay yet again. But before he could, Rionazen grabbed hold of his arm, inciting his displeasure. **"Are you still defying me?"**

"I don't defy you, your excellency. Only offering to relieve you of this burden. Engaging in battle with this impostor is unfit for someone as great as you. Though his strength is great, he is still an imperfect being."

"**I am aware of this. If you're going to do something, do it quickly before he regains his strength.**"

"So that's it? You joined up with them now? Is that why you helped my parents find me back then? So you could keep a close eye on me? Just whose side are you on? Apeay asked.

"That's what I'm thinking. I agree, your excellency," said Nepcizyr. "Don't wait any longer."

"**I'm not in conversation with you. Empress, speak quickly before I lose interest.**"

"Like I said, he's imperfect, and we have him surrounded. Therefore..." Thorel flew behind Apeay and pinned his wrist to his back, "order your Gihan to open fire on him, his imperfect body will be vaporized in an instant! Nepcizyr, Valus, you morons hurry and help me restrain him so he can't take off!"

Stunned, Nepcizyr rushed to her assistance as did Valus, all too pleased to destroy anything that was of value to his former friend.

It was but a moment too long for Apeay. Once again, he was overwhelmed by his opposition, who had the unfair advantage over him. Even with all of his might, he couldn't break free of their abnormally strong grasp.

"**As it should be. As it always was. As it will be. Now, all will be made as iz...*Gihan hydrilzheon Apeay marxian astiox*!**"

From the foregrounds came the call, "Gihan accepts this perfection!"

From the tzierhan heading skyward the flash of 144 hytradilihan rays discharged, all trained on Apeay, converged to one focal point.

"Get down!" Thorel shouted.

In less than a jhenta, in less time than it takes to blink, Rionazen released her grip on Apeay, flinging him aside as she smashed Nepcizyr and Valus' heads into one another, causing them to fall away. By doing so, all the hytradilihan rays were absorbed by her perfected body. All around her, the rays swirled. And being that it was not one but many, she felt great power surging through her. The intensity was so great that it heated the atmosphere around them, creating various fields of inexplicable weather.

"I knew you were no different from him," said Valus. "You have the insight, the edge, everything it takes to make it this level where only the diamonds shine. But like him, a soft-hearted fool, you tricky, condescending binnal!"

"I'm soft-hearted, you say? Alright then, your mind must not have been perfected with your body. You forgot what I said I'd do to you if you ever degraded me again. And I keep my word."

Faster than light itself, she zipped past Command, snagging up Valus and Nepcizyr by their collars. They were helpless in her grasp. The rays she'd absorbed multiplied her alignment with the star a hundred times over.

"After everything I did for you, this is how you repay me?! You choose to save what shouldn't exist?! I made so many sacrifices for us, for us to be in perfection together as it should be. You deny the perfect us?"

"You still don't see," said Rionazen. "I don't deny the perfect anything; But what you want, what you call 'perfection' is beyond our control, so I accepted it for what it is. Maybe one day you will too...Apeay, when we're here once again, we can break free. Take care of your people." Thorel twirled away from the duo, while jerking Valus and Nepcizyr up to eye level with her. "Hold on you two. Zennite's cabera sequence: diamond decimation!"

Flying, soaring with reckless abandon, Thorel propelled herself along with the treacherous pair towards the crown jewel of Command's ultimate design. It was so sudden that neither he nor Apeay had time to comprehend her actions.

Her friends, her comrades, most of whom knew her as family were frozen, dumbstruck by grief, as their beautiful gem of a friend collided with the grand diamond sioleh as she uttered the chant, "*Nadee ah'seh gxos!*"

The star energy contained within her cosmic body destabilized as she made contact with the sioleh, causing diamond statue to shatter into billions if not trillions of reflective fragments of stardust that were instantly drawn to an invisible center. From one side of the horizon to the other, there appeared a great rift surging from the north like a storm. Then, at once, all the energy that at one time swirled about imploded at the center. Every region from all ages, all realms of space and time space itself, converged at the absolute center, disappearing into the dark schism.

From the greatest nikashiro to the most brilliant shototu and despised mystic, all were gone. The life they knew had vanished into a space unknown. There was nothing left but a desolate, uninhabited region. A region without light or darkness, without knowledge or ignorance. There were no stars, atmosphere, no tzierhan above or below, no alignments, no dreams of perfection.

And yet, somehow, they remained.

He sat himself down upon nothing staring intently at this one. The other did likewise. Both were confounded, for there was nothing to see and nowhere to go. Only between their thoughts could there be seen a faint light. It was impossible to know if anything had been saved or not. After what could be considered an infinite measure of time, a question arose.

"Was this it?"

"I don't know. I don't know what this is."

"You do know! It's the very reason you were created; to destroy everything I worked for."

"I said I don't know. I never wanted to destroy anything. All I ever wanted was to be where I belonged. I've been chased from here, pushed there, forced to fight battles that I never wanted to be a part of. And, I don't know who this 'they' is, you're talking about. I just want to go home."

"There's no home for you. You're a fantasy, a myth conjured by mystic ignorance. They only dreamed of a perfect world. Now, because of them and you and everyone that slept, everything's ruined. Eons of arduous work had finally come to pay off. So close to that perfect moment. And now all of it, all gone." Command stood to his feet, staring into a bleak, unknown opening. **"I was the only one that knew; the only one to stay awake, watching, guiding, making perfection a reality. The only one..."**

Apeay watched Command as he paced to and fro upon a path of emptiness, with a look of despair in his diamond-like eyes. The feet of Command shuffled as he shook his head in bewilderment. Command was stuck, murmuring the same words over and over again. **"The only one to stay awake, the only one...awake to perfection was I...the only one to stay awake..."**

Apeay noticed an imprint on the side of Command's pants, and without regard for how Command might react, he reached in his side pocket. To his surprise, Command did not admonish, or resist him. Instead, for the first time, he simply observed Apeay in silence. Apeay reached into the depths of the inner folds of his pouch and retrieved a phenomenal paradox. It was a single golden writing utensil. Emblazed on the side facing him was the word, *AWAKE*. Apeay shook his head in disbelief. Yet there was no other explanation. It was the same golden utensil that he found back then.

"Where did you get this?" said Apeay.

Command ceased his pacing to look over his shoulder back at Apeay. He peered over at him for but a moment more. He turned back to where Apeay rested and took his grand seat on the throne of the void.

"I've had it all my life."

"All your life?"

"Yes."

"How?"

"One day I woke up and there it was..."

"Not possible or...Wait...Like from a dream?"

"If only there were such things as dreams. **Dreams are only a dream themselves, and nothing more!**"

"You're wrong...But I know how you feel. Dreams are only dreams. They come, then they go."

"You understand how I feel?"

"As I stand here, I do."

"Tell me then, please tell me, who are you?"

"I could ask you the same, because I've never known...I am Apeay."

"Dream of Zjvxenozb..."

He leaned forward extending his hand as he did the same. The other's eyes widened and shouted, "Wait!..." A violent gust of wind tore through the invisible spectrum, leaving only him and himself there alone.

He stood on in a place of pure thought, as his body was neither perfect nor imperfect. He wore no silver-laced garments, hooded tops or anything for that matter. There was nothing else left for him to see as he said to himself, "You should have nowhere to take me."

Within the pits of utter bleakness, a cool wind gently caressed his cheek. Not letting a jhenta go by, with a swift movement he caught the gentle breeze, cupping it in his palm. Though it was cool, the wind in his hand gained heat until it was hotter than the star, Heyliun. Invoked to action by this sensation, Apeay using both his hands, held the breeze high as he spun himself round and round, in multiple spherical alignments until a great whirlwind surrounded his center. It seemed to dance about as the wind pirouetted to the direction of his center. "For my life, there is but one place you should take me."

While spinning, Apeay threw the wind into the empty space before him.

Both plasma and lightning appeared, giving light to the darkness within the great twister of wind. Spreading far and wide, the exploding winds revealed an ethereal masterpiece. Powerful sky, sea, and land creatures emerged, raging among the flames. Civilizations rose and fell within the blink of an eye.

Beautiful songs overlaid the seamless cadence of marching men. The seas and the rivers flourished with life fixed between cascades of mountains of rubies, emeralds, topaz, and opals. Icy blasts somersaulted over clouds crashing headlong into lofty pillars of ivory. It was uninhabited and rare, yet common.

The panorama that engulfed him shot out in all directions with sonorous thunder. Clouds of blue diamonds, scorching flames, and dusty winds were scattered abroad by a cosmic shockwave going so fast that light trailed behind its expanse. Before his eyes, luminous orbs appeared out the clouds, until one shone at a great distance some 2,187,309 reels away. The orb rapidly expanded until it dominated the cosmic horizon.

Staring upon the brilliant crystal-blue sea, he knew it was true.

"Zjvxenozb, my life is Apeay? That can't be right. I am Apeay... I am...well..." He knew something he'd forgotten long ago at his admission. "I left him right there. I have to hurry."

He looked to the star, raising both arms upwards and out. *"Zjzhbe'han Xenoshiiox!"*

Twin flames rose from the core spinning in opposite congruent directions. The tail end of each took hold of him with each passing. Gradually, he found himself caught up in the throes of its immense gravity. With each pass, with each crisscrossing orbit, his velocity increased ten-thousand-fold. Timing the orbit, he calculated the correct alignment, at the precise moment to make his leap as he lunged forward and kicked off.

Clouds of dust were ignited by the soles of his feet as he made his way back. Everything became but a blur around him. He was gliding through an endless river of liquid starlight. At this point, he wasn't even sure how far he was along. He ran with highly ordered swiftness until he felt his legs beneath him once again.

Then...

There was a clearing...

Within a mist, a lush field of fruit flowers among tufts of honey kissed straw lay before him. Wrapped around them were lush exotic trees. Overhead, the sky was a brilliant cobalt blue, lit by the yellow-orange star. He proceeded on his journey, feeling the pull to explore as he crossed through the field until he reached the edge of the sea. In the distance, he saw a vast place, and set off along the edge of the waters. All at once, he became aware of his location.

This seems about right.

Off in the distance, he heard an odd noise coming from several sannos away. Observing his surroundings again, he was sure that this sound was very much out of place for there was only him standing alone in the field.

Whoosh...whoosh...whoosh...

Out of an invisible alignment, the radiant cabera appeared before him. The capsyint was among its surroundings, sharing their alignment. A window on the side of the capsyint slid open, allowing a man to poke his head out the side.

"You need a lift fella?" said the man. He appeared to be young but slightly older than him. The man's eyes were kind yet full of wild ambition, with a countenance that suggested a great sense of self-assurance. The man wore a shiny silver-topped hat upon his head, though the rest of his outfit looked plain.

He stood there for a moment, silently observing the man.

"Well, do you need a lift or not? Sheesh, she told me you might turn down the ride, but if so, just say the word, man. I don't have all day to wait for someone who thinks they're too good to speak."

"You knew I would be here? Who told you? What's your name?"

"That's too many questions for just one passenger. Look, I don't have all day. Too many stops to make. How about you hop on board and I'll tell you just who sent for you. It's not like it's a secret."

With a shrug of his shoulders, he replied, "Why not."

The man pushed on a crystal cord and the doors slid open. "The name's Selhu, welcome aboard."

"Selhu?" At first, he thought he knew him, but something about the man's essence seemed atypical. "Have we met before? Sometime long ago?"

Selhu took his hands off the controls and leaned back in his seat. "You know, we have a saying around here: There is no such thing as 'long ago.' Either you know a person or you do not.

"You said someone sent you to pick me up. What's their name? He stared intently at Selhu. He wanted to hear it for himself.

"You know who she is. And don't get the wrong idea. I'm no personal transport for you love sick-fools. I just owe her one."

"So you know me as well?"

"Don't start that amnesia crap again. We have a life to live too, ya know?" said Selhu. He pushed one crystal cord, then another. The doors slid closed. "Just one little favor, she said. Sheesh. I knew it couldn't be that simple. Never is with you, Apeay..."

CHAPTER 25

They were all there was to see. The capsyint absorbed the surrounding alignments of the waters and atmosphere into its own, propelling it with extraordinary ease across the great sea until arriving the welcoming coast adorned with flowers. In fact, the commute was so quick that Apeay wasn't sure if he'd actually experienced it or merely imagined it.

Ssshhhh...Whooossshhh...Ssshhhh...Whooossshhh

"Thanks, fella," said Apeay

"Eh, it's just a thing," said Selhu.

Apeay stood to his feet as the door slid open. He made his way to the exit, but Selhu hadn't budged. Surely, he would come and join him, he thought. However Selhu simply sat in place, going over the various controls of the capsyint.

"Well, we're here," said Apeay

"Yes, yes you're here," said Selhu. "Better get a move on."

"I am, but aren't you coming?"

"Me?" Selhu turned about in his seat. He scratched his chin, eyeing Apeay. "You know, I'm flattered that you'd invite me to your grand festival; however, I have to stay on schedule."

Beep, beep

The capsyint signal was going off. "Already? Looks like I have to go. See you around."

Apeay idly nodded back. "Sure man." Continuing alone, he headed into the lush cascading fields. Oh so bright, so brilliant indeed. The flowers were more vivid than he remembered. It was nearly perfect, but something about Selhu irked him. Surely this character was playing a trick on him, saying one thing to hide another. If he was indeed who he thought him to be, Selhu wouldn't miss a festival for such a trivial reason.

Apeay snapped about thinking he'd catch Selhu sneaking up from behind. But to his astonishment, the capsyint bolted away with a grand charge. The capsyint merged into the invisible alignment between the trees blowing in the breeze. The same breezing blowing across the field turned the dew on the grass into a mist that blanketed Apeay's bare feet. He looked towards the middle where a river flowed directly to the center of a great plain. Out of the river emerged yet another alignment. This alignment was unlike the one that swallowed the capsyint. This one was based on the location of the central area and went only in one direction. The transparent silver portal opened as the crystal river waters were drawn in and emanated from the same side of the opal tabanger.

The tabangers aerating power core whirred, churning the river water into a fine mist-like fog. The obscure scenery made it difficult for Apeay to determine the identity of the individual navigating the vessel. Once again he sensed a familiar essence with an uncommon characteristic. However, the surrounding ambience registered true.

"Must I challenge you for a ride across the river?" said Apeay.

"You know, that sounds like fun to me. But I promised them I wouldn't. So you have a free pass...this time. Just don't get comfortable, because I may change my mind."

"Really now?"

"Don't test me. I'll hit you so hard that you'll cry until you need a tabanger to travel on your own tears."

"And you are?"

"Dexzhil, your guide."

"I don't know if I believe you, but you are pretty funny."

"Now you think I'm funny?" said Dexzhil.

"If the life of guardian ever gets old, consider becoming a performer. That's all I'm saying."

"You would say something like silly that. Anyway, it's good to see you."

"You too, fella."

"But, I'm not really who you want to see, am I?" Apeay crossed his arms, cocking his head with indifference. Dexzhil considered this pose to be nothing more than pretense, for he knew Apeay all too well. "Hop on already, before they think we really did get into a fight."

"Where do I sit?" Apeay asked.

"You don't, boy."

"Now I'm a boy. That's something."

"It made you think about what I said instead of where we're going. You don't realize it, but we're already here."

Apeay looked down to see the waters flowing through the tabanger, sealing up the alignment behind them while opening the one ahead of them simultaneously, bringing them directly to the center of a field.

"The living dream," Apeay whispered to himself. It was exactly like nothing he remembered. The open field was flat. There was no valley. Overhead the sky was clear. No ornamental object occupied its space.

Overhead, between two clouds an alignment unsealed. One by one, they came through the opening, until there were thousands standing in the field.

"Like I said, he's going to be just fine," said the man to the lady at his side.

"Of course. After all, he always manages to find his way back. How he does it? I don't think we'll ever know," said the lady.

"Good to see you too," said Apeay, taking a knee. The royal leaders of the land had come to greet him.

"We're in need of your service," said the man. "Please stand."

"What do you need from me?"

"Actually, it's both of you."

Apeay was at a loss. "He and I?"

The man burst into laughter. "Oh no, not you and him. Khexa, if you would please summon for her, it is time."

"Zharden, my dear I sent the signal the moment he arrived," said Khexa. "And her travel will be most swift with the one I chose."

"If it's who I think you're talking about, that may have been unwise. He has a passion for recklessness," said Zharden.

"There you go again with the worrying. He's just a speedster that's all. And speaking of which..."

A hanging cloud resting about 100 shawaras above them, opened up to a precise alignment aimed directly at the ground behind them. From the alignment shot out a glowing six-winged apparition. The startled crowd ducked as the silver, spectral glizhix cut through the air overhead. It jetted from one side of the field to the other, bringing itself to a slow before coming to rest on the plains. The cockpit opened up, and a slender, wild-eyed fellow leapt out of his seat to stand on the nose of the glizhix.

" Hello, folks. I hope you weren't waiting too long."

"Not at all," said Zharden. "Had you gone any faster, you may have just taken us out. It's difficult to be disappointed if you're not alive to realize it."

"Well, my apologies, emperor. I'll try harder to be a normal pilot next time."

"Levenjhi'enel, don't bother, I...we like you just the way you are," said Khexa. "However, you may want to tone it down for him. You know how he gets."

Zharden was taken aback. "How *I* get?" Zharden asked.

"Moving on, this is a most special day, for he has return-ed." Khexa motioned to Apeay standing before them.

"I know. She's been talking about him the whole way here," said Levenjhi'enel. He turned back, extending his hand towards the rear seat of the cock pit. "My lady."

With his help, she stood to her feet. Her beautiful locks hid her face for but a jhenta, until a breeze blew across the field. Then he saw her. He saw her emerald eyes, and her charming smile gazed at him. She was one with the flowers of the plains. The sleek goddess looked upon him as she posed herself, be-fore gracefully leaping off the side of the glizhix.

Apeay felt the rhythm of her steps as she nonchalantly strolled towards him. Could it be? Could it be real this time? "Is that you?"

Her cool stroll gradually sped up. Now, she was strutting most lively as her steps evolved into sprinting.

Apeay approached her as she leapt into his arms.

"The one and only Xaeshii, my love."

"Xaeshii?" *That can't be right. I'm sure she has another name, but what?*

He held her aloft and gave her a kiss. It felt wonderful, but something was missing.

Xaeshii wrapped her arms around him. "It seemed like forever. I missed you so much."

"Me too," said Apeay.

"I see you still have it," said Dexzhil. "Still, don't think I'll let you put all the ladies under your spell. We can't have the new emperor making a disgrace of himself!"

"*Ahem*," Zharden cleared his throat. "I believe I'll be making the official statements from here on out."

Dexzhil nodded. "Of course, your excellency."

"Don't you have something to give him?"

"Oh, right. I was getting to that. Heads up, Apeay." He reached into his satchel at his side, and with the snap of his fingers he flung the crystal corded ornament with laser speed towards Apeay's head. Apeay caught it in midair not a moment before it would've struck him. "Just like I thought, you're still faster than light."

"And what if I wasn't?" said Apeay.

"Then it wouldn't be you."

"I've been guarding it ever since the last time."

Apeay juggled the ornament in his hands. "It feels sort of light."

"Are you ready?" Khexa asked.

"Yes, with so many here to be the first, we need a place among the new tzierhan, here in the middle of these great plains. We need you do make this real for us."

"Alright," said Apeay. "I think I understand." He turned to Xaeshii as he extended the alignment of the crystal cord of the ornament, until it was large enough to wrap around both of their necks. "Together now."

"As it should be," said Xaeshii. "It's what you wanted to show me all along. I'm excited. I finally get to see it for myself."

Apeay nodded. Then, in one voice the two of them spoke:

"*Tehnzillxheda Xhalhominha Xenoniallax!*"

From the ornament, the winds blew in several directions among the alignment of the atmosphere between the ground and the highest reaches of the cosmos. The river that brought them there split in half by the lower winds, with one side folding over on itself until it became like multiple interwoven circles. The middle winds blew across the center winds as they absorbed the essence of Dexzhil's gauntlets into their vortex. Out of vortex came a rainbow, from both visible and invisible alignments. The light in the sky shot straight down towards the liquid palladium circles, reflecting back, converging in the middle of the air. For each interwoven circle, the light materialized as an alignment of gold.

Rays from the setting star bounced off the inverted pyramid from every direction. The intwined alignment between the pyramid and the atmosphere obscured its appearance.

From the pyramid's inferior an infinite stairwell cascaded down towards the middle where they stood.

"It is time to take your place," said Zharden. Both he and Khexa removed their signet rings and held them out for Apeay and Xaeshii to take, whilst the two stared at each other for a moment. To Apeay, she was more beautiful than he remembered. He was where he wanted to be, but unsure of what to do next.

"Well now, are we going in or are we going to stand here all day?" said Dexzhil

"Sure, fella, but..."

"What's the matter?" said Xaeshii.

Apeay looked about his surroundings, at the people all standing there in the most perfect arrangement, and at the woman by his side. "None of you can sense a familiar essence approaching?"

From nearby, an alignment opened up revealing a man navigating a capsyint their way. The capsyint, came to rest and the man got out and dashed up to where they stood.

"Who is that?" asked Dexzhil

"Yes, I need to know as well," Zharden called to the man. "Who are you, and how did you navigate all the way into this area?"

The stranger tipped his hat forward, tilting it at an angle and posted one leg up on a large stone. "None of that matters. All you need to know is I'm the one that keeps everything up and running. I have a schedule to keep. And this guy," he said, pointing to Apeay, "has something to do."

"But he just returned," said Khexa. "And, as you see, the palace is as it will be, as are all things new."

"You see that's the thing. He always returns. But, truth be told, he never really leaves either, like the one I do my task for. So it's never what you think."

"Is that you, my man?" said Apeay. "Haru, it is you. What happened to Selhu?"

"Selhu?" Haru looked around, seeing the gorgeous people surrounding him in the picturesque grasslands and shook his head. Only he and the lady who sent for him knew exactly what was happening. Apeay wasn't where he needed to be, not even close. "I Couldn't have arrived at a better time. Don't worry about these folks. It's what's happening with you that's the matter." Apeay looked stunned, awaiting Haru's explanation. "I came back for you like I promised."

"Mister, whatever this business with Apeay is, it will have to wait," said Zharden "We need to establish a new foundation before it's too late."

"Yes, the foundation, we already know all that," Haru said. But the lady needs to see him. Know what I'm saying? Actually, you probably don't. If he doesn't come with me, right this moment, there won't be anything to establish. Don't worry, we'll be right back."

Apeay nodded to Zharden. "I've got this. We won't be gone long."

"Are you sure?"

"You should learn to be more trusting," said Khexa. "You'll help him stay on course, won't you, Xaeshii?"

"You know it," said Xaeshii.

"I'd keep an eye on both of them," said Dexzhil. "We can't have them creating life in inappropriate places."

"Okay now," said Apeay, "you don't have to take it that far."

"He doesn't, because there's no reason for her to come along," said Haru.

"Haru, she's coming with us."

"Oh boy. Well, guess she's coming along. All aboard, folks.

With Haru at the helm, and a pull of the string, they bolted off.

Apeay looked out the viewport of the capsyint into the endless spectrum of the surrounding alignment. It was clear to him where they were headed. The capsyint was on the center alignment, heading south, which leads to only one place. "So, that's where we're going."

"You know it, fella. Eos Express at your service," said Haru. "She said you had to be the one. I offered to do it myself, but she was quite insistent. Well, I guess it's best this way. I can only go so far in this. Who knows what might happen if I miss the mark."

"It's the thought that counts," said Apeay. "You know, I haven't seen her in quite some time."

"Who is that?" asked Xaeshii.

"Someone I knew a long time ago. We were children then."

The capsyint came to rest on the outskirts, surrounding a small valley. The doors slid open and hopped off. They glided above towards the edge of the hill. From there, they took the path of radiance from the outer corridors to the Silver Lake at the center of the valley.

CHAPTER 26

I always say "see you again," because it's so much easier than saying goodbye.

"Hey there, lady," Haru shouted. "You mind sitting still for a bit?"

"Why should I? What's the matter, fella?"

"You're getting my new hat all wet, that's the matter."

The young lady was causing a commotion with every move she made. She appeared to be about nine cycles in age, with the personality to match.

"I don't care about your bahba. I'm having fun."

The lake splashed against the shore, its waters churned by the swift winds that blew in accordance with her movements

In waiting, she couldn't contain her lively energy which filled her young being with a spirit of reckless abandon. And with her task complete, she had nothing else to do, but give chase to the vovajxio flying through the valley.

"Come on lady, get serious. Why'd you have me bring him if you're just gonna play around?

"If it bothers you that much." She stopped running, then looked up at Apeay and smiled. But her smile was tinged by a faint trace of melancholy and soon faded away. The young lady pulled on Apeay's sleeve. "Did you forget something? You forgot something, didn't you? Why are you so old?"

"I...I don't know," said Apeay.

She released her grip on his sleeve and took him by the hand. "Come with me. You too," she said to Haru. She led them along to the edge of the lake. "Look into lake. Tell me, what do you see?"

Apeay stood tall above the waters of the lake, but the light cast from the setting Heyliun made it difficult to see what it was she wanted him to see. He knelt down for a closer look, and saw a strange sight. "I see you, Haru, but..."

"But not yourself. Why is it that you have no reflection? Why can't you see yourself, Apeay?"

Apeay patted his body, feeling that he was still there. But was he? Not only did he not reflect, he also felt that his ornament was no longer around his neck. "My ornament, it's gone!"

Xaeshii covered her mouth as she gasped. "Little girl, does this have something to do with why you called for him?"

"Do I look like a little girl to you?"

"Well, sort of. You're definitely not a woman."

"You shouldn't even be able to see me. That tells me he's further along than he should be, which is why I sent for him. I wish I could take care of this myself, but I'm ill-equipped look after more than one," said the young lady.

Xaeshii looked up at Apeay as he turned away from her gaze. She sensed his grief as she felt it herself. "Girl, I mean lady, just what do you need with him?"

"It's not me, it's him. He needs himself. Someone may need to tell him about himself." The young lady looked up at Apeay. "Look below, look deep into the water, and tell me what you see."

Apeay peered into the water, but saw nothing more than what he'd seen before. "Nothing. I still don't have a reflection."

"Will you remain to be withdrawn from what's within you? Are you afraid?"

"I've never been afraid of anything."

"Yet you don't remember me. If you have no fears as you say, then why not look below the surface?"

"Alright, I will." Apeay took a deep breath and submerged his head beneath the surface of the lake. He opened his eyes and saw the life below. Caldazhians swam in between the dark, verdant plant life scattered among the reef. Beyond the reef there was an unfathomable drop, revealing a greater depth to the lake than what could be seen from the surface. From that depth, many tiny lights appeared as if they were from some far off land. One of those lights began to shine brightly. So bright in fact that Apeay had to shield his eyes.

When he opened them, he saw a baby boy, resting on the surface of Silver Lake. A gentle spinning alignment of water kept the child afloat fixed in one place. The baby did not make a sound as he looked at Apeay. The boy's eyes spoke loudly in an inaudible whisper that said everything.

"Do you have somewhere to take him?" said the young lady. Before he could answer her, Xaeshii walked into the lake, and lifted the baby from the waters.

"He'll stay with us at the palace. We'll raise him as our own," said Xaeshii. "Apeay, he could be the first of several, if we'd like."

Apeay dismissed the idea because he knew there would be no place for the child here, at the moment, in that place. For this child was speaking to him in a voice that only he and the young lady could hear and understand.

"That would've been *magnificent*," said Apeay.

"It will be," said Xaeshii. Apeay did not acknowledge her sentiment. Instead, he sat down on the edge of the lake and peered into the water a second time. "What's the matter? I'm not trying to rush you into anything you're not ready for. I just thought it would be ideal."

"It is," said Apeay. "But not for this place."

"I don't see why not." Xaeshii held the boy up to the sky and spun him around. The baby boy laughed with glee. "See, he wants to stay with us. Don't you, little one?"

"Xaeshii, look at me," said Apeay as he engineered the waters of the lake with his hands. He'd come to the reality of his situation not but a few moments ago, deciphering what the young lady had been telling him all along. "Don't be disappointed by what I'm about to say, but we, as in you and I, can't keep him. It would be impossible here. A child has to be raised somewhere, and we're nowhere."

"We're standing right here, at a lake."

"That's not what I mean. You wouldn't understand."

Xaeshii sighed, and sat the boy down among the flowers near her feet. The boy pouted and reached up for her.

"You'll be fine. I got something for ya." Xaeshii picked a flower and placed it in his hands. "Here, little one. Hold on to this, and it will be like holding on to me. You may even find it sweet." The baby squeezed the flower in his hands and put it to his mouth and began to nibble on its petals.

"No, no," said Xaeshii. "That's not the part you eat. You have to open the flower." Xaeshii pulled apart the petals to reveal the sweet center of the fruit flower. The baby boy instinctively lapped up the juices that flowed from within, while keeping a tight grip on the flower.

"Haru, would you pass me an empty bottle?" said Apeay.

"Who says I have one?" said Haru.

"I know you keep a few with you."

"I suppose." Haru felt around in one of his oversized pockets, retrieved a clear blue bottle and opened it with a three-piece device that separated the lid into four pieces and gave it to Apeay.

"Thank you." Apeay submerged the bottle under, filling it with the water he'd stirred and resealed it, placing it in a pouch on his side. "That's all we need. Haru is your capsyint ready to take us where need be?"

"My friend, we're charged for endless travel. Just say the word."

"Xaeshii, I'll be back soon," said Apeay.

"Of course you will. And I'll be right here when you get back," said Xaeshii.

"Can you sense his essence? Can you feel his intentions?" said the young lady.

"I can feel his intentions like they're my own. I'm his heart, his love. That's why I'm here."

The young lady reached out and felt the soft fabric of Xaeshii's sleeve. "You're here, but it's his desire that made you real. Be his heart, and give him what he needs."

Xaeshii picked up the baby boy who was already reaching up for her and placed him in Apeay's arms. "Go where you will, my love. I'll be looking for you."

Apeay pulled her to him and kissed her. "I won't be hard to find, trust me."

"If it's alright with you, I'm ready, my friend. It looks like he is, too," said Haru. The baby was fast asleep in Apeay's arms. "I like 'em that way. It makes for a nice quiet capsyint ride. And, lady can you please grant me an unrestricted alignment just once?"

"So you can disturb my tranquil valley with that thing?"

"Come on, lady, we go way back. You're not gonna make me walk all the way back, are you?"

"Alright, just this once, I'll grant you permission...*Xhenhil cabjheranal astianha*." At her summoning, the capsyint's alignment opened in front of them. The glowing violet light beam protruded from the alignment across the lake and beyond the horizon.

"Thank you, thank you. Now, all those bound for the next destination, hop aboard."

Apeay looked the capsyint over. "A grand cabera. I'd expect nothing less from you, Haru, but this time..." Apeay carefully tucked the baby close with both his arms, and leapt from the ground to the top of the capsyint.

"Are you out of your mind?" said Haru "Do you know what dust does to a person when they're going 200,000 reels a jhenta and they get curious and poke their head out a viewport? Their head turns into dust! If you sit up there, you and that baby will become a dusty memory scattered among the stars."

"We'll be fine. Let's be on our way, before we miss our mark."

Haru shrugged his shoulders. "It's your life, kid. I'm just looking out."

"No, my friend. It's your life, too. And I wouldn't dare let any of you down. So take me…take me to a place where dreams come to life."

"Alright then fella, hold on to whatever you can. It's time to fly!" Haru took to the controls and waved to the two ladies on the edge of the lake as it reflected the violet and gold aura from the capsyint's power unit. The aura spread from the unit, enveloping the capsyint, Apeay and the child.

Apeay took his outer garment off and wrapped the baby within its folds. Then skillfully wrapped the ends around his arms, securing the sleeping baby to his back. He looked over to Xaeshii. "Meet me on the hill next Oros. Know that!"

"What hill?" Xaeshii asked.

"The only one," replied the young lady.

"You'll know it when you see it," said Apeay "It's here in…" Before he could complete his thought, the capsyint bolted away into the twilight.

All around him, the stars highlighted the realm of empty space. His mind raced as he peered, awaiting to see the proper destination. The land below them was too fleeting to be the proper place, and the land above seemed too rigid, leaving no open space. Then, there appeared an opening, a faint place between both the upper and lower lands that shared the great heights and depths of each.

"Haru, go to full!"

"I'd usually object to such a reckless request, but seeing as how you're still in one piece up there, I'll entertain your foolishness and oblige." Haru pushed on the cord closest to him all the way.

The capsyint accelerated to an incalculable velocity until it became impossible to see in front because they were ahead of where they were heading to, which is precisely what Apeay wanted. He looked to the rear of the capsyint, where a single point in existence trailed behind. "This is where I get off," said Apeay, standing to his feet.

"Looks like we made the full circuit," said Haru. "Take care of yourself, kid."

"You too, fella. Thanks for everything. Later, my friend."

With a single bound, Apeay jumped headlong into the space between the upper and lower places, into an ambience of starlight. The light merged at the singular point, then back out again like a liquid that cut into the rigid upper land like a blade, forming a gateway. Apeay snugged the garment even tighter to his body before soaring through the open path. On the way through he rotated upside down. The land below was now above as the starlight found its proper alignment among the clouds.

"Here we are," said Apeay.

Apeay slowed his being until both the upper and lower lands disappeared, leaving but one place. He touched down, and there he stood, his feet immersed in the cool water of the stream.

"It's too cold to carry on like this." Apeay stepped out of the river and carefully loosened the garment holding the child to his back. Gently, he laid the child within the garment on the grass as he retrieved the bottle from his pouch. "I knew it wasn't my imagination. This bottles been getting hot since we left." The bottle glowed bright cerulean as the water inside boiled. He opened the lid slowly to let the steam seep out rather than explode out with a loud noise, and meticulously poured out the water in six alignments onto the edges of the garment. "*Xjenahn yahashi gxoh.* There, that's better."

Apeay lifted the child from the ground, and took the path of the trail that led him away from the river into an open field. From the field, he made his way to a place of high hills where the tree tops of a lush forest were lit by the night stars. The flowers along the edge of the pathway were frosted over by an ice cold breeze. As Apeay strolled up the last hill, the baby awoke and started to cry.

"Hey...hey there, little guy. There's no need for that. Everything's alright." Apeay set the lapis-lazuli cradle down. "Look, I think there's something in here for you," Apeay said as he reached into a fold of the cloth at the child's side. "Just like I thought." He retrieved an ornament that contained a fiery blue light within, bound to a single crystal cord, and placed it around the baby's neck.

The child stopped crying as he held the ornament in his tiny hands and looked up at Apeay.

"I don't need it, but one day you may. These are good people. They'll always be here for you... Apeay."

He took one last look at the picturesque house on the hill before stepping back into the ultimate alignment. "Goodbye Mother, goodbye Father..."

As the alignment sealed, it rang out in perfect pitch with a chime that resounded throughout the forest.

"Did we order a new artaghan for the door?"

"No, I don't believe so."

"Are you sure?"

"My love, I'd be the first to know..."

Oh, it feels good to stretch my legs. How long have I been sitting under this tree? Twilight has caught up to me once again.

That man...I wonder where he was headed? Where could he be now? He was definitely in a hurry to get somewhere when he left me. Now that I think about it, I don't believe he told me all there is to know. But would he honestly hold out when he shared so much? Is he afraid of something, or perhaps someone else finding out what he's up to? It's hard to tell. So, then, I've decided. I have more questions that need answering, and I'm going to pry until I'm satisfied that I've got the whole truth out of him.

Oh, my stomach is screaming at me. I probably should go back home and grab a bite to eat, but I'm afraid I won't catch up to him if I do. Ah well, what's one more day? I still have plenty of water left in my jug so, I'll be fine.

Alright, here we go.

∞Δ∞

The girl sat on the edge of the lake, feeding kronozel seeds to the vovajxios from the palm of her hand, when something caused them to become alarmed. The brilliant orange plumage on the underside of their tails was the last to be seen as they flew off into Heyliun.

The young lady turned around to see what frightened the vovajxio. "Oh, is it you? Did you rest well?"

The boy appeared flipping a golden utensil through his fingers. "Of course it's me. I think I overslept, but the dream I had, it was amazing. I saw everything. I know exactly what to do. Everything will be...

Perfect..."

A MAN'S DREAMS, MISUNDERSTOOD. HIS LIFE EXPECTATIONS, FULL OF DISAPPOINTMENT LEADING TO ONE TRAGIC EVENT AFTER ANOTHER.

BEFORE there were two, there was one. One man with a forgotten past and an identity lost to time, on a mission to right the wrongs of existence.

ZJVXENOZB, fed up with a world of uncontrolled chaos, sets out to create the perfect life, even at the risk of destroying his own.

The legend continues in **BOOK II** OF III:

"I AM COMMAND"

www.ingramcontent.com/pod-product-compliance
Lightning Source LLC
Chambersburg PA
CBHW021121260626
47169CB00005B/1384